Hybrid of the Pale Race

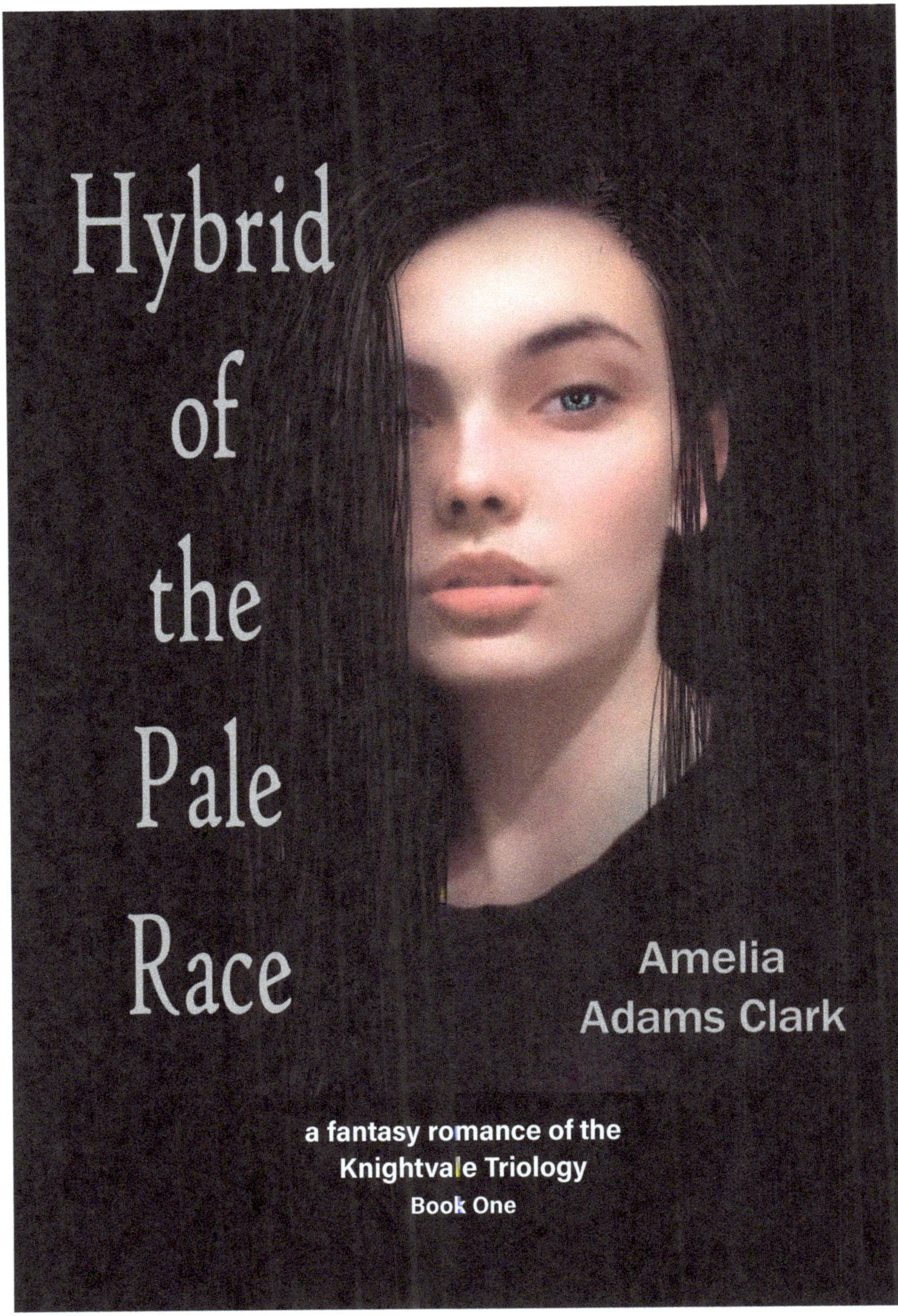

Hybrid of the Pale Race

Amelia Adams Clark

**a fantasy romance of the
Knightvale Triology
Book One**

Haley's

Athol, Massachusetts

Copy edited by Debra Ellis.
Cover photo of Shyanne Hill courtesy of Shyanne Hill.
Cover designed by Amelia Adams Clark

Haley's
488 South Main Street
Athol, Massachusetts 01331
marcia2gagliardi@gmail.com

International Standard Book Number, trade paperback: 978-1-956055-09-2
International Standard Book Number, e-book Adobe PDF: 978-1-956055-10-8
International Standard Book Number, ebook, ePub: 978-1-956055-12-2
InternationalStandard Book Number ebook, Kindle: 978-1956055-13-9

Library of Congress Control Number: 2024910812

for my husband, Adam—
until the stars burn out!
You never appreciate true happiness
until you experience the other side of the spectrum.

Though I wrote this first novel eighteen months prior to
finding my way back to you, Adam,
you have been my escape since the day we met.
Now I wake up and drift to sleep embraced in my escape.
I love you.

Nothing begins, and nothing ends
that is not paid with moan.
For we are born in others' pain
and perish in our own.

—Francis Thompson

Contents

Illustrations

Duck Pond

Lesai

"So, when do you leave?" Willow asks Ivy, an enormous meadow of wildflowers surrounding them.

Ivy shrugs. "I think I leave after my ceremony. I haven't really asked my mother much about it."

Aster pinches her nose in annoyance. "Stop talking all this sadness! What are you going to do about Finn?"

Ivy rolls her eyes. "That guy can't take a hint if his life depends on it." Looking up at the clouds as they pass by and wondering if she is really doing the right thing, Ivy rolls over to her back.

"I know, but he's adorable, and he's totally in love with you." Willow attempts to hide her jealousy of love, but her wavering voice betrays her.

Ivy rolls her eyes. "He is in love with the idea of me, not the person who is me. He doesn't know me from a hole in the wall. He's too worried about what he looks like on my arm to concern himself with what an actual marriage looks like. Don't get me started on the pushy side of him. He hides it well."

Aster eyes her. "He doesn't hide it as well as you think!"

Willow huffs. "I wish I could go to the ball." She toys with a flower petal that has expired. "Instead, I have to spend the night meeting my soon-to-be husband and his family in Vespira."

"I'm never getting married," Aster says, smiling at the sky. "There are too many men out there that I want to explore. I would be a terrible wife." Willow and Ivy laugh at her flippant ways. "I'm dead serious. My mother said that if I want to flooze, I am more than welcome. She has six other daughters to marry off, and I am the last one she is worried about."

Yeah, right! Ivy looks at her friend with concern.

"You are crazy!" Willow says, throwing her shawl over Aster's head.

Aster gets serious. "What does your mother have to say about Mr. Naese?"

"She said that it's up to me. I'm not expected to take over the throne because I have cousins who are more than willing to do it." She's quiet for a moment as she flicks a blade of grass. "It's because I am sick."

Willow and Aster are quiet, both putting a hand on Ivy's back for comfort. Willow cheers up a bit. "Why don't we sing a tree into existence right here in the middle of the meadow?"

"Why?" Aster flips her hair over her shoulder irritably as she looks at Willow.

"Because this might be the last time we get to just hang out in our meadow without kids or other life crap hanging in the air," her peppy attitude becoming law as she makes her point clearly.

Willow pulls her two friends up next to her and walks to the spot she thinks is perfect. "Sit, you two. This is something that we all need. I can't go to the ball, and this is the last time we will be together."

Aster and Ivy sit reluctantly as Willow smiles ear to ear. "Hands." The three of them clasp hands the way they were taught as children. "Now focus on a white birch and think of all the happiness we have had."

Ivy does as she is told and grounds herself, bringing her roots into the ground while they clasp hands. Feeling the connection among the three of them mixed in with the elemental magic of the earth, she sings.

The low notes of sorrow and high notes of passion intertwined together create a pact among friends that would hold a lifetime in the form of a tree releasing a feeling of friendship to be seen and felt for all who come here.

At the end of the song, an eight-foot-tall sapling sits right in the middle of the meadow, its leaves different shades of green as it radiates the happiness of the living. The sight almost causes Ivy to regret her intent to leave Lesai.

Iveliis awakes to the sun shining through her window of her tower bedroom overlooking the ancient city of Lesai, sung into the trees of a forest. The homes, that look like burls to the naked eye of anyone without ancient blood, are high up in the treetops. The ancient race, having been on the earth much longer than the human, Pale or animal races combined, know the only way to preserve the living earth is to collaborate with it to build their communities. From the food they eat to the weapons they use to protect themselves, they make sure that the living earth is not harmed in the harvest. Working with the Elemental Mother to heal is first and foremost in any ancient's way of life.

Iveliis sits up in bed, knowing all too well that today will be a busy day for her. It's the day before her twenty-first birthday, which means she will come of age and no longer be under her mother's thumb. She's excited to know she will be joining the Scavenger guild but also nervous, as she's never been allowed to venture out of the city. It isn't allowed due to her royal bloodline to leave before she's fully trained and of age to make her own decisions in the field. She's been training for the Scavengers since she was five years old, basically since she was old enough to handle a wooden sword.

Her maid, Wren, comes bustling into the room, and Ivy puts the blankets over her head. "Ivy, there is too much to do today, and you well know it."

"I am perfectly capable of dressing myself, Wren," Ivy muffles through the blankets.

A chiming little bark of laughter comes out of Wren as she says, "Yes, you are capable. However, then your mother would make you come right back into your room and change into the outfit that she's picked out."

Ivy peeks her head out of the covers and gives Wren a sharp look. Wren holds up the long satin dress that must have come from the recent venture of the Scavenger guild. "Isn't it beautiful?"

Ivy scoffs. "Do you realize how hard it is to wear my back scabbard in those ridiculous things?"

"According to your mother, and I quote, 'If she thinks that she's wearing anything other than what I have picked out for the last two days that she's a child in the eyes of the law, then she's sadly mistaken. Make sure that scabbard is hidden in her closet.'

"Now, I'm not about to hide the scabbard, but you won't be able to wear it today or tomorrow."

The uncanny imitation of Queen Diannicalyn Grenedich gives Ivy the heebie-jeebies. The difference is that she also knows how much these two last days of her childhood mean to her mother and it won't necessarily kill her to deal with it. *It's just two days.*

Knowing full well that with the dress comes a hairdo that will take more than an hour to achieve, Ivy gets out of bed and bathes. It's the nightmare that haunts her. She hates the way women are in Lesai. Then again, she hears from other Scavengers and her studies of humans that human women are the same way, so it's safe to say that she hates the way most women are obsessed about being. Their constant worry that every hair on their head is precisely in place and that there is not a single bit of dirt on their overly extravagant clothing has been the bane of her existence since childhood. It's one thing to be feminine but a whole other ball game to be beautiful at all times.

After showering, Ivy puts on the shift she's given and sits for her hair to be groomed. After twenty minutes of torture with the charmed brush given her as a toddler, Ivy's wet hair renders it useless. The ancient charm will only keep her dry hair from tangling. The only problem is when her hair is wet, because then it's too heavy for the charmed air sheaths to hold strands apart from one another.

She feels a tingling sensation in her scalp as Wren individually detangles each strand and crafts her jet-black hair into an intricate braid with beads and flowers sewn in. It hangs neatly past her right shoulder and almost to her waist. Her grey, almost white eyes, with eerie black rings around the edges of the iris, stare back at her from the bedroom mirror, and she barely recognizes herself.

She knows Finn, her date, will love the look on her, but then again, the boy she's kept around for the past year always seems to push her towards staying in Lesai. It doesn't matter that it's the last thing she wants to do, but he wants to marry her. He wants to be on her arm for the next several millennia, since he figures she will rule over Lesai. Not that she's necessarily opposed to the idea of him being there, but he's always a bit too pushy for Ivy to trust him completely, and the last thing she wants is to be stuck unfulfilled in Lesai for the rest of her life. The idea that Finn would expect her to take the throne is annoying by itself, seeing that an ancient ruler's reign doesn't end until they wish it or they pass on, and she has no expectation that the previous ruler plans to abdicate.

Wren interrupts Ivy's thoughts when she comes in with the gown. Ivy dons the extravagance that reaches the floor as well as flats that feel constricting on her feet. The result after an hour and a half of prepping is picturesque Iveliis Grenedich, Princess of Lesai.

Wren steps back and sighs in approval. "I am happy with the outcome," she says.

"I'm glad you are," Ivy says, rolling her eyes. She figures she may as well get it out of her system before she's to do the whole I-am-a-royal routine that she despises about as much as she does dressing to perfection.

Wren laughs. "I am enjoying this. Get over it and realize that tomorrow will probably be the last time you let me get you ready."

Besides her close friends, Wren is the only person in Lesai who knows everything about Ivy, including the occasional hurtful, uncontrollable, blinding blackouts. A few times, Ivy's had to be kept prisoner in her own room so there wouldn't be any collateral damage. Sometimes, her mother made her sit for hours meditating while drawing elemental magic in to calm herself. Ivy is quite sure that the tea her mother has the Scavengers get is also part of the solution.

All the while, knowing how out of sorts and unpredictable Ivy can be, Wren never acts skittish around her. It's as if she knows Ivy will never hurt her, and it's the reason Ivy considers her more of a friend than a maid.

It's a mystery how she's the only ancient she's ever heard of who has such episodes. Even the wise ones and their fits don't come close to the all-encompassing sickness that makes Ivy's eyes turn red. She never remembers any of it happening. She eventually snaps out of it in shambles, clothes torn, and room destroyed with someone she's known since childhood cowering in a corner. It's like her mother knows what is happening to her but hasn't ever said what causes it. Her mother always tells her, "When you feel different, retreat to your room and send for me. We will do what we must to snap you out of it." Ivy doesn't know how long the occurrence lasts but knows only that her mother and Wren are always there when it's over.

She's about to open the door when she hears a knock on it. "Ivy, are you decent?" Ivy hears Finn's voice.

"Yes," she replies, wondering how he got to her bedroom door without someone catching him.

The door to her bedroom opens, and Finn strides into the room with all the grace of an alley cat. "Oh! I didn't realize that you aren't alone." He backs up a few steps towards the door and bows formally, back-pedaling to save his grace.

"You shouldn't be in here, sir. Please wait out in the hallway. I will be having a conversation with the guard stationed outside." Wren taps her foot in annoyance at the forwardness.

Finn almost blushes. "So sorry for the intrusion. I slipped past the guard when he wasn't looking. I was waiting downstairs for over an hour now, and I wanted to speed up the process."

Finn looks Ivy up and down and smiles appreciatively. "The queen is waiting for you in her study." He holds his hand out for Ivy to take it as he waits impatiently while completely dismissing Wren's direction.

"You really should go to the parlor and wait, sir."

Finn rolls his eyes at Ivy. "Can you believe that a maid is telling me what to do?"

Wren looks as if she's going to argue her point. Ivy ever so slightly shakes her head "No" then gives Wren the look that means they will discuss his rudeness later in detail so they can laugh it off and move on. Men in Lesai royal circles always assume they're in charge, which the women allow them to think. However, when someone is not even a part of a family yet, no matter who it is, disrespecting a maid's directive for a man to leave a woman's bedroom is a straight up no-no, one even Ivy is concerned he isn't heeding.

Ivy takes his hand and looks back at Wren, "Thank you."

"Always, Princess Iveliis," Wren says in her formal tone that she always uses when they aren't alone. "I will see you again before the night ends."

Ivy nods.

Ivy and Finn take the spiral staircase down to the bottom floor of the royal quarters. Ivy lifts her hand to knock on the office door of the queen, but Finn puts his hand over hers.

"Let me."

Ivy isn't sure she likes the way he presumes that it's allowed, but she doesn't fight it. In ancient formality, males usually do the knocking. It's some outdated patriarchal thing that irks Ivy.

Finn knocks, and Reed, her mother's guard, opens the door to the queen's immaculate office. Not looking up as Ivy and Finn enter, Ivy's mother sits behind her desk looking over a few details needed for the next day's ceremony. "Please sit."

Finn gestures to Ivy to go ahead and sit first, then sits himself to her right.

The queen looks up from her work and says, "Oh, Finn." She looks at Ivy with her eyebrows raised. "I didn't realize that you would be here," she tells Finn.

Finn looks sheepish. "I assumed you wouldn't mind. I have a question for you."

Finn looks at Ivy. Sensing what he will do, she shakes her head no.

"What is your question, Finn Naese?"

Finn stands in front of Ivy's mother's desk and puts his chin up. "Queen Diannicalyn Grenedich, I'd like to ask for your daughter's hand in marriage.

Dumbstruck, Ivy's mother looks at her and asks, "Have you not told him of your plans to join the Scavenger guild?"

Finn doesn't let her answer. "She's spoken of nothing but the Scavengers since we first met, my queen." He hesitates a moment and then resumes his speech. "My hope is that upon an agreement from you for our formal engagement, she can take a year to ponder whether she would like to be a wife and a mother more than someone who seeks to tarnish your family name, a year during which she would have to stay in Lesai to explore her options. Such a request is perfectly acceptable in the eyes of the law, and I know that you do not want your daughter killed in the line of duty. I agree with you on that and would like you to consider it."

Ivy watches more than a few emotions play swiftly across her mother's face, and none of them good. However, there is no way Finn will read the face of a queen he has only seen a few times.

Ivy knows she's going to have to be blunt with him. There is no going around it. It's one thing to ask Ivy herself if she will consider staying, but to exclude Ivy from making her own decisions makes Ivy's temper rise. The air sucks out of the room as her sight begins to glow red.

The queen must have seen her daughter fighting to maintain control and says quickly, "I need to speak to my daughter alone, Finn. Please leave." Finn looks as if he's going to argue his point a little further but thinks the better of it. She's the queen, after all.

"I will leave you to review my proposal, Your Highness." Finn bows himself out of the room as if reverence is what's needed to get what he wants in this situation. He doesn't bother to look over at Ivy before he leaves.

Once he's out of the room and the queen hears her guard escort Finn out of the royal domain, she stares at her daughter. Ivy's eyes return to their natural grey. The queen looks at Ivy with a sly smile and says "It looks as if you will have to let that boy down a little bit harder than you already have. I've heard you tell him repeatedly that you want to join the Scavenger guild. It's something that I believe you will accomplish amazingly."

Ivy rolls her eyes. "I am starting to think that it doesn't matter what I say. In truth, you may have to do it."

Her mother shakes her head. "Nope. Sorry, honey, but there will be more in the future you will have to let down, so it's better to have practice now. That one is persistent, though."

Her mother is quiet for a moment. Then, "It makes me wonder why. You have never really led him to believe that you want to follow me to become a queen. Ancients live to be eons old. You may have great-grand-children before I pass. Not only that, but Wren also tells me he's never asked to be a boyfriend. He just tells everyone that he is and bullies anyone who goes near you."

Ivy shrugs. "It's true. He assumes that his word is law. Even if I were staying in Lesai, there is no way I'd marry him. He has no care for anyone other than himself, and he just made that perfectly clear." Ivy stands up and looks out her mother's office window. "I doubt I will even have children, Mother. But I will follow in your footsteps. The Scavenger's guild is where you started as well."

The queen smiles as if remembering times long ago that bring happiness to her even now. After a moment, her face becomes serene again. "Enough of that now. I won't be giving him an answer. You will have to do that.

"The ball is tonight," the queen continues, "and the ceremony is tomorrow morning. How are you feeling?"

"Well, I am wondering if I should do a session with the tea before I have to face him tonight. I don't want to have a blackout if I get upset—and as you just witnessed, if there is any more of him walking over female decisions, I might let myself beat him to a pulp."

Her mother nods knowingly.

"Reed?" she calls.

Not speaking a word, the guard who opens the door approaches her. "Have Wren bring a tea up to Ivy's room. She will be headed up shortly."

The queen looks back at Ivy, "By the way, the dress is perfect on you."

Ivy stands and does a twirl for her mother. "Take it in while you can. After tomorrow, I won't be wearing another one of these."

Reminding Ivy that she once had the same attitude toward her attire, her mother rolls her eyes in the most unqueenly of manners. Ivy wonders if it's the throne that made her so conscious about the dress codes of royals.

"Make me one promise, Iveliis." Ivy cleans the smile off her face to look her mother seriously in the eye. "Remember that, no matter how harsh I have been over the years or how much I have kept to myself, it has been to protect you."

"I will remember, Mother." Ivy's hair stands on end, as she senses that something is coming that will change everything. Her stomach lurches as her mother's admission that she has been keeping things from her solidifies in her mind. Swallowing nausea and refusing to dwell on the thought, she curtsies to her mother and makes her way back up to her bedroom.

The tea she requested sits on the small table next to the window. The leaves and dark amber coloring making her salivate even before she can smell the liquid. Even though it tastes like dirt, she anticipates the feeling of it soaring through her veins. It creates a sense of calm as it awakens every sense in her body.

Ivy walks over to the cup and tips it to her mouth, observing as told to drink it slowly and feel the effects wash over her as a preemptive way to relax before the meditation.

After the tea is gone, Ivy forces herself to close her eyes and ground herself. She can feel her roots blending with the roots of the tree surrounding her. They spread out into the forest and soak up the magics to rejuvenate her.

It never ceases to amaze her how much power the earth holds.

During training, the Ancients are taught everything there is to know about the human world and how as time passed, most of the humans abandoned worship of the earth to worship a new being they called *God*.

They reframed rituals to celebrate the life and magics of the elements construed into a different type of holiday nevertheless originating in nature but given different meaning. But if they would reach out around themselves, they would feel the magic for themselves even if they can't use it to its full capabilities.

The awe-inspiring hum that tells Ivy she's full to maximum capacity of the elemental magic she loves so much comes to her all of a sudden. The music of it causes her to want to sit a while longer to enjoy it, but she knows she needs to step away from it. That is one thing that some of the Ancients have a problem with. It's like the problem that the humans have with plants they've made into what they call medicines. The music and hum of the elements calling you can be addicting if you aren't careful. There are Ancients that will sit in the woods for decades even, listening to the sounds of the different elements dancing together within the earth.

Ivy opens her eyes and confronts the sun beginning to hit the horizon. She's meditated the day away and hadn't realized it happening. As she contemplates why it has taken so long to come out of the meditation, she hears "Princess Iveliis?" as Wren calls from the other side of her door.

"Enter," Ivy responds. The door opens, and in walks Wren with a dress featuring a very large amount of silk taffeta.

"You have got to be kidding me!" Ivy complains. "The other one is perfectly fine!"

Wren smiles widely, then sees that Ivy remains sitting by the window. "You haven't been meditating this whole time, have you?" A look of concern hides quickly behind Wren's poised smile.

Ivy sighs. "I was, actually. It makes no sense to me, though." Ivy scratches her head annoyed. "It hasn't taken this long since I was a kid."

"Knock that off! You will ruin your hair."

Fixing the pins so there is no evidence of Ivy messing with it, Wren swats Ivy's hand away from her head again. "You are fine. Now let's get you ready for your party."

"It's not a party, Wren. It's a ball," Ivy says winking at her friend. "There will be nothing fun and entertaining about having to dance all night long and tell a boy who apparently wants to trap me into staying here that he's dreaming."

Wren tsks, "Get a grip, miss. All will work itself out."

Ivy shrugs. She has a gut feeling that Finn will not listen to her.

It doesn't take as long as the morning to get Ivy into proper dancing attire. Her hair has only to be adorned with the tiara her mother has had specially made for the evening. As Ivy stands, she feels lightheaded as her lack of oxygen causes her to hold the back of the chair for balance.

"You okay?" Wren asks, concerned.

Ivy nods. "Just nerves, I think. I'll be fine in a few minutes."

"That's the spirit," Wren grins, holding the dress for Ivy to step into. The dress is the corset type that allows no one to breathe with a skirt so full that it rubs up against everything when Ivy moves. For a warrior-trained young woman used to walking without a sound, the rustle of the dress sounds almost deafening in comparison.

Her shoes are heels this time. With all the Scavenger training, her mother thankfully insisted that she also learn everything there is to know about being royal, walking in any type of heeled shoe imaginable as well as being able to walk with books on her head and without dropping one.

The walk down to her mother's office is tedious, especially while trying to make sure her dress doesn't get snagged on anything on the way through. She fulfills one of her mother's requests before she goes outside to meet Finn. Queen Diannicalyn wants to be the first to see her daughter's beauty before her coming-of-age ball. At exactly midnight, she will be considered an adult in the eyes of ancient Law.

As Ivy approaches her mother's office, she finds the door already open wide and her mother sitting at the desk and smiling at her as she walks in.

"You look absolutely beautiful, my daughter. Thank you for letting me dress you."

Ivy looks at her mother with a sly smile. "As if I have a choice!"

Knowing all too well the tension they've endured throughout the years as it hangs heavily in the air, the two of them laugh together. Iveliis knows that she's a handful. All the same, her mother takes her hands and holds them out to the sides.

"You will make sure he knows you will not be marrying him?"

Ivy nods.

"Good. That boy needs to understand that in the ancient tradition, that not all royals have to serve. You have two aunts and six cousins who will be able to continue the Grenedich line."

Ivy smiles. "I know. I will never be able to keep up with all these rules you have to follow, anyhow."

"I'd say that one day you can try it, but I know all too well that you are not someone who will want to take a throne. You would much rather sit in the back corner and make faces as the magistrate speaks."

"His mustache is way too long for his face," Ivy argues with a chuckle.

Her mother makes herself serious again. "As long as you truly know that I am always here for you in any matter you need."

"I'm going to be a Scavenger, Mother. It's not like I won't be here half the year."

She notices a tear in her mother's eye. "There is no need for that," Ivy says. "I'm walking out the door to go to a ball, not leaving forever."

She makes light of the situation to help her mother keep her composure, but the fear and sorrow in her mother's features makes Ivy wonder what exactly is going on in her mother's mind.

"I love you, Mother."

Kissing her cheek, her mother says, "I love you, too, Iveliis."

Yearly Round

Clockwork

"I will consider it for duty. But I will not decide until I meet her. Can the Pale Council accept these terms?"

The three council members nod in unison as if knowing that it would be his answer. Knowing better than to outright defy the wishes of the Pale Council, Asher has crossed his arms over his chest in irritation. On the night of his transition, the council members give him a direct order. "Is there anything else, councilman?"

Ash's dad looks at him from the podium of three council members, the distinction between father and council member made when he was a youth in training, thus separating roles. From his position between the other two, his father nods. "We will be asking you to join the Protectors after your trial."

Beyond happy that the one career he focused on since boyhood has come to fruition. Ash lifts himself to his full height and nods to his father but reveals no evidence of his elation. As the sole heir to the Vale name and son of a councilman, he knows the constant necessity of decorum.

The day of minimal sleep hovering over his features, Ash answers his phone with. "Yeah?" An overwhelming anxiety surrounds memories he has been plagued with since he transitioned. Every year, he finds himself having the same dream, but somehow it is different this time.

"Hi, honey!" His mom's voice startles him out of his sleepless stupor.

"Is everything okay?" he asks concerned, remembering with urgency the knot in his stomach.

Aurora chuckles. "Of course it is! I am calling because there is this woman I would like you to meet." She waits for a reply.

"I don't want another blind date, Mom," Ash tells his mother earnestly.

Aurora laughs. "There is no reason to fight it, Sweety. You need to keep your options open, and you are never going to meet your lifemate at work. Especially when you work with only males!"

Ash rolls his eyes in annoyance. "You are aware that I don't want a lifemate, right?"

"Why on earth wouldn't you?" Aurora asks seriously.

Ash huffs, "You know why."

"It's just a prophecy." His mother dismisses the notion as Ash pictures her hand flying through the air as she says it.

Ash laughs. "It's a prophecy you have been studying for over a millennium, Mom. You can't tell me that it is unimportant. Otherwise, I would not have been given the ultimatum Dad gave me."

He chuckles at catching her haphazard lie.

"Then look at it this way. Consider it practice for dealing with women. Use it to your advantage that I'm willing to interfere because I care about your mental state," she huffs. "I don't need a sap who hides in the corner when a woman approaches him!"

"What's her name?" Ash asks, sighing in resignation with the fate of his night off in shambles due to the Terrors having their own crap to deal with. He can hear his mother smiling as she tells him the address of the female and that her name is Lola Stewart.

"Are you talking the daughter of councilman Jameson Stewart?" Remembering her well, he isn't too sure he wanted to be around her. If he remembered correctly, she was the one who used to stab the other little girls with pencils if she didn't like what they said to her. The obnoxious royal vibe always made him uneasy.

Aurora says, "Yes! You remember her! That's a good sign."

"Not so sure about that," he mumbles under his breath. "I've got to go, Mom. I have some other stuff I need to do before midnight."

"I love you, Asher," she says in her sing-song voice, knowing that she has gotten her way.

Ash rolls his eyes. "You too, Mom."

Ash runs through his errands, not dreading the date, but knowing that it's going to make him want to hide for another decade all the same. At the grocery store, he grabs the essential junk food that he sees the human women eye enviously with their need to keep calories low. Being of the Pale Race means that nutrients in his blood sustain his body, but that doesn't mean he doesn't like the taste of their more toxic food choices.

He stops into the hair salon he goes to every three weeks like clockwork. The vampire stylist knows exactly what he wants, as she has helped with his disguising for the past two hundred years. It's part of the cultural norm and law of the Pale Race to keep humans in the dark with regard to age. His millennial style favors a tapered cut with three inches on top, perfect for spiking his millennial style.

"Hey, Ash!" Gwen says as he walks into the salon.

Ash smiles, happy to see a face that he doesn't mind having a conversation with. Even though he can smell the attraction she has for him, she never shows it. Her husband of the past century and a half is enough for her that she stays faithful in all conceivable ways. Something he has noticed is rare when it comes to most of the Pale, humans and vampires. The Pale Race is different when someone finds a lifemate with the blood bond so strong they never seek out anyone else to fulfill their needs.

"Hello, Gwen."

"Same as usual?" she asks, draping the cloth over him and snapping it into place.

Ash rolls his eyes. "I really think I like this look. It works better than any of the others I've gone for."

Gwen chuckles. "Well, I can imagine that there aren't many people who would approach the goth you. However, I'm quite sure that they don't even sell those pants anymore."

Ash shrugs. "Maybe I'll stick with them anyway."

"Ash, it's been twenty years. You will have to change it up pretty soon, and you know it."

The general rule of anyone Pale or vampire is to change the appearance and location every ten years. "I'll let you decide on my next look at the next solstice. Will that work for you?"

Gwen smiles and, as she begins planning the next hair style out loud, he loses himself in thought, wondering why his stomach is still in knots.

Ash eventually shows up at the door of Lola Stewart, daughter of a councilman and of the Pale Race. He has dressed as his normal self, which is pretty much a 2000s Gothic store, the spikes on his head always frowned upon. However, in the grand scheme of things, they do the trick when it comes to anyone approaching him. Fashion changes and he doesn't, so he makes it his main goal always to pick the fashion that aggravates the mainstream, which in turn makes him less approachable.

He rings the doorbell on the mansion and steps back, waiting for the usual vampire employee to open the door for their Pale employer, but instead, "Asher Vale!" councilman Stewart says, surprised to see him standing there. "What are you doing here?"

Before Ash can say anything, a pretty blonde with blue eyes runs up to the door. "It's okay, Daddy. He's here for me." She gives her dad a peck on the cheek, and he glares at Asher with the look of a pissed-off boss.

Asher shrugs. "Ask my mother," he explains, not wanting to deal with a tirade.

With a stern look, the councilman nods, letting him know that he will be calling Aurora and that he does not approve of what is happening.

"Who is it, Jamie?" Lola's mother, Patricia, approaches the door and smiles brightly when she sees Ash standing there. "Oh, Asher!" What a pleasant surprise! Would you like a drink?"

"No, thank you, Mrs. Stewart. I will have her back by four o'clock, sir," Ash adds, knowing that it isn't going to be one of those other kinds of dates. On a usual date with a Pale female, he can expect to get a little bit of casual sex, but when considering he is on a date with the boss's daughter, he knows better.

Lola grabs Ash by the arm and drags him out of the house. "Let's go, Asher! I'm famished!" Ash gives one last look back at Mr. Stewart and nods, unable to make eye contact. "Oh! Is this a Jaguar?" Lola asks as she eyes his BMW540i.

"Something like that," he says, opening her door for her and offering his hand for her to step into the car. It's not like he has forgotten his manners, though it's safe to say that his mother was right about him needing to keep up on them. *But I will never admit that!* He says to himself.

Ash seems to find himself nodding and agreeing as there is a running commentary the entire way to his restaurant. The problem with human restaurants: they are rarely open when the Pale Race wants to eat. Ash had decided in the forties that he needed a place open for him. Never having time to cook his own meals but getting hungry just as the humans do was a problem.

They arrive at the nearest Beacham's, one of several he's opened over the years. Knowing the table that he always takes, Ash parks in front of the main window. When he parks in the right spot, he can always keep an eye on the car from his table, which is necessary for the neighborhood.

He goes to the passenger door and opens it for Lola, who steps a scantily clad leg out the door, showing off her black heels. She rises out of the car as if she is stepping onto the red carpet as she smooths her short red dress and smiles with poise.

"I like your dress," he says with a polite smile.

Lola smiles as she takes his arm. "I thought you would have commented on the shoes."

Ash looks down, seeing them and not wanting to have a conversation about shoes. With a small shrug, he says, "They're nice."

"Nice?" Lola asks with a foul look on her face. "They're Louboutin peep-toe pumps. For the price, they are always more than just nice." She haughtily tosses her hair, and Ash looks up to the sky in terror. *Kill me now!*

Ash calms himself down and smiles again with the polite smile he was taught as a child. "I'm sorry. I'm not much of a fashion person."

Lola giggles, looking at his Tripp pants with a raised eyebrow. "I can tell."

Did she just diss the pants! Oh, it's on! He eyes her as she carefully steps over a manhole, probably afraid either to break her neck or get stuck in the tread. The shoes barely bring her height to his shoulder, and it floors him, because she is wearing heels that need platforms in the front to get the heel positioned well.

Ash laughs to himself as Lola looks around the restaurant in dismay. Ash glances around, seeing the old restaurant clean but slightly run down. "Is this where we are eating?"

"Yes. It has amazing food," he says, knowing that most women would turn their noses up at the idea of actually eating, which helps him assess them and rule out the stuck-up ones at the same time. This one is worse than the stuck-up ones, because she doesn't even wait for the food to arrive before she takes on the appearance of a shrew.

They sit down in his favorite booth, and he almost starts laughing when her hand sticks to the table because of an unremoved dollop of maple syrup. "Eew," she complains, shaking her hand to get it off.

"Hang on," Ash says to her, grabbing a wet nap from the carousel at the inside edge of the table. Handing it to her, he says, "It was probably a family with kids sitting here before us." He smiles, trying to lessen the blow for her.

"Kids are always so gross," she mutters, then, realizing herself, bats her eyelashes at him. "When they are the innocent beauties that I love so much, that is." *Wow!*

"I'm sorry, Lola. I should have looked."

There is horror in her eyes as she wipes her hands. "Why would you have me sit at a table that hasn't been cleaned yet?"

Ash shrugs. "I didn't think it was going to be dirty."

"That's right. You didn't think," she says to herself and widens her eyes as she inspects her hands in annoyance.

The waitress comes to the table and asks what they would like to order.

Lola sits up straighter and smiles politely with scrutiny in her eyes. "I would like the Caesar salad without croutons or dressing." *Isn't that just lettuce?* "And I would also like a water with extra lemon." Appearing around forty years ago, females of the Pale Race began basically starving themselves, as they worry about getting fat, though it's baffling why, since they metabolize so quickly it's impossible for them to gain too much weight.

Members of the Pale Race have to eat due to having a heartbeat. Nutrients in food help their organs function. They need blood in their diet because their bodily functions rely on it. Vampires, however, do not eat food, have no heartbeat, and can't tolerate sunlight. They have to drink blood to sustain the blood magic the Pale Race uses to transition them into vampires.

"How about you, sir?" the waitress asks him with a patient smile. Ash has made sure that his staff knows he is to be treated like a customer, especially in the presence of a female. All his staff are vampires or Pale during the night shift and humans during the day so that he can keep the restaurant open twenty-four hours.

Ash smiles, getting his usual. "I would like the porterhouse with mash and broccoli. Rare."

She nods. "And to drink?"

"I would like a large chocolate milkshake with three cherries." He smiles and hands her the menu. "Thank you."

Twenty minutes later, the food arrives. It couldn't have been soon enough, either. The woman's constant ramble is enough for him to chew his arm off. *At least if she's eating something, her mouth will be full of food and not words.*

Lola looks down at the lettuce she had ordered and looks up at him with irritation. "That woman isn't getting a tip!" Ash eyes her over a bite of broccoli, and she mutters rude comments under her breath as she picks croutons out of her salad one at a time in distaste.

Stabbing the last piece of broccoli and putting it in his mouth, Ash chews his food as he wonders why Lola is so determined not to eat a tiny bread bite. He sees terror in the eyes of his date as she realizes he will eat his meal, he chokes back a laugh by stuffing a chunk of meat in his mouth.

Lola is in front of him, smiling shyly, though Ash can tell from the look through her lashes that it's an act. Her blue eyes seem like oceans, but if you get close enough, you can see the icebergs within. She is there for one of the three things that women always want from him: sex, money, or power. The problem worsens when one realizes that he has all three in spades.

Every ten years, he faces the same thing as he reminisces about the past thirty-some-odd dates he has been forced into. There are only so many royals in the Pale Race, and he fears he's getting to the bottom rungs as he peers over at her.

After centuries knowing that, if he finds his lifemate he can never marry her, the idea of intimacy beyond the physical puts a sour taste in his mouth. Even as he sits in front of a woman who will probably make any other man whistle on the way to work, it doesn't matter. The secret he has been forced to keep since he was twenty-one nags at him, even if there is no chance he will ever choose to be with her.

"So, you are a general?" The lettuce moves here and there on her plate as she debates taking a bite.

Ash nods. "Yes. I have a team of Protectors that work under me." He sees the wheels rolling around in her mind.

"Is the pay good?" *Did she really just ask me that?*

"It's decent."

"You will make a woman happy some night, you know, making sure that she is pampered and safe." The calculating smile she gives him is enough to throw him off his game.

"So, what do you do for work?" Ash asks forgetting himself.

Lola cocks a perfectly manicured eyebrow at him in annoyance. "I am a female. I don't need to work." She moves her food around more earnestly on her plate, eyeing it like it's the last thing she wants to eat as he scarfs down his steak.

Ash forces himself to look sheepish, though internally he wants to run. "I don't date much. Sorry if I offended you."

Lola smiles at him. "It's not a problem. I do some charity here and there, some babysitting for my sister." She doesn't meet his eye, and he remembers the statement she made earlier about kids, which prompts him the think she's lying through her teeth. Never understanding what females do with their lives is a constant reason that he doesn't date.

"That's very nice of you," he replies, digging into the mashed potatoes and shoveling them into his mouth. The idleness women have expected from him is torture. One time he risked a second date only to sit on a veranda for six hours while she had her pedicure.

Lola grins, "Want to take our dinner to go?" She pauses a moment as she seductively eyes him. "I don't have to be home for a few hours."

Ash can smell her arousal.

Jeez! Already? I haven't even had my dessert

Slightly uneasy about the look in her eye, Ash looks up as he figures that she probably has a plan to trap him. He shoves the last piece of steak and two bites of potatoes into his mouth, then looks in his wallet to pay the check, including a decent tip for his employee. It also gives him an excuse to make sure he put a condom in his wallet that morning. *At least I can get something out of these dates.*

"Let's get out of here."

Thorns with Every Rose

True Colors

"Mr. Finn Naese here to pick up Princess Iveliis," Hawk, Ivy's mother's other guard announces as Finn approaches the open door.

Her mother nods to the guard and looks up into her daughter's eyes. "Let's see how this young man cleans up, shall we?"

Ivy nods reluctantly.

"Even if he is an ass," her mother mutters under her breath.

Ivy chokes back laughter as the two of them walk into the foyer and see Finn standing there. He's dressed in a goldish green tuxedo and holding a rose. They decide that he does clean up well with his shoulder length, pin straight, golden blond hair tied to the back of his head. He doesn't bother to look at Ivy as he walks past her and hands the flower to her mother.

"Thank you, Your Highness, for allowing me to take your daughter to the ball and for considering my proposal."

The look of amazement in her mother's eyes makes Ivy want to deck him. The preposterous idea that her mother would force her to stay in Lesai after she becomes an adult does not sit well with Ivy at all. She knows that her mother would never push her to stay of course, but Finn's audacity in thinking she will stay grates on her last nerve.

"Let's go," Ivy says rudely to Finn, almost dragging him out of her mother's dwelling.

"What is your issue, Princess?" Finn asks, disgruntled.

Ivy swings around and gives him the hardest glare she can. "I will not be pushed around tonight. Nor will I allow you to make my coming-of-age ball about your ego. There will not be another word of me staying in Lesai until I bring it up. Do I make myself clear?"

Finn looks away, huffing in the silence of the forest, then meets her gaze again. "When will we speak of it, then? I want a specific time. You are not going to keep putting me off."

"I have made it clear since day one what my plans are, Finn. If you are still unable to see them for what they are, then I beg you to walk away."

"I need a time."

Ivy throws up her hands in defeat. "I will give you my answer before midnight. Don't ask again." She immediately spins around and stalks towards the ball tents on the other side of the meadow. She knows full well that she will be stalking away for about a quarter mile in heels no less.

About thirty seconds before Ivy reaches the opening of the rose tent, Finn, out of breath, catches up with her,. "Stop, please, Ivy! I've asked you ten times by now!"

Ivy stops, if only to get him to stop pouting like a child.

"Thank you. Now can we please forget the conversation and have a fun time?"

Ivy gives in and nods. She wants to be surrounded by other people. Her nerves are getting itchier by the minute. The ball means goodbye to people she's known her whole life, and even if she sees a few of them in the next few years, many of them she will never see again.

Finn tucks her hand into the crook of his elbow and smiles grandly as he escorts her into the entryway. He speaks to the man doing introductions. After raising an eyebrow at Ivy, he enters the hall on the other side and projects his voice. Ivy and Finn hear, "Introducing the reason we have all gathered here tonight, Iveliis Grenedich, Princess of Lesai, and her fiancée, Mr. Finn Naese."

There is a roar of applause and cheering as Finn, having to pull Ivy into the room, takes on the royal airs of a king at court. Ivy looks at Finn with contempt while he smiles ear to ear and loving every minute of being the center of attention.

Why would I ask a princess if I could have us introduced together? Ivy imagines Finn never having thought, since she had never accepted his proposal. The loathing makes Ivy queasy as she looks around, realizing that she is in a room filled with people she knows but has never been close to. The room feels as if it is closing in around her, and she looks for the nearest corner to hide in.

Squashing the overwhelming urge to pull her hand out of the crook in his arm, she refuses to draw attention to her own insecurities. Instead, Ivy walks forward into the center of the room, away from all the people she knows. She pulls Finn right out onto the dance floor. She knows for the first thirty seconds, it will be just them, according to custom. Once the first thirty seconds of music have passed, her peers follow suit, swaying to violins and harps. The dances of the Ancients are the oldest created, intricate enough to include formal steps. Skirts float around to the careful placing of silent feet excluding the possibility of talking.

To Ivy, there is nothing worse than having everyone stare at her. It's bad enough that she will always be the oddball, black hair to their white, alabaster skin to their tans, only making friends when her peers want some of the limelight. Even at the moment, though, she realizes that the only people she trusts are her mother, Willow, Aster, and Wren.

She eyes the side of the dance floor and spots Aster flirting with a few men and enjoying her night. As Ivy catches Aster's eye, though, she sees Aster turn so that she's facing away from the dance floor as the others she's with watch Ivy with odd looks. Refusing to eavesdrop and fearing the worst, Ivy dances, making the music a part of her. As much as she gets along as an adult with others, she knows that her sickness makes her different. The sadness she feels bleeds into the music as she dances on.

The dance ends, and another five dashing men in their traditional attire ask Ivy to dance. Finn does not approve, but she's happy she's able to get away from him for at least a short while as the dancing progresses. They all seem to want to dance with her because she's a promised woman, especially when they remember all the times they and others teased her throughout the years. They will never again have the chance to dance with her not that they genuinely want one, of course. The last one bows in honor to her royalty, and she goes to the drink table. She hears a couple of women whispering about her and smiles at them to let them know she can hear. They scurry away, not wanting to risk her wrath, after all, since that is what she has always been known for.

Nursing a glass of mead, she walks to a corner, not the head table where she's supposed to sit to watch the ball. She feels dizzy yet again, so she sits as well as the taffeta will allow and puts her feet up on a chair under the table. She wards off a couple more men seeking her out to dance and watches as people she has known her whole life enjoy the night.

She notices a few people in the corner whooping and hollering about who knows what and smiles to herself, wishing that she could be so carefree. *They're probably drunk!* She thinks to herself idly before she sees Finn standing in the middle of them boasting about something in a ridiculous manner. Ivy silently moans to herself, knowing that even if she were staying in Lesai, an ice age could arrive and she would flash freeze before marrying him.

Finn catches her eye, and she looks away quickly, hoping he will skim right past her, but to no avail. She senses him coming purposefully towards her and pretends not to notice.

"May I have this dance, Iveliis?" Finn asks, hand out.

"Can I sit this one out? My feet need a break, and I'm not feeling all that well." Taking another sip, she smiles gently and gestures to the others around them. "Take a seat with me."

"I don't want to sit this one out. You shouldn't have wasted your energy on other men." Finn grabs her hand and pulls her out of her seat, causing her foot to get tangled in the chair she had used to prop her feet. The mead that she held has become a stain on the gown, yet he doesn't seem to notice as he half drags her towards the side door of the tent.

"You owe me an answer."

The tenor of his voice makes the hair on her neck stand up.

It's much later than Ivy thought from the position of the stars and the full moon above her. She curses to herself as she feels pain in her ankle and the headache starting behind her eyes.

As Finn pulls Ivy through the woods, she glares at his back while thanking the Elemental Mother that he's showing Ivy who he truly is before she ever trusts him with her heart. As they near a secluded spot under a giant oak tree, she decides that enough is enough. Not allowing Finn to pull her any further, Ivy stops dead in her tracks. Realizing that her strength exceeds his even after his decade of male growth, she pulls her hand from his grip.

"I am not sure what you want me to say to you, Finn," she tells him. "I have made myself clear from the start. I will be a Scavenger, and I have no intention of doing anything else."

Finn laughs at her. "You women don't know what you have in front of your faces."

"I know exactly what's standing in front of me: a power-hungry ass, whose mother never taught him the word no"

Finn slaps her across the face with all the force he can muster. "If you will not agree with me, then I will force your hand." Crossing his arms over his chest, he puffs himself up.

Ivy smiles. "You really think that you can hurt me? I have been training with children who can hit harder than you. There is no way that you can possibly force my hand into marriage. I am a royal. I have my pick of the litter, as long as the litter is worthy of the elders' approval."

Her hands fly everywhere as she yells at him. "You have never been nor will you ever be worthy of a royal marriage. It doesn't matter if you bully every male in Lesai. I'd stay a spinster with cats before I would marry you, you presumptuous tart!"

Thinking that he still has the upper hand, he gives her a look that says, *don't be so naive.* "If I plant a child in you, you won't be able to leave." The look on his face becomes menacing as he feels he has the upper hand. "If your mother won't stop you from leaving, then I will. I have worked too hard to get to this point."

Unwavering, Ivy takes a step towards him. "I dare you to try!" Ivy shouts. "You think that forcing yourself on me will make me marry you?"

She could take off his head and not flinch.

She reaches back both hands to draw her swords, ready for the battle to begin and forgetting the admonition to leave them in her room that night.

Shit! A moment of panic floats through her mind as she realizes that her swords are lying on her bed at home. *That's it. I am never leaving without my swords again. I'm going to have to do this the old-fashioned way.*

The thought makes her square her stance and smile menacingly at the little shit. "You have no idea what you are getting into. I am going to kick your—"

She sees red, and a searing pain starts in her fingertips and slowly envelopes her entire right arm. Her eyes flash red and gold, making her queasy, as she holds on to the oak tree. Without the support, she won't be able to stop herself from falling over. *This surely hasn't happened to me before.* The pain level keeps rising and begins coiling itself around her neck, eventually searing her entire body. Setting every nerve ending on fire, it creates a sensitivity as it ebbs and she feels the air move every tiny hair on her skin.

She experiences an ache as she puts her finger to her mouth and feels a painful bulge in her gums. Something sharper and longer slowly slides out, wrenching sobs from her as they grow. Her ears blow up in pain as she hears everything that is going on at the party and around her—laughs in the ballroom tent, birds chirping, burrowing mice, and everything in between so that she can't differentiate one sound from another amid the growing cacophony.

She smells dense earth pure and thriving beneath her feet, allowing herself to kneel as she tries meditation. Ivy's head tips back as she begins drawing elemental magic in waves of strength to dissipate the pain and calm the churning nausea. The intensity of chaos makes her focus sporadic at best, and her eyes blur in and out, pupils dilating with a new searing pain. She bows down, laying her head on the earth, asking the Elemental Mother to stop the agony.

She doesn't know how long she is there, only that she's panting on her hands and knees as internal panic grips every facet of her body. *What on the mother's green earth was that?* she asks herself as pain slowly ebbs away. She hears ants skittering beneath the surface of the soil under her as she feels the movement of the air around her.

I must be going nuts.

The smell of the grass between her fingers overwhelms her nose, and she tries to hold her breath to stifle it but ends up sneezing instead. The echo of the sneeze hurts her eardrums as it becomes louder than all other noise. She covers her ears, and a heart-wrenching sob escapes her as, her mind too foggy to get a grip, she tries to understand what's happening.

Hunched over, Ivy feels a new excruciating pain. It explodes repeatedly throughout her sides. She feels herself ripped off the ground and thrown over a shoulder, and it takes her a moment to remember that she isn't alone. She's being carried like a sack of grain as her hip bone grinds into Finn's shoulder.

"Put me down!" she yells, the sound echoing off the trees and making her dizzy as she beats his back and fights through his attack.

"I am bringing you directly to the queen. I don't know what that was, but I am sure that it isn't supposed to happen.

He starts to talk to himself. "This one is defective. I should have known that it would never work when she flew off the handle at a whim."

She feels him shaking his head.

"And who in their right mind wouldn't want to be with me? No one who is worth anything, that's who. I hope the queen makes sure she's locked away, or better yet, rid Lesai of the trouble of a psychotic heir."

All of the pain thrust upon her is more than enough to handle without the running commentary of an egotistical jerk. His words echoing all around her, she agonizes.

She opens her eyes a little bit to try to get a bearing on her surroundings. What had once been a night of darkness, illuminated by the full moon and the luscious stars, has become as brilliantly lit as a gloomy day. She can see everything even as movement tempts her body to vomit. She finds every nuance of color staining a tiny leaf or flower so breathtaking that she's able to drown out the sound of Finn.

Ivy returns to real time as she hears, "I rescind my marriage proposal. I do not know what just happened, but I can tell you right now that I will not marry or breed with an ancient psycho," Finn rants as he walks into her mother's office. Dumping Ivy onto the floor, he places his hands on his hips, tapping his foot impatiently. "This defective, she devil needs to be put in a cage at the very least."

Queen Diannicalyn sneers at him and runs to Ivy. "She isn't going to marry you, anyway. Mind your tongue or you will have no station in Lesai ever."

Concern etched on every feature, she turns to her daughter. "Are you okay?"

Ivy looks at her and smiles, her new fangs showing brightly in the room. Her mother nods, seeming to understand what is going on. *What in the hell is happening to me?* "Guards!"

Reed and Hawk enter the room and wait on her mother for directives. "Take him to the guest bedroom and make him comfortable. He's to speak to no one." The look of shock on Finn's face pleases Ivy, her abdomen still fighting pain from the abuse.

Reed and Hawk nod and escort Finn out of the office. The doors close with a thud that makes Ivy jump and wince as she covers her ears. It isn't just the sound but the air movement as she feels as if her eardrums are being plucked from her skull.

Quietly and calmly, her mother asks, "When did this happen?"

Ivy shrugs as she curls into herself in a daze.

"A little bit ago."

Her mother looks at the clock on the wall. "It wasn't supposed to happen until after the ceremony. Your father said that it happens at the exact time of the birth." She shakes her head. "I didn't want to believe that it would be this soon. I am so sorry that you went through that by yourself."

Ivy looks at her mother with a thousand questions racing through her muddled mind. "My father?"

Her mother nods.

"You said that my father was a human who died."

"I had to lie to protect you. If I hadn't, you would have been left to die at birth."

The queen pulls out her cell phone. "There's no time. I need to get you out of here. It's not safe for you to be here anymore.

"Is everything okay?" a male voice asks on the other end of the phone.

"No. She changed at midnight. I thought you said —"

The man's heated rant interrupts her mother.

"I told you repeatedly that the time of her change will be unpredictable, especially with the way time flows in Lesai. It doesn't matter that she is not twenty-one out here for another few months. She's a hybrid fledgling. Shit! I'll be at the spot in an hour."

He sounds more worried than angry, but Ivy worries more at the idea that someone has spoken to a queen as if she isn't any better than him.

"I am so sorry, Soren," the queen says into the phone. She hugs Ivy, prompting Ivy's internal panic. "I wish all of this was different."

The queen sniffs, and Ivy jumps at the sound. *My mother doesn't cry.*

"She will be there," the queen says into the phone.

The phone goes silent. With all the vigor of an icy heart, the queen calls to her guards.

Reed and Hawk return and eye Ivy carefully. "Bring my daughter to this meadow right here." She points to a map on her desk. "There will be a man there who will make sure she remains safe."

They nod in unison.

"You know what this is about. I will never forget the loyalty the two of you have shown me over the years, and you will be compensated." She pauses a moment.

"I also need the two of you to take care of the Finn problem. He made it perfectly clear to me that he will not be discreet about what he just saw."

They look uneasy, and she continues. "He just saw what Ivy's teeth look like. He will gain favor in any way that he can, even if it means sending his queen to the viper's nest."

Ivy hears the observation and clears her throat, drawing their attention to herself even though she doesn't want to. "Before I transformed," she says, "he told me that he will force me to stay by making sure that I have his child in me." She lifts the remnants of her ravaged gown from her stomach to show them red bruises with hints of purple seeping in.

Ivy sees ice cover her mother's features. Looking as if she wants to take care of the Finn problem herself, the queen glares at the door to her office,

Hawk lays a gentle hand on the queen's shoulder. "Consider it taken care of," he says.

The queen eyes them with the cold look that has taken the edge out of many enemies and whispers, "Do not go easy on him. At least this helps with the plan."

Reed and Hawk give a little smile and look back at Ivy before heading out to prepare horses for departure. Realizing that she has just signed Finn's death warrant, Ivy stares at the door after they leave.

Her mother approaches her and shifts her dress even further again to reveal much more bruising than she had shown the guards.

"He really said that?" the queen asks with an air of menace that makes Ivy's hair stand on end.

"What is all this?" Ivy asks, gazing down at the mark of vines creeping up her arm.

Tracing the lines as if mesmerized by them, her mother stares at Ivy's arm but catches herself and looks at the clock. An eerie feeling travels up

Ivy's spine. "Your father can tell you all of that when you get to him. I want to make our last few minutes count."

"Wait what do you mean?"

"Iveliis, we don't have time for this. We need to get you packed and out of here before the Elders realize what you are."

Ivy nods reluctantly as she understands that time is of the essence, even if she has absolutely no idea what is happening.

The two of them go up to Ivy's bedroom. When they arrive, Wren hands Ivy a cup of the tea. Ivy smells the meditation tea as her mother watches her daughter's features.

"You've been giving me blood?" Ivy looks at her mother's face and sees the truth. She smells it again, gagging at the thought that it came out of someone else.

"Drink it," her mother insists. "We don't have time for thinking too much."

Knowing that it's really not new considering she has been drinking it for years, Ivy gulps in disgust. In a quick tip of the cup and two swallows, she downs it. Ivy can feel color creep into her cheeks as whatever its made from quells the sickness.

Her mother nods, focusing her attention elsewhere. "It was the only way for us to keep you from hurting others, especially when you started biting other kids. We tried the blood, knowing your heritage, and it seemed to work for a while." Her mother goes through her closet, packing a bag. "We don't have time for this, sweetheart. Get dressed. Fighting attire, please."

Ivy looks at her mother shocked and goes to speak, but her mother puts her hand up. "Just do it. Scabbard too."

Ivy does what she's told even though she knows that her mother won't answer all her questions.

Wren looks back and forth between them. "Where is she going?"

Ivy shrugs. Her mother looks over Ivy's head at Wren as Ivy stuffs her bag with items and clothing. "She will be safe."

"But with who? No one else will know how to handle her."

Ivy raises her eyebrows, offended as Wren continues to speak as if she isn't standing right there.

"I can go with her."

Ivy goes to speak, and her mother interrupts her. "Iveliis will be perfectly fine. The place she is staying has everything she will need. Now, get her hairbrush from the bathroom."

"She needs to be with family," Wren insists, standing up to Ivy's mother in a way that Ivy has never seen.

Ivy watches as her mother seems to grow six inches, towering over Wren. "You will do as asked, and you will keep your mouth shut. I will not tolerate the help getting into my family affairs."

Wren whips around and stomps into the bathroom.

"That was harsh," Ivy says.

Seeming to have information she isn't sharing, Ivy's mother looks at her daughter with pity. "Sometimes you have to be offensive to get things accomplished."

"But Wren is like family."

Trying not to make her mother even more angry, Ivy shuffles her feet. Her mother approaches her and whispers quickly, "Like family is not family, Iveliis. There will come a time when you understand why I have made the decisions that I have. Please understand that and, no matter what, do not discuss any of this with anyone except for those whom your true family trusts."

Ivy nods and her mother walks back to the other side of the room as Ivy gets back to getting dressed.

Her mother looks at her, wearing her usual black leggings and soft boots, and interrupts her putting on a tank top with, "Long sleeve. No one can see that." She refers to the vines climbing Ivy's arm and circling her neck on her collar bones.

"Okay."

Ten minutes later, Wren says goodbye as she tries to smile through tears. "We will meet again, Miss." Ivy feels that the friendship between them will never be bested, even though her mother chooses not to trust her.

"I sure hope so," Ivy says as she turns Wren's curtsy into a giant hug. Her mother looks at Ivy, gives her a deep hug, and walks into her office, closing the door. Ivy knows that her mother can't let her subjects see her emotional, so she doesn't fight it when her mother disappears.

Finn rides a horse looking like a snake, eyes slit with distaste. As she mounts the beautiful mare she's always ridden and strokes her mane, Finn says, "I knew Queen Diannicalyn would agree that you need to be put away until death."

Ivy wants to crush him. Apparently, Reed and Hawk fed him a few lies to make him compliant.

Reed and Hawk look between the two of them and then do the last thing she ever expects. They in turn make her laugh as they play rock paper scissors to see who gets to take him out. Finn glares indignantly at Ivy, then seems to dismiss her laughter as another crazed thing to add to the reason she should be locked away.

"When your mother's guard asked if I would accompany them to deliver you to the loony bin, I almost didn't agree." The haughty attitude oozes from him. "Something about dignity and the like. It wasn't until I realized that you might come back one day to haunt me that I decided to make sure you will stay locked up." He hefts a bag of coins. "I intend to make sure that you never see the light of day again."

Ivy seethes about a mile from the meadow. She knows they are too far away to be overheard. "You are a loathsome little tyrant, aren't you?" She hates herself for not making it clear years ago that he had no chance. Even as a child, he was a little jerk.

Finn has the nerve to look mortified at the accusation. "Are you kidding me? You are the one who is a tyrant, Throwing tantrums when you don't get what you want—a spoiled and completely psychotic royal who will be the end of Lesai."

"I have no intention of ever ruling, which you know well, since I have said as much since the first day we met."

Ivy laughs at his idiocy.

Finn looks out at the forest. "You could have had everything. All you had to do was marry me, pop out a few babies, and do whatever you wanted after. I know that was my plan!"

"You really think that I would ever let you touch me?"

Finn grins to himself. "We have kissed a thousand times. So yes, you have let me touch you.

"A kiss is nothing if it is not wanted." Ivy looks daggers at him. "How many times did I push you off me because you thought it was your right to take what you want?"

Finn looks right at her. "I had every right the moment that you became my girlfriend. There is a reason that men ruled for a millennium. It's because men are not fraught with the emotional baggage that women are. The moment they allowed a woman to rule Lesai was the moment that the realm became tainted. After all, look at what the queen birthed!"

Ivy laughs as the horses continue to move forward under them. "You are a real piece of work, dude."

"Me? You grew fangs! What kind of ancient grows fangs?"

"The kind you don't want to mess with, half wit," Ivy says, feeling an ache in her teeth.

Finn laughs with jovial sarcasm. "If only there was something you could do. But there isn't. You are screwed, my lady, your long life ending as we have this lover's quarrel."

"Lover's quarrel? Are you really that dim? I have never loved nor will I ever love you. You are a self-righteous ass who actually believes himself worthy of affection. Never once have I ever considered you a prospect as a husband, and I sure as shit would *never* have you sitting under me on the throne of Lesai!" Ivy yells.

"Sugar, I would never have been under you in bed or on the throne. You would have been in your place from the day that ring was around your finger."

"You are aware that you are a piece of shit, right?" She watches his face as he lifts his chin in utter defiance.

"It's better than being crazy! To think that I was planning to impregnate you tonight so you can't leave. Thank the Elemental Mother for small favors."

"Fat chance of that. You couldn't force me if it were your only mission in life."

"I'd have to force myself and you. You are royalty, which begs me to ask, how the hell are you so gross looking? The fair-haired princess my parents promised me is definitely not what I am looking at." Finn grimaces and looks ahead.

It isn't her intention to get so angry that she'd hurt him, since she knows there's already a plan in place. Reed and Hawk have already decided, but she realizes her mistake too late. She can feel anger coming in waves along with the intense urge to rip his throat out.

"The Elemental Mother won't do any favors for you. You probably couldn't even fertilize anything if you wanted to," Ivy says as she dismounts her mare.

They have arrived at the meadow. Finn jumps down lithely and barges into her space. "You will rot, you ugly, bit—ahhhhh!" Smiling, Ivy punches him in the face. Her fangs pulse painfully.

"I've been meaning to do that."

Reed and Hawk look at her with pride, and she sees that Finn's nose has erupted with his blood.

"You foul leper!" she cries as she roundhouse kicks him in the head, his blood spattering her face as she makes impact. He staggers back, then charges her with elf speed and tackles her. Ivy feels him hitting her in the face, and everything turns red. She can still see everything and smell everything. The artery on the side of his neck pulses, just begging her to bite it.

She cringes inwardly as the thought of blood in her mouth repulses her. Finn's heartbeat picks up in pace when he meets her eyes and sees them bright red. Uncontrolled, she feels a pull of hunger never before experienced so forcefully.

Frantically he tries to get away from her, he fumbles back and falls in the grass. "Please don't hurt me," he begs, cowardice showing bright on his face. But even as she comprehends that she should rein in her temper with her stomach in knots at the thought, nothing can stop the need for sustenance that has gripped every muscle in her body.

Ivy stalks him like prey as she hears his blood rush louder and faster. She smiles knowing that her anger serves a purpose. She hovers over him as he freezes in fear, and a moment later, she feels her teeth pierce his skin, puncturing the vein she's been watching.

Blood flows as she pulls her teeth slightly out of the holes, her lips to his neck. Ivy drinks deep to suck every drop of lifeblood from his body, the magic in him creeping out into her limbs. She can feel it begin to flow through her veins as her body absorbs it.

She's on fire, and Finn is dead.

His eyes have struck with horror before she pulls herself off him. Thick black, almost blue, non-oxygenated blood covers his neck. She tilts her head to the side and observes her handiwork.

I am going to need more practice if I don't want to bring a change of clothes to every feeding, she thinks. The fact that she doesn't see red anymore puts her nerves on edge.

I remembered it all! She holds her stomach, slightly nauseated, with the initial rush of blood over.

She looks over and sees Reed and Hawk gulp with a mix of fear and revulsion. "Are you okay?" she asks?

They both nod and turn around, making themselves busy with her mother's plan.

Ivy loves the energy she's feeling, and even more, she loves being able to see so well at night!

As she peers around, she sees a man watching from the edge of the meadow. He's taller than Ivy and has jet-black hair like hers. She can see every line on his face and notices quickly that she looks just like him.

She can hear his breath hitch when he gets close enough to see that their eyes mark the only similarity between herself and her mother. She has her mother's eyes, gray with black rings, but Ivy's switch to a glowing red the moment she begins to feel the sickness.

To Protect the Hybrid

Protectors

Four men and two women stand in the parking lot of the retired mental ward used as a holding cell. Soren, general of the Beasts, waits at the front of their group for everyone to gather.

"Okay. We have at least one known female inside. Getting her home safely is our top priority. Sonya, distract the guards. Calyn, while she has their attention, sneak in and unlock the door at the back hall for us to enter."

The women nod, disappearing into the dark as the three who stay consider their jobs.

Ash's blood burns as always before a fight. With the last few decades of females going missing, the night carries high need of a win. "Ash, you have the female. As soon as you find her, get her out and gone. Do not wait for us."

Ash nods and asks, "You two are heading for the guards?"

"Yes," Soren says with finality. "Stone and I are the front line. Cason is the man on deck."

Soren looks up over the huddle as Ash also sees the silhouette of Calyn sliding a knife across the throat of a guard attempting to yell out.

"It's a go," confirms Soren.

Ash turns off everything else in his mind as he heads into the brightly lit hall with doors on every wall. Ignoring the commotion, he starts to open each door. The effort proves pointless as he realizes how many doors in all to open.

Ash closes his eyes and begins walking down the hall. He ignores the sound of racing human male heartbeats as he searches for the distinct sound of a Pale female's heart. He hears the slow beat to his right, and he opens his eyes as he walks straight into the room.

He opens a curtain and sees the woman's eyes wide in panic as a human quickly attempts to drain her blood. Ash rips the IV out of her hand. Before the human has time to consider escaping death, Ash rips the human's throat out with a slash. He doesn't bother to ingest any of the blood.

"Are you okay to move?"

The woman nods and glances down at her slightly distended belly.

Ash can hear the quick pace of the little one inside her womb. "Is the baby going to be okay?" she asks.

As much as he wants to reassure the mother that no harm has been done, he can't. He doesn't know how much blood the human has taken from her. "Let's get you to a healer so they can let you know," Ash says. "I'm not a doctor. I'm a Protector."

"Okay."

Ash sees the woman limp out of the bed, the dirty johnny she wears in tatters. Her foot looks as if it's been broken.

Without asking the woman if it's okay, he lifts her up into his arms. If she's limping, he won't be able to get her through the clashing battle happening just outside the room.

"I am going to run," Ash tells her. "Hold on, okay?"

The woman nods, not saying a word as she grips his neck tightly, hiding her face in his collar.

Ash awakes to the sunset as he remembers the different rescues he's completed successfully with the Beasts and the Terrors as well as the ones that went badly. Shaking such thoughts from his mind, remembrance of the horrible, earlier date remains. If it wasn't bad enough that she constantly complained, it was even worse when she tried to bite him. Now granted, that is how a lot of the Pale Race date as they attempt to find out if they are lifemates. In fact, Cason, one of Ash's Terrors, found his lifemate that way. The issue is, Ash doesn't ever want to find out if he has a lifemate. That would mean he would know the woman he is blood-bonded to but won't be able to keep for the eternal life they will both endure. The Pale Race is the only race gifted with the lifemate bond and Ash is of the Pale Race.

Ugh! Stop thinking about depressing crap, Ash! He gets out of bed and takes a shower. The feeling of something terribly wrong still upsetting him, he dresses quickly and sets out on his average Monday. Taking his phone out of his pocket, he calls Stone.

"Hello?"

"Hey, contact the informant from the other night. I have a gut feeling we are missing something with our recon."

"Okay, Boss. Is there anything else?"

Ash looks out the window, deciding that he may have to visit his father that night as well. "If you can't get through, text me with any updates you get."

"Heading to your parents'?"

"I might be."

"Copy that. Tell your sister I say hi."

Ash growls, "Knock that shit off, Stone." Stone chuckles as Ash hangs up on him, exits his apartment, and heads down to the mailboxes. Without looking carefully at it and figuring that he can go through it when he gets to the club, he grabs the mail and tosses it on the seat of his car.

Traffic in the city is horrible as he goes, aggravating him, but not because it's taking forever. Idiots who get too close to his car make him want to throw a penny out the window at them. Time moves so slowly for the Pale Race that sitting for an hour in traffic means nothing.

He gets to the club and parks in the garage. He sees that just as with every night, a few dozen people wait for the doors to open. He looks down the line and sees a full-figured woman in her mid-to-late twenties and appearing shy as she waits for the line to move. Ash sees a few glamour bots cut in front of her and, even though he can see that she is upset by it, she doesn't say anything.

Not ever having to deal with not being noticed, Ash feels for her and walks over to her. "Come with me, please."

The woman looks around, not expecting that he's addressing her. "Me?"

Ash nods and holds his hand out to her. He feels her jump a little bit at the difference in temperature. Those of the Pale Race aren't really cold, but due to their slower heartbeat, they are not as warm.

She takes his hand, and he leads her to the front of the line. "You don't have to do that," she mumbles.

"Alfonse, please make sure that this woman gets a VIP spot up top." He lets go of her hand and leaves Alfonse do his job. The giant vampire nods, smiling at her as she beams.

"Thank you."

Ash smiles politely. "Don't let anyone walk all over you. Everyone is worth it." With that, he heads into the club with the bundle of mail he brought from his apartment building. He can hear the woman asking who he is and knows that it won't be the last time he sees her. He shakes his head.

The office in his club is on the first floor and decked out in the décor of the previous owner, which works for him. He sits behind the desk and filters through the last week's mail, tossing most of it into the shredder.

Opening bills, he begins writing checks for each of them. There is a knock on the door to his office, and Ash cocks an eyebrow. "Come in."

"Hi." It's the woman from the cue line sooner than expected. Nervous as she looks around the office and her heart racing, she has a mission. She closes the door and smiles a little. "I wanted to let you know that I am awakened."

That perks Ash's interest. "I am awakened" means that she has been informed at some point of the presence of the Pale Race and vampires. The phrase was invented so that people of blood magic will know who has been trusted. Otherwise, humans have the memory of feeding erased.

"What is your name?"

She smiles a little bit. "Silvia."

"What can I do for you, Silvia?"

She shifts her feet. "I am offering to have you feed on me."

That's a first. Ash hears his stomach growl. "Come on over here."

"Just so you understand, I am not offering more."

Ash chuckles. "I wasn't either." Sylvia honors him with a blush and approaches him.

"How do you want me?" she asks.

Ash gestures to his knees, and her heart speeds up. She sits sideways on his lap, moving her hair to the side.

"You know that I don't expect this, right? I didn't give you the VIP for favors," he tells her.

Smiling, she nods her head. "I know that. Otherwise, I would have been brought straight here."

Ash nods okay. Before she can say anything else, his fangs drop into view, and he pulls her to lean into him as he bites into her neck. Her quiet gasp and fast heartbeat tell him what he had suspected. She is addicted to the rush that comes with being fed from.

Chances are, he imagines, she once dated a vampire who never sought someone of the Pale Race to transition her to vampire. When a vampire experiences a relationship with a human, it becomes a problem only when the vampire does not intend to transition the human to vampire. Vampire venom, similar to an addictive drug, is hard to go without. Whether vampire and human consent to the interaction, intense sensations intoxicate the one fed from, creating an addiction to the act of giving blood.

If the human turns into a vampire, craving human blood causes no anxiety. If a vampire leaves a human fed from but unturned into a vampire, the human actively craves being fed from a vampire.

Because vampires cannot transition a human into a vampire without assistance, the vampire must find someone of the Pale Race to complete the transition. Because members of the Pale Race must accept responsibility for those they change to vampire, transitions are based on the trustworthiness of the vampire. No Pale will consider contributing to the change of a human if the vampire concerned has not proven honest enough to train the newly created vampire.

Not wanting her to get passionate about his nourishment, Ash feeds quickly, not moving a muscle as he takes the smallest amount necessary for survival.

When satisfied, he pulls his fangs from her and pricks his finger to bring his blood to the surface. To eliminate obvious signs of her donation, Ash rubs his blood over her wound to close the punctures.

"Thank you," he says in a neutral tone as he wipes the trail of blood from her neck.

She stands up smiling. "Anytime." Leaving Ash to finish his work, she walks wistfully from the office, the glow of her face affirming exactly what he suspected.

The rest of the night, he writes checks and makes out deposit slips. He finds it tedious to get all the information squared away for his new identity that will take effect in the next few months. He wants to make sure that every name, location, and bit of tax data will fall under the name Ashton Vale, the twenty-one-year-old heir to his "grandfather's" fortune. Ash finds times exhausting with the humans keeping records of everything, but in order to own a business in the human world, it means his identity and place of residence must change every twenty years to avoid their inquiry.

A few decades ago, he watched as some of his close friends were tracked down by the vamp-ops, a human government sector bent on eradicating vampires. As a precaution against the threat and in accordance to Pale mandates, he remains scarce, rotating where he keeps his main office every decade or so. Even though humans can stay employed at clubs or restaurants for more than fifteen years, only one has previously recognized him.

Ash glances into the mirror on the other side of the room. He doesn't want to drop the dangerous appearance he's perfected for two decades. *This sucks!*

He puts the password into his computer and does an internet search for "rebellious clothing." He turns up only women, most scantily clad and displaying everything.

What happened to people keeping their bodies to themselves? Ash wonders. Ash himself once wondered about the centuries-old obsession with covering skin over the top, but as he considers it, he wonders if the change in clothing trends has to do with different religions and what they allow.

He directs the internet to bring up men only. *Is that guy wearing tights?* Ash makes the image larger, the pixels on the screen making it impossible to focus his keen eyesight. *Yes, he is, and he isn't wearing anything under them either. Your own fault for looking closer.* Ash scrolls through, seeing a few other styles he may like. One catches his eye.

"Biker fashion is one that may vary but will never disappear," reads the label. Ash clicks on the image and sees a leather coat with a pair of ripped jeans and a pair of black boots. The model leans against his Harley.

Now that I can work with, thinks Ash.

Ash takes the vendor checks with him and, bypassing the screaming techno and moving bodies, heads down to the kitchen. Not bothering to knock since the sound can't be heard over the thumping music, he stops at his manager's office next to the exit.

"Hey, boss," Corine says from behind the desk as, apparently interested in a fight that may break out. she studies her monitors.

"You need me to go out there?"

Corine gawks at him. "Now why in the world are you going to do that? You have ten bouncers, and half of them just chill there."

"If they aren't here when you need them, problems will become much worse," Ash says, referencing the blowout-turned-mob-scene during the prohibition. "I would much rather have them here and getting paid for nothing than have to rebuild another club after a few Molotov cocktails."

Corine shrugs and asks, "What do you have for me?"

"Vendor checks you will need for the week. You said it's been packed all week?"

She nods.

"I put a request in for the armored truck to stop nightly this week instead of every other," Ash tells her. "Don't remove any money from the safes. They will do it."

"Copy that," she says grinning and going back to the monitor. "Anything else?"

Liking that Corine is always about getting her job done correctly the first time, Ash shakes his head. With the raids and random stabbings always on the news, her all-business attitude saves him time, money, and public relations issues.

Ash finishes up at the club and heads over to the bank, another Pale Race operation, so it's open twenty-four hours. The owner's son smiles as Ash walks in. Like clockwork, he gestures to the office behind him, which tells Ash that the young man's father is free to speak.

Looking up from the desk when he hears Ash walk in and close the door, the man bellows jovially, "Asher! What can I help you with tonight?"

Asher smiles at the friendly face he has known for centuries. He opened his first account with him when the bank was established in 1798, less than a decade after the first United States bank started in DC.

"Well, Bertrand, I need to do a transfer of funds to my heir," Asher says, making sure to use the cover story. The owner finds humans nosy who work during daylight hours, so he forbids speaking of anything Pale- or vampire-related. Considering that the Pale are unlikely to perform mundane work at all and the vampires cannot work in daylight, the humans are necessary. Once, a human faction of the municipality's police had bugged his office and attempted to blackmail him.

Bertrand nods. "I'll just have you sign a few forms, and then I can do everything on my end to keep it smooth. Sound good?"

Ash nods. "Has there been anything of concern in your neck of the woods?" he asks, referring to the vamp-op situation confronting everyone. Bertrand lost his granddaughter a couple of decades ago, and the recent intel suggests the possibility of her rescue.

"Not any more than I have said." His features fall as he thinks about his granddaughter.

"I'm sorry to ask. I just need to have a clear image of everything before we can move. That being said, if there is anything you see or hear about anything in that area, let me know. Okay?"

Bertrand nods and hands Ash the paperwork to sign.

"I am going to need a few grand to keep on hand," Ash informs Bertrand. Then, his signature in place, he stands up.

"Go see Joshua. He will help you with the withdrawal."

"Okay. I'll be back next week for the final signing."

Carlos nods, and Ash takes his leave, fills out the slip, and heads over to Joshua to get his money.

The drive up to his parents' house calms him the closer he gets. They live on the top of a mountain, surrounded by forest and streams. As a child, he escaped from the mundane into the outlying expanse of trees. The lush evergreens provided sticks to battle with, and the ledges gave him practice for long, strenuous treks. He even learned how to kiss a girl properly near the immense waterfalls that fell off the mountains—a human girl, yes, but a girl all the same.

"Asher!" his mom cries when he pulls up to the front stoop. Out front with pruning shears, she cuts flowers for the dinner table.

Asher walks over and gives her a hug. "Do not ever set me up on a date again," he urges as he squeezes her petite frame.

"You—"

"Oh, no, you don't," he interrupts her anticipated reasoning. "You will promise me right now that you will never set me up on a date again."

She nods ever so slightly.

"Say it," he insists.

His mom looks at him innocently. "I promise to never set you up on a blind date again."

Cocking an eyebrow, knowing her intelligence, and not letting her escape the promise, Ash stares at her.

"Fine!" she exclaims. "I will never set up a date for you again. I promise."

"Thank you. Now let's see what we can get for info from Dad. I have a weird feeling."

His mom looks up at him with concern. "What kind of weird feeling?"

Ash shrugs. "I can feel something is wrong. I can't put my finger on it, though."

His mom appears thoughtful with wide eyes but quickly hides it behind an impenetrable mask.

"What?" Ash asks her.

"Nothing. Your dad is in his office. I'll be there in a minute."

Heading into the house to go over plans for the next night's raid, Ash nods. They can't miss anything, especially not with the knot in his stomach urging him to go over everything again.

"Unit one, report," Ash says into the mic as his Terrors ready themselves for the drop. The male beside him moves his foot a mile a minute as he anticipates results. He glues his eyes to surveillance screens and watches as ordered for signs.

Two more in the van with him will accept their loved ones at completion of the mission. They know the slim chance of getting them back, especially over the past few decades and the humans getting better at what they do. The two Pale males share a look as Ash recognizes one of the males as Bertrand's son. Fear pains their faces as they wait for their loved ones. The daunting reality makes the air around them cold.

"One, ready," they hear over the mic. He hears the heartbeats of the men pick up as angst thickens the air in the van. They will attempt to get three Pale females out of captivity that night, three hurt mothers who need freedom and comfort during their pregnancies.

One of the females they hope to rescue is the granddaughter of his banker, Bertrand. Her father, Joshua, sits in the back of the van waiting for the return of his daughter.

"Unit two, report."

"Two, ready." Ash is relieved to hear that the rooftop team sits in wait. He had the most difficulty placing them without attracting the guards' attention.

The four men wait camped out in a van a quarter mile away from an abandoned warehouse on the outskirts of a human city. They have a clear mission, to free three females inside held captive and guarded by six humans and an ancient. The ancient's presence makes the mission so risky. The ancient can feel air move and will know immediately that the guard team must react.

Ancients don't work with humans, though, so the circumstances mean that something bigger is at play. Therefore, Ash and his team have reconned the mission for five months.

"Unit three, report."

"Three, ready."

Ash watches the feed as the guards switch out. He feels adrenaline wash through him in his mad wish to save them. Timing must be perfect, or the team risks all the females inside the makeshift holding cell.

The screen shows the ancient walking out the door and getting into his tiny car, revving the engine, and shooting out of the parking lot at high speed.

One, two, three, four, five . . .

"It's time. Go. Go. Go," Ash shouts as the ancient and previous shift of humans drives down the street past his van.

Ash's team of Protectors begins pouring into the building from all exits. Ash stays quiet, knowing the high risk of them losing focus as they do their jobs. The males in the van cause it to shift with their weight as they hover over the monitors. He would have asked them not to crowd him, but if push came to shove, he would do the same thing. In fact, he would be right in there with the Terrors lopping off heads if his sisters and mother were in that building. The strength those males show to resist the urge impresses Ash as they allow the Protectors to do their job.

Every Protector knows the stakes as the team risks their lives for the survival of their kind. The war with the humans became an issue over the past century as the humans began to find new ways to capture members of the Pale Race, mainly the females, and use their science to study it. The males, losing their families and having to live an eternity without them, caused quite a few lifemates to take their own lives as they refused to live without the prospect of their other halves at their side.

Loud bangs and shouts blast through the mics as the Protectors make their way through the building and incidentally keep Ash at the edge of his seat. He knows that asking questions will only distract his warriors. The chaos agonizing, he awaits the results of the mission with five months of recon put into play—five months when husbands and fathers awaited the homecoming of their loved ones.

"Two. All clear. There is no one in the east wing." Ash's heart drops into the pit of his stomach as he waits for more information from the others. More failures than successes have occurred when dealing with rescues mostly due to changing tactics that make tracking much harder than in the past. Worse, some of the females give birth to their children only for the children to be taken and brought somewhere else for study.

"One. I have a female in bad condition. Getting her out of here."

"Copy that. You know where to come," Ash says, relieved that they've found at least one. *Breathe*, he thinks. *This is better than the last time.* The back door to the van opens, and the males jump out to wait by the makeshift EMS vehicle they brought to get the females home.

"Ivania!" Ash hears Roman cry as he reunites with his lifemate. The weeping of the two sounds relief to his ears as the other two climb back into the van.

"Three. I have one alive. The other is drained."

"Bring them all here. I will meet you at base."

Ash rips the headset off. "Fuck!" he yells, slamming his hand down on the table in front of him. Knowing that one of them will go home to a funeral, he hears the two males jump back out of the van in anticipation.

They look at each other and hug, not caring that they show emotion as they wait.

He knows when they arrive, because he hears the wail of grief from one male, and unable to contain it, Ash feels a tear fall from his eye as he realizes that he had failed to bring her home to him. The realization washes over him that Carlos's granddaughter, a woman he grew up with, is dead.

"You need to stop beating yourself up over this," Dayton says gruffly. "We did everything in our power to make sure no harm came to those females."

Still hearing the mother's cries, Ash shakes his head. "Every female we lose is a child without a mother, a parent without their daughter, or a mate without their mission in life." He places his head in his hand. "I don't allow myself to fail."

Stone approaches the table with a double shot of bourbon, which Ash hastily drinks, feeling the burn as it quickly begins to do its work. Only the men know that alcohol affects him in an odd way. Anyone else who has ever seen him like that is dead. "We did our best."

Ash shrugs off the sentiment. "Sometimes the best planning still isn't good enough to save the night."

Not wanting to deal with the remorse plaguing him and determined to drown the feeling of inadequacy in a female who won't ever ask for more from him, he heads out to the dance floor.

As rave music and blinding lights pulse, Ash manages to attract three females within two minutes, and he smiles back at their table. The Terrors know that he works like that after any mission that doesn't completely succeed. He gets piss drunk and buries all his hidden emotion into a female as he takes her to the back room of the club, Vines.

Not caring what his comrades think of his actions, Ash sways to the beat. He slowly starts sweating out the alcohol as his body speeds up the healing of his liver. Ash knows it's childish but doesn't care as he grinds himself into the three young women who return the favor. His thoughts disappear with the only thing he can think of: bloodlust and the situation in his pants.

As humans, the young women have no idea what he is or his station in life, and it exhilarates him in a way that no average Joe can imagine. One of the women shouts in his ear to ask if he wants to go into the bathroom, and he nods, smiling ear to ear as he holds his teeth in.

The woman pulls his hand with her as they dance their way to the bathroom only for him to pull her into the back room instead. The woman looks at him, a question in her eyes.

He points to himself and the name on the door off the main room. Her eyes widen as she realizes he's the owner. Her eyes gleaming, she nods her head, hoping behind her ecstasy-induced eyes that she will land a wealthy man.

The thought makes Ash cringe, but he craves only the blood and sex promised him by her walking into the soundproof back room.

Silence sobers Ash up as she starts stripping while walking to the black leather couch in the middle of the room. Thankful for no pretenses, Ash goes to her and takes off his shirt. He picks her up so that she will straddle his waist, then settles into the couch as he kisses her, and she kisses him right back.

They shriek as someone throws a lamp at them.

"Asher Vale! What the hell is going on?"

The young woman on his lap pulls back and searches his eyes, then continues to kiss his neck as she realizes that the woman means nothing.

"Get out," he says, letting his fangs drop and then biting the young woman on his lap. Immediately she tenses, tips her head back in an erotic fit, and grinds into him.

Glaring through the haze of his dire situation, he can feel Lola's eyes on him as he eats,. The woman on his lap opens his pants and settles herself on him, moving solely to gain her own climax as he feeds.

Her blood soars through him, creating his own drug euphoria as he swallows, then biting his lip and closing her wound as he kisses her neck.

Seeking to end his internal torture, he picks up the movement when he has had his fill.

He grunts, spilling himself inside the young woman, knowing that he has no reason to be concerned about rare hybrid humans.

The young woman pulls back and smiles at him with a look of amazement. "That was the best I've ever had!"

Ash pulls her into him with his gaze, and her pupils dilate slightly as her mind settles in for the mesmer. "You only came to have an amazing time. You danced the night away with your girlfriends. That's all you remember."

"That's all I remember." The woman stands up and searches for her clothes while Ash fixes his pants. She gets dressed and disappears from the room without a glance back at him.

"How could you?" Lola's petulant foot stomps on the floor.

Ash, completely sober with the Pale metabolization and his liver healing too quickly for his liking, goes to the safe in the corner and covers his hand as he dials the fifteen-digit passcode he's memorized. Pulling out paperwork he has to sign for Bertrand, he sighs as thoughts of the meeting's outcome wreaks havoc in his mind. He never hides from his responsibility to own his failures even when ignoring them might hurt less.

Setting dismal thoughts aside, he doesn't respond to Lola, who stands in shock as he walks out of his office and leaves the club. She follows him until he gets to his car, and her pout reminds him of a spoiled child. *I'm so done with this!* he thinks, annoyed, knowing that it won't end. Women like that don't budge once their claws are dug in. He prays she will never find him with his guard down. One more time in bed, he figures, and she will insist on marriage, something he can never give her or any other female.

He hears his phone's ring. "Yeah?"

"Where are you? I thought we are all meeting here for poker."

Ash thinks to himself a minute, not wanting to go home just then, and eyes Lola. "Sounds good." Ash ends the call.

"Why can't you admit that there is something between us?" she asks as her face contorts with manipulative sadness.

Ash laughs to himself. "Because, Lola. I have already told you; we are friends." Getting in the car and starting it, he watches her pretty face screaming at him over the intro to "Falling Away from Me." He mouths, "I can't hear you" as he drives away.

In the rearview, he watches her stomp, turn, and run to her car. He assumes she hopes to follow him. He turns down an alleyway and shuts his lights off, hoping to God that she hadn't looked back to see the trick. Her car speeds past him, and he sighs in relief. He wants nothing to do with her. He gets that she may believe she feels something for him, but stalking him is just messed up.

Invitation

Duneskil

"Ivy, I presume," he says in the same voice she heard over the phone. Ivy nods and turns to Reed and Hawk.

"I am all set, guys. Thanks for bringing me. If the two of you want to take credit for him," she gestures to Finn lying on the ground and staring up at the stars, "you are more than welcome to."

"Your mother will be proud," Reed says. It's been nice knowing you, miss."

"And may we always be on the same side of the battlefield," Hawk says under his breath.

"Now that is one scary woman!" Reed mutters. Hawk nods in agreement as they fall silent and take the two horses with them on their way out of the clearing.

"And likewise," Ivy says. "I presume that you are my father then?"

Soren nods. He looks past her to the dead ancient lying on the ground and lifts an eyebrow.

Ivy shrugs. "He pissed me off."

"Ready to go?" he asks with a chuckle.

Ivy looks back, imagining Lesai sitting beyond the trees and knowing that she will never see the city again. It pains her that she can never go back, never again see anyone to whom she has been accustomed. Even though she has more questions than she'd thought possible, she can only move forward.

"Yeah." She says solemnly. "Where to?"

He grins. "It's time you get to know the other half of your story. As I am certain you have figured out, you are also of the Pale Race."

"I heard you say that I am a hybrid though. How so?" She asks as they begin walking through the woods.

He thinks a moment, "Well first, a hybrid is half of one and half the other. So, you are half ancient and half Pale Race. The birth of you is forbidden in ancient law for reasons of a prophecy that doesn't make sense. So, basically, you were never supposed to be born."

"Thanks!" Ivy twists her face in sarcasm.

"You don't understand," he says defensively. "It's not that we didn't want you. Honestly, I only found out I have a daughter about a month ago, and at the same time, I found out that your mother is an ancient. She never told me. Of course, she's aware that I am of the Pale Race, since I told her when we first met, but apparently it wasn't important to her for me to know her ancestry." He takes on a brooding look as his sarcasm hides the hurt he feels.

"So, we are vampires," she says in a huff. "We suck blood and only come out at night?" She startles herself as she realizes that drinking blood doesn't feel as gross to her as it would have before that night. She glances back at the meadow, her thoughts on Finn and what she did.

"No," he says as he scrubs his hand through his chin-length hair. She points to her teeth, and he chuckles. "There is more to it than that. We are born with the genetics for vampirism, but our sunlight issue is more of a sensitivity for most, so we sleep when the sun is up. We need blood and food for sustenance, yet we can also have children and pass our children our genetics. Almost all children who survive being a hybrid never get a mark of heritage. Vampires, as in those who are turned using our blood's magic, are unable to go into sunlight, sleep like the dead during the highest point of the day, and cannot have children or transition humans into vampires."

It doesn't help that she has even more questions flowing through her brain than before. "So only the Pales can turn vampires?"

"The Pale Race. And yes. You are another story altogether. You have both elemental magic and blood magic that your body attempts to sustain.

Most of the Pale Race can only be in the sun for a little while before enduring a splitting migraine or worse even during youth. Your mother says that you can be out in the sun the entire day without any issues?" It's a question more than a statement.

Ivy nods. "I've never had an issue with the sun. Ever. But it is annoying that I can't even get a tan!" Ivy huffs. "I do think I might need sunglasses at least now, though, since the night now looks like a cloudy day."

"I have a few pairs at the compound you can choose from," he says, watching her instead of where he's walking. "With the ability to use the elemental magic of the Ancients, you are basically unstoppable unless you are up against another, older ancient." He seems overwhelmed at the idea. "Even if the Ancients will want you dead, the Pale Race has been waiting for you."

Ivy lifts an eyebrow in question, "What do you mean, waiting for me?" When Soren looks up at the sky to ponder the stars, she senses that she won't get the answer that night, so she puts the question to the side and continues prodding him. "Even an elder ancient has a tough time getting the better of my skills," she says with the assuredness of a cocky adolescent.

Then Ivy stops dead and looks at him. "You mean to say that by having me, my mother created my death sentence?"

"Yes."

Ivy smiles. "Sweet!"

Soren gapes.

"I am sure she also told you about my training," Ivy says.

He nods.

"Good. So, you know that it will take more than someone screwing with me to take me out and that's without elemental magic."

"Reed and Hawk are right," Soren answers. "Your mother should be proud, though I have to say, you are sounding about as reckless as she used to."

Ivy smiles, knowing all too well her own recklessness but has only ever heard stories about her mother's youth. "You are taking this in stride, but we need to figure out how to explain this to the coven," he says. "I forgot to ask, Can you show me your heritage mark?"

Ivy looks at him quizzically, and he smiles, gesturing to her arm. "The mark that appeared on your skin when you transitioned."

"You mean the searing hot, ass hat of a mark that goes from my wrist up and around my neck?"

He seems a bit scared as he nods uncertainly.

He pulls the sleeve up on his arm. "Does it look like this?" He shows her the vine work as well as the coat of arms nestled just under his elbow."

Thankful she's wearing a workout sports bra, Ivy pulls her arm out of her sleeve and stretches it over her head. "I haven't gotten a good look at it yet, honestly."

"Holy shit! How in the bloody hell did that happen?" he says as he looks at her arm. Ivy doesn't see that the emblems match.

"I thought you just showed me a coat of arms," she says as she looks for it. She can see only coils of vines and, upon closer inspection, long thorns throughout as well.

He walks around her to look at her back, moving her braid over to the front of her shoulder. "You do have a coat of arms. It's on the back of your neck. What is really weird is that I have never seen a heritage mark look so intricate, nor have I seen one extend past the bicep. It must be something to do with the elemental magic coursing through your veins." She visibly sees him force himself to look away from it. "I will do some research on this."

She thinks a moment, then says, "I was topping myself off when it happened. Well, it's more like the pain knocked me on my ass so I did what any ancient will do. I drew from the elements to dull the pain. It still hurt, though."

She can tell by the look on his face that he doesn't understand but doesn't seem to want to talk about it.

"You will have to walk me through it at some point," he says, "but it will have to wait for now. We need to get you back before the rest of the coven goes to rest for the day.

Ivy can hear her stomach rumbling again, reminding her that she hasn't eaten anything most of the day.

Her father laughs. "How are you hungry? You just ate an ancient?"

Ivy shrugs. "I eat normal food, too, duh. Don't tell me I'm the only one."

"No, you're not the only one, but it usually curbs the craving for human food when you take in that much blood. Do you still feel hungry?"

Ivy thinks a moment as she assesses her stomach. "I feel a little sloshy. Not really satisfied."

His eyebrows raise. "We will get you some more when we get home."

Ivy nods, not sure why the thought of blood makes her salivate again, then remembers that she is a blood sucker. *Why does my life have to be so freaking weird!* Her stomach flips over as the thought of more blood also makes her queasy.

It doesn't take long for the two of them to reach the one thing she's always wondered about. She walks around the car and touches it, pulling her hand back as if burned when her hand feels the metal. "This is a car?"

Her dad laughs at her astonishment. "Yes, Ivy. This is a car. Get in."

She cocks her head to the side, looking for how exactly to *get* in. Shaking his head at her, he approaches the passenger door and opens it for her. He waits for her to settle in and closes the door. He then gets into the driver's side.

Put on your seatbelt." She looks around and then back at him with no clue what he means, and he chuckles, then shows her the little metal piece on a strap that retracts from the car, and then where it buckles.

She does *not* like it. *It's too constricting*, she thinks "Do I really have to wear this?" she asks, hopelessly plucking at the contraption.

He nods. "Yes. Even if we can't die, it doesn't matter, because in an accident, a hurt vampire or someone of the Pale Race tends to be more feral and cannot control the blood lust. They end up killing humans that they don't intend to kill."

"Um, there is something you should know, then," Ivy says looking at her feet.

When he doesn't respond, she looks up at him. He scrutinizes her, waiting for her to tell him.

"I can't control my sickness at all," she says. "Apparently, my mother has been feeding me blood without me knowing since I was a little kid to keep it at bay, but I have never been able to stop the sickness from consuming me."

"Is that what happened in the meadow?" he asks understandingly.

Ivy shrugs. "Technically, yes. No matter how disgusting it is for me to drink blood, I couldn't stop myself. I could have drawn a sword and taken his head off, but his blood called to me. On the other hand, the queen said he must die, so Reed and Hawk were going to do it anyway."

"Your mother wanted him dead?" he asks in surprise.

Ivy lifts her chin. "Yes. He intended to make me have a baby to keep me in Lesai indefinitely, knowing that I am joining the Scavenger guild." She hears a low growl and at first doesn't realize where it's coming from but then sees that it's coming from Soren. "Don't worry. He won't be able to turn my mother in to the Ancient Elders. I took care of it." The satisfaction she felt in protecting her mother from imminent death surprises her, but she pushes it to the back of her mind with other matters she has yet to process.

"Did you enjoy the kill?"

"Did you really just growl?" Ivy avoids the question.

Soren shrugs. "It's a Pale Race thing."

Ivy giggles. "That definitely won't be me!"

"Now answer the question."

"Is it that bad if I did?" she asks self-consciously.

He shrugs. "Not bad per se, but until you get a grip on the hunger, you won't be able to leave the compound. Do I need to keep the catty baby vamps from you, too?" His grinning face makes Ivy smile.

"I doubt it. I'm rather good at holding my cool as long as someone isn't insulting my family and I'm not hungry." She looks out the window as the car starts to move. Things begin to move quickly past her window, and she tries her best to follow them with her eyes before they disappear. Then, as the car begins moving faster, her grip on the door handle makes her knuckles turn white. "Slow down!" she cries. She's not used to anything faster than a horse.

"You are aware that we are going slow, right?" *It's too much.* She closes her eyes to keep the scenery around her from screwing with her ultra-sensitive sight. "Just tell me when we are there," she says, "because I can't handle the movement."

"Do you have any other questions?"

"Yes," she croaks, feeling the immediate need to upchuck the blood she drank. "You need to stop."

The car jerks to a stop, and Ivy fumbles around looking for the door handle. Soren reaches across her and throws the door open just as she vomits all the blood out the door. She looks down at the ground and sees that it's black and clotted looking.

"Do you feel a little better?" Soren reaches over again and shuts the door as he maneuvers the seat to lay down. Trying to keep the dry heaves from returning, Ivy curls into a ball

"Do it as fast as you can, please," Ivy says about the seat. The sooner I'm out of this thing the better."

"It won't be long. Oddly enough, Duneskil is only fifteen minutes from the clearing where your mother insisted I pick you up." Ivy peeks her eye open and closes it again quickly.

Her stomach in knots, Ivy wants to vomit again. "I do not like this at all. Please tell me I never have to get into one of these again, please."

"Can't do that. It's a downfall to the human existence. Fast moving lives. Humans die so quickly that they are always in a hurry to live. You will actually have to learn to drive one of these at some point soon. First, we will get you settled in, though."

"Ugh. But I'm not human!" Then a thought hits Ivy, "How long will I live?"

Soren remains silent for a bit. "I don't know. I haven't thought of that, though I assume you will live at least as long as an ancient. If you live as long as the Pale Race, you won't die at all unless there is a rare circumstance. Once you decide you have lived as long as you want, you will allow yourself to dry up. The process takes decades, but we of the Pale Race decide when we have had enough."

"Huh." A few questions remain for Ivy, and figures she can distract herself from the discomfort of riding in the car.

"What is considered a rare circumstance?"

Quiet hesitation sits in the air until finally Soren says, "That is a discussion for another time."

Ivy shrugs. "How does the next coven leader get picked?"

He laughs. "Already wishing me to die?"

"No," she says seriously. "I just know that in Lesai, when the ruling king or queen dies, each of the five families put up a choice for who should rule. Once they have named the five candidates, the Ancient Elders choose one as the king or queen."

In the car, she feels the air move, indicating Soren's nod. "Okay, then. I am a duke. However, we don't use such terms. We try to refer to ourselves in modern terms so that if we are overheard, it doesn't sound like some form of cult issue. Everyone refers to me as the commander of Duneskil or Soren, and when they refer to you, it will probably be by your given name if that is okay."

Ivy sighs in relief. "It definitely is, though I'd prefer Ivy. I've been a princess for way too long, and Iveliis is a mouthful."

"I get that," he chuckles. "Duneskil has a pecking order just as within all compounds. I am first rank. Then there are others who sit below. Only the Pale Council sits above me unless I am at another compound where the commander there outranks me. There are two more compounds in New England alone. To be a ruler, you must be able to create vampire underlings, aka you have to be of the Pale Race. Simply because you have that mark on your arm, you will be revered. And some humans who may see you out and about will know exactly what it means and that you can turn them."

"I think I'm going to be sick again."

The car stops, and Ivy risks opening her eyes to see a field with nothing around them, just an expanse of grass. Opening the door the way he had done and leaning out, she feels herself dry heave a few times. After she's sure she won't retch again, she closes the door and looks at him sideways, cocking an eyebrow at him when the car remains still. "We can get going again."

"You look like your mother did as a Scavenger."

Ivy laughs at him. "I doubt that my mother ever vomited due to being in a car. Not to mention, I look nothing like her. She is all blonde with perfectly golden skin, and I look like you."

"You'd be surprised how much I see of her in you, then." He smiles, then says, "Iveliis Grenedich Knight, I invite you into my home and welcome you to Duneskil." Like the snap of a finger, the ancient veil lifts in front of her eyes, and she sees a ginormous compound directly in front of her.

It's her turn to say, "Holy shit!" *Why couldn't I see the magic before he dropped the veil? I can always see the veil in Lesai.* She fumbles as she opens the door, gets out, and slams it shut. Unable to look away, she stares at stone walls with vines growing up the sides. Lights in every window make the entire place look inviting.

"Do you like your new home?" Soren asks, coming up behind her. She nods her head. She's never seen anything like it. Told about human-made homes that harm the environment, she hadn't considered they could be so stunning.

She glances around with her new super sensitive eyesight at rolling hills in front of the house and sees flowers and hedges molded to perfection.

"Why did you have to invite me in? Only Ancients use elemental magic," She observes still taking it all in.

He clears his throat. "It's a gift to me from your mother, actually, though I didn't know until I found out about you. Only I can invite someone to see past the veil that hides us from the outside world. No humans, vampires, or Ancients can sense that our home exists here."

Ivy scoffs. "So that would be the reason I couldn't see it, but how did you not know she did it?"

"I had no idea she was an ancient. She created the veil twenty years ago and sent word through one of her messengers that one day I'd be required to keep a gift safe from the world. The only stipulation is that I have to explicitly trust everyone I invite to come in. Otherwise, they have to stay in the shack over there by the road."

He points to a house next to the giant gate with a light on. His use of the word shack understates reality. The castle-like compound dwarfs the house, itself grand. "All who have not earned my trust stay in the shack until they win my favor."

Ivy doesn't have much expression left in her. With everything so new, a heaviness in the air encourages a craving. Then it hits her. She can smell blood somewhere. She feels her eyes shift as she lifts her nose and inhales deeply. She feels Soren's hand grip her shoulder.

"You never know whose blood it is. Back down." He pulls his kerchief from his pocket and wonders if he came prepared, since the pungent smell masks any other. "Come with me. We will get you a glass of blood."

Though drinking blood doesn't upset her as much as it used to, her stomach turns at the words. Knowing that Wren made her blood-tinged tea that kept her sickness away, she accepts the offer.

"Thank you," She muffles through the cloth, and he nods.

"Jynx", Soren says loudly. A short, mousy woman with a bob cut comes out of the front door.

"You called me, commander?" She missteps when she sees Ivy. "And who is this?" she asks, trying to hide her surprise.

"Jynx, my daughter Ivy. Ivy, my corporal Jynx," Soren says.

"Daughter?" Jynx asks half under her breath.

"Yes. She needs two glasses of blood, please. I am not sure of her appetite yet, but for now we will start with two."

Jynx nods, a thousand questions skittering through her eyes. You can tell she wants to stay and ask them, but she does as she's told.

Ivy looks at Soren. "Does anyone know I exist?"

"No. I haven't known long enough to prep anyone. I was going to do it tonight, since I was supposed to pick you up tomorrow, but the heritage mark came quicker than your mother expected. If any of the Ancients, not to mention the ancient's elders, hear of a random tattoo appearing at the age of twenty-one, they would kill you on sight. It's bad enough that your birthday is technically in a couple months out here. Lesai has a different time schedule than the outside world, which sped up your transition."

Soren seems annoyed. "Do you know how much blood your mother has been giving you?"

Ivy shakes her head. "No. As far as I can tell, it's not much. I could barely smell it in the tea Wren made me earlier. I usually get one tea per week if I need it."

Ivy cringes as another thought comes to mind. "Please don't make a big deal out of my birthday."

"Crap," he says under his breath. "If your mother had asked, I'd have told her that you needed more than that. It's no wonder you are unable to control your thirst. The average fledgling drinks three full glasses per night."

He turns to Ivy and directs, "Show me your teeth."

Ivy blushes. She's not used to that kind of attention. "Is that necessary?"

"Yes."

Ivy opens her mouth and shows him the two-inch-long fangs protruding from her gums. He pushes on one as if to push it back in her face.

"Ouch!" she grabs her mouth. "What was that for?"

He looks concerned. "Have they been like that since earlier?"

"Yes."

"Maybe they will retract after you have enough blood."

Apparently wanting to yell about something, he looks up at the new moon, takes a few deep breaths, and looks back at her.

She looks at him questioningly. "Retract? Like suck back up into my face? That's weird."

Soren opens his mouth to show her his normal-sized teeth. He stands a moment, and his teeth grow larger. They are as sharp as hers but aren't as long. Her teeth overhang her bottom gums and feel like razor blades. When she shuts her mouth without care, her sharp teeth puncture her gums and bottom lip, thus drawing her own blood.

"Huh," she murmurs as she takes in the new information.

High Standards

Females!

"What the hell do you mean, you don't want to go on another date?" Lola yells from the other end of the line.

Ash grimaces, his face reddening as he rubs the back of his neck. Everyone on his team of Terrors, all of them his friends and fellow Protectors, sit around the poker table and hear every word. The unsaid rule when it comes to a gaming table on dudes' night is, *If your phone rings, don't answer it.* Since Ash's phone had blown up with unrelenting annoyance for over an hour, the importance of his work keeping him from muting the ringer, they told him he had to answer it.

"Can we do this another time?" Ash speaks nonchalantly into the phone.

The guys around him poke each other and silently laugh at his predicament. Ash deals with it every time his mother forces him on a date. It doesn't help that his mother sets him up with the worst ones. It's like she's trying to make him hate women.

Mom, you suck, he thinks to himself as he takes a breath and lets it out slowly.

"No!" Lola retorts. She sounds pissed to a degree he hadn't thought her capable, considering she lives in a mansion where her mom and dad spoil her. "You can't go and blow me off after having sex with me. I am not a whore, so do not treat me like one, Asher."

Since Pale and vampires have acute hearing, his friends can clearly hear, and the snickering continues at the use of his formal name. Where on earth did his mother find that chick?

Teeth clenched, Ash glances at the clock. He grows irritated as her tirade continues without pause. "I am promised to someone else," he says, not technically lying but not telling the full truth. "I am not looking for anything other than what we discussed the other night, Lola. Friends. Nothing more and nothing less." *Far less but I won't start more shit with a nut job,* Ash thinks.

"That's unlikely, since your mother set us up!"

Dayton mimics the caller and starts hand puppet motions with his hands, becoming more manic as her rant continues.

Graham snorts with laughter.

"You have me on speaker phone?" she inquires in a wounded tone.

Her high and mighty tone of offense sets Ash off.

"No," he replies. "You are yelling so loud that the entire poker game can hear you."

"Poker isn't for men in a relationship, Asher Vale!" All four of the men turn bone white and wait for the shoe to drop.

"There is no relationship! What is wrong with your hearing?" Asher yells. "What I do is my own damn business. Stop calling me!"

A sob breaks through the momentary silence as her crying starts. "You are so horrible, so spoiled, and you treat females so poorly! I introduced you to my parents."

Kill me now! Asher thinks.

"You had to. You live with your parents. Obviously, I have to meet them when they answer the damn door," he says, smacking himself in the forehead for not thinking before he spoke. Everyone else laughs at full bore, and Ash wants to start flicking quarters at their heads. He would do the same thing if it were someone else in his place. They know it and he knows it, so he can't say anything about it.

"Asher tell them to stop laughing at me!" Lola shrieks into the phone.

Dead silent, Asher stares at the phone dumbstruck. *This woman is a fruit cake!* he thinks.

"Sorry, but it's not my house, Lola. I can't control other people. I also can't control when a woman lets her parents answer the door for a blind date."

The rage returns in a tornado as she shrieks. "You are a *Protector*. You know damn well that a female without a mate can't live on her own!"

He pulls the phone away from his ear as the men nod and point to the phone.

"Why did I have to fall in love with an asshole?" she sobs into the phone, refusing to hang up as she blows snots into a tissue.

"She's right," Graham mouths as he grins in satisfaction. "Total asshole!"

Ash balls the fist of his unused hand, and his short nails bite into the flesh of his palm.

"I really can't do this right now, Lola. I have to get back to the game."

"You drank from another woman in front of me!" she screams. "Then you have the nerve to walk away without giving your girlfriend an explanation!"

Ash scoffs, "I am Pale, and you are not my girlfriend." He says it with conviction.

"You haven't even bothered to drink from me, but you will do it with a human!"

"I have a game to get back to," he declares while exchanging looks with his poker crew.

"How dare you put a stupid poker game in front of your female, Asher? That's the rudest thing you can ever do!"

She takes a breath, snorts something nasty enough to cause Cason to gag and continues as if she hadn't been screaming at him for the past half hour. "I need you to come over so we can talk."

He thinks for a minute and smiles as he replies, "Why don't you give my mom a call and see if she can come and talk to you about it, since it seems that she is the culprit in this debacle."

"Don't you dare put me off for your mother to deal with. We made love and it was blissful. I think you might be my lifemate," Lola demands as the whole table hears her little feet stomping on tile floors.

"Give her a call! You have her number, I am sure. I bet she knows a bunch of males interested in being more than friends and the possibility of lifemates, too!"

"You asshole!" She screams as she ends the call.

"Thank god" He exclaims in relief at the headache her voice alone caused. He rubs his temples as the guys around the table can't stop laughing.

"Where the hell did your mom find that?" Cason eyes the phone with disgust. "My Sierra is not anything to behold in the manners department after we've being married for a century, but god forbid any man should be forced into that situation. Ugh."

Ash stares at him blandly and says, "Thanks, dick!"

Cason shakes goosebumps off his back and considers his cards.

"She is the worst one I've dealt with so far. I should have known when I was sitting at the table and she was offended when I asked what she does for work."

"It's your turn, Ash," Cason says from his right.

Ash looks down at the two aces in his hand. Throwing chips into the middle, he says, "Call."

The other men toss their cards into the middle and he pulls in the small pile of chips towards himself. "She wouldn't even eat. Do women of the Pale Race even have a fat gene?"

Graham laughs. "Hell, no. I have watched the most gorgeous thing eat about three bags of chips and two ice creams because she loves the taste, and she gains nothing. Not one pound. At 250-some-odd years old, she looks the same as always!"

Ash nods. "That's what I mean. So why, all of a sudden, are the females not eating anything? Like really—salad? *We are carnivores!*"

As usual, Dayton pipes in quietly. "I love me a woman who can eat. Hey, Stone, what do you like about women?" he asks, smiling.

"God, if I don't love me a beautiful set of fangs for those teeth to just . . ."

The guys, every one of them, take that in.

"Your mom is one crazy lady," Dayton says to Ash as he begins shuffling and dealing. Dayton has long, dirty blond hair with a red beard.

"Every ten years, like clockwork," Ash says with sarcasm. "She hates me."

With the baby face women go crazy for, Graham, all olive skin and dark eyes, looks at Ash and says, "The least you can do is keep them around for more than one date! Try to be a gentleman and woo them. Well not *that* one, but someone. I have never even seen you with a chick!"

"Then I would have to put up with the boredom that comes with dating in the royal circles," Ash says as he looks at his cards. "Not to mention, they stick like cling wrap as soon as they realize I have my own bank account. Better yet, my general-of-Protector status makes them swoon. It's all over from there."

Chuckling, the men nod.

"Amen to that!" Cason says, eyeing his own lifemate mark. "I swear if you can make it, they can spend it."

Ash looks around, "So is there any new chatter going around?"

"Dude, its poker night," Stone, his friend since boyhood, complains, "unless we get an order from above your head, we are off for the next four hours."

The other guys nod in agreement.

Dayton reveals the cards Ash needs to work with, and he tosses his into the center of the table, folding before the game even begins. "Man, this is getting to me. How on earth can a woman be so dim?" Ash says.

Every one of them laughs.

"Dude," Stone says, looking up at him. "That woman is not dim. She is a snake. Every one of those tears, every syllable from her mouth and every face she makes is part of a plan."

The other men nod in unison.

Ash looks at them like they're crazy. Stone continues. "You wait! She wants something, and this isn't the last time you will hear from her."

Ash spaces out as he watches the rest of the deal. He knows that he will have to contend with Lola at some point. The average Pale Race woman has never been enough for him, so even if Lola hadn't been clingy and obnoxious, her chances were already slim. He disdained their constant need for men to be perfect along with their incessant need to be around their mate. Hell, even Cason had issues getting to poker night when Sierra had a meltdown about her needs being met.

It was even worse when Sierra was in her haze that overcomes a female every twelve years or so, making her body go through a process of hyper ovulation. Then he couldn't leave the house for a week, because the needs of the female become so strong that any male near her will come running without thought. Even if a woman doesn't personally need her mate present during every minute she goes through it, he has to be there to ward off any other males. It's so bad that, whether a male intends to show up or not, he joins men who gather waiting. Sensing her needs, they will comply with anything—in the physical sense.

The thought of being needed that much by a female scares the shit out of Ash to the point that he jumps when Stone yells his name.

"What?"

The guys laugh at him, and his ears to turn red.

"What is up with you lately?" they chorus.

"I have no idea," Ash replies as he tries to figure it out. "I can feel something changing, and I can't figure out whether it's good or bad."

Stone asks, "Have you talked to your father about it?"

Ash shakes his head, "No. I don't want to until I know what it is."

The others agree, all in their own usual way of nods or "Yups."

"Dude, when was the last time you slept?" Stone asks in his stoner way. Ash swears that if the kid's workplace permitted board shorts on the job, he totally would wear them.

Ash takes a minute to think about it. Then, "Not sure."

"Dude, get out of here," Dayton tells him. "If we are expected to be ready, so are you."

"But he has most of the chips!" Graham complains.

Ash laughs at his buddies and pushes the chips to the middle of the table for them to split. "Don't be up too late, boys!" Walking out of the kitchen, he chides them. He knows that none of them will get the sleep, just as he doesn't plan to. He looks at his watch. As it's only midnight, he decides he needs to clear his head.

Traffic is light during the five-minute drive to the gym, and it calms him a little. With his favorite gym empty the way he likes it, he grabs his bag from the trunk and heads inside. Ash finds himself looking in the mirror as he changes his clothes, the days when no one remembered a face so easily long gone. His long, dark red hair never made anyone look twice when he walked through a village. Now with cameras and fingerprinting, he has to be constantly aware. The style Gwen has been throwing around, a style that will attract attention, freaks him out a little after a century of trying to hide. Shaking his head, he goes into the main room filled with treadmills and ellipticals.

He looks at his phone for the time, again forgetting he has just seen it. He thinks to himself, *At least I won't have to worry about humans for a while.* He sets his phone down on his towel next to his water bottle, his mind occupied. He can think in the gym, expel pent-up energy, and figure out his issues with the world.

On a treadmill, Ash thinks about everything work-wise that bugs him. It's as if a block of lead sits in front of his face and he can't figure out what's on the other side. He doesn't know whether the feeling has to do with someone to protect or someone to rescue, but he knows it's something to do with work. All his gut feelings seem to concern work, and he always attempts to heed his inner warnings.

That was the thing, though, he thinks. *The Protectors are supposed to protect more than rescue.* Protection of the Pale Race once ranked as their first task, but now, rescues of those captured are to ensure that the Pale Race cannot be eradicated from the face of the earth. With dwindling numbers of children born, the fate of the Pale Race can't change for the better until something significant comes along.

The day before, his father informed Ash of the prophesy coming into play, a prophesy that dictates whom he will marry as well as the races uniting as one. Therefore, he and his four warriors, the Terrors, will have to head out when they receive the call to protect the hybrid who will be stronger than all and will lead the armies, —a man who will guarantee the safety of the Pale Race.

Ash doesn't know when he will get the call to glory, but he knows he will. The many teams of Protectors throughout the world have assembled, awaiting the order to protect the hybrid as soon as it makes itself known.

He looks down at the digital numbers on the treadmill and pushes the arrow to increase the speed. Staring at the wall again with a grimace, he contemplates the growing knot in his stomach. *Could it be because I felt the hybrid coming or even because I sensed my fate of marriage?*

Just another obstacle to face when it comes to women, he figures. His mother and father both know what his future holds, so his mother attempting to fill the void comes as pure torture for him. If he does find a mate he wishes to be with, then he can't marry her. And if he doesn't marry the mate chosen for him, he will still have to procreate with her. *My fate as a male is a Catch-22 in a damned handbasket from hell.*

He feels a tap on his shoulder. It stops him mid stride and almost causes him to faceplant into the treadmill. He pulls the earbuds out of his ears and waits for the human female to speak to him.

She meets his gaze and becomes instantly aroused. "Um, are you almost done? I've been waiting for almost a half an hour."

With doe eyes, she bats her fake eyelashes at him.

Humans! he thinks to himself, pissed because he only comes to the particular gym because it's open twenty-four hours and is close to his house. *The rarity of a human in here at past 2:00 a.m.,* he thinks as he looks at his phone and swears at himself. *Even at this hour, it's still odd that a human is working out. She must have a different work schedule,* he thinks as he turns the speed down.

"Shit. Yeah, sorry about that," Ash says as he gets off the treadmill. "I didn't realize the time." Not bothering to show his distaste for the human's typical observance of time and day, he wipes it down and heads for the locker room. With members of the Pale Race never dying unless they choose to dry out, he understands that humans have an expiration date, but that doesn't mean he likes consistently hearing about it.

The woman runs up and taps his shoulder again. "Can I get your number?" she asks coyly, causing Ash to take a step back in annoyance.

"Nope," he says with sideways smile. "I'm not interested."

He isn't trying to be a jerk, but he's found that anytime he tries to let down a human female easily, she tends to get offended.

She scrunches up her face with a look that said "are you kidding me?" It makes him grin after he turns again to leave. *It was cute that she's interested,* he thinks, *even though she definitely isn't my type.*

Another tap on his shoulder.

"Yess?" he says, trying not to hiss at her. He turns as slowly as he can, not wanting to spook her.

"May I ask why?"

Ash thinks a moment about how to let her down easily but falls short when he realizes he has to go and really doesn't give two shits. "I am not interested because, from the very small conversation we've had, I now know that you are pushy, rude, and full of yourself."

He turns and walks away, calling over his shoulder, "But have a great workout!"

He hears her stomp back over to the treadmill in a huff as his phone rings.

"Where the hell are you, son?" his father asks loudly. Ash wonders what he has forgotten to do. After realizing he hasn't missed anything important, he switches the phone to the other shoulder so he can get his things together.

"I'm at the gym. I don't have work for a few hours. What's up?"

His father laughs. "You and your working out! Our kind has no need for that kind of thing. We are already stronger and faster than the humans."

"It feels good and helps me focus, Dad," Ash says glancing at the ceiling and waiting for his father to get to the point.

His father barks with laughter. "Get over here. Your mother and I want to chit-chat."

What is it now? Ash complains to himself.

"I'll be there in an hour. That, okay?"

"Sure."

Just a Taste

Hunger

"Shouldn't I feel better by now?" Ivy asks, removing her scabbard so she can get ready for sleep. The past couple weeks of nausea and headaches have wrought havoc on her motivation even to move, and dark circles have erupted under her eyes. A lot of the time, she barfs up the blood that is supposed to sustain her, and neither her or her father can figure out why as they switch up blood types to see if it may be just a sensitivity. Ivy feels her system struggling, but nothing works with her mind as grossed out as her body about the thought of more nausea and headaches.

Quiet as he looks into her eyes, Soren sits at her feet. "There has never been a hybrid before. You're the first, and I'm not sure how to answer. I have been looking into it, though."

Breaking eye contact and changing the subject, Ivy nods. "Is there a warriors guild in this coven?"

"It's something like that, though usually, females of the Pale Race are protected, not serving as Protectors." His gruff tone concerns Ivy, as she debates whether it's a patriarchal rule or more. With nothing more to do, Ivy has been reading nonstop about Pale history. The sickness causes her not to want to get out of bed most of the time and sometimes even makes her put down a book to stop her mind from spinning. Soren goes into her room most mornings and lets her ask all the questions she can think of.

Ivy looks up at him and smiles wistfully. "You are aware that I'm trained in several ways of combat. I fully intend to be a Protector, as you called it. But first, I need to figure out why I can't eat."

Ivy knows deep down that she must prove her fighting skills to Soren yet fears he will never trust her enough to defend more than herself. With no getting around the aspect of being the daughter of yet another leader, even as her sickness has her weak, she sighs in resignation.

Almost at the same time, Soren huffs out a breath. "Can I at least get to know you for a bit before you go running off?"

Ivy shrugs. "I guess. I thought you said the Pale Race can only die when they choose to." Wondering if she can actually die from her sickness, she looks at her feet. "And why do females need protection?"

Soren scrubs his fingers through his hair. "Some humans out there know we exist—some good and some bad. Even if we can't die, we can be captured."

He pauses.

"The blood of the Pale Race has magic," he continues, "literally called blood magic, and it's the way we can turn a human to a vampire. The magic of our blood creates venom that we can inject to allow a vampire to keep living. Our venom has to be fed with blood to keep it from decaying, though. It's also why it can heal a human of ailments that the humans haven't been able to cure with their medicines."

Ivy thinks for a moment about that. "So why would they seek only the females. Don't the males have the same blood?"

"Yes and no. When a female of the Pale Race gets pregnant, she's pregnant for twenty-nine moon cycles. During the pregnancy, she can be bled to cure a human's cancer or illness. The blood of a pregnant Pale Race female has extreme amounts of what the humans call HGH, the hormone helps our fledglings grow at the rate of a human. The blood of a pregnant Pale Race female won't turn the human to a vampire.

"If a Pale Race female loses more than a few ounces in a week," Soren continues, "the baby will spontaneously abort. If she loses even just under a pint, it will kill her as well, and her blood will be tainted."

Soren's eyes meet Ivy's as she combats an overwhelming feeling of wanting more information.

Realization widens her eyes. "They hold Pale Race females captive and keep making them have babies?"

"Yes. They don't need many males to make the process work. Just one would suffice in most cases," Soren says with a grief-stricken face. "They starve male babies of the Pale Race. They raise female babies to breeding age, and the cycle repeats itself."

"I'm going to be sick."

Ivy runs to the bathroom and yet again vomits all of the blood up she's consumed. Ivy usually has a strong stomach, so she knows the story isn't what has made her sick. She opens her eyes as the last of her dry heaving ebbs.

"Soren!" she calls.

She panics, making herself sit on the tiled floor before she falls into the porcelain bowl.

Ivy sweats profusely, holds her legs to herself, and begins to shake uncontrollably. *Something is wrong with me*, she thinks as she feels something creeping through her limbs like a black slime, stopping her conscious thought, except for, *This has never happened before.*

"You can call me *Dad*, you know," he says, annoyed. "It wasn't my choice not to . . ." He stops in his tracks, "Now this," he says, seeing the mess, "I have never heard of before."

He flushes the toilet and turns on the shower. She gags at the smell of her vomit. He picks her up and puts her, still fully clothed, inside the shower stall and shuts the door.

"You speak to no one about this," he instructs. "I will be right back."

Ivy sits in the warm shower shivering uncontrollably. She can feel the sickness coming worse than anything she has ever experienced, like a red fog clouding the shower stall. It starts differently than ever before, but after years of a mellower version, she knows.

She starts to freak out, grasping for anything that can help her focus.

She opens the shower stall door and tries to keep her mind focused on her breathing and looks around for anything alive. If she can even touch a plant or some dirt, she can draw strength from it. Through the red haze, however, she can see nothing even remotely alive. *The Scavenger guild was right*, she thinks. *Humans don't care about the living.*

She finds her last thought dismal as she loses consciousness. Even meditative breaths and attempts to draw in the elements have given her no control over what happens.

She can no longer feel around her. Her sight darkens as her breathing grows ragged. She's about to black out and feebly resigns herself, knowing that she will kill someone. She lets it take over.

Ivy comes to. One at a time, her senses kick into motion. She can hear a horrific gurgle of someone coughing. She feels the cold tiles beneath her hands and body as she lies facedown. She can taste heaven even as she smells blood pooling sticky and sweet around her. Her eyes focus on the room as everything gleams red—not the red fog that goes with a sickness. The red of blood splattering everything within sight all over the walls, ceilings, and floor. A woman lies on the ground struggling to breathe, a look of hatred across her features as Ivy finds herself licking blood up off the bathroom floor.

Ivy forces herself away from the floor as she fights the urge to keep licking the surfaces of the bathroom. Looking around, she assesses the situation. Without knowing what she's doing, she bites her wrist and feeds it to the woman who looks like she's dying. The woman shakes her head, "No," but Ivy forces her to take it. The woman tastes the blood, and then, as if her fight or flight kicks in, swallows in large gulps. Like magic, the gaping and gruesome hole in the woman's neck closes itself.

Once the woman heals enough to move, she backs herself against the wall away from Ivy, condemning her with her eyes. She then frantically looks around for an escape as Ivy sits back, watching her. The need for more blood screaming in the back of her mind, she sits, not able to move again. The fear of biting the woman again holds her back to the wall.

Ivy wants to go to her and explain what happened, but as if reading Ivy's mind, the woman begins screaming, "Stay the fuck away from me!" Soren and Jynx careen into the room as they slip on blood that coats every surface.

Soren gets to Ivy and madly checks her for injuries, but he's confused. "What happened?"

"That psycho bit me!" the woman screams, slamming her fist on the blood-covered tiles, causing blood to spatter the walls all over again. Ivy can feel the repeating pull of blood and squints her eyes shut, forcing herself to center and relax even as her teeth begin to ache fiercely.

"Nova, you are a vampire and will respect your betters, or you will be removed."

Still dazed and not comprehending the event or why it happened, Ivy knows she has to get out of there. But she can't move. She watches her hand as it mechanically rises up to her mouth automatically licking the blood from her fingers.

Soren scrubs his hand through his hair and looks around. "Jynx?"

"Here, boss," she says as she attempts to mop up some of the mess that Ivy made, the ick factor showing clearly on her face.

"I need you to get a hold of Asher for me. Tell him, 'It's here.' Then I need you to send Sebastian to me."

"Thank god. Guess there was a reason you asked me to fill the glass." Jynx gestures at the space around her and says, "This place is nasty. Ugh."

The woman called Nova backs further against the wall. She shakily holds her measured tone as she slowly says, "Soren, that thing is not your daughter. You have been my mate for almost twenty years. I heard the shower and came in here, and she attacked me."

"Did that happen?" Soren asks Ivy.

Nova jumps to her feet. "Why the fuck are you asking the psycho that bit your mate if it happened? I just said that's what happened!"

Without looking at Nova, Soren growls at her, "You have never been my mate, Nova. The agreement between us was comfort. This woman is my daughter. She's of the Pale Race. That means she has command over you. If she wants to bite you, which by the way, I don't see any evidence of, she can do so without your permission." He seems to dare her to question his authority.

Feeling a pull she can't control, Ivy looks up at Nova and says, "Come to me."

Panic in her eyes and against her will, Nova moves closer. As she approaches, Ivy can see that her eyes have relaxed into large pupils.

"Shut your pretty little mouth and don't speak to anyone of this. Go sit in your room until Soren comes to find you," Ivy smiles as she touches Nova's neck, her eyes turning red with her sickness calling for more—more of the vampire blood that she smells around her, rivulets staining every surface as the spray rolls slowly down the walls.

Why isn't this gross? Ivy wonders. She feels fog enveloping her will, and it takes every bit of composure for her not to lick every surface of the bathroom clean.

"Yes, your highness," Nova retorts as she walks purposefully but dazed out of the room.

Soren shakes his head and looks at Ivy. "Did you really bite her?" A sly sideways grin replaces his look of concern.

Still slightly out of it, Ivy shrugs, "Yeah, but I gave her my blood. She's healed."

He coughs to cover his shock. "Your blood?"

Soren looks at her sideways, the shower still running to cover their conversation in case anyone can hear. "So did it satisfy you?"

Ivy shakes her head. "Yes to the blood and no to the satisfaction." Her eyes change to a glowing red as her vision begins to redden with them. "I want so much more."

She breathes in deeply, the need for more causing her teeth to ache. "I can't move. If I do, I might go after someone else. Now that I know what the blood of a vampire tastes like, I can smell the blood in everyone here. I can hear it rushing through their veins as we speak. How do I get more?" Through a haze of bloodlust, she breathes in deeply, her nostrils flaring with the intensity.

He takes a step back. "I was hoping this wouldn't be the case, but when you started to yack up all the blood, I started to suspect it. I left to figure out who I can trust to fill a glass for you to try. Jynx did the honors."

Soren hands her a glass of blood he had been holding in his hand. "We will have to figure something out." He looks at the room around them. "So, your ability to mesmerize vampires, or mesmer as we refer to it, must come from them being your prey . . . This is so weird."

Ivy takes a momentary breath as she chugs the glass of blood Soren handed her. No remorse tempts her as she closes her eyes and sighs. "You try being the freak and then get back to me on what's weird," she tells him between gulps. She can't do anything else but gulp it all.

"Commander?" a male voice calls from the other room.

"In here, Sebastian," Soren answers.

Ivy eyes the empty glass in her hands and wishes she had more but also feels the ache in her mouth ebbing. The new voice has her full attention.

The sound of footfalls echo and then a very drawn out, "Fuccckkkkkk!" Smash! The newcomer, apparently Sebastian, slips on the bloody floor and takes out a shelf full of soap bottles.

Ivy and Soren laugh almost maniacally with anxiety. "What a mess!" Sebastian exclaims, pulling his clothes away from himself in disgust. He grimaces at Ivy and Soren as he realizes that blood covers them.

Ivy knows that she and Soren must look horrible as they nevertheless grin at his clumsiness.

"What the hell are you two doing in here?" Sebastian demands. "It looks like you've committed mass murder!"

"No murder," Ivy giggles. "More like an overzealous baby vamp."

Sebastian looks confused. "But you're not a vampire."

"I'm not talking about me," Ivy says with a wink as she licks a single, blood-covered finger. Her eyes turn red with bloodlust and she feels herself lifting from the floor as, in her mind, she stalks him.

He steps back, apparently hoping to escape. "Whose blood is this?" he asks frantically, looking to Soren for support.

Immediately, Soren wraps his arms around Ivy and stops her from moving. Ivy looks at him and feels herself panic as she snaps back to reality.

"Nova's," Soren says. "Ivy, stop scaring him."

Ivy looks at the floor and, instead of focusing on the blood rushing through the new guy's veins, plops down in the middle of Nova's blood.

"Baz," says Soren, "you are my second in command. I need you to take this to your grave."

Baz looks from Soren to Ivy then back to Soren slowly as if trying to figure out the secret for himself. "I'll be right back," he says.

Baz goes out into the bedroom and turns on some extremely loud racket that Ivy assumes humans consider music. The deep sounds of it shake the house with a loud thump. In agony, Ivy covers her ears. She watches the air vibrate as her new senses reject the reverberations.

Baz returns to the room, and Soren tells him as much as he can. They leave out the parts that include Ivy's ancient heritage.

The two work diligently to get the bathroom back to perfection as they try to figure out the best course of action. Not wanting another bloodbath to contend with, they speak quickly and don't allow Ivy to get a word in. Ivy sadly gazes at the blood-sodden towels soaking up her meal. The banging in the other room gives her a migraine while she can only sit watching. Ivy coughs and sputters at the scent of the cleaner her father uses, and the pungent smell only worsens the pain in her mind.

Still so hungry! she thinks. When they finish the bathroom, she goes back into the shower and cleans herself up yet again. She throws the only towel left on the shelf around herself she walks out of the bathroom and into the bedroom.

"Ivy! You aren't decent!" Soren announces in agony while averting his eyes. Baz stands and blatantly takes in the sight of her. She notices that, when you look beneath the blood he's covered in, that he's aware of his handsomeness. His egotistical air to him makes Ivy look quickly away as she refuses, even with his attractiveness, to give him the time of day.

Soren observes Baz staring at Ivy and smacks him hard in the back of the head.

"Ow!" Baz complains.

Feeling her ego puff up a little bit as she sees his diminish slightly, Ivy smiles a little.

"Have some common decency, kid," directs Soren.

Not sure which kid Soren refers to, Ivy whisks past them and heads towards the closet. "I need clothes. It's not my fault you are still in my room," she asserts as she enters and, ready to pass out from nourishment rushing through her veins, shuts the closet door.

Her hands shake as she stares with concern at a long mirror inside the closet. Energy she has never had in her life hits hard, and she can imagine that her teeth will begin to chatter. Not sated in the least even with the potent power she consumed with Nova's blood, her stomach growls again in consternation, *What will I feel like when I am satisfied?* she wonders as she shuffles through the small amount of clothing in the tiny room.

They continue their conversation through the closed door while she searches for a pair of shorts and a t-shirt. Her stomach growls again, and she sighs. She can sense that dawn will come soon and, as vibrant as she feels from feeding, she is exhausted as well. She's sad about not seeing the sun as much as she once did. It pains her that a couple of weeks before, she awoke in Lesai, the only home she'd known her entire life, and she'll never see it again.

A feeling of helplessness hits her hard in the chest. In determination to resist the feeling, she decides to have plants in every window and corner of her room. *I will never be in a position where the elemental magics are not close enough to reach. In Lesai the very walls of the homes are the trees themselves, giving life and magic to the dwellers.*

Human music still plays when she emerges from the closet. She turns off the radio her father showed her weeks before when giving her a tour of his favorite human gadgets. *Thank the Elemental Mother for the off button,* she thinks. She takes a deep breath, tips her head to the ceiling, and, thankful to feel even a little better than she has in weeks, slowly lets the breath out.

Her father sits on a couch in her room, and she looks around to find that the other male has vanished. *Drats!* She thinks. *He was good eye candy! Even if he has the weirdest vibe.*

"We have figured out a plan for you to get sustenance," Soren says. "For a while, at least, we will have random vampires come visit you to play chess, and you'll mesmer them to make them forget. They'll only remember that you play a good game."

Ivy smiles. "Can we try it tonight?"

"Baz will find someone now. Just so we are on the same page, though, you cannot bite anyone until we know the full consequences," Soren says with a sigh. "I know it will be hard, but you must stop yourself. If you can't, either Baz, Ash, or I will be here to stop you."

Ivy looks annoyed. "Why can't I bite someone? I can mesmer them to forget."

For the first time, Ivy sees Soren irritated. He bunches his fists and says, "For the love of all things holy, do as I say."

Ivy stands, hands on her hips, and challenges him with a stare. He stares right back at her.

"I will only say this once," she retorts. "I am not helpless. I am not stupid. If there is something I need to know, then tell me. Otherwise, I will make my own decision—even if, for some reason, I have to leave to make the right decision for me."

Ivy stalks around him to the bed. She pulls back the blankets and shuts out the lights when she settles in.

Soren walks over and turns the lights right back on. "Vampires don't sleep, Ivy. We cannot have half of the coven snoring during the night because you fed from them. We can't keep a secret with that happening." He inhales sharply and lets his breath out slowly as he adds, "We also don't know what it will take to make more hybrids. You could very well transition someone without knowing."

"You said, and I quote, 'Vampires sleep like the dead at the highest point of the day.' End quote." Ivy repeats his words back to him as she meets his eyes in defiance.

Soren chuckles at Ivy, and it throws her from her high horse. "And that, my daughter, is why I say you look like your mother. By the way, you act like her, too—more stubborn than you know what to do with."

Ivy's eyes go flat as she narrows her eyebrows at Soren. "Biting is more nutritious, though."

Soren shakes his head as he pats Ivy on the leg through the blanket. "A blood bag is just as nutritious, which you would know if you read anything from this century. There is a difference between sleeping and sleeping like the dead, Ivy. The vampire you just fed from is snoring before dawn, whereas normally only after the sun has risen, one would be similar to a cadaver."

Ivy shrugs. "Okay. Well, that makes sense. Next time, lead with the facts. And in no way do I want to make another hybrid. That would be cruel."

"I don't suspect you can create a hybrid, since what you just did only caused sleep, but what you just did is exactly how the Pale Race creates a vampire."

Ivy's jaw drops. She keeps her arms folded in front of her. "Oh." Shaking herself a little, she asks, "Now, who is Ash?"

Soren smiles. "Ash is a friend of your mother and me from back in the day when she was a Scavenger."

Ivy groans. "So, basically, some old fogey coming to babysit me. So much for fun."

Her cranky attitude makes Soren laugh. "Something tells me you will be surprised." A knowing look in his eyes says there's more, but he doesn't plan to tell her.

I feel good enough to run miles, Ivy thinks. *I bet I can give an old man a run for his money, especially if he thinks he can always have eyes on me.*

The idea that her father will bring someone to protect her like a child unsettles her. The last time someone had to protect her was when she was eight. After she bit one of the guards, no one would even try, though they told her mother that she needed a tighter leash before they could keep her in check.

Suddenly, she smells blood somewhere, and her mouth begins to ache again as her fangs of their own accord dig into her bottom gums.

"Are cravings always going to be this strong?" she asks, wiping a trickle of her own blood from her mouth. Her eyes turn red as she thinks about the feel of it sliding down her throat, and she salivates. *Eew, get a grip, Ivy,* she thinks.

She hears a knock on her bedroom door. "Enter," she says as she gets out of bed and heads over to the coffee table.

Baz walks into the room with a male vampire who looks around twenty. Feeling her instincts begin to push her for what her body needs, Ivy smiles grandly at him.

"Hi. I'm Ivy. Who are you?"

"Taz," the guy says. He sees her red eyes and hesitates a moment before Baz gently urges him forward.

Ivy waits until he meets her eyes again, then allows herself to assert her will. "You will open your vein into this bottle until you begin to feel dizzy," she tells him. "Then you will remember nothing and return to your room to sleep."

Taz nods, cuts his wrist, and allows his blood to flow into the wide top of a Nalgene bottle she provides. The wrist quickly heals a couple times as the bottle fills, and he reopens the wound each time it stops flowing. When the bottle fills to about three quarters, Taz starts getting a bit wobbly but keeps going until the blood level nears the top.

Once done, he stands up, and hands Baz the bottle. In turn, Baz hands him a bag of human blood, which he downs at once. His wrist heals to unblemished skin, and he walks out of the room in a trance.

Ivy feels the saliva glands in her mouth begin to water. "I thought we agreed on chess?" Soren says in a huff.

"Just before dawn, I am going to invite a stranger to a game of chess. Because that's believable, right?" Shaking her head and tossing it back against the pillows, she looks at her father. "Trust me," she says. "I don't want to be found out any more than you want me to. The freak is secure. From now on, I will use our cover, but for this morning. I went with what I knew would be believable."

The blood distracts her from more comments as Baz hands her the bottle of vampire blood. His face a stone mask, Baz makes eye contact with Ivy.

She hastily takes the bottle and gulps the liquid gold. She feels her eyes glow not just any red but vibrant, vivid red. She lifts the bottle to her lips again and drinks deeply.

Through the haze of crimson, she sees a look of disgust float across Baz's face, but he recovers quickly. The moment causes Ivy to wonder if she sees imaginary things as the blood flows to every vein in her body and seeps into her limbs. She savors every feeling even as she misses the rush that comes with taking it from a vein. Even once was enough for her to want it again, the sparkling feeling of complete authority over the other life she can take or let survive.

Is it always going to feel like that? she wonders.

Making the best of the bottled blood, she doesn't take a breath until the entire bottle empties, then closes her eyes and drifts away in bliss. She barely remembers her father checking on her teeth again and whispering, "Well, at least she's good now. Her teeth are in place."

ᵛᶠ ᵛᶠ ᵛᶠ

For the first time in her life, Ivy feels fully revitalized, wants to eat actual food, and decides she wants to explore the kitchen. She finds that the kitchen, created to feed an enormous number of humans, lacks the items necessary to prepare food. *Well, it* is *a compound filled with vampires.*

They don't eat, but what do the Pales do? The massive grills and counters have collected dust and debris from minimal use over the years.

Rummaging through the refrigerator and cabinets, all but bare as well, she finds some crackers, cheese, and peanut butter. Not knowing how long the cheese has been in the refrigerator, she sticks to the crackers and peanut butter after smelling the stuff and realizing it is just a smooth textured form of the nuts she has eaten in Lesai.

Ivy walks out the door at the rear of the expansive foyer and onto a patio with benches placed throughout. Fountains and hedges surround her, creating a maze of majestic and manicured space. *There is nothing natural about the flow of the gardens, but it's still beautiful,* she thinks as the sunshine above her head and smell of the trees around the area, cause her to sigh in relief. Even as the sun feels impossibly bright, she closes her eyes and lifts her face to allow it to penetrate her skin. *I may need a pair of sunglasses, now that I think of it,* she imagines.

Even if the trees and shrubs don't naturally pair, she can see past the humans' attempts to create beauty as long as she can feel nature in the place. She walks a little further and sees a hammock next to an apple tree. Since it's morning, the tree will supply shade, but she isn't interested in hiding from the sun. Instead, she sits down on the ground and looks around at the peaceful garden as she chomps on a freshly picked apple.

Can't Escape It

Road Trip

"What do you mean, it's here?" Ash asks reluctantly as Jynx explains herself on the phone. *She was always kind of awkward in the way she spoke,* he thought.

"All Soren said was, 'It's here.' He told me to tell you that exact wording. He didn't say anything else except to 'get Baz.'" She hesitates, not wanting to say something else on her mind.

Knowing that she waits for the go-ahead, Ash says "I am alone, and no one can hear me."

"Thank God," she says in a huff. "I'm in Soren's office, so I'm good, too. We ran into Ivy's room to see what all the hubbub was, and there was a layer of vampire blood from one end to the other. Nova was screaming that Ivy bit her. There were no marks on the baby vamp, but it was really weird. Ivy looking like a kicked rabid dog sitting on the floor in the mess. Ash, she was licking the blood off her fingers, and I don't even think she realized she was doing it."

Confused, Ash asks, "Who the hell is Ivy?"

"Soren's daughter," Jynx replies chuffing. "Keep up."

Ash wonders, *Is this is all really happening?* as he stares at the pool laid out in front of him. For three centuries, he has been waiting to make the decision now facing him—three hundred years of solitude, refusing to get close to a woman out of fear he would have to let her go.

"Ash? Ash—?" Jynx asks, annoyed.

Ash comes back to real time. "When did Soren have a daughter?"

"Just get here!" Jynx says impatiently as she hangs up the phone.

His mother's hand touches his shoulder. "What's the fuss?" Even in times of stress, her voice can soothe him (except when she's trying to fix him up with a date). She sits down in the lawn chair next to his as they feel the last dregs of night fade away.

"Is this the councilman's right hand asking or my mom?" he asks, eyeing her sideways.

"Both. But start with business."

Ash sighs. "Well, Mrs. Aurora Vale, there are several issues I am dealing with right now. First, I am pretty sure that the prophecy has manifested itself. That was Jynx telling me that Soren said, "Its here.""

His mother sat up straight. "You need to get to Duneskil before tonight." She starts mumbling to herself, but even with his perfect hearing, Ash can't make out the syllables.

Interrupting her, he looks up at the sky. "She also said that Soren's daughter Ivy is there too." Ash looks back at her as a look of hope crosses his mother's features.

"Is it true? Has your wife finally come to us?" his mother asks.

Ash wants to crawl into a hole and die. He will tell the Pale Council to suck it before he marries an entitled royal, A female who acts like a lamppost all night and never assumes any functional roles in society.

"Mom, you know that I am not okay with someone having chosen whom I will marry three hundred years before they are even born. There is no way that's normal. In fact, the Pale Council is crazy if they think that it's going to work." Trying to hold his cool, Ash grits his teeth.

Aurora smiles faintly. "I understand."

She is the last person ever to push him into anything—bluntly into anything, that is. A gentle nudge is her custom. "Make me one promise, though," she says.

Ash waits for the catch.

She continues slowly, "Before you ask her, you need to tell me."

Ash feels his blood heat with irritation. "I am not going to marry a woman I've never met. Nor am I going to do what the Pale Council dictates. I will be a Protector for my entire existence. Believe me when I say that I will protect as my job description warrants, but marrying Soren's daughter is out of the question."

Waiting for the promise she has asked for, his mother gives him a pleading look. "Alright, mother. If on the off chance I ask her, I will call you first," he retorts sarcastically. His mother laughs and knocks him off his lawn chair with her foot.

"Go see Soren," she tells him.

After kissing his mother's cheek, Ash leaves the patio and gets into his BMW and speeds off. The sun comes over the horizon, and he smiles, happy that he can tolerate the sun on this day. The aftermarket UV filtered glass he installed makes life bearable when he wants to get out of a funk.

After an hour, he struggles to find a distraction from his stress. so he begins a game he and his sisters started as children. He sees a street sign that reads, Ridge Avenue. He thinks to himself in the singsong way he used to as a child, *A ridge is a bluff is a ruse is a fraud is a deception is a lie . . .* He startles himself a little . . . *that got dark quick.*

Back to the stress at hand, he thinks about the woman at Duneskil he has been fated to marry since he was born. The prophecy, hanging in the air since the beginning of time, gnaws at his insides.

A hybrid to unite the races with fear and loyalty as one, he remembers from a line read to him when he came of age. The Protectors, created to defend and help the hybrid, had grown into little more than rescuers. For the last hundred years or so, Ash's sole responsibility has been to rescue and protect the Pale Race from vamp-op teams. Vamp-ops came from other races, mainly human, and wished to eradicate the Pale Race from the world while using Pale Race blood to cure ailments.

Ash's father is one of the three councilmen with Ash first general and next in line for the councilman. He's never wanted the power of the Pale Council. Going into the line of danger to protect and bring families together defines his calling.

Remembering a few of the faces that he's helped over the years, Ash momentarily forgets his problems, then passes a street named Ivy Terrace. *I swear fate wants to torment me,* he thinks, narrowing his eyes with determination. *Watch this! I can ignore fate!*

Twenty minutes later, he misses his exit and has to drive ten minutes to get himself back on track. The next street name he passes is Webb Circle as he stares glassy-eyed out the window. Ash renews his game in his mind as he drives on, *a web is a snare is a trap is a ploy is a plan . . . no way.*

After driving halfway to his destination, Ash can't get his mind off his fate of marriage nor the knot winding tighter in his stomach. A thought occurs to him, and he fumes with anger. Hoping that he'll wake his father in the middle of the day, he clicks the call button on the dash of his car.

"Yeah?" His father asks, obviously awakened by his ringing phone.

"How long have you known?" Ash demands. His father always knows everything. His mother may have been surprised, but Ash doubted she was any more in the dark than his father.

He hears his dad tell his mom that Ash is on the phone. "To what are you referring?" his father asks.

"You know damn well what I'm asking," Ash grits through clenched teeth.

"I have known since she was eight," his father says, irritated.

Ash grips the steering wheel tighter, knuckles turning white. "And Mom?"

"Same time, honey, but we didn't know she would get a heritage mark," his mother answers with a yawn.

"I don't give a crap what you thought. You continued to make me date other women when you knew the woman you want me to marry is alive."

His mom doesn't say anything as his dad speaks with a harsh tone. "For one, if she didn't get her mark, you would not be marrying her, and for two you need to rein that temper in before you make me angry. Do not speak to your mother that way!"

Ash takes a breath and eases his words out slowly. "The least you could have done is tell me that the woman might be the one I am fated to."

Ash's mom speaks calmly into the speaker phone. "Once you meet her, you might find that you like her after all, honey."

"I am not going to be a pawn in the council's game to make sure that the bloodlines stay pure and untainted by incest! I am a Protector, and I don't have time to be worrying about what a female may or may not want for a pedicure or as an addition onto an already gigantic estate her parents own."

"You promised to at least give her a chance before you make your decision, Asher," his mom says in a serious tone.

Ash laughs without humor. "I made that promise before realizing the two of you have been playing me. For the near future, my entire field of work will be protecting the hybrid, no matter the cost."

He can hear the smile in his mom's voice as she says, "I understand, Asher. Please make sure to call after you arrive so we know you've made it safely." *Why isn't she fighting me on this?*

"Fine." Asher slams his finger into the dash as he hangs up the phone. "Why in the hell was she just laughing at me? I have a job to do." He has a feeling it will be the longest twenty-four hours of his long life.

It dawns on Ash that he hasn't let the Terrors know that it's a go. He scrolls to recent calls and dials Stone. As the call goes to voicemail, he realizes it's just after noon so, as a vampire, Stone can't answer his phone. Instead, Ash dials Cason, who like himself is Pale and answers on the second ring.

"Boss?" Cason asks, his voice croaking a little sleepily.

Ash takes a breath and pushes his irritation into the back of his head. "The hybrid is in play."

"Wait, what?" Ash hears Cason move in the background.

Ash repeats himself.

After a pause, Cason asks, "What's the plan, Boss?"

Ash thinks a moment. "Be on the road at nightfall. Meet me at Duneskil."

"Um, okay. What are we going to do about the veil, though?" Ash received an invitation when Soren found the veil in place that hides Duneskil from the eyes of anyone uninvited, so Ash always forgets about it. "Wait in the shack until I send Soren to you. He will get you in."

"Copy."

Ash freaks out privately again, not knowing what they will be walking into. "Better yet, I will assess the situation first and then let you know when to get there. Camp out in the nearest hotel until I call you."

"Copy. We still leave at dusk?"

"Yes."

Cason yawns. "Okay. I'm going back to sleep."

"Fine, but as soon as the sun sets, you call Stone. I couldn't reach him."

"Who is it, babe?" Ash hears Sierra asking in the background.

"The boss," Cason tells Sierra, then says to Ash, "And fine, I'll take care of it."

Ash hangs the phone up. It immediately rings. The car automatically answers before he can reject the call.

Shit!

"Hello?" Ash answers with annoyance.

"Ash?" asks Lola's poised voice.

Ash wonders if he still has the manual for the stereo in the glove box. "Who else would it be? You called my cell."

Lola giggles. "I was making sure. You never know."

"Can I help you with something?"

After a quiet moment, she says, "I miss you."

What in the hell? "I am heading out of town. I probably won't be back for a while," he replies, suddenly elated that he won't be around to deal with her.

"Why didn't you tell me? I would have come to see you before you left." The lilt in her voice makes his stomach queasy.

Ash thinks of a decent answer. "It was a last-minute thing. There was no time for goodbyes."

"There is always time to say goodbye to a girlfriend."

Ash grits his teeth as he stares at the road in front of him. "You are not my girlfriend, and I am a Protector. I will never know my schedule or when I will be in any city."

"Then maybe you should be in a different line of work," she suggests with a haughty tone that leaves Ash boiling.

"What do you want from me?" Ash huffs.

She sobs as the waterworks start, only serving to piss him off even more. "I want you to take my needs into account."

"There is no reason for me to do that, Lola. We are not together. I told you the night that it happened, it was only sex."

The sniffles continue. "What we have is monumental! I have never felt this way before. How can you deny the love I have for you when there are so few females out there?"

"I can because I am not looking to be with anyone." He pauses for a moment. "I am promised to someone already. There is no marriage unless it's her, and even that isn't going to happen because I am not going to be told who to marry."

The truth comes falling out of him without his control.

Lola shrieks into the car's speakers. "How can you do this to me?"

Ash avoids the impending migraine her voice might give him by turning the volume down on the car speaker.

"I am not doing anything to you, Lola. I am simply being realistic. I do not feel for you in any way other than a friend, and that won't change. It can't change," he persists, gripping the steering wheel.

She sobs more fake than a three-dollar bill and makes sure he can hear everything.

The gruff voice of her father comes into the room. "What is wrong, honey?"

"Asher won't return my feelings! He is so mean, and he says he is promised to another woman, so even if he likes me, it can never worrrk!" Her cries resemble those of a petulant child and seize Ash's nerves. He gets the sudden urge to toss his phone out the window.

"I told you not to persist. He has a different path!" her father, the councilman, rages at her.

Ash hears shuffling on the other end of the line as Lola's father takes the phone from her hand, and the councilman speaks, "I am sorry about this. I am doing my best to explain it, but I can't."

Ash nods still pissed but understanding his place. "It will only be an issue in the field. I am going where you need me right now. Please make sure she doesn't interrupt what is happening."

"Thank you for taking this so seriously, General. I will make sure she doesn't call you again."

The phone hangs up, and Ash feels only slightly relieved.

Sanctuaries

Unwanted Advances

While meditating next to the grove of oak trees in the gardens, Ivy chants, bringing all her worry and sorrow into herself as she sings the song of life. Vibrant and full of energy that she never could have imagined, she feels stronger than ever.

She has to obey the irresistible draw to the stand of oaks as she opens herself to the gardens and allows everything in her to reawaken. The pain of devastation coming from the life around her puts her off balance, but as she progresses, she intuits what the Elemental Mother requires: healing of the old and creation of the new, which forces her sorrows to the back of her mind.

The air around her swirls as dewdrops on the grass lift, dancing to the melancholy sound of her voice. Her voice, the mid-tone alto of the Ancient Elders, not the high soprano of a classic ancient song, vibrates everything it touches. Ivy can feel the earth move beneath her, animals and insects nourishing the womb of the Elemental Mother. The heat of fires that flow beneath the surface rises as she pulls shapes into being. The tree wood she touches with each hand begins to give, allowing her to reach into the center and withdraw its offerings.

Her eyes closed, she finishes her song as she feels the air around her resume the earlier sadness that had engulfed her. Realizing that the Elemental Mother has created a gift for her efforts to heal her, she smiles when she opens her eyes.

She finds herself determined to explore the entire compound as she twirls the gift in her hands. She hasn't yet had the energy to explore the rest of the compound, but enlivened by her meditation, she decides to explore it.

Starting with the bottom floor, she makes her way through double doors into a room next to the kitchen which she skips, since she knows it's empty. Her stomach growls in complaint, reminding her that she needs to ask Soren to fill the kitchen. There are some thirty, round tables stacked at one side of a giant room with high-mounted ceilings, chandeliers, and intricate woodwork. The delicate designs painted onto the ceilings have begun to fade and crack in places, leaving little crumbles littered around. With no need for chairs, someone has stacked them in the corner.

The thought of every tree killed and ripped apart to create such intricate things upsets Ivy. She can allow her mind to justify their death if people use them, but leaving them lifeless and forgotten?

I have to rectify this, she thinks. Even if nature doesn't cross the minds of the Pale Race or vampires, Ivy will not tolerate wasted death, no matter the species.

Remembering her human studies class in Lesai, she wonders if she can gift the chairs to humans who will use them. She gazes around the beautiful if somewhat shabby room once used for eating as she hefts the staffs bestowed on her during meditation. She twirls one in her hand and speaks to the Elemental Mother aloud, her voice dimly echoing, "You think of everything."

Ivy finds herself in the hallway at the bottom of the stairs. She opens each of the doors one at a time along the corridor. All but one enter into empty offices, furniture and electronics covered in dust. Years of decaying wood unsettle her nerves as she adds the items to her list. The years they have been forgotten scream at her as she attempts to think of a good use for the rooms. Muttering to herself about the injustice, she moves on down the hall, stopping at the only locked door.

Forgetting that she's the only one awake in the daylight, she looks around to see if anyone is watching. She touches her sword and uses her other hand to reach toward the door as she lets the element of air flow into the lock. She feels around and finds little pins she slowly pushes and pulls until she can turn the cylinder. She hears the definitive click from the sprung lock and slowly enters her father's office. Light from outside brightens the room, which seems airy, though she can sense that the opposite effect comes at night.

Her father's office is set up like the others and not dusted very often, probably because it's used so frequently or locked when he isn't present. His dark wood desk sits at the center of the room with a cluster of paperwork and electronics. She smiles at the bookcase on the wall laden with books on many subjects. She paws the titles, plucking a few from their homes as she decides to read anything she hasn't already, especially anything with hybrid lore. She holds the books in her arms and peruses a little more, stopping quickly when her eyes fall upon a photograph sitting among the books on a shelf near his desk. She sets the books down on the corner of the desk beside her and picks up the picture. Undeniable love in her mother and Soren's eyes as they gaze into each other's souls makes Ivy's heart skip a beat.

Ivy feels a tear slip down her face as she misses her mother more than she could have contemplated. She'd long known that she would be leaving, but the prospect of never seeing her mother again makes her ache.

She realizes she isn't the only one who has looked at the photo recently as she puts the picture back in its place. Rearranged where the frame lay, dust gives her some insight into the man who gave her life.

Not finding much aside from a few more books to explore, she pokes around the room for a couple more minutes. She creeps out silently and, after closing the door, touches her sword with her free hand to lock it again. She returns to her room to drop off all but one book and then continues her journey.

She steps into a door across from Soren's office and feels her heart beat rapidly. She breaks into a sweat at the number of books there. *This must be what the humans call a library.* Ivy has seen books before, but the Ancients have Scavengers who bring books between the cities as they protect the ancient race. Hundreds of Ancients read one copy of a book by the time it earns retirement to the elder's tomb. Considering the number of dead trees in the room, she decides at once that it will be her favorite place in the entire compound, if only to give their deaths meaning.

On the other side of the foyer, she finds a room with many closets. In no way does she understand why on earth anyone needs so many closets, but she decides she's going to have to ask someone.

Now this I can work with! she thinks, walking into a training room. She swipes her finger across the dust built up on the punching bag and grimaces to herself, *What a waste.* Some of the equipment puzzles her, but if she's the only one awake during the daytime, she knows she will figure it all out. *Even if the Pale Race and vampires are superior in strength, that doesn't mean they shouldn't improve it. Reflexes take time to hone.*

Ivy stops in front of a set of double doors with the word POOL written above it. *No freaking way!* She's always wanted to see what a pool looks like, but none of the teachers of human studies had any pictures. She pushes the doors open and walks over to the edge of the gigantic rectangle of blue water. As the smell of salt fills her nose, she smiles ear to ear.

She kneels next to the edge and puts her hand into the water. It's warm and feels wonderful as she imagines herself bathing in it without a care in the world. In Lesai, the pond outside the village grows a rare form of water hemlock making it toxic for swimming, or so the Ancient Elders would say. And even though she secretly learned to swim there, it was too risky to let down her guard to relax in that pond.

Ivy realizes that she's only gotten a few hours of rest when she begins to feel her legs getting tired. Her mind doesn't want to rest, though, with her newfound knowledge. Wanting at least to attempt to stay up the whole next night, she thinks about her bed but wants to enjoy one last place while the sun still shines.

She lies down in the hammock and looks up at the sky, the sun bright enough to cause her to squint. She wants to let the sun warm her the way it always did in Lesai. She realizes that not only does she see the sky's billowing clouds but also three floors of balconies that overlook the gardens. Every bedroom, including hers on the east side of the compound, sits facing the lush gardens.

The clouds hypnotize Ivy as they float above her head, and even with the full intent of letting her legs rest while she reads a book, the clouds gently lull her to sleep. *What do you mean you want to fight?* *Little Willow wrinkles her nose at Iveliis.* *"Fighting is for the boys."*

"Mommy was a Scavenger, and now she's a queen. Fighting is for girls, too!" *In an effort to provoke a sword fight, Iveliis pokes Willow in the arm with a stick.*

"Ow!" Willow squeals as she runs away from Iveliis.

Calyn speaks up over her needlework. "Iveliis, honey, put the stick down. You know Master Phoenix will be disappointed should he find out you are sparring without a trained partner."

"Fine." Iveliis puts the stick down and, her mind unwavering from her dreams of turmoil and defeating enemies, uses her boot to draw a battle scene in the dirt.

"I'll smash your face! For the king!" she cries victoriously as she stomps the little stick figures into smudges of dirt.

"Iveliis. This isn't nice," her mother chuckles, looking up. "There are many reasons to defeat enemies other than for a king, Sweetheart."

Ivy smiles, drawing another battlefield with a girl on the throne. As they gather in her mind, her soldiers await her orders. "Kill those soul-sucking tarts!" Ivy takes the makeshift sword and begins battering a stone bench across from the one her mother sits on. "Take that, Buttface!"

"Iveliis Grenedich!" her mother cries, setting her project to the side. "You need to be a lady in all situations, even while alone. You never know who may be watching."

Ivy sits in the grass and plays with the laces on her boots as her mother lectures her on being a royal. Knowing better than to mock the speech to her mother's face, she does so in her mind, wishing that she weren't bearing the title of Princess. Her mother finally calms down, and Ivy looks up a little. Seeing her mother go back to her needlework, she smiles.

She stands up, testing to see whether her mother will catch her escape. Ivy ducks behind the bench when she sees her mom again occupied with her needlework. She peeks through the slats and sees her mother still busy pulling threads. Creeping slowly through the bushes, Ivy disappears. She congratulates herself on her stealth, knowing that Master Phoenix would be proud.

She looks around the open meadow all the young ones play in while their mothers do other things. She looks around herself and sees a couple boys sword-fighting by one of the saplings. "Can I play?"

"We are not playing with a girl." The tallest one has a hand on his hip. Ivy, still taller than him, smiles a little, knowing she can take him.

Arms crossed in front of her, Ivy shifts her weight in the way she sees Master Phoenix stand as he watches them train. "I am training to be a Scavenger. So, I can play if I want to."

The boy laughs. "Did you hear that, Rian? The princess thinks she can play because Master Phoenix trains her. It's like she doesn't know she's a girl who won't ever be able to fight."

"I've seen her fight, Finn. She is good." Rian looks worried.

The boy named Finn laughs again, this time, raising his sword to the ready. "Let's see if she can fend me off. I don't even train!"

"I wouldn't, Finn."

Ivy smiles. "Can I borrow your sword, Rian?"

Rian hands Ivy his sword and, not wanting to be in the way, backs to the edge of the clearing. Ivy tests the weight as she was taught and chokes up on the handle a little bit, creating a better balance.

Before Ivy can get into the ready, Finn comes at her with his sword above his head. Ducking and tripping him with her foot, she swings around and watches him fall on his face. He stands up, dusting off his pants and giving her a cold glare that has her smiling.

The best way to win in a fight is to make them emotional. *In her mind, she repeats what Master Phoenix has said to her so many times.* Ivy steps into the ready, squaring herself up for Finn to try his best again. Slashing his wooden sword, he comes at her, and Ivy blocks every blow with a finesse that comes only from practice. She delivers a few blows but wants him to tire himself out. His anger boils as he can't get a single hit in.

As she sees him beginning to lose oomph, she begins sending blows his way, hitting the mark almost every time and watching him flinch more as she comes at him.

"This isn't fair!" he yells as Ivy knocks him in the arm again with the sword. "It's fair. You just stink!"

Finn glares at her a final time and, covered in red welts from where she had gotten him, stalks out of the meadow. As he passes Rian, he pushes him into the bushes.

"Ow!" Ivy hears as Rian bashes his knee on a rock as he falls. Ivy goes to investigate, upset that her enemy has retreated. She sees that Rian holds his knee in pain. "Are you . . . ?" Ivy smells something different but doesn't recognize the scent. She lifts her nose into the air, then brings her face back to his knee. She touches the blood and brings it to her face, licking the red drop from her finger. She begins to panic as everything around her goes dark . . .

Startled out of her slumber, Ivy goes back into the compound. *I'd just be more freakish if they found me in direct sunlight.*

"What in the world are you doing?"

Baz interrupts Ivy's groove, and she jumps. She's been pondering the prospect of one day being well enough that she can leave the compound. The past week has been nothing but boredom until she sets her sights on cleaning and rearranging shared areas. She remains on lockdown, even though she has all the energy in the world. She stands on a ladder to clean a bookshelf.

Ivy shrugs after almost falling off the ladder from jumping in shock. *He's as quiet as an ancient!*

"Cleaning."

She grabs a handful of books from the shelf and passes them down to Baz, who eyes them annoyed. "There are maids we can hire to do that."

"Why? Because we are such busy people that we can't thank the trees for their sacrifice and the books for their knowledge?" Ivy shakes her head at the audacity of him acting like a putz.

Baz looks confused. "Paper is paper."

"To you, maybe, but to me it's more. Now if you want to help me out, that's fine. Otherwise, I'd kind of like to be alone."

Ivy's stares at him fully aware of his internal debate.

Baz puts his stack of books on the table as Ivy brings another pile down the ladder. She climbs back up with her dusting cloth and wipes down the shelf until it shines. Satisfied, she goes back down and begins meticulously wiping the books.

"I want to talk to you," Baz says, approaching her.

Ivy looks up at him, keeping her expression neutral. "Go ahead," she says, wondering what it's about. He's been keeping the vampires coming to her on a regular basis, usually at least two per night, but other than that, he stays away. Once in a while he hangs out with her for the occasional movie they laugh at together. And even though he isn't always there in an obvious way, she can always feel his eyes watching her.

He gets even closer and pulls the book and cloth from her hands. Putting them down on the table, he takes her hands into his. "I like you," he says, meeting her eyes.

"I like you, too." she says smiling. "You're a good friend."

He looks confused as if her words do not compute with his thoughts. Ivy experiences a strange feeling as the hair on her neck stands up. *Don't do it! Don't you dare!*

"No," he continues, "I really like you. Like, I would like to take you on a date," he finishes, blushing slightly.

Ivy pulls her hands from his. He tries to take them back, so she steps back a few feet. "I am not in any position to date. I can't leave the compound, let alone go a night without wanting to kill someone from bloodlust." Ivy throws her hands out, unable to really describe her frustration. "I am the equivalent of a baby vamp in a house full of blood bags while being told 'You can look, but you can't touch!'"

Ivy can swear she hears a chuckle from the third floor of the library and looks up. After concluding that she must be hearing things, she continues. "I will kill anyone who gets close to me. I am a freak. Nothing anyone *feels* will change that."

Baz looks at her with irritation. "So, what I feel has no bearing on you at all?" he asks, shifting his feet, a hand on his hip.

"The problem, Baz, is that even if I did have a more-than-friend feeling for you,—which I don't, by the way—it would never happen. I am incapable of feeling for anyone because all I see is dinner." Ivy shrugs as she steps back over to the table and starts wiping down another book.

"You could always bite me," Baz says with an edge of something she can't place in his voice.

"Fat chance of that happening. I am forbidden to bite anyone." *Elemental Mother, it would be amazing to sink my fangs into an artery right now!*

Baz doesn't take the hint, though. "You seriously feel nothing for me?" He approaches her and turns her face to meet his eyes. If any other woman were in her shoes, they would melt at his handsome face and give in to defeat. He leans in for a kiss, hovering ever so slightly before firmly planting his lips on hers. She feels nothing—not a thing, and she thanks the Elemental Mother for that.

Ivy steels herself, knowing she will lose the only person in the place she thought she could call a friend. "I feel nothing except blood lust for anyone. And that will never change."

A look of contempt replaces the earlier adoration, and he inhales quickly to speak. "I feed you. I went out and picked up clothes for you. I make sure that you have someone to talk to. All because I am in love with you, Ivy" he yells, flailing his arms in aggravation.

"You can't love someone after a few weeks, Baz!"

"Ivy, what I feel for you is something I can't ignore. Time has nothing to do with it."

Ivy repeats herself, irritated. "It's been less than a month. No one falls in love that quick."

"I'm still in love with you."

Ivy shrugs, returning to the books that have earned her feelings and trust. "Then you are mistaken," she responds to his reasoning, "because any real man who actually loves a woman will accept her feelings. If you have only been faking friendship to have more, then that is not love. It's manipulation, and you should leave."

Baz grabs her by the arm and turns her to face him, really losing his temper and forcing Ivy to look at him. "Do you think you are better than me? Is that what this is? You have no idea what you are losing," he yells into her face, causing her hair to move with his breath and spit.

"Oh, yes I do," she says, smiling, her fangs in full view and aching. Thankful that the bruise will heal before the end of the night, Ivy plucks his fingers from her arm. "You are a conniving little puke who thinks that he can go up against me and is sadly mistaken." Hissing with anger, she moves in closer to his face. "If you *ever* think you can touch me again, I will end you."

Baz's eyes are wide with fear, something she knows wouldn't be the case with someone who loves her. "Get out of here before I drain you." She pushes him back towards the door. He falls on his ass, stunned.

Baz retreats, As the door closes behind him he mumbles, "Crazy bitch!"

Ivy backs up, fighting the urge to follow him and drain him in front of the entire coven. Her back hits the wall of shelves, and she sits down forcefully, the wood scraping her spine as she falls.

A feeling of hopelessness and despair overwhelms her, the same as it always has, and she knows she will never have the life that every woman dreams of having. In her moment of grief, she thinks about running after Baz and apologizing as she glances at the door, but she can't make herself lie to anyone about the prospect of a future with her. No one can see past her inner freak if she can't do it herself.

"Why do I have to be a freak?" she cries, slamming her fists into the tile floors." She pulls her legs in close, wrapping her arms around them and beginning to cry.

Pent-up emotion washes over her as she lets tension out. "I miss my mom!" she sobs, her head buried in her arms.

Shadows

Initiation

He leaves his car sitting in the driveway and can hear the heartbeat of someone not inside the compound. It's the slow heartbeat of the Pale Race, so that means that the someone must need help. When he goes around the back of the compound, carefully keeping to the shadows, he sees a stunning woman— jet black hair and curves in all the right places,—sleeping soundly in direct sunlight. She sleeps with no concern for the UV rays usually cause pain, and no burns can be seen. In fact, she's still as alabaster as any of their kind.

Ash steps closer so he can breathe in her scent, and she starts to stir. There is no way she could have known I was there, *he thinks. He hisses when the sun catches his hand, burning it a little as he jumps up to the roof. He continues to watch her fall back to sleep in the shadows of a dormer. The woman snuggles herself back into a hammock, her book falling to her side.*

He sees she wears nothing really from the current period of style. She has a tight, long-sleeved black turtleneck, loose enough to hide her features. The leggings she wears are also black and a hundred percent wool. Then she has on a pair of knee-high, soft-souled boots that lace all the way up. He looks closer and realizes that they don't have zippers on them for easy on.

Who the hell is this woman? *he wonders.*

Her breath hitches as if something in her mind causes her to laugh, and he realizes that she dreams, something the Pale Race rarely does. The sigh afterwards forces him to adjust the situation in his boxers a bit. Her face turns up in a smile as something in her mind gives her happiness. Ash can't take his eyes off her as he stands in the shadows watching every breath she takes.

The only way this can be possible is if it's true, *he thinks.* It's here. *The words echo in his mind. The prophecy's merit has always been a debate among his people. However, every single person who knows about its validity, who has read it—even the people who study it—think the hybrid will be male. A Protector. Why on earth would the hybrid be a female who can be captured and tortured?*

As he stares at her, she opens her eyes, they flash quickly from grey to red and then back again, making him jump out of his skin. She smiles and stretches in the hammock, showing him more details of her curves. She is tall, he thinks as she stands and stretches more—taller than any female he has ever known aside from Calyn. Watching her eyes flash to red as she stares straight into the shadow he stands in, Ash doesn't make a move.

Ash awakes with a start, having slept half the night away, driving most of the day to get there. *Why am I dreaming all of a sudden?* he wonders as he remembers the details of getting to Duneskil earlier in the day. The dream has him all hot and bothered, so he decides to shower before he speaks to Soren. The image of the woman burns in his brain, and he does not want to leave any time soon.

Ash glances out the window on his way to the bathroom to see the woman. Her tall, lean body, sways in moves like tai chi, yet different in the forms. As she pushes and pulls her arms around her, leaves, shrubs, and grass sway with her. It's as if she moves the air as she moves, mesmerizing everything around her, including the squirrels who watch from a nearby branch—and Ash. The sky suddenly opens to rain around her as she does her makeshift dance, yet none of the drops fall on her. They simply avoid her altogether, creating a dome of dryness as she smiles to herself.

Ash shakes his head, trying to rid himself of the compulsion to watch her longer. *Places to be, Dude! Knock it off,* he chides himself as the back of his mind wonders, *How is that even possible?*

Ash sits in a chair opposite Soren and waits for him to speak, having busted into his office moments earlier. Ash feels impatient as he keeps coming back to the woman who sleeps in the sun, but because Soren employs the title of Commander of Duneskil, Ash remains quiet.

"Do you remember Calyn?" Soren asks, a look of remorse on his face while eyeing the picture of Soren and Calyn.

Remembering the spitfire they fought with a couple decades before, Ash smiles a little. The one woman his friend ever loved disappeared without a trace one night.

"Yes. I wonder what happened to her. She was a riot!" Soren's features go a few shades closer to paper white. "What is it?" Ash asks.

"She had my child." Before Ash can express his confusion and congratulations, Soren continues. "She disappeared because she had to take the throne of Lesai."

Ash sputters a moment. "She's a fucking ancient?"

Soren nods. Then it clicks.

"Your daughter is the hybrid," Ash says awkwardly, realizing that he had been checking out his best friend's daughter and the woman the Pale Council fated him to marry. "Did you know? Did she know? How did you find out? And most of all, do the Ancients know?" *I came here to protect the hybrid and let Soren's daughter plead her case before turning the match down,* Ash thinks.

Soren bursts at the seams. "I had no fucking clue that she is an ancient. She was fully aware that I am of the Pale Race. She told me a month ago that I have a daughter and that she was sure that Ivy's heritage mark would show up eventually. With times flowing differently between the realms, we didn't know if it would be during her twenty-first there or here. The Ancients don't know anything. Only four people in Lesai have known about it. Two of them are guards for Calyn herself. Ivy ripped out the other's throat in front of me. Ivy had a maid who knew a lot, but not everything."

"So she transitioned when?"

Soren scrubbed a hand through his hair. "She transitioned in Lesai on her coming of age."

"Wait. So she isn't of age out here?"

Soren shakes his head.

"But she has a heritage mark," Ash says.

"Ash, that mark is so strong, it wraps around her neck."

Jeez! Ash thinks as he remembers the pain of his mark magnified if it wraps around the woman's neck.

"You said she killed the boy who knew about her. So—she has a bloodlust." He recognizes his need to adjust. *Get a grip and do your job, idiot.*

"Not to anything we do," Soren says under his breath.

Ash pulls himself from his thoughts. "What do you mean by that?"

"She killed the ancient kid because he pissed her off." Soren hesitates a moment. "She sustains herself with vampire blood."

Ash stares at him for a moment, waiting for the gotcha!, but it doesn't come. "You're not joking?"

"Nope. She had a blackout from starvation last night after about two weeks of us filling her full of blood. Calyn fed her about three ounces a week. After vomiting the ancient up in my car and then vomiting the rest over the past two weeks, she ripped into Nova." Soren scrubs a hand through his hair, the telltale sign that he's freaking out inside.

"So, Nova is dead?"

"Nope," Soren sighs, "though it would have made things easier. The answer is even more complicated. Nova was mesmerized not to speak of what happened to anyone but me after Ivy healed the gaping hole in Nova's neck."

Pale topics have never confused Ash, but he feels confused. "I thought the prophecy speaks of a warrior who will bridge the gap between races, not eat them."

Soren thinks a moment. "I believe that she is capable of doing that. She receives sustenance through blood magic, and she uses elemental magic. The vampires who drink her blood can dream, Ash. Nova said as much to me after Ivy gave her blood."

How is it possible that she healed a vampire with her blood? But thinking of the connection between the Pale Race drinking human blood and in turn able to heal humans, he figures it normal in its own oddity. Even though Ash knows deep down that he should run from the woman, his career and the survival of the Pale Race depend on his protecting her. Not to mention that he can't think of another female in his 332 years who has intrigued him. The very thought of her lying in the hammock the previous night has him dreaming. *What in the hell is happening to me?*

He shakes his head to clear it.

Stick to your damn job, Ash! You are not letting the council dictate who you are with. You have already decided!

Ash sits in Soren's office again waiting for the phone call to end. For the past week, they have been covering strategy on keeping the hybrid safe and checking in with all known players. His Terrors run errands for them as Ash and Soren work from Duneskil.

Between phone calls, Soren and Ash have covered information and details about Ivy. For some reason, it never feels like enough information to keep the hybrid safe.

"Have you figured out how Calyn has kept her hidden from the Ancient Elders all this time?" Ash asks. From everything they have heard of the ancient prophesies over the years, it has always been that a hybrid will break the magics of the ancient race.

Soren shakes his head. "No. She only told me about fifteen times that if Ivy is discovered by the Ancient Elders that she will be killed immediately."

Annoyed with the lack of intel regarding the imminent threat, Ash compresses his lips with a frown. Not only does Ivy need protection from vamp-op teams but also from the Ancients.

"Can you try to call her again to get more information?" Ash asks.

Soren nods. "I can try."

"Good. We need to figure out all the angles she is at risk from . . ." He trails off as Soren holds up his index finger to silence him.

Soren answers his cell phone as Ash thinks about the ongoing recon. Ash finds himself almost ready for introductions and training the hybrid to start, but first he has to assess her and get permission from the council.

There have been reports that a vamp-op team has been assembling in the state. Making notes of the conversation, Jynx stands to Soren's right even though those of the Pale Race have impeccable memories. Every time Soren has reminded her, though, she explains to him that the night she doesn't have the information will be the night they need it. As the conversation nears conclusion, Ash stares at the pages of the book he's pretending to read so he can think.

He finds himself lost in thoughts about Ivy. To his dismay, he likes Ivy, but it does not mean he wants to marry her. He thinks back to watching her as she cleaned books one at a time in the library. The act was something he has never seen a female of the Pale Race do aside from his mom. Vampires who need work usually do the cleaning, though they do not take the work very seriously.

Though she hides it well from those around her, he can see her depression while he watches her from afar. The day he watched her deal with Baz had been entertaining, even if Ash had wanted to deck Baz. The jerk had the nerve to talk to royalty like she was nothing because she wasn't interested in more than friendship. It was the same heinous fight that he has with women every time he goes on a blind date. Not to mention that Baz put her down because she wasn't like other females. *That is what makes her so intriguing!* he thinks. She meticulously made sure that all the book bindings were also clean and intact, setting aside the ones that needed attention.

When Ivy blocked the only escape, he'd had to endure the entirety of her sadness that night. The heart-wrenching sorrow he had witnessed caused tears to fall down his own cheeks without realizing what was happening. He had no explanation for it, since he had grown up with three sisters, all of whom cried a lot. Then there were the women his mom always set him up with always crying when they didn't get what they wanted. Ivy was different, though. It was as if he was looking into her soul that night, and it scared the shit out of him.

Soren hangs up the phone and asks, "What's up with you? You're brooding again."

Ash shrugs, not really wanting to go into detail about what he'd seen. But as he relives it, a thought hits him. "Does she know how to fight?" Her fists had cracked the tiles that night. *The aftershocks shook the building.*

His mind keeps telling him to stay away from her, to delay their meeting. Then the Protector in him knows he has to protect her and that means training her. *Man, she can knock a man off his feet!* Ash laughing at his own pun as he remembers her throwing Baz on his ass when he'd tried to kiss her.

A look crosses Soren's face as he thinks about Ash's question. "I am sure she does. Calyn said she's been training with the Scavenger guild since she was five. Something tells me that we will be pleasantly surprised about that part."

Ash chuckles to himself, determined to give the woman a challenge. How smart can she really be in battle? Few people have both brains and brawn and use both to their advantage like he does.

"Ahhh . . . But you see, she's only had her heritage mark for a couple weeks!" Ash grins overconfidently. "So, any practice she's had in the past will need honing. You said her senses and her strength are off kilter from the change, plus she was bed-bound starving for a couple weeks."

A thoughtful look on his face, Soren leans back in his chair. "Ash, I think you might be right about this one."

Knowing full well that Ivy needs training, Ash stares at the ceiling. "When was the last time she got to spar with someone stronger than her?"

Soren's face lifts with the knowing smile of a father who wants to give his kid a run for their money. "She is strong, just so you know. But do you remember how cocky Calyn was?"

Ash nods while smiling slowly. "How pissed do you think she will get if we mess with her?"

Soren looks at Ash with a grimace that makes Ash laugh.

"Let's do this shit!" Ash says, standing up quickly.

"She might bite one of us." Soren's twists his face, and Ash can swear that Ivy intimidates him.

"Do you realize how stupid you sound right now?"

Ash laughs at Soren.

Soren shrugs and eyes Ash with concern. "She's the hybrid we've been waiting for. No one knows what she can or will be able to do, Ash."

Ash shrugs. "No better time than now to find out, right? Let's go!"

Soren nods with a grin on his face as the two determined guys walk out of the office.

They go to the workout room to grab staffs and make sure they devise a plan. Assessing her is their main priority, and they can leave nothing out. The style of one's fighting and thinking is always the most fun the first time because you have never before glimpsed what they have to offer.

Unexpected Gifts

Sparring

Ivy opens her eyes after dusk and feels eyes watching her. She glances around and sees that every vampire in Duneskil is staring at her. It isn't the first time she has slept out in the sunlight, but it is the first time she's slept into the night. *Oh, Elemental Mother!* she curses to herself.

Every single one of them are either curious, furious, or jealous, the varying degrees made obvious as she scans her surroundings. A vampire woman with a pixie haircut speaks up. "How can you do that?" she asks. "No one of the Pale Race I have ever seen can pull off anything close to that."

Ivy shrugs. "Maybe its genetic?"

She doesn't know what else to say, and technically it's the truth. As those around her come closer with a parade of questions, she quickly attempts to make a break for it.

"If you'll excuse me, I think I'll go for a walk."

Always hating the feeling that comes with stares, she does her best to walk slowly out of the limelight. When free of onlookers, Ivy finds a decent hiding spot within the maze of hedges. The large square, seemingly the center, is perfect with four benches overlooking a small pond. Settling into a nook in the bushes instead of a bench, she sits down to read her book, *The History of All Things Pale* by Styx.

That is a funny name, she thinks, but she suspects that during the era when he was an author, there wasn't much need for surnames. *Or is that his last name?* Either way, she settles into the book easily and absorbs every single syllable as she reads.

There are seven surnames of the Pale Race. Each of the Pale Race is of royal heritage traced back to the Great Mother. The Pale Race can create children of their loins and vampires, children of their blood. Children of their blood cannot produce heirs, but instead aid in the protection of their Pale parent. The vampire is unable to function during the apex of the day and is impaired in ability when the sun is in the sky. They do not sleep and cease to function only against their will.

When a child of the loins comes of age, they will receive a mark on their arm to announce their heritage. Once their true heritage is known to the Pale Council, the Pale Council will choose a mate in order to continue the lineage without taint.

The life of the Pale Race is eternal, only perishing when they choose to do so. Allowing blood magic to drain from their bodies through decades of self-induced torture, there are not many who choose that fate.

The Pale females who are in confinement are at risk if they are hurt, it being the only exception to the eternal life. Should a Pale female lose enough blood, the child within will not come to fruition, and if they lose more, the body of the Pale female will cease working, leaving her soul to be reborn into another child of their lineage.

What in the world does that mean? Ivy thinks as she looks up. *I swear I just heard chains rattling.* Seeing nothing in the vicinity, she looks back down to read and feels a shift in the air. She instinctively catches a staff hurtling towards to her. She sets her book down beside her without looking up. She knows that it's her father. None of the others ever come up to her to really get to know her. Well, they do, but not this way. Ivy takes a moment to draw some elemental magic into her and touches each of her swords to check their levels. After the little sparring match, she will have to fill them back up again.

Standing to her full height as she twirls the staff in her hands, Ivy looks up and smiles at her father. Feigning innocence, she puts on a meek look. Something about anticipation of a fight feels like an unscripted dance. She has felt nothing like it, and she knows deep down nothing will compare with it. She feels her energy surging as the little hairs on the back of her neck come to full attention.

Out of the corner of her eye, she sees a newcomer with dark hair. It glints red in the moonlight as he tries to gain ground on her. She looks directly at him as he approaches her, and she smiles at him while baring her longer-than-normal fangs and red eyes. He slows down for a moment but recovers quickly, enduring the waiting game as he listens to Soren for direction.

Soren speaks up, "Ivy, meet Ash. He's the first general of Protectors, and we will see what you've got."

He smiles at her with the challenge.

"So, the elusive Ash finally makes his debut. He isn't as old and stuffy as you said he would be, Soren."

She watches Ash stiffen and look at Soren with annoyance. "Really?"

"I never said that. It's a ploy!" Ash visibly relaxes and sidles closer to her again.

Ivy giggles a little, watching their faces as she throws them off guard. They look at each other oddly, as they reconsider whether their spar will be fair. Soren and Ash search each other's expression for an okay as Ivy taps her toe.

Ivy brings them back to attention. "But you did say that I would be surprised, Soren! Either way, it's your funeral, boys."

She changes her stance square between the two of them and allows them to come at her. She lives for the feeling she's trained for her entire life. She keeps her feet moving to avoid any missteps, her soft-soled boots allowing her the balance she needs for a good fight on the uneven turf.

Ivy stands between them as she closes her eyes and waits for the first strike. Swift and barely seen as he leads with a calculated blow to her head, Soren moves in with the speed of the Pale Race.

Surging forward and out of the middle of the two men, she sidesteps before Soren's staff makes contact. She deflects Soren's immediate reverse roundhouse kick and finds herself stunned when she's tossed as he uses her own body weight against her. Ivy goes flying up and backwards, careening through the air so quickly she almost panics. Twisting with a spinning backfist to Ash's face as she moves through the air over him, she shocks him out of his macho superiority.

She lands in a crouch to wait for more. Soren comes up behind her while she lingers. Feeling the air move around her, she moves into a low sweep just before he is on her. Ivy brings her staff up to the front of her as Ash brings his down, mid-spin. She handsprings out of the way, plunging her staff towards his midsection immediately after he moved.

Soren comes at her again. He spins his staff just as a volley of raindrops hit her skin all at once. Every drop bruises her skin and throws her off her game. As the drops overwhelm her, Ash comes in from the side, lashing out with a crippling blow to her back. Recoiling like a snake about to strike, Ivy stops the rain from hitting her as she drops her staff and takes her swords out of her back scabbard.

Waiting for the next subterfuge, Ivy bristles, her eyes peeled for any movement since the rain has interrupted her sensors. She ducks, and a staff hits a tree as Soren and Ash steamroll her with blows, The intent obvious, they want to know if she will break. The two men back Ivy towards a pond and she does what any ancient in this situation would do.

Weaving air behind her, she blocks and steps backwards out on the water, allowing the two men to follow her without awareness. The push, causes them to smile with their thoughts of having the upper hand while Ivy continues to block, parry, and render blows. Her smile widens the closer to the middle of the pond she gets. The moment comes, and she giggles as the men slow down and realize where they stand. she wiggles her fingers at them and chortles "Bye, bye, boys."

Shock etches their features as they both drop into the pond. Pretending to preen her nails, Ivy sits cross-legged on top of the water waiting for them to come sputtering back to the surface.

"I told you, it's your funeral . . . or should I have said bath time?" she gloats. "Either way."

She grins from ear to ear. "Priceless."

"Want to see something priceless?" asks an unexpected voice.

Ivy sees Nova on the other side of the water putting something to her mouth.

Shrieking as she covers her ears in pain, Ivy realizes everyone else around her is wincing but otherwise unaffected. She drops right into the water, and as soon as her head comes above the surface for air, Ivy screams again.

Someone is pulling her out of the water, so cold that she tingles at the warmth of the hands. Her own hands remain over her ears.

Suddenly the piercing sound stops. Smelling blood dripping down the side of her neck, Ivy sits at the edge of the water. "What the hell just happened?" she asks.

"That was me," Nova says with a sneer. "You have some explaining to do. And even if I can't talk about it, it doesn't mean I won't make your life a living hell until I get answers."

Soren roars at Nova and plucks the dog whistle out of her hand as she's about to blow it again.

"Hey!" she complains. "That's mine."

Soren grabs Nova's arm and drags her into the compound as Ash crouches beside Ivy. "You really are a damn good fighter" he says with a smirk.

"I am okay, I guess. This whole Pale Race change is throwing me for a loop though." She plucks at her boot lace, refusing to meet Ash's eyes. "A month ago, neither of you would have even gotten close, and I was starving then!"

Ash sits down. "So, I'm guessing that hurt, huh?"

Ivy widens her eyes as she looks over at him, then holds a hand up to him so he can observe blood leaking from her ears. "Duh," she says.

"Is there anything else you think will mess you up in a fight?" he asks without irony.

"Why? Do you want to know how to take me out?" she asks slyly, looking up to meet his eyes.

She finds the depths of them searing into her as she hears him say, "Actually, the Terrors and I are here to protect you. The best way to do that is to make sure you can protect yourself, too, and since you know your weaknesses best, that's where we need to start."

"Terrors?"

"Ivy," he says, looking around in angst. "We will need to have a discussion in Soren's office soon." Meeting her eyes with an intensity she has never felt, Ash puts a hand on her shoulder. "There is too much at stake to speak freely."

Ivy nods slightly, not knowing why her eyes suddenly flash red, but they do as she stares into his. *I am not hungry, though.* Her cheeks flushed, she looks around to see that the rest of the vampires surrounding the sparring match have left. With her wet shirt, she cleans the blood that dripped from her ears. *Ugh! Why are women always so spiteful?* she wonders, irritated.

She looks up. Ash studies her, then looks away as if trying to hide something he's thinking.

Ivy continues staring at Ash, who is one hunk of man meat, all jokes aside. He has green eyes and dark red, spiked hair, He's at least six inches taller than she is. With black baggy pants and chains hanging off them, he doesn't look like much of a general. Then again, she's seen his skills, and he can take on an ancient Scavenger just as precisely as she can, aside from how loud he is when he moves.

The difference between the Ancients and the Pale Race are significant. Finn, the ancient, was tall and thin, his pointed tips giving him an air of authority and poise. Golden hair suggested a soft-hearted and humble being, the total opposite of his actual character.

Ash, however, has massive shoulders and is taller than even Soren. Everyone within eyesight recognizes his presence with the "mess-with-me—I-dare-you!" look in his eyes. He has precise but not garish fighting skills no matter how much she wants to deny it. In fact, if she hadn't tricked them with the air floor, she would have lost their first spar.

Something about him feels dangerous as if cautioning her that, if she goes there, she will never come back out of the depths, which freaks her out. *I'm not interested in more than looking at him,* she says to herself. *I have too much other shit going on and I will kill someone if they get too close.*

Ivy decides that she will avoid Soren's friend, no matter how adorable he will look after she messes up his carefully spiked up hair. *How does he get it to spike up like that anyway?* she asks herself. *You will not find out, so drop the thought, Ivy.* The promise of pain she will cause anyone she comes close to weighs heavily on her heart.

Baz, who also must have been watching them spar, interrupts her thought. "Ivy, I was wondering if you want to play chess with Pierce." Her eyes flash to red, then back to grey as she nods her head, Ivy looks at Baz.

Not waiting for a reply nor looking his way, she declares, "I'm heading in, Ash."

Baz nods, a look of annoyance in his eyes vanishing in a flash. Not dwelling on it, she realizes that Baz is trying to feed her still. *Why is Baz being nice? I totally put him in his place the other night.*

Carefully hiding her bloodlust, she looks at Pierce. "Ready? Let's go to my room. I have a really well taken-care-of chess board in there."

Pierce nods with a look of satisfaction. Up close, she can smell his arousal and realizes that he thinks that chess means something completely different. *Eew.* The smell emanating from Pierce practically gags Ivy as they walk to her bedroom.

Knowing that those of the Pale Race have an especially perfect sense of smell, she eyes Baz from the side as they walk. *If Baz is so interested in me, why is he okay with a dude lusting after me?* The thought stops abruptly when Baz, not wanting to intrude, waits outside the door.

Ivy takes out the chessboard and sets up the pieces, wondering if she will finally get in a game of chess. The air around Pierce sickens her, so she walks to the window and opens it all the way. *Is this always going to happen? Jeez!* She sticks her head outside and breathes a few untainted breaths before joining Pierce at the small table set up with the chess game.

The look on Pierce's face tells her that he has absolutely no idea how to play. It disappoints her a bit as she moves her first pawn. Part of her is annoyed while the other part is happy to imagine the guy leaving after bleeding out a bottle of blood.

The idea upsets her because she knows that she will never have enough control simply to hang out with friends. If in the room with a vampire, she craves their lifeblood with a blinding force. Thankfully, the smells of soil, grass, and plants mute the scent of blood while she is outside.

Ivy catches Pierce's eye and imposes her thoughts on him. *You played a quick game of chess with Ivy,* she transmits. *She's cool once you get to know her. You will forget everything else that happens in this room from this point forward.*

"I will forget everything," he repeats with adoration for her.

Ivy cringes, and says aloud, "Good. Fill this bottle with your blood, then sit quietly on the couch while you drink a bag of human A positive for yourself, slowly. Then you will leave and continue your night."

Pierce fills the bottle much the same way that Taz did the night before. Pierce, however, bites himself over and over, gazing into her eyes like a lost puppy, which totally gives her the creeps. As soon as he's done filling the bottle, Ivy takes it from him and drinks it as slowly as she can this time, attempting to savor it. Much to her dismay, its effect doesn't last long at all. Pierce does as instructed and leaves about fifteen minutes later.

Baz returns and chills in her room with her as she's reading, trying to stay away from the eyes of the coven. Even though he remains quiet for most of the time, he stares at her as if studying the lines of her face. He acts as if he has no memory of her tossing him out of the library, and she finds it awkward. The least he could do is acknowledge that he understands her action. Instead, it's like it never happened as she feels him staring at her.

She can feel the interest he has in her and, as much as she can get past his rude behavior the other night, it can never amount to more than their being friends. She doesn't see anything in him that would ever make her want to date him. It's even less than friendship because it's uncomfortable.

Tired of feeling eyeballs on her, she hands him a book.

"What am I supposed to do with this?" he asks. "Clean it?"

Ivy smiles sarcastically. "You read it. I am trying to figure some stuff out, see if there has ever been anyone else like me."

"What do you mean like you?" he asks eyeing the book, turning his eyes on her as if she is daft.

Ivy shrugs. "Like anyone in the Pale Race who has ever needed to drink from vampires. You know, like freak stuff."

He shrugs and starts reading quietly, though she feels his gaze return to her occasionally. She realizes that he is pretending. *Does he not know how to read?*

The night progresses in quite a mundane way considering she's living with a coven of the Pale Race and vampires. Instead of enjoying the outside and seeing more people, she curls up on one of her couches, while Baz sits on the other.

As she approaches the last chapter in the monotonous book, skimming more than reading, there is a knock on the door.

"Enter," she says, glancing up at the door.

A woman, the one with the pixie cut, peeks her head inside the room. "Hi."

Ivy perks up a little bit, not wanting to scare her away, but also not wanting to seem too eager to please. The whole etiquette of Lesai is forefront in her mind.

"Can I help you?" Ivy asks.

The woman straightens her shoulders and speaks, trying to hide the uneasiness she's obviously feeling. "I am wondering if you would like to hang out with me and a couple of the other girls tonight. We realize that Nova is not the best first impression you should have gotten at Duneskil, and we want to welcome you the best way we know how." The woman shrugs. "Popcorn and a couple scary movies."

Ivy is all for it. *I was just invited to watch one of those moving pictures!* she's thinks as she smiles. The little voice in her head whispers loudly, *Your life has no place for friends.*

"I will have to talk to Soren about it, but I think we can do that!" In a happy tone, Ivy ignores the voice. She misses the infrequent slumber parties that the other women threw in Lesai. She was technically friends with only two women, but it doesn't matter to her. She's a quality-over-quantity type.

She glances at Baz, who looks like his eyes will bug out of his head.

The woman jumps up and down excited as she leaves the room to tell the other women.

Ivy glances back at Baz and asks, "Can you go get Soren for me?"

He nods, shaking his head, and as he walks out of the room, sneers ever so slightly, "I'm not your fucking maid" barely audibly even with her extreme hearing.

Ivy smiles knowing that his avoidance of the other night was just an act. *Two can play at that game,* she thinks.

Mind Meld

Mesmers

Reliving the memory, Ash is back in the maze as he watches the scene play out in his head for the tenth time. He sees Ivy walk away with a vampire named Pierce on her arm and smelling the vampire's lust for her. He figures that she feeds to hide her secret, but he has a sudden urge to beat the guy to a pulp.

Ash feels a territorial pull as his mind wanders to images of her pulling another male's blood into her. *If only she would realize that I would taste so much better.* He startles himself back to the present. *Get a grip,* he demands harshly of himself.

"What the hell is wrong with you, Ash?" Soren asks with concern, done dealing with Nova.

"Nothing."

"Bullshit, Ash."

There is no getting anything past his friend of centuries. "I really don't want to get into it."

"Fine," he responds gruffly. "Then come with me. After Ivy feeds, we need to teach her how to mesmer correctly. Nova needs a little bit of work."

"Why can't you teach her yourself?" Ash asks pointedly.

Soren shrugs. "Because then we won't know if she can mesmer the Pale Race as well."

Ash stops in his tracks as they're heading back to the compound. "You really think she can do that?"

"Yes," Soren replies. "I believe there is a lot left to uncover about who she is. There is also the issue of what will happen if she turns a human into a hybrid like herself."

"Shit!" Ash exclaims, back to the thought of Ivy's fangs in another person again. Snapping himself out of it he continues walking. "Isn't Nova your mate?"

"Hell, no! From night one, I have told her that we are only an in-the-moment thing, no matter how many moments there are. It's not my fault she thinks that she can bypass the whole Pale Race card and become more than that."

Ash laughs. "You do realize how hypocritical you sound right now, right?"

Soren eyes him with a questioning look.

"You have a daughter with someone not of the Pale Race, and you are expecting a woman who has been with you on and off for almost twenty years not to think into it?" Ash asks with a smile.

Soren shrugs. "I never thought of it that way. Calyn was never supposed to be out of my life. And I have tried to love others. When that never worked, I went with the next best thing, a bed buddy." Soren pauses a moment, thoughtful. "And now that is becoming quite the problem."

Did he say bed buddy? Ash giggles inside. "You will have your daughter mesmer your ex lover to leave you alone, right?"

Soren shrugs again. "It's that or have that little, crazy baby vamp thinking that she has a right to demand the attention of my daughter who, if you haven't figured it out already, is stronger than you and me both."

"Oh, I realize it," Ash says with concern almost to himself.

It's Soren's turn to laugh. "Do you have a thing for Ivy?"

Ash shakes his head. "No."

Soren gazes at him a moment longer, analyzing Ash's face. Ash sees him smile a little. "You do know that you are as worthy of happiness as anyone else, right?" Soren asks.

Ash shrugs. *There can never be happiness in my life without having to accept that the Pale Council was right to give me orders.*

Soren must have sensed Ash's refusal to accept the idea as he continues, "Something is happening in Lesai."

Ash cocks his head to the side. "What do you mean?"

"Calyn called me today. The Ancient Elders are pulling some shady shit. There are Ancients asking for resident information to make lives in the human world every day. She can't figure out what is happening, and it's scaring her."

But what? "Lesai has been a thriving city since the beginning of the Ancients. So, what is different now?" Ash asks. He knows the answer. *Ivy.* "Do you think it could be that your daughter isn't in Lesai anymore? That maybe they are looking for her?" Ash inquires.

"I am wondering the same thing. We've had vamp-op teams relocating to the area and, oddly enough, there is chatter that the Ancients are with them."

Ash curses aloud. "But Calyn led them all to believe that Ivy is dead."

"She said that it doesn't make sense, that the Ancients are drawing other Ancients out to fight the war against humans, not joining them. Ancients have been leaving Lesai ever since Ivy came here, but there hasn't been a clue as to why," Soren says, sharing his thoughts aloud.

"Do you think they know, Soren?"

Soren shakes his head and meets Ash's eyes. "No. If they did, Calyn would be dead by now. I told her that I'll look into this on my end." He pauses a moment and asks, "Can you see if you can find anything out as well? I have a shit feeling about this."

Ash nods in agreement.

Soren looks around and meets Ash's eyes. "Okay I need to get back inside to see what Jynx has heard." He pauses, then asks, "You coming?"

"I think I'm going to give my dad a call, then take a run to clear my head. Give me a text when you need me."

Soren nods, so Ash makes sure he has no tail on him as he takes off running to the outskirts of the property. He listens for sounds in the distance, and when sure that only the animals can hear him, he dials his dad's phone number.

"What is it, now?" his dad asks.

"I need to speak to the councilman first, please," Ash says to categorize the reason for his calling as official business.

"Go ahead, Ash."

"Lesai is losing their Ancients for a war against humans. The hybrid is a female who survives off vampire blood. Lastly, I would like permission to move forward in training the hybrid for the field."

There is silence as his dad absorbs the information. "Permission granted. Be sure to keep me updated on the Ancients. Something isn't jibing with the information I have sitting on my desk."

"Copy that."

"Now, Asher," his father asks him without the official overlay. "What do you need to speak to me about?"

Wishing that he didn't have to keep finding out their secrets, Asher stares up at the sky. "You knew that the woman I am supposed to marry is the hybrid."

"Yes, Ash. We knew that the girl is a hybrid, which is why we were not sure she would transition with a heritage mark. Have you seen it?"

Ash sighs. "No, I haven't seen the mark. She wears turtlenecks no matter how warm it is outside. Soren did mention that it wraps around her neck, though." Pausing a moment to keep his composure, he continues. "With all due respect, I feel like I have been lied to for the past fifteen years."

Ash hears his mother clear her voice. She may not have a title in the Pale Council, but she is very much a deciding voice in many areas of the government. "We understand your reasoning, and we apologize for not taking your feelings into account. There is more at play than you know, though."

Ash perks up. "What are you talking about?"

"Just know that only four people have read the entire prophecy, and all four of us have been sworn to absolute secrecy. The final result of everything depends on it. If we could inform you of the role we all play, then we would, but from here on out, it is up to you to understand that there is a reason for everything."

"God, Mom! I hate when you are vague!" Ash complains, knowing that there is no way to sway her resolve. She is too old and wise to go against what is for the greater good, so arguing is moot.

His Mom chuckles. "We say this with love. Forget that you have been fated. Get to know that girl and protect her with your life. Everything depends on it. Stubbornness won't change what fate has in store. It will only make things take longer."

"Fine, Mom." Ash really needs to clear his head after that. "I will be in touch once I have more information."

He hangs the phone up and looks at the night sky, a thousand things cluttering his mind. He drops the phone into one of the lower cargo pockets and starts jogging around the outskirts of Duneskil, chains jangling with each step.

〰 〰 〰

The moment he and Soren set foot in Ivy's room, Ash wants to escape. It smells like her, and it's intoxicating. Trying to keep to the edges of the room, Ash can feel Ivy's eyes on him as he tries to distract himself. All items uniquely hers litter around, the most obvious a pair of panties chilling by the bathroom door.

So messy! He thinks, looking over at her and regretting it. He feels himself smiling at her without realizing it, smelling something he shouldn't coming off her in waves.

She blushes, and his groin reacts with a shock wave. Temptation hits him like a ten-pound brick. Her eyes flash to red, and he realizes she lusts for him even if she doesn't know it. Totally against everything in him, he looks away, not wanting even to contemplate getting involved with her.

The council is not right.

Nova stands nearby petrified with fear as her eyes dart around looking for a way out.

"What's up?" Ivy asks, watching Nova carefully.

"You asked me to come here," Soren says to her, even though Ash knew otherwise. They were already on their way when she summoned him.

Ivy gives a nod in Ash's direction. "And he came because . . . ?" *She is a total smart ass!* Ash thinks, imagining all the things that he shouldn't. *And I'm an idiot,* he tells himself, forcing himself to calm down before she smells him. *There is no way she wouldn't smell me either with her heightened senses.*

Against his will, Ivy's eyes pin him down with their intensity.

"Ash is here to help with something."

"Ok-a-a-a-a-y." Ivy moves her eyes to Soren. "A couple women want to watch a movie with me tonight. That's okay. Right?"

Soren thinks a moment. "Blackouts?"

Ivy shakes her head no.

"Then sure. Can you do something for me?"

Ivy nods. "Anything."

Will you do anything for me? Then, pushing down the errant thought, Ash gulps.

"Make Nova forget what she knows. Then make her lose interest in me, please."

Ivy nods and looks over at Nova.

Soren interrupts what she is about to do. "We need to help you fully access that gift first."

Ivy cocks her head to the side, "What do you mean?"

"Ash will guide you through a mesmer first."

She turns bright red and looks over at him out of the corner of her eyes. "Really? Why not you?" she asks.

"It's also a test of sorts."

Ivy laughs. "You want me to mesmer you?"

Oh, she's good! Ash thinks.

Soren nods with a grin. "We need to know if it works on the Pale Race, and it will help with learning the proper way to do it." He eyes Nova and nods. "She is your first and not properly completed, which I expected. Ready, Ash?"

Ash nods. Then, keeping every nuance of thought at bay that is not on target, he walks to Ivy and sits next to her on the couch. He taps each of her legs, feeling tingles as he does it. *That's weird.* "You will need to have full relaxation," he tells Ivy. "Nothing crossed."

Ivy nods. "Okay, what next?"

The intensity of her student mind makes Ash want to smile. Having never been someone's teacher, Ash finds the experience fresh and even fascinating. Trying to remain serious, he half smiles.

"You draw their eyes to yours, even if you have to will it from far away. You bring them to you." The intoxicating stare he feels all the way to the pit of his stomach is hot enough to melt iron. *Holy shit!* "Once they are trapped, you push your will into their mind, forcing your will to overpower theirs as you make your thought their thought."

Ash mentally puts a hand on Ivy's back as he pulls her to him. "If you are making them forget, you tell them what they will remember. Avoid using negative words, because that can cause confusion."

Ivy's face turns bright red, and her eyes flash red.

She can smell me! Shit! He pulls her deeper to him, not actually able to mesmer her but pretending to.

Her voice begins panicking in his head. *Why do I feel like this? This has never happened before!* Then he feels it, the searing heat of her body on fire for him causing his body to react the same way.

Ash can't stop the pull that causes him to want more from her. They have spent some time together, but there is no reason that he should have such heat for her. He begins searching her eyes for something more to go on and hears her again, transferring her thought, *That hair will look adorable all ruffled.* And then, her further transferred thought: *Ivy shut up! There is no hope for anyone to feel like this for you. Get a grip!*

Ash feels scalded by hot lava as Ivy moves her eyes out of his trance. *She is attracted to me! Wait! How in the bloody hell did that happen!* There is no way he will allow more than lust, but he feels himself longing to see how her face would look as she explores the fire burning within her.

Ivy glances back up to his face, her nostrils flaring as she inhales his arousal again, causing him to burn as red as she does. The air between them drains from the room as Ash stands up to put some distance between them. There is something happening that he can't quite place, but that something is strong.

The council is not right!

Soren brings him back. "Okay did you get that, or does he need to show you again?"

Soren has a smile in his voice that draws their eyes to him. He laughs at them while covering his face with his handkerchief.

"What do you think?" Ivy asks with a scowl. The look is adorable, though he would never tell her that when she looks so annoyed.

Ivy stares at Soren and draws him to her. Ash sees his friend's pupils dilate until he can't see color in the eye anymore. *Holy crap!*

She smiles, instructing Soren, "You will let Ivy pick out her own clothes sometime this week."

Oh, you little minx! Ash thinks, snorting back a laugh.

Ivy pulls back and gives Ash a sideways grin as she waits for Soren to shake the fog from his brain. "So did you do it?" Soren asks with anticipation.

Ash laughs. "That depends. Are you going to let Ivy pick out her own clothes soon?"

Soren screws up his face. "Obviously! She is going to this week!" After a moment, he says, "Shit. Ash! Why didn't you stop her?"

Ash chuckles as he says, "Don't worry. The princess will have at least one warrior at her side." He meets her eye, and she looks away, bestowing on him the honor of her blush. *Protectors protect, no matter where they are,* Ash thinks, refusing to admit even to himself that the Pale Council may have been on to something.

"I do not want to be referred to as a princess, please. Ivy is fine." She has her feet tucked under her again as she fidgets with a bootlace.

"Ivy." Ash waits for her to look up at him before continuing. "You are a royal. Even if we don't use the terms as much in this century, it doesn't mean that you aren't above most others of our kind."

Ivy shrugs. "Being a princess has been the bane of my existence since I was a child. Soren said I can go by just Ivy. I'd like to stick with that, if you don't mind."

Seriously? Suddenly, Ash finds himself of his own free will willing to listen to his mother for once. Never has he met a female who isn't interested in the pretenses of being more important than someone else. Sure, he would see a few of them befriending those of lower stations, *but the refusal to be addressed as a royal, even in private . . .* The idea of it has him utterly confused.

"Nothing can stop me from loving you, Soren," Nova announces as she glares at Ivy and Ash, one at a time, her doe eyes lingering on Soren. The outburst brings Ash right out of his own head.

Ivy smiles as she zeroes her eyes in on Nova, the most defiant person Ash has ever met.

"Nova," Ivy says in her chiming tone. Nova walks to her as if possessed.

"Be honest. Why are you interested in Soren?"

Nova blurts without thought, "I expect to be a commander's wife one night. I don't care about the law of the classes. I will get what I want."

Holy shit!

Ash sees Ivy's face turn menacing. Ash can feel the air around him heat as her temper comes into play. He witnesses something similar to Ivy's demeanor when Baz all but admitted to manipulating her and that she had ripped into the ancient when said ancient had bad intentions towards her and her mother.

Ash steps closer, not sure whether to help Ivy or Nova, the baby vamp.

"Nova, when you leave my room, you will remember nothing about me. You played chess with me and almost won, but I took your queen, which condemned you. You have no ill will towards anyone at Duneskil, and even though you and Soren have had a good roll around, you are destined to be happy in life. Soren makes you sad when you think of a future, because you are a vampire, and he is a royal."

Nova glares at her once Ivy finishes and restores Nova's own mind.

"Why did you tell Nova to wait until she's out of the room to forget?" Ash asks thoughtfully.

Her eyes glowing red and her fangs at full length with bloodlust, Ivy grins at him.

Oh my god she is beautiful!

"You won't get away with this, bitch." Nova spits on the ground at Ivy's feet.

Ew! thinks Ash.

Ivy stands to her full height, towering over Nova. "Don't make a sound."

Nova's face makes the full shriek face without sound as Ivy pounces on her and sinks her fangs into her neck.

Ash stares. He knows that, as a Protector, he should do something to save the baby vampire from the bite of a hybrid, but he finds himself unable to take his eyes off Ivy as she feeds. The way she's hunched over, breathing through her nose as she pulls Nova's blood through her lips, has Ash hard as a rock. Her eyes are wide open and glowing, the scent of her arousal hanging in the air in waves.

He heaves breaths into his lungs by sheer force of will and tries to tear his gaze from Ivy. After what feels like an eternity, she releases Nova. The look of satisfaction lights her face as she looks at the ceiling, feeling energy rush through her.

Knowing the feeling well, Ash throbs with the need to take her right there in the middle of the room.

Ivy turns her face to look directly at him, her nostrils flaring in the aftermath of her dinner. Blood smears the corners of her mouth, her teeth dripping. She licks her lips instinctively, turning a bright shade of red as she inhales, her eyes flashing to red.

She knows! She knows! Shit, I want her! He watches her still, thus prolonging his torment as he fights against every cell in his body that wants to claim her as his own.

The panicked retreat he sees in Ivy's eyes tells him she's pure. Her teeth retract as she smiles sweetly down at the heavy-lidded glare of Nova. He feels pride that he doesn't deserve as she drags the vampire through the room and throws her out into the hall onto her ass.

Nova's confusion is clear as Ivy shuts the door in her face.

Unable to hide his need to have her, Ash decides to use the bathroom and regrets the decision as soon as he closes the door. Ivy's inability to clean up after herself, an endearing trait, becomes a burden in his awkward situation. A solitary white towel lies on the floor next to the shower, and he can smell her on it.

Usually, women of this century cover their scent in layers of chemicals. Not Ivy. There is no mistaking the feminine musk radiating from the towel. He stands over it and debates with himself about whether to pick it up and smell it more deeply. Instead stepping over it, he lifts the lid of the toilet to relieve himself. He has to wait a good forty-five seconds for his situation to ebb. He realizes that, of all the women he has ever been with, he cannot single even one of them out of his memory as special. Women of every size, shape, color, and race dance through his mind, none of them comparing to the woman in the next room.

As his brain begins working again, he hastily exits the bathroom to make his departure. He holds his breath and fears that he would take her without a second thought even with her father standing there. Feeling Ivy's eyes on him makes him walk faster.

This has never happened to me! he thinks, reminded of the phrase he heard Ivy say in his head.

The knot in his stomach tightens as he closes her door and enters his own suite across the hall. As he paces back and forth, there is nothing he wants more than to run.

The council could not have known that this would happen. There is no way.

Knowledge

Decisions

"I thought I said not to bite anyone, Iveliis." Soren folds his arms in front, his glare causing Ivy to shrink back ever so slightly.

Ivy looks at him and says, "I thought we agreed that Ivy is suited better for my life here."

She takes a moment to continue as she wipes blood smears from her face with her shirt. "And as for the sleep thing, I really think that has more to do with ingesting my blood than me biting."

"Not the point, Ivy."

Ivy shrugs with acceptance of her shortcomings. "She pissed me off! She has been using you for years to get ahead." Then, with a sidelong look at Soren, she asks, "Is it still okay if I have my movie night?"

He chokes out a laugh. "Would you allow it?"

"Yes," Ivy says, her chin lifted. "I would actually say, 'As long as you have a glass of blood handy for cravings.'"

Ivy smiles innocence. "Please? I promise I won't bite anyone."

"Mhmm. Because that held the first time.," he retorts with a sarcastic smile.

Sulking a little, Ivy looks at him sheepishly.

"That probably would have worked ten years ago," he tells her, "but you're a little too big to be spoiled."

"I tried," Ivy says with a sigh.

Soren relents slightly. "If you can make it a week without biting anyone, you can have all the women in the coven make the dining hall into a movie theater for the night."

Contemplating for a long moment, Ivy says, "Add popcorn and soda to it, and you have yourself a deal." She holds out her hand for a shake.

"Oh, and this week, you can take either Baz or Ash to the mall to find some clothes."

Ivy looks at him funny. "Mall?"

Soren laughs, his face lighting up. "Wow. By the time you come back, whoever you take will want to kill me."

Grinning, Ivy thinks a moment about who she wants to torment more. "Can I take both of them?"

The smile lighting Soren's face would blind the faint of heart.

"You're mean!" He laughs as he walks out of her room, shutting the lights out. "Goodnight, Daughter."

"Goodnight, Dad." She grins as she sees him miss a step and smile back at her.

Ivy tips her head back and feels her own pulse send Nova's blood to all the places she needs it. She can feel Ash's eyes on her. He's mesmerized with her reaction to her dinner.

Smelling her arousal, he tries to hide, and Ivy looks up to meet his eyes. He is on fire, his eyes glimmering with the need for release as he steps towards her. He hesitates only because her father stands right there. His breath comes in bursts as he struggles to gain control.

She smiles, licking blood off her mouth, wishing the blood were his own regardless of the council's intent. In a blur that she doesn't understand in her state of mind, she jumps off Nova and onto Ash, taking him down. He looks shocked. Her body writhes with the need for release as she grinds herself down onto him. She captures his mouth, not stopping as he goes still in shock. He begins kissing her back, and she feels herself raised to new heights as her body convulses.

Ivy wakes up panting. The erotic dream has her in pain. *What the heck!* She freaks out as she comes back down to earth. She feels herself and realizes she's just had her first wet dream.

She darts to the shower to cool off the lingering ache. *What is it about that man that has my body betraying me? After a week you'd think that I'd be over it. Instead, it's worse! What the hell is wrong with me?*

Once fully calm and back to herself, Ivy dresses and leaves her room. She glances sadly at the bed and leaves to approach the night.

She walks into the dining room and starts washing each one of the tables and chairs until they are beautiful dead things again. Even with their misuse of the earth, she thinks, the humans do know how to create beautiful things.

Maybe their need to cause death in nature comes from a subconscious obsession with their short lives, she thinks idly as she scrubs. She takes the tables apart with a wrench she found in a maid's closet and puts them into the foyer to deal with later.

As she cleans one of the intricate chairs, Soren walks into the grand room. "What are you doing?" he asks, smiling and looking around at the considerably emptier room.

"I am taking initiative," she says with a smile, completely happy that Soren isn't giving her a ration of crap at the disarray in the foyer. He nears her, grabs a rag and another chair, and cleans them with just as much fervor. "Want to explain what I'm doing?" he asks with a chuckle.

"This room has so much potential as a training room. The tables and chairs are a waste in comparison to the life they once had." She eyes him to see if he will make fun of her reasoning.

Soren stops scrubbing and stands up straight to look around. "Why didn't I think of that?" he asks, a light in his eyes.

"Because you were busy doing what needed to be done in other ways," Ivy grins, happy that they are on the same page with the space. "I want to give the tables and chairs to humans who may need them."

Soren looks down at her. "So, a charity?"

He laughs when he sees her questioning look. "A charity is a place where humans help humans."

She nods. "Yes. A charity."

"Sounds like the perfect idea. I will get someone to pick them up from the shack sometime this week."

Soren quiets for a moment, and she feels his eyes on her as she finishes one of the items he is working on.

"I know you didn't come to help me clean," she says to him, "so what's up?"

Soren sighs and sits down in the chair that he's been working on. "Can you sit for a minute? I have something to discuss with you."

"Um, yeah," Ivy replies as she puts the cloth down and rearranges her chair to face him.

Soren studies his hand as she waits for his answer, and she feels alarm bells in her head.

"There is something you need to know about being a royal in the Pale Race," he tells her.

"Okay," Ivy says, drawing out the last syllable.

Soren takes a deep breath and lets it out slowly. "This will be something you don't want to hear, but it's something I can't control, so listen before yelling at me, okay?"

Ivy nods.

"The reason I sent for Ash was to protect you. I was informed shortly after his arrival that he is the mate the Pale Council has chosen for you in marriage."

Ivy takes a breath to argue, and he holds up a finger to admonish her to let him finish.

She sucks in her rant.

"The royals in the Pale Race do not have to marry the individual chosen by the Pale Council, but if they don't, they will never marry. Females are expected to find a suitable male who will give them children to continue the line."

Ivy feels herself boiling, and Soren sees it, so he quickly adds, "No one else nor I expect to tell you that you have to marry."

He falls silent for a moment, and she looks at him for permission to speak. He nods, sighing in resignation.

"Why Ash though?" Her fate as a royal evidently creates as much turmoil in Duneskil as much as it had in Lesai.

"I do not know why the council chose Ash. However, he is the general of the Protectors, and nothing is more important than protecting the hybrid of the Pale Race. His team, called the Terrors, are the best of the best."

"How does Ash feel about this?" Ivy looks at her feet.

How is anyone going to love me? I don't even have the strength to fight a craving.

Soren laughs. "That is a question you will have to ask Ash, although I do know that Baz is also an interested party."

Ivy sneers at Baz's name.

"Baz proposed marriage," Soren continues. "However, I informed him that you are spoken for in that respect. Baz doesn't seem to mind that, though. I'm just saying that he wants to give you the best life."

"I am not interested in Baz at all."

"But you're interested in Ash?"

Ivy shrugs. "It's not like I'm blind."

Soren laughs and she goes on, feeling odd about discussing the situation with her father.

"I will hurt anyone I am close to," she says. "That to me is a problem that I am trying to avoid. Me accepting this marriage would be giving Ash a death sentence. At some point I am going to snap."

Soren puts a hand on top of hers. "I think you will be surprised. I have known Ash a long time, and he is harder to kill than you may think."

Ivy nods, though completely at odds about her situation. She knows that she feels curiosity at least about Ash, but wanting more, she figures, invites sorrow.

"Why are you so okay with me not marrying?" Ivy asks. "A marriage of protection is something I can understand getting forced into, what with the vamp-op teams out there."

Soren is quiet for a moment, and Ivy waits for him to speak. She looks away, expecting him not to continue, but he does. "I was forced to marry," he tells her, "and it didn't end well. Neither of us wanted it. Her especially, since she had already found her lifemate."

Ivy considers her words carefully as she asks, "How long do I have to think about it?" She knows deep down that Soren would not have brought it up unless he agreed with the council.

The idea is absurd, she thinks, *especially forcing a man to marry an unhinged girl with a biting problem.* The history books she's read speak of the Pale Race dwindling in numbers and of a woman's ideal potential for fertility when she's with a lifemate. Her problem is that she isn't sure she wants to pass on messed-up genetics to defenseless children, thus forcing them to go through her challenges.

"The council has decided to be lenient with you since you have only just come into the fold. You had one month to decide."

Ivy looks up at the ceiling in dismay. "What do you mean, Dad?"

Her father huffs in annoyance as he looks away. "They gave you one month as of last week."

"That's crazy!" Ivy complains, wringing the rag she holds. "How am I supposed to know within three weeks? And more importantly, why did you wait?"

"I waited because you had just gotten here."

Soren becomes quiet, holding something back.

"What is it?" Ivy asks, sensing the negative her father hasn't told her yet.

"If you don't marry Ash, the council will still expect you to bring children into the world. That means you will have to have at least two children before you are fifty. If you don't, they have the authority to make you become pregnant through magical means, but it also means you will have no choice about the child's heritage."

Ivy mutters under her breath. "What kind of patriarchal bullshit is that?"

"That's what you take from this?"

Soren laughs without thinking as Ivy shoots a deathly glare at him.

"I'm glad you think it's so funny!" Ivy says. She thinks a moment and decides she needs more information. "What happened to your wife?"

Soren turns ashen. Ivy watches his countenance as memories dance through his mind. "We got married. We got pregnant. We raised our little one happily together, and when he came of age, he got his heritage mark." Soren takes a long, ragged breath and continues, "When a child of the Pale Race comes of age, they get a mark of their paternal heritage. He was not my child. He was the child of her lifemate, Finch."

"I loved the boy regardless. He was my son whether he had my bloodline or not, but once she realized that she'd had her lifemate's baby, she called it fate. She took Knox to spend her eternal life with her lifemate at Desdemona. I haven't heard from any of them since then."

"How long ago did this happen?" she asks. Sympathy for the pain he must have dealt with raced through her.

Soren clears his throat and scrubs a hand through his hair. "It was almost a century ago. I thought we were good together, but it seems that her relationship with Finch never ended when we married." He inhales sharply as if reminding himself to say something else. "You need to know that I met your mother several decades later, and if she were Pale, I know she would be my lifemate."

Ivy looks at her father with empathy and horror. "That is messed up. You must have been in so much pain not only being left by the woman you married but also by my mother."

"It's why I won't force you to marry. If you make this decision, it should be for life. Not on a whim. Beyond that, though, know also that I regret none of the time I had with your mother. The years after were lonely, but the happiness of that time stayed with me and kept me going."

Ivy nods. "I have one more nagging question, though," Ivy says, scanning the room around her instead of looking her father in the eye.

"What is it?" Soren asks with concern.

"What does this mean for me joining the Terrors? If I marry Ash, is he going to make it so that I cannot fulfill my desire to fight?"

"That's a question you will have to ask Ash."

"Does he know that we have been matched, Dad?"

"His father says that he has been informed of the match, so yes."

🙰 🙰 🙰

After waiting for the sun to almost come to the horizon, Ivy finds herself sneaking out of her room, the rest of Duneskil asleep for the day. She grabs a book she found the other day in the back of the library. Another book written by Styx, it doesn't have a title, just seven coats of arms in a circle on the front cover. Ducking out the front door of the compound, she finds a bench and opens the book to read:

> At the date of this record, there are sixty-three children of the Pale Race. The seven families of the Pale Race are at a precipice of becoming tainted. Females are finding lifemates closer and closer to their own lineage. Of course, we have all traced back to the Great Mother, and as such, we are all distant cousins of sorts.
>
> To curb the debacle of taint and low birth rates, the Pale Council will choose the mate when the child comes of age. If a child does not accept the advice of the Pale Council, the child will still be required to produce heirs without taint. Two children in the first fifty years will suffice in effort to grow a population without taint. If the couple accepts their union, they must produce children.
>
> Finding a lifemate who will nourish the other through time will supersede any prior marriage. In the case of a lifemate found before marriage to someone else, no matter the reason the lifemate is forfeit and the female will bear the heirs to the marriage partner.

So why did her father marry a woman who already had a lifemate? She wonders, even more confused than she was before she began reading. *Was she forced into it, or was her lifemate too close to her heritage that to produce heirs with him would taint the lineage? Great. Now I have to go through the lineage books and see what that is all about.* Even more perplexed about the decision she will have to make in three weeks, Ivy puts her index fingers to her temples.

Ugh, she groans. She knows she must sort through the information she's gleaned. She stands from her perch and walks until she finds a spot on the lawn in front of the compound, where the elements are humming.

Sitting so she's facing the rising sun, Ivy allows it to warm her as she grounds herself. She pushes the tendrils of her spinal column into the earth as deep as she can get them while expanding herself up into the air as if a beautiful live oak during summer. She begins feeling the pulse of the elements and pulls the magic into her swords and herself.

The Elemental Mother can give me some insight into what I need to do, she thinks.

Invasion

Bloody Hell!

Ash is still reeling even after his walk. *Why in the hell is this happening to me?* he keeps asking himself. In all his life, he has never experienced a draw like it. He feels as though there is nothing he can do to abate the gnawing sensation that he has to go to her. His skin burns with trepidation even after an hour of jogging through the woods. Images of her fangs and the way she will look after being satisfied in his arms fleet through his mind in waves even after forcing himself to think of other things. She seeps into his every thought, and a fog has fallen over him, forcing him to realize that it isn't going to end.

The icy shower beats on his body in his attempt to cool down the ache he feels, but it isn't enough. He shuts the water off and grabs a towel from the shelf next to the shower door. It reminds him of the one that smells like her on her bathroom floor. Pacing his room, he finds some clothes and, as he pulls his t-shirt down into place, he sees a giant oak tree sitting in front of the compound.

What the fuck? he thinks as he steps up to the window for a closer look. *There is no way that a damn tree could have grown in a night.* Since the compound is filled with vampires and the Pale Race, all the windows are now UV resistant glass, but brilliant sun coming over the horizon causes his eyes to squint against the glare and does nothing to sharpen his view.

Bloody hell! he sighs as he leaves the window and walks down the hall to Soren's rooms. With a look of concern, Soren opens the door before Ash even knocks.

"Why the hell is there a bloody oak tree in front of the compound?" Ash demands.

"Are you okay?" Soren asks, reaching out to feel Ash's forehead. Ash knocks his hand away before it touches his head and walks into the suite across the hall from Soren's and leads him to the window.

"Bloody hell!" exclaims Soren

"That's what I said!" Ash insists as they both try to figure out is happening.

Soren pulls his cell from his pocket. "Go look out the window," Soren orders someone. "Can you see the compound?"

A pissed off groggy voice answers, "No," and hangs up on him.

They both assume correctly that they are under some form of magical siege. The changes the hybrid will bring threaten the old school way of life they live.

Soren has his phone back out and about to dial a number when Ash says, "Look!" Soren returns to the window.

The tree-shaped mist falls into itself as if collapsing into a black hole, and the oak-tree vision disappears.

Glowing in the sunlight with an aura of complete power whipping her hair around her in a black tornado, Ivy walks towards the compound.

Speechless, the two men gape at each other unsure of what happened and knowing they had both seen it, so neither of them has gone mad.

Shaking his head sleepily, Ash says "So you know, she may not want to do that when anyone else is awake. Otherwise, there won't be a secret to keep anymore. The swords' holding magic is believable, but the Pale Race holding magic of their own is not."

Soren stops Ash with his hand on his shoulder. "I understand if it's too much."

Ash is silent.

"Calyn called," continues Soren. "There is a war coming between the Ancients and the humans."

"What kind of war?"

Soren shrugs. "The only thing she was able to tell me before she had to go is that it's between the humans and Ancients and won't be pretty. There are very few Ancients left in the cities."

Ash thinks aloud, "What could draw Ancients from their homes?"

"Fear."

Worrying that he's in over his head, Ash glances back out the window. He doesn't have a clue about some things pertaining to Ivy, whose face is grave as she approaches the front door of the compound. He feels a rush of anger flow through him. *Why is fate such a bitch that it would pair me with a girl who can either end the world or save it?*

"Dude," Ash says to Soren, "I need to think."

Soren eyes him with a smirk. "So *that* is what you are so irritated about. You have your eye on my daughter," he says slyly.

"No."

"Yes, you do."

"No, I don't," Ash groans.

"If there is anyone that deserves happiness, it's you," observes Soren. "The council approves the match. The members said so the night you arrived."

Not willing to admit Ivy's attraction for him and knowing full well what the council has for motives, Ash looks up at the stars.

"If she's to choose you," Soren continues, "I will approve, but know this: I will ruin any man that hurts her."

The only words Ash can find, and he has no idea why, are "Dude, you and me both."

"That's all I needed to know. Go for it." Ash looks at him and shakes his head incredulously. "She's your daughter! And I don't even know if I am even going to, yet."

Soren rakes a hand through his hair. "I realize that. Her new heritage mark means she needs a mate. I want her to choose her fate if that can happen. And if not, we know that the Pale Council will insist that she have a baby—no matter who the father is or whether she goes the way of your sister and is given a child by magical means."

Ash growls, scaring himself.

"Now you understand," Soren sighs. "I missed my daughter growing up and learning. I missed all the moments that a father cherishes for his endless life. That being said, I will not interrupt her happiness. My only desire is to see her become the warrior heiress that she is and give me lots and lots of grandbabies to watch and help grow."

Ash loses himself thinking about the prospect of kids, something he hasn't considered before.

While Ash reflects on parenthood, Soren continues, "Both her mother and I will truly be happy if she chooses you. But that's the thing. She has to be the one to choose you, because we won't do it for her nor insist that she do it."

"Even if I were to obey the council's directive, I don't think she could ever love me."

"Asher Vale, I have never known you to give up before trying."

Offended, Ash replies. "I never said I have been trying."

"Okay, buddy," Soren says with the look of an all-knowing father.

"Even if I were to move forward, she is so far out of my league that I wouldn't even know where to start," Ash says.

They both laugh. They both know he would be signing up for the ride of his life if he chooses to follow the path as Ivy's husband. What's worse is that he will have to teach her not to hate herself before she can learn to love others.

You are a dumbass! Ash thinks. *You are not interested in allowing the council to be right. Stop!*

"Want to teach her how to drive?" Soren asks with his eyebrow raised.

Unsure why he even considers embarking on life with Ivy, Ash eyes Soren.

"Isn't that the father's job?"

"Well, I guess it should be, but it will give her a little bit of freedom and help her adjust to the human world. Not to mention, how else are you going to get time alone with her since Baz always shows up to feed her." Running a hand through his dark hair, Soren clears his throat. "Hell, he asked for my blessing to propose to her the other night."

Ash growls, "That idiot doesn't have his head screwed on tight."

"What do you mean by that?" Soren asks.

Ash clears his throat. "Only that he needs to back off with the 'date me' stuff, or she will rip his head off . . . or better yet, I might."

"He's been pressuring her?" Soren asks, annoyed. "I told him she is spoken for. When did this happen?"

"A few weeks ago. Before I introduced myself."

"Well, don't make me pry it out of you, Ash"

Ash nods, deciding it probably best to fill his friend in on the library incident. "When Ivy told him that she isn't ready for anything more than friends, he got in her face." Soren begins to stand, and Ash puts a hand on his arm. "She took care of it," Ash continues "I don't know if he's done pestering her, and I want to be there if he does again."

Tough as nails, Soren asks. "What did she do?"

"Essentially told him that she would rip his throat out if he touched her again," Ash says with a grin.

"He touched her?" Soren says, enraged.

Ash nods. "And she threw him across the room for it."

Ash takes it in as Soren relaxes a bit. "She is a fighter, that one. I do have to tell you to be careful."

Ash laughs. "As much as I am heeding your advice, know that she intrigues me, so if I get bit that's my own fault," he says, admitting that he has been thinking about her biting him. He blushes.

"So true, brother. You will have time to think when you and Baz bring her to the mall."

"You have to be kidding me." he groans, knowing that the cloud of lust will be even harder to hide when he sits next to her in a car.

Soren chuckles with no remorse. "Baz feels that he is fair game, Ash, though I'm not sure why. She made it clear that she isn't interested?"

"She did, though I am not too worried about it. That little shit can't compete," Ash says, jealous, likely without reason.

"I don't know. He feeds her," Soren says with a shrug, leaving Ash to his own thoughts.

They keep coming back to her though! Ash thinks, pissed that rational thought of her completely evades him as he returns to his room.

"Oh!" Ivy says, startled. "I thought I was the only one awake!" She eyes her door and shakes her head as if disappointed with something.

Ash smiles at her without realizing he's doing it. "No worries. The giant tree out front didn't freak anyone out at all."

"The what?" Ivy asks, her eyebrows scrunched together in confusion.

Wondering if she really doesn't understand what her power entails, Ash tilts his head to the side. "Whatever you were just doing planted a giant tree in front of the compound for the past hour," he says with astonishment and a bit of sarcasm.

"Great!" she says looking at her feet. "Even more freaky shit out of the number one freak of nature," she comments, referring to herself. Shaking her head in aggravation, Ivy grabs her sword. The movement makes Ash uneasy, but he hears a click, and the door to her room unlocks, apparently because of something to do with the sword.

That's convenient, he thinks.

A moment later, as she's about to disappear into her room, her shoulders tense. He sees a tear slipping down her cheek. "Ivy."

She pauses before shutting the door. "What is it?" she asks.

He can hear her voice straining with emotion as she hides her face from view.

"You are nature's perfection. Uniquely you." He pauses for a response but doesn't get one. "Don't let anyone make you feel less than that."

"Sure," she responds softly as she closes the door gently. Moments later, from her suite he hears music playing softly enough not to wake anyone and loudly enough that if she were crying, no one can hear her.

The abilities and the magic that she's given be damned. She's still a woman, Ash mumbles. *If nothing else, I am going to make her believe that she is amazing.*

Realizing that he has just made up his mind, he gives himself an imaginary slap on the back of his head.

Brotherhood

The Terrors

"Guys, this is Ivy." All at once, six gigantic warriors stare at her and assess how much protection she will need.

Eyeing them, Ivy stands a little taller.

"Hey, Ivy. I'm Stone," says the one the same height as Ivy and just as muscular.

"Hi. I'm Cason," says the tall thin one with a half smile.

Another warrior nods, "Dayton." Reserved in his expression as if embarrassed to speak too loudly. Ivy looks up a little bit to find his eyes.

"Wow, you're beautiful!" says the Ken doll with a baby face.

Without thinking, Ash growls, "Zip it, Graham"

Each of the warriors stops looking at her, shock on their faces as if in awe of something Ash said. They look back at her, and every one of them again looks at Ash, a wordless conversation occurring among them. Ivy has never experienced a more awkward moment, and she doesn't know why.

Anxiety creeps up her spine as she looks from warrior to warrior. She does what she always does during tension, applying the maxim, "For a fungus to grow, you must give it as mushroom as possible." She smiles disingenuously as the Terrors respond unanimously with skepticism.

Ash lifts an eyebrow at her.

Stone asks Ash, "Is this chick crazy?"

"That was a good one!" Ivy giggles. "You guys are too serious."

Without a word, Cason looks wide-eyed at Ash.

"Wait! How about this one? What has a mouth but can't eat?" she asks smiling and waiting for one of them to join in. Getting shrugs from them all, she says, "A river."

Cason's face contorts into a smile as he chuckles to himself.

"Of course, *you* would laugh." Stone says dramatically. "You're a dad."

Ivy puffs up. "That's sexist!"

Dayton looks at her as if she has two heads. "They're called dad jokes for a reason."

Putting a hand on her hip in annoyance with barely a grin, she asks, "Where does a tree store their stuff?" as she breaks the ice. "Their trunk, duh."

Ash grins with a weird look on his face, "Where is this coming from?"

Ivy smiles brightly, knowing that her eyes must look like coins. "The internet!" She spreads out her arms. "It's full of awesome stuff!"

Ash laughs at her, and she pouts.

Graham asks Ivy, "Want a joke about tree -free paper?

"Sure!" Ivy replies, cheering up.

"It's tear-able."

Ivy cocks her head to the side thinking about it, then says, "No, it's not." *In fact,* she thinks, *that's the only paper that the Ancients will use if it's not in a book!* Missing the joke, she glances at Ash. The guys laugh as she filters the joke through her head and finally understands. The guys laugh again.

Reminding herself that she can't tell anyone about her ancient side, Ivy looks up at the ceiling. "What shorts do clouds wear?"

"What kind?" Dayton asks, for the first time showing interest.

The quiet one, she thinks

"Thunder wear!" Ivy says with a giggle.

Cason laughs with her. "I need to tell that one to the littles. They will love it!"

"Why did the tree get in trouble?" Graham asks straight-faced.

Ivy thinks and produces nothing, so she waits.

"It was knotty," Graham informs everyone.

Unable to hold it back, Ivy snorts with laughter. "Good one!"

Cason smiles as he asks, "So what must tree's drink responsibly?"

Water? Ivy wonders.

Dayton shrugs, nodding as he says, "Water. Drought sucks."

Happy she isn't the only one thinking about it, Ivy nods with him.

Cason shakes his head no. "Root beer," he says.

Everyone laughs except Ash, who looks around at them with wide eyes. "What has gotten into you guys?" he asks, his face scrunched up.

Stone inquires, "Where do saplings learn?"

Ivy yells out, "Elementree school!" while Stone giggles uncontrollably.

"You, too?" Ash shakes his head as Ivy smiles in a childlike manner.

Stone pipes in again "Why does the leaf need a healer?"

"Why?" asks Dayton.

"It was feeling green!"

Trying to see the funny in it, the others stare at him.

"What is a tree's least favorite month?" Graham asks.

No one answers.

"Sep*timber*." The other guys except Ash laugh. He goes stock still as he watches Ivy's expression.

Then it hits her.

"That's not funny," Ivy says, punching Graham in the arm.

"Kind of is," Graham argues, rubbing the bruised area and looking at her funny.

Ivy shakes her head in disappointment. "Not even a little bit." She tsks him, and the others laugh at him.

Graham gets defensive. "It *was* funny!"

The men, laughing a moment before, shake their heads in agreement with her. That they have her back and not his causes her to puff up a little.

"Are we done now?" Ash asks, annoyed.

The men look at Ivy, and she shrugs. They nod in assent.

Ash clears his throat. "Guys, again. This is Ivy. The council has told me that I am to brief all of you at once about the hybrid."

"Then why in the hell is she here?" Stone asks, disgruntled. "She isn't a Terror."

Earlier comradery evaporates.

Then Ivy sees the general her father told her about. Ash looks suddenly as if he's grown another three inches as he growls, "Can I finish now?"

The warriors immediately shut up and no longer look her way. Every single one of them nods acknowledging his authority.

"Ivy needs to train with us as she will eventually fight with us both as Terror and as hybrid," Ash tells them.

All eight eyes plus Ash's snap to her at once. They stare quietly at her, and she sees Cason inhale deeply as if to see if she smells different.

"The hybrid is supposed to be a male," Dayton says seriously. "How are we supposed to keep a female hybrid safe? It's hard enough to keep normal females safe!" His angst shreds his usually quiet demeanor.

Dayton comes closer. "She doesn't look like much." As if to assess if Ivy's real, he pokes her in the arm.

She glares at Ash as if to ask, "Are you serious?"

He smiles at her and nods his head in the go-ahead to drop Dayton.

She smiles. Dayton walks to the other side of her and sees that her mark goes up under the sleeve of her shirt. As he has his finger ready to pull back the material. Eyes turning red with annoyance, Ivy bares her fangs and hisses at him.

Dayton jumps back so fast that she cracks up. Bending at the waist, Ash laughs with her until he's almost out of breath.

Each of the Terrors eye them with a mix of concern and anger.

"I'm going to pee!" she laughs, trying to catch her breath. "Your face!" She doubles back over. "I can't take it. "Oh, my Elemental Mother, that was so funny! I needed that! Thank you, Ash."

Still laughing, she sits down where she had stood and tries to pull herself together. Another wave of laughter hits her just as she seems to have regained her composure.

The guys stare incredulously at Ash, who laughs so hard that he also has to sit down.

"Dude!" Ash exclaims. "She's right! Your face!"

Their looks of utter astonishment keep Ivy going.

Dayton goes to leave.

"No!" Ash orders. "You can't go! We have important shit to discuss," he says between hiccupping breaths as he attempts to get himself back together.

"Ivy," he tells her, "stop laughing. It's making me laugh."

Ivy does the internal poise trick her mother taught her. Closing her eyes, she takes three deep breaths and relaxes every muscle in her face. Once she feels the trembling stop, she opens her eyes. Around her, every single one of the Terrors kneels in front of her.

"Wow, boys!" she tells them. "This is a little too fast for my taste. Polygamy isn't my style!"

They look at her puzzled, as if she has five heads. Then Graham starts laughing, snorting himself to a composed face.

They speak in unison. "As the hybrid of the Pale Race, we will train you to be one with us, work with us, and fight with us. We will teach you to protect our kind from all that can harm it. From this night until the end of nights, the Terrors and all our nightmares will protect you with our lives."

Dead silence follows. Not knowing what to say, Ivy puts her hand to her throat. She looks up at Ash to see him smiling at her. She wishes she knew what he is thinking but knows better than to ask.

The Terrors stand up and look down at her, so she stands. Each warrior comes forward and shakes her hand as she makes sure to use the Warriors grip, Master Phoenix taught her. Each one of them nods approval.

Ash clears his throat, drawing her attention to him. "Ivy, from this night forward, as the Pale Council has requested, you will be sparring every night. You will do your best to get past any weaknesses you have and do as you need to when the time comes."

Ivy nods, smiling. "Place and time, and I am there."

"The time will be midnight every night, starting tomorrow. At dawn, you will do your meditation as well. Then on the side, you will collaborate with me on weaknesses and strategy for when those weaknesses overwhelm your senses."

Ivy nods, looking at the clock, seeing that it's well past two in the morning. *I was hoping to train tonight,* she thinks.

Ash looks to the others. "This goes nowhere. No one in the compound can know this information. No one can eavesdrop on this office, so we use the code word "comrade." We will discuss it here. You are dismissed for now."

He pauses a moment and continues, "Also, Ivy, I need to talk to you about something."

Ivy sees that the other men look as if they want to stay. But knowing better than to do it, they walk out of the room and close the door. "How much you want to bet at least two ears are to the door right now?" she asks, smiling.

She's right. As whoever it is listening hightails it from the vicinity, she and Ash hear the door make a slight noise.

"I thought this room is soundproof," Ash says as he stares at the door.

Ivy shrugs. "It is if you don't know what I know. You can listen through vibrations if an ear is to the door."

"You're good!" Ash says with a grin. "Royalty problems?"

"Always." She shrugs, thinking about the conversation she should bring up but setting it aside. "Part of the reason I am not so keen on being a royal in yet another circle. It's bad enough when you are a freak in one place, but when you're also a freak in the other, it makes for a shit show."

Trying to hide her face as she reminisces her past, Ivy walks over to the window. "What's up?" she asks.

Ash sighs, leaning against his desk. "I need you to know something." Ivy nods for him to go ahead. "Should you decide to marry me or not, you will still be a Terror. You will still be a warrior, and you will still be the hybrid."

When she doesn't turn to look at him, he goes to her. He touches her shoulder gently, and Ivy turns to him but doesn't meet his eyes. The last thing she expects happens when he lifts her face to his. Her chin almost goes numb with the tingles his touch invokes. "You are extraordinary, and no one can say different," he tells her.

"I am a freak, as I always will be, but thank you for saying that. Ever since I could hold a sword, I've had one in my hand."

"Ivy, you were born to unite the races. Your differences are honorable, not freakish," he whispers.

The tingles grow stronger as they shoot down her throat. Their breaths mingle, and the prickles make her shiver uncontrollably as she waits for his next move. She imagines him taking her mouth possessively and biting her lip as he devours her.

Idiot! her body reacts, not listening to her mind. She isn't the only one. She can smell him, too.

Ash registers her reaction as her eyes flash to red and lets go of her chin, the moment over.

I am not mad! She thinks. *Please do that again!*

She mentally checks herself, and he smiles at her sweetly, not giving her any clue about his thoughts.

"Enjoy your training tomorrow night, Ivy." He steps back and waits for her to reply.

Ivy smiles weakly and says, "I will." *How many cold showers do I need to take in one day?* she groans as she wonders why the hell she wants him to kiss her. *Stop with the puppies and rainbows, Ivy. It isn't happening.*

Thwack goes the staff on the back of Ivy's head.

"Whatcha thinking about that has me able to ambush you?" Jynx asks as she steps in front of Ivy and twirls the staff in her hand with ease.

Forgetting she sits in the middle of the garden, Ivy shrugs while rubbing her head in pain. "Nothing important."

"Seems mighty important to me if it has your head out of the game. Spill," Jynx says in a serious tone, as she plops down beside Ivy.

"I can't." Ivy says, staring straight through the rock in front of her. *There is no way for me to come out unscathed if I even think that it's a possibility.*

Jynx cocks her head and sits next to Ivy. "Now, there is no escaping it. I like to know everything. If I don't, it will drive me crazy. And by me, I mean you."

Ivy eyes at her with dread at the thought of Jynx up her ass all the time until she tells her. *It isn't pretty.* "I think there is a chance that Ash may like me more than as a match made by the council."

"Is that a problem?" Jynx asks.

Ivy shrugs. "Not necessarily, but that means that if I marry him and I am wrong, I will seal his fate of resentfulness forever. If I am right and I don't end up feeling for him the way that he feels for me, then we are in the same boat."

Jynx smiles and thinks a moment. "It feels to me like you need to see if you actually like each other. Forget the match for a night, Ivy. Don't think about obligations, marriage, or babies. Think about what you feel inside and get the same from him."

"That's harder than you think, Jynx. He has only showed me glimpses that he might. I can't make this decision by myself, and I have three weeks to make my decision," Ivy complains as she buries her head in her hands.

Jynx takes a breath and lets it out in a huff. "It seems to me that you need to get him to kiss you, then. Literally make him kiss you, even if you must get on top of him to do it. A kiss will say a thousand words that the voice cannot."

"Think you can give me some pointers on how to accomplish this?"

Jynx smiles with a ferocity Ivy could never have pictured on that mousy face. "Absolutely."

Dirt Roads

Strategies

Doing somersaults and cartwheels, Ivy blocks, parries, and counters the four male warriors attacking her from all sides. The battle has advanced for a good half hour with no stopping her.

Ash watches as, here and there, Ivy flicks her sword hand one way or another. He laughs when he realizes she throws magic to trip them.

Intending to disparage Ivy, Graham complains about cheaters never making it in the real world. Ash grins, knowing she does cheat in her own way and they have no idea. Once, Dayton swings his battle-ax through the air and misses only by a hair. Without touching the ground, she throws herself into a backbend, then stands up to face him. The shock makes him falter and allows Ivy to send him hurtling into a rosebush.

"What the hell is this, *The Matrix*?" Stone cries, awestruck and shaking his head.

Ivy does a no-handed cartwheel and kicks Cason in the head, almost knocking him out. As she skips away taunting them, she steps on a flower. "I'm so sorry," she says as she bends, remorse etched into her features, to stand the plant back up.

Thinking Ivy distracted, Dayton runs full speed at her back. At the last moment, she does a handstand and uses her feet to spring Dayton over the flower.

Stone mocks Ivy to the others. "Cheaters always fall harder! Watch, she will face-plant concrete."

Ash sees Ivy's mischievous grin and knows she heard the remark. She lets him grab her and then throws her weight as she launches into a backflip off the patio. When she lands, she sits on his back ruffling his hair and asks, "What was that about face-planting?" She smooshes his cheek into the concrete with a giggle. She jumps off him and squares up to Dayton and Graham.

Graham trips again and looks for the culprit. Not seeing anything, he looks up just in time to see Ivy's staff hit him square between the eyes.

"Those baby blues will match the bruise," she says, smiling as she skips away.

Lying on the ground, Graham groans and holds his forehead. After rubbing his eyes to clear the spots from his vision, he peeks his eyes open. From what Ash can tell, Graham has decided to stop for the day.

Ash watches from the sidelines as Cason pulls back from the fray to eye both Ash and Ivy. Ash feels the eyes of the other man and plasters his general's expression on his face. He watches the wheels turn in Cason's mind as Cason notices that Ivy relies on her swords and thus succeeds in knocking one away from her. With a wide grin, he goes to pick it up before Ash can warn him, and he gets zapped. "What the hell!"

Ivy giggles and stretches out her hand, bringing the sword whipping back to her as it almost takes Dayton's hand off when he tries to stop it. Ash shakes his head and shrugs as the guys all stare at him in shock. The determined faces magnify as they realize that she really challenges them. For so long, they have outmatched anyone and anything they have come across.

The men try and try, unable to sway her hold on the sparring match against four grown warriors. Finally, Dayton looks at Ash, dropping his battle ax and sitting on his butt with a thud. "Does this chick have any tells?"

Ash shakes his head, knowing full well that he has never seen her moves before she gives them.

"Weaknesses?"

Ash grins, and nods slowly, perking Dayton up. "What?"

Ash pulls out the small Bluetooth speaker he brought for just that reason. Dayton cocks an eyebrow at him, so Ash puts a finger up to hold on a moment. The sound of a thunderstorm starts to play. Knowing it will shake her up a little, Ash turns the volume up halfway. Dayton stands and moves beside Ash to watch.

Ash turns the sound up one more notch, and thunder echoing on the speaker causes Ivy to shake her head a bit. Looking at the speaker, she huffs a little, sensing an ending to her reign over the Terrors. "Soren doesn't want to do it too much yet," Ash tells the others, "but we need to know everything."

Perplexed, Dayton watches as the loud parts cause her to falter. "Sound is a weakness?"

Ash nods. "This can't get out though. No one can know that we are testing her in this way in order to figure out how to protect her."

Dayton nods seriously. "We can work with it." He grabs his battle ax and runs back into the match, smacking the ax off different things to see her reactions as the ax makes different noises. After a few minutes of defending herself, Ivy backs into a ring the Terrors have made. During a lightning strike on the recording, Graham approaches her from behind and puts her in a headlock, and her eyes grow wide. He gives her a noogie that messes up her braid. She glares at him with the same look his sisters always give Ash when he annoys them.

Every one of the guys has a grin on his face as they knock Ivy back and forth among them. The pout on her face has Ash chuckling as they all come back in for a huddle.

"Stupid noise," she groans, rubbing the noogie spot on her head and wincing as another loud lightning crack echoes around them. "Turn that off, please."

Ash turns the music off and waits as the Terrors continue to take advantage of her uneven equilibrium. Ash becomes nervous as he watches Dayton stare at Ivy, but he needn't worry.

Dayton clears his throat and grins, "My little sister would love to learn from you."

"My daughter is first," Cason tells her.

Stone looks confused. "What fighting style is that? I have never seen it before . . . well, a little here and there throughout history, but you've smooshed it all together."

"An . . . an old style," Ivy says, glancing around at the onlookers. Stone's eyes look like saucers. and Ivy giggles. "I have been training with an old sect of fighters since I was five."

Offended, Graham confronts Ash. "You knew this?"

Ash nods, grinning ear to ear.

"You couldn't have said anything?" Graham persists."

"Who do you think I've been sparring with?" Ash grins, not realizing that he looks like a little kid. "She's good, isn't she?"

All four Terrors nod as Ivy lifts her chin in satisfaction. She looks like a kitten who caught a mouse.

Dayton whispers uneasily, "And the noise?"

"When I transitioned, my hearing heightened more than my ancestors'. Touch and sight are the same."

Cason glances at her swords. "Why do those things zap me?"

Ivy giggles. "It's also an . . . old item."

"Fucking cheater!"

Ivy crosses her arms over her chest. "Nope. It's not cheating to use those swords and take advantage of everything they can do when I am in battle."

Stone looks at Ash. "Weaknesses need to be addressed, right, Ash? She has to spar without relying on magic."

Ivy seems like a deer caught in headlights. "I'm not sparring without them!"

"Ivy," Ash says with hesitation. He knows that she has always used magic weapons. Ivy's reliance on the magic she wields with them makes her easier to capture if she is confronted without them.

"Don't even ask." Fear shows through her eyes and breaks Ash without his understanding why.

Crushing the feeling that he should give in, Ash barks in his general's tone, "Ivy."

"What?" She doesn't give a typical pout but looks more like a beaten dog.

As he sticks to his own orders, Ash reins in the pain he feels at her distress. "We address all weaknesses to make sure that you can defend yourself in any situation. You will set the swords down at the edge of the field for the next sparring practice."

"But . . ." Ivy protests.

Ash holds up a finger to stop her.

"If you do not reach for them during an entire hour, you will never have to train again without them."

Ivy nods, eyes flashing red as she battles her inner fury. "Copy that." Without another word, she stalks into the compound. "This is bullshit," she mutters. "Little babies can't take defeat." She slams the door behind her.

Stone grimaces. "She is scary when pissed. Remind me not to be on the receiving end of her wrath."

"Scratch that. She is scary when she isn't pissed, too," Dayton pipes in as he watches the door vibrate. "She can fight."

Graham smiles. "That's because you assholes don't understand women."

Stone elbows Graham in the rib. "Speak for yourself, Ass!"

Ash listens to the men as he looks around. If he could do something to change things, he would. Stone is right, though. As soon as any weaknesses show, they must be addressed. Otherwise, she could end up dead, which will never happen if he has anything to do with it. In that moment, he realizes it's not his career that wants to keep her alive but his heart.

"You should check on her," Cason says, still watching the door.

Ash looks at the door as Graham starts walking towards the house. "Not you, Asshole!"

Graham shrugs. "I'm good with women!"

All four men look at Ash as he growls before he realizes his teeth have elongated at the thought of Graham calming Ivy down. "No one approaches Ivy without consulting with me first." Ash stares down each of the men to emphasize order.

Dayton looks back at him and nods to accept the order even though he doesn't understand Ash's demanding tone.

Stone chuckles. "What are you, in love with her?"

The Terrors go quiet, including Stone, as Cason gasps, "Shit, Ash! You are!"

"No one's business. Have I made myself clear?" *Why did I not deny that?* They all nod at Ash, and he relaxes a little bit though not fully understanding what exactly has just happened.

Stone nudges his shoulder. "You've got it bad."

"I have what?"

Stone chimes in a little singsong voice, "You're in love."

"Mind your business, Stone," Ash directs as he stares at the door. "She is mine whether she knows it yet or not. Be ready to spar with Ivy every night at midnight like we are supposed to be doing. I want an itemized list of where she needs work, what shows that she's under pressure, and everything you can think of to train her effectively."

The warriors nod in agreement. Dayton snaps his fingers in front of Ash's face, bringing his eyes away from the door to the compound. Ash cocks an eyebrow at Dayton.

"What is her story?"

"She will tell you when she is ready."

Stone grins at Ash. "When did you know?"

"Know what, Stone?"

"That you've fallen for her."

Ash tries to brush off the statement. "Immediately." *That isn't what I was going to say. What the hell?*

"You really think so, Ash?" Cason asks as he surveys the door and then looks Ash in the eyes.

Realizing how stupid he would be to attempt to keep anything from his brothers, Ash nods.

"We will protect her until our last breath," Cason says, his determination and loyalty evident.

Ash straightens up his form, looking his Terrors in the eyes one by one. "Thank you."

Shit! Shit! Shit!

Ash holds the "oh-shit handle" in the passenger seat of the topless SUV as Ivy plows through a logging road at dusk. If he weren't immortal, he would be having a heart attack. He looks over at Ivy's face smiling like a banshee as she dodges a tree. *There were six spots on that lady bug's back!* He thinks as they fly past it rip-roaring fast.

"What happened to you being motion sick?" he asks, remembering what Soren had warned him about. The rhino lining will make washing vomit from the jeep much easier than from any other vehicle.

Ivy giggles as she scrapes the skid plate on a jagged rock. "It's different when you aren't starving, and you get to control it!" she says.

Ash groans. *This chick is an adrenaline junkie.* She wears no seatbelt, apparently without a care in the world for safety as she bounces so high in the seat that her foot leaves the pedal. As she bounces back down, her foot revs the engine, and they peel out some more.

Having had time to plan the excursion, Ash picked his favorite place to off-road. Soren had begged him not to take her anywhere that might have people she could kill, and he had agreed. Her cravings were more manageable, but that didn't rule it out altogether, not to mention her less than proficient driving ability. Though good at dodging trees, she should not be on the open road just yet.

Even at risk of reckless endangerment charges as she does thirty-five mph on a logging road, she looks like a goddess, jet black hair flying in the wind, a smile across her face from ear to ear. He debates whether hitting a rock form turned jump at their speed or her beauty will end up knocking him out of the SUV.

They ride a roller coaster with no rails to keep them in line, and as many times as he can count, she narrowly misses a boulder or a tree. His heart races as fast as the SUV, and he refuses to freak out as something scrapes down the side of the SUV.

He knows better than to lean out to check the damage. *I'd lose my head!* he mutters to himself.

Getting close to the turnaround, Ash puts his hand on her arm and points to the end of the road as he motions a circle with his finger.

She nods and watches more closely as they approach the end. Ivy shrieks as they fly over a knoll with the tires off the ground and the vehicle unable to stop immediately. With a cliff right in front of them, she slams on the brake. When it catches, the SUV leans dangerously to the right as she turns the wheel, causing Ash unnatural panic as he frets over her protection. The SUV stops and slams back down to four wheels. Ash lets out the breath he wasn't aware of holding. *Thank God for roll bars.*

They park the SUV in front of a crystal clear freshwater quarry where a small waterfall drains, causing ripples.

Her breath hitches in her throat and without thinking, she opens the door and steps out into the tall grass of the road. "Beautiful!" she whispers.

Ash smiles. He hoped she would find the place as sublime as he did. "Yep," he agrees, as he turns the key in the SUV and puts the key above the visor.

He reaches into the back seat to grab the cooler he brought. He knows that he doesn't want her hungry but finds her gone when he looks around.

"Ivy?" he calls, looking around the SUV to see if she's hiding.

"Down here!" she calls out. He steps to the edge of the cliff and looks down. Sure enough, about forty feet below him she sits on the ledge, hugging her knees to her chest.

"Want company?" he asks, smiling.

Ivy looks up at him, putting her arms to the side in a motion to show the space around her. "Duh!"

Ash carefully climbs down and thuds as he lands. His pants jingle, and she laughs. "Man, you could use some stealth skills!"

The sound of her laughing at him stirs something in him that wasn't there before. Sure, he lusts for her and has a feeling that she needs protection at all costs. *But this is different*, he thinks, wanting to pull her to him.

He pushes the thought aside. After hearing her in the garden with Jynx wanting to know if he feels more than duty, his mind and body start to sync.

"I wish I'd brought my bathing suit," she says mostly to herself as she watches the water ripple below her.

Ash smiles. "You don't need a suit when you are this far from civilization." Ivy looks down at her feet. A blush creeps up her neck and stains her face in a crimson glow. Her hair begins to fall forward. Without thinking, he tucks the strands behind her ears. *Oh, my god, her ears are adorable.*

Ivy looks at him, her ears turning red, too. She smiles shyly. "They're weird, I know," she says as she pulls her hair back over them.

"Actually, they're really cute," he replies.

Her forehead wrinkles as she cocks an eyebrow at him. Not believing him, she shakes her head and looks out over the quarry.

Ash reaches into the cooler and hands her a bottle of blood. "Ooh," she says with delight. "A picnic by the water!"

He chuckles and grabs a blood bag for himself. "Kinda. More like I don't want you hungry enough to bite me if you get mad!"

Ivy slaps him in the chest, startling him at the contact. "Ass!" she laughs as his chest tingles where she touched it. They quietly sip their supper and take in the moon's distorted reflection over the water. It's not the awkward silence that needs small talk but the easy silence that comes with familiarity.

Ivy eventually says, "I don't want you to think that you have to marry me out of duty. I know that I am a freak and if anything—" She fiddles with the lace of a soft soled boot but doesn't look at him. "—I want there to be more than duty in a marriage."

"You are not a freak. You are a hybrid," Ash says, trying to get her to understand her worth. *If she only knew how important she is.*

Ivy shrugs. "Semantics."

"Ivy, who will respect you if you don't respect yourself?"

"I don't care what anyone thinks of me. I can fight better than anyone I know. My skills in that area far outweigh my need to be liked."

"You are unique."

Ivy looks away. "Same difference."

"Why are you so difficult?"

"I am not difficult, Ash! You don't get it. Listen this time. People can think what they want. I drink the blood of vampires. I have read every history book at Duneskil. Twice. There is not one recollection of the Pale Race having a vampire blood fetish, hybrid or otherwise. So it is simple. That labels me a what? Oh, wait. Yes. That's correct. I am a freak."

"God damn it, Ivy. You are not a freak. You are part of a prophecy written before the birth of the Pale Race."

Ivy stops her mocking and becomes defensive. "What are you talking about?"

"Never mind." *Shit!*

"Oh, no, you don't! What in the hell are you talking about?" Her look could scare a councilman into loud chatter.

Ash steels himself and takes a breath. He expects backlash. "You are the fruition of an age old prophecy that foretells of a magical hybrid who will protect and unite the races."

Ivy starts laughing. "By whom? An idiot?"

"No by the Great Mother."

"You mean the Elemental Mother."

Ash shakes his head "No. The Great Mother. The first of our kind. You are also a first, Ivy."

Ivy throws her hands up, "The first of what? Freaks! I bet when I turn a human, it's going to transition into a zombie."

"Where did you hear about zombies?" *She is nuts.*

"Well, Ash, I discovered streaming movies." Her haughty tone reveals her upbringing in the royal circles as she manages to look down her nose at him.

"You will not make zombies. Zombies are different," Ash says seriously.

Ivy's eyes open wide. "Zombies are real?"

"Don't change the subject."

"What subject, General?"

Ash feels his temper getting the better of him. "*You are not a freak, Ivy!*"

Ivy winces at his shout and quickly recoups her indifference. "Yet to be determined, I guess," she replies.

Speaking slowly and softly to bring her to understanding, Ash reins in his fury. "You, having no self-worth, will give no one reassurance in the field."

She plays with her boot lace and doesn't look him in the eyes as she says, "As long as I am assured that I will win in the fight, who cares?"

"I do."

"But, why? Why is it so important to you?"

"Ivy, you are royalty. You will change the world. The prophecy says you'll change the Pale Race—save it. You can't do that with your head up your own ass."

Ash watches as she peeks behind her. "That's weird. I didn't realize that I could bend that way."

Ash feels himself smiling. "Why can't you stay serious about this?"

Ivy shrugs without answering.

During their silence, Ash knows that he has only two-and-a half-weeks to get her to accept someone loving her. Otherwise, she will assume that any proposal he makes originates in wrong reasons.

Blushing again for no apparent reason, Ivy stands. "Close your eyes," she says with a mischievous grin.

Ash stands with eyes shut, opening them only when he hears a barely audible splash below. At his feet sit her boots, socks, and clothes. Peeking over the edge, he looks down through the darkness to see her giggling as her head pops up out of the water. He can't stop himself from staring at her pale skin as it peeks from the water in the moonlight. Her hair obscures her in waves as it fans out around her body.

"You coming?" she yells up to him as she swims away. Without thinking it through, he unlaces his boots and pulls them off. In his haste, he snags his shirt on a branch as he rips it off over his head. Pulling off his pants, he debates whether he should keep his boxers when he notices her underwear on top of her boots. He does a double take at the lace and peers back down at her as he squints through the night and sees that it's true.

Bloody hell! He sees her shapely butt as she kicks away from him. She flips over to her back, her hair wrapping around her torso. His brain shuts off momentarily as he gapes at her naked breasts.

He kicks his boxers off as she swims determinedly away from him. He does a running jump into the water to cause a tidal wave as he hits a cannonball right next to her.

A sputter of shock and splash in his face greet him as he resurfaces. He grins.

"I've decided you are getting some pointers in the art of stealth, Mr.," she laughs.

Ash chuckles, treading water in the quarry as she swims around him in circles. "I am stealthy," he tells her with a straight face.

Ivy snorts, covering her face with her hand in embarrassment. She recovers quickly with, "Do you own pants that don't rattle?" She raises her eyebrow at him. "Then again, I see that your hair isn't permanently sticking straight up." She giggles.

"Hey! Don't diss the do!" Ash admonishes, splashing her in the face.

"What the hell do you put in it to get it to do that, anyway?" Ivy asks, and Ash swears she's blushing but isn't close enough to be sure.

Ash shrugs. "Glue."

Ivy sputters. "You put *glue* in your hair?" She swims over to him and touches his sopping wet hair. "Eww!" she pulls back quickly. "It's slimy!"

"That's because its water soluble," Ash replies, offended. "Why don't you ever cut your hair?" he asks, attempting to poke her back.

"Because I had to hide my ears from the Ancients," Ivy says as she begins floating on her back, providing a view that makes Ash uncomfortable.

Ash tries to distract himself. "Why would you have to hide them?"

"If you saw my mother's ears, you would know why."

Ash realizes that in all the years he has known Calyn he doesn't remember ever seeing her ears.

"Hers are extra pointy," Ivy tells him, "like all the Ancients of Lesai. Whenever anyone saw my ears, they would ask why they were so tiny, so I grew my hair long enough to always have them covered."

His intention to pick on her seems crude as he realizes that it's something she gets no matter where she is.

"Is it possible to hide your ears around others?" Ash asks, wondering if that's what Calyn had done.

"It's more of an intangible charm you wear. It makes it so that if you become distracted, the glamour still holds for all races aside from the Ancients."

"How is it that you can swim but Calyn couldn't?" he asks as she effortlessly treads water.

Ivy laughs and blushes a little. "There is one pond in Lesai that no one was allowed to swim in because of a special plant that grows in it." She looks up at the stars and grins a little. "On one night every month, the elder would meet with the healers, and no one would be watching the pond."

Ash grins back. "So you just break more rules than your mother."

Ivy chuckles and nods. "I think she is on par with me, considering she had a child she wasn't supposed to."

The melancholy in her voice gives Ash a chill, and not wanting to ruin the time they have, he changes the subject. "Your dad wants me to start preparing you for the human world, too. Would you be willing to use a charm in case we are around humans?" Ash asks, trying to distract himself from looking at the parts of her body skimming the surface as she begins floating again.

Ivy makes ripples as she shrugs, bringing Ash's eyes right back to where they were previously. "I don't mind. I hide them anyway."

He can't help but hear a hoarseness to her voice when she says it. He feels annoyed at her lack of self-confidence. It has him wishing he could show her how she looks to him. Certain she won't believe any compliment he gives her, he leaves it alone. After their disagreement on the cliff face, it's obvious, he has his work cut out for him.

He grabs a foot and tickles it, making her squeal and flail in the water. "Stop! Stop!" she begs, giggling.

Ash stops and grins from ear to ear. On the outside, he's begun a war, but on the inside, he has made sure he will feel her body on him at some point. After all, she can't resist fighting back.

When she launches out of the water full speed at him, Ash looks up shell-shocked at her naked body. She lands directly on him and dunks his head under the water. Not fighting her as she holds him under the water, he enjoys the view. Free for him to ogle, her entire body puts a smile on his face.

Eventually she lets him pop up out of the water, and she dives down before he can open his eyes. He looks everywhere for her next move. As he begins to panic that she hasn't popped up, His lungs fill with water on a sharp inhale of shock when she pulls him under the water faster than he can blink. *That little vixen,* he thinks, eyeing her from twenty feet away as her giggles overtake his coughing fit.

"It's a good thing we can't die, right?" she says, still giggling.

Ash coughs up some more water. She treads water just out of reach as he attempts to think of a plan. "You do realize that you are not going to get away with that, right?"

"Psh!" she says, tossing her hand to the side. "I think my Protector needs to be protected." Ivy covers her mouth in mock surprise. "Someone come and help him!" Her yell echoes off the cliff face "The scary hybrid will drown my immortal ass," she yells before erupting again in giggles.

She is baiting me, Ash thinks, attempting to ignore how turned on he is as he looks around for her plan. Not seeing anything she can use as a weapon, he catches his breath and dives under water chasing her, intent on regaining his aplomb. He opens his eyes underwater and can barely make out her feet as she kicks strongly away from him.

He comes up for air and goes back under, gaining on her. Before he knows it, he can feel the current of the water she pushes behind her. He smiles with satisfaction that he swims faster than she does. *There has to be something I can do better than she does.*

She stops quickly, and from under the water, he sees the edge of the cliffs in front of her. *She's trapped!*

She pops out up from the water, and Ash meets her eyes as he maneuvers slowly towards her. Her doe eyes attempt to seduce him into leniency as she calculates. She looks up at the cliffs and down at herself, and he knows he has her. *If I go back under, she's going to climb the cliff.* He watches her dip below the surface as she assesses how deep she is and smiles before submerging.

Ash watches her go under and knows exactly what she's about to do. He feels a rock under his foot and jumps to where she went under. As she launches out of the water, he covers her body with his own, and a look of shock covers her face as they collide. Ash dives back down while holding on to her, memorizing the feel of her bare skin on his.

The tingles aren't the gentle kind. They cover every part of his body that touches her. It shocks him, and he can see that she feels it too. He lets her go as fast as he can, scrambling away and seeing her in a new light.

Now that is an unexpected outcome!

Overlook

Heart to Heart

"Why wasn't Ash at practice? Is he too good for us now?" Ivy asks the men. She had sparred without her swords and totally failed when it came to not reaching for them. Thoughts of the other night tempt her, but she smooshes them back down.

Cason laughs at her. "Why are you so worried about Ash?"

The inquisitive look on his face makes her blush. "I am not worried. He is just always at practice."

Stone elbows Ivy. "Do you like him?"

"What are you, ten?" Ivy scoffs, not wanting to admit to herself let alone anyone else that she misses him. She hadn't even known she would until he wasn't there.

The other guys laugh as Graham looks at her and sighs. "You do know that because you reached for your swords that you have to train more without them, right?"

"Yes. I am aware. As much as I hate not having them, it is a weakness. Especially since I can't trip you up to give myself time to react." She shrugs her shoulders in defeat.

Graham slams his hand down into the concrete of the patio where they're resting. "I knew I wasn't imagining that!"

Ivy laughs. "You dudes are clueless to the art of war. It's life or death, and to keep the edge, you do what you have to."

"We are not clueless, my lady. We have been fighting a war for centuries. The difference is that we don't take the magical aspect into account unless we are up against an ancient."

Ivy cringes, as the warriors exchange glances. "Don't call me 'my lady.'"

"But you're an heiress. Just as Ash is an heir."

Ivy scrunches up her face in distaste. "I'm good with my name. Ivy is fine. Not Iveliis, not my lady, not anything but Ivy. Just plain Ivy."

Dayton laughs. "What kind of royal are you?"

"One that doesn't want to be looked at funny because I'm an heiress on top of being a freak."

Cason lifts his eyebrows. "You are not a freak. A little cocky and a lot stubborn, but not a freak."

Ivy tosses her hands into the air. "There is nothing about me that is normal in any way. I am—different. I eat—different. I smell more and feel more. My eyes turn red, and my fangs are longer than any pair I have seen thus far. I am a—freak."

The four guys look oddly at each other without saying what they want to say but nevertheless communicating.

Ivy groans in irritation, "Spit it out."

"You know that you are revered, right, Ivy?" Ivy doesn't say anything, just looks away not wanting to give away her inner fears. "You fight better than every single one of us. It takes all four of us maneuvering you to take you down without your swords. There is no way that you will fail with them."

Ivy shrugs. "I know that I am a good fighter, but that doesn't mean that I am not weird as well. I have never met anyone like me before, and I never will. There is nothing that makes anyone able to relate to me."

Graham pipes in. "You are beautiful. Not hitting on you. Ash would—" Cason elbows Graham in the ribs. "Never mind that. Just know that you can have anyone you want. You are witty and beautiful. I will leave it at that."

"Ash would what?" Ivy asks, her eyes narrowing.

"What Graham is trying to say," Stone says without his normal grin, "is that there is nothing stopping you from being happy. You have more to offer to a male than any female I know. All that is stopping you is you."

Ivy smiles, hefting her sword in her hand, causing all the men to back up.

She chuckles. "If I am fighting, I will be happy for the rest of my life. There is nothing I want more than to help people who can't help themselves."

Dayton laughs. "You really need to train some females to have your mindset."

"You really think that females are that bad?" Ivy looks at them warily.

Graham smiles. "I don't, but a lot of females get a bad rep because they gave up fighting for their survival."

"Of course, you wouldn't think females are bad. You have the baby face that makes them swoon." Ivy says slapping his cheek and giggling at his wide eyes and red face. The other guys start laughing, too, making him burn even brighter.

"You are cold, my lady."

"It's Ivy, shithead," she scolds Graham, smiling. "So, in all seriousness, what do I need to work on?"

The guys look back and forth among themselves and all at once say, "No swords."

"Seriously?"

They all nod. Dayton looks contrite when he offers, "Every time you reach for them, you falter for half a second and open yourself up for attack. Until you fill that gap, you need to train without them."

"So my greatest strength is my biggest weakness?"

All four of them nod.

"Oddly enough that makes sense," she says, remembering that the one time she didn't have them, Finn hurt her during her transition. "Looks like these two need to stay home from now on."

Stone shakes his head. "No. When we are not training, they will be on you. There is no safe place. Not with all the vamp-op intel we have been getting. We are not always here."

"But Ash is," Ivy says before she can stop herself. Looks pass over each of the men's faces as she turns bright red.

"I am not relying on him, obviously, she says. "I can protect myself." As she looks around at the warriors who have sworn to protect her, she realizes that she has said too much.

"Don't say anything to Ash. I shouldn't even be thinking like this," she says.

The warriors all nod. Stone grabs her and gives her another noogie, distracting her from her thoughts of Ash.

Will you stop that?" she complains. "You keep making me have to re-braid my hair and it takes forever, man!"

They all laugh at her. She feels like their kid sister created only for them to torment.

Graham looks at Ivy seriously as she takes her braid out and begins the work all over again. "Have you ever wondered if Ash might feel the same way?" he asks.

Dayton elbows Graham in the rib, knocking the breath out of him. Ivy can feel something at play but can't put her finger on what.

"That isn't something I'll even let my mind consider. I mean, the Pale Council has matched us, so it could be that he will do his duty," Ivy says looking down at the braid she quickly weaves.

Graham starts to speak, but Dayton elbows him again. Cason smiles solemnly at her. "What if that is something he wants to do?"

Knowing that she looks just like her mother as she copies the way she speaks, Ivy looks Cason in the eye. "I will never allow someone to resent me because they are unhappy for not just a lifetime but an eternity. Duty doesn't keep the heart content. There needs to be more than just duty in a marriage."

Cason smiles at her and nods, grabbing her braid and tugging it like a little kid. "This could be considered a weakness as well, you know."

"Ow! Ass! I am not cutting my hair." There are shocked gasps around the circle as she tucks a strand behind her ear. Quickly, Ivy covers her ears again, not knowing how she had forgotten to keep her hair over them.

"Holy ears!" Stone points as he shrieks with wide eyes.

Ivy turns red and shrugs off the insult.

Graham smacks Stone in the back of the head. "Don't be a jerk."

Stone shuts up, then asks, "Is that how you hear so good?"

Ivy rolls her eyes, a tear falling before she knows it's there. She swipes it away with a serene look.

"Oh, my god. I didn't mean to hurt your feelings. I'm sorry."

"It's fine, Stone. You're not the first or going to be the last. I have this one handled." She gets up, and Stone pulls her back down.

"I am serious. I was just playing. They are cute—like a little leprechaun."

Ivy bursts out laughing. "You are not funny, asshole!"

Stone grabs her in a bear hug that makes her gasp for breath. "It made your stubborn ass laugh, so it did the trick."

"Can't breathe!"

"Guys! I'm sensing another weakness!" Stone yells, making the other guys grab her by the legs and pull in the other direction.

"We've got you, Ivy."

Ivy freaks out. "Let me down, you shitheads!" When they chuckle and keep holding her, she summons a sword.

Dayton must have seen it move, because he yells, "Scatter!" and they all drop her like a sack of potatoes. All at once, training continues and Ivy refuses to drop her swords.

With a grin, she squares her stance and gestures them forward. "Your funeral, boys."

Every one of them doubles over laughing, unable to continue.

"What did I do?" she asks without guile.

They walk away laughing, while leaving Ivy in confusion at the ready.

Ivy lies in the hammock she loves. Thoughts about the night at the water weigh heavily on her as she rocks back and forth in the wind. Clouds above her billow lazily as she considers the feeling that zapped through her body when Ash caught her that night. Something about it keeps her awake during the day trying to figure out what happened.

After a sleepless day, she'd gone into the library where she filtered through as many books as she could to find information to lead to an explanation. The only material she found referred to a lifemate bond. *Whatever that is.* She racks her brain, figuring she must ask Ash but unsure he will even want to talk about it.

His distance has increased since it happened not in the way of avoidance but in the way that he tries not to be alone with her.

"Sorry to interrupt," the woman with a pixie cut says to her, bringing Ivy out of her internal debate. "I've been meaning to properly introduce myself. I realized that I forgot to tell you my name the other night. I'm Jenny."

Ivy lays down the book she's been holding propped up on her chest but not reading. "Ivy."

Jenny looks at her feet. "I know. Everyone does." She looks back at Ivy and lifts her chin up. "I want you to know that you are welcome to come and hang out with us, too. You always seem so lonely, and I feel like we haven't done enough to include you."

Ivy smiles a little as she tries to hide the anxiety she feels about eating one of them on accident. "Not really lonely per se." Ivy pauses, trying to figure out a way to explain the situation without seeming rude. "I think I just enjoy the quiet of the night, that's all."

Jenny looks upset. "Sorry. I can leave you alone then." She turns to leave.

"No!" Seeing the misunderstanding in the girl's eyes, Ivy backpedals. "Not at all. I didn't mean it like that."

Jenny turns back to Ivy. "What did you mean it like, then?"

"I've never had anyone who understands the sickness."

"Sickness?"

Ivy rolls her eyes to herself. "You know." She turns red as she explains. "The bloodlust."

Jenny perks up a bit and smiles. "Oh, I get that completely. But you thought you were sick?"

Ivy nods. "I figured you would get it. I grew up around people who didn't understand it. They all thought I was crazy."

"Really?" Jenny asks, incredulous.

Ivy nods, looking away.

"Ever since I was transitioned," Jenny says, "I have lived with vampires and the Pale Race, so I knew what to expect."

Thoughtful, Ivy asks, "Did you know or choose to be turned?"

"Yes. I was given the choice. Your dad is my Pale parent."

Ivy laughs as she realizes, "So we are kind of like sisters."

"Exactly." Jenny sits on the hammock next to Ivy.

Ivy shuffles a little to give her room. "I've never had a sister."

"I do." Jenny says, looking forlorn. "She is in her eighties now, though. I visit her every now and then as her nurse. She swears she knows me but only realizes it's me once a year or so. She has Alzheimer's disease."

"What is that?"

Jenny clears her throat, holding back the emotion that Ivy sees trying to escape. "It's a human disease where you forget who you are after it sets in. It's a dreadful existence. I make sure that she is comfortable."

"I hope someday they find a cure for it."

Jenny's expression changes. "There is one, but I would never consider it an option."

Realization clicks for Ivy. "Oh, I am so sorry. I forgot."

"It's okay. You didn't put two and two together. You are new to our world."

"Maybe sometime soon you can show me a picture of her?"

Jenny smiles. "I have a bunch. We can make a date of it, and you can show your family too."

Ivy realizes that she doesn't have any pictures of her mother and her and wishes she did. "I don't think there are any of me as a child. My . . . parents didn't believe in them."

"That's odd," Jenny says, quietly leaning back and looking up at the clouds. "I can see why you like it out here so much. It reminds me of my human life, just staring up at the sky and wondering if the boy I have a crush on is kissing another girl."

Ivy barks out a laugh. "I wouldn't say that's the only thing I am thinking about."

"I'm surprised!" Jenny says giggling.

"And why is that?"

"Because," she says, wiggling her eyebrows, "I see how Ash looks at you."

Ivy scoffs. "I highly doubt that is the case. He's an enigma."

"A what?"

"A mystery I won't be solving anytime soon," Ivy says sighing and returning to her thoughts about the other night. "Men are annoying."

"I second that!" Jenny laughs. It makes Ivy smile knowing that she isn't the only one perplexed by the male population.

Gardens

Contemplation

Ash sits on the roof watching Ivy as he has spent most of his nights lately. *You are not a stalker. You are doing your job,* he reminds himself after watching Jenny leave.

He finds it endearing to watch Ivy just lie for hours on end while reading or watching the stars. Even after years of complaining that females just lie around doing nothing all night, it doesn't matter. She trains and meditates every dawn. For reasons he can't fathom, she will even clean the library for hours on end. *Maybe cleaning calms her, dummy.*

It's entertaining to watch her swing in the hammock and chit chat with another female. His irritation that he's a bodyguard and not out on recon with his team every night fades as he watches. His concerns about becoming stir crazy appear far from correct as he makes sure to stay out of her sightline.

Tonight she has another history book about events predating his own birthdate, and he imagines the boredom that comes with it. As if on cue, her book falls onto her chest, waking her with a start as she looks around, burning red in embarrassment. Ash smiles as he realizes his assumption was spot on.

Her hair hangs in a long braid beside her face tonight and has little black wisps that sway in the breeze. Brushing them aside, she places a bookmark at her place and sets the book on the stone slab under the hammock. She has a look of peace as she closes her eyes and allows herself to fall back asleep.

Ash sees Baz approach from beneath him and perks up a little. The last time he had seen Baz talk to Ivy, Ash wanted to deck him. *Ivy is the hybrid and should be addressed as such.*

Ash observes Ivy visibly tense when Baz gets close enough for her to smell him, and Ash knows she avoids his presence as she feigns sleep.

"Hey, beautiful," Ash hears Baz say as he goes up to the hammock. Seeming to want him to give up and go away, Ivy ignores him. Baz pokes her shoulder twice, and she gives him no response, so he shakes her. "Ivy. You awake?"

Ivy fakes a stretch, pretending to wake up from a nap. "What is it?"

"It's the middle of the night. You have all day to sleep," Baz says smiling and plopping down in the hammock, causing Ivy to bounce towards him.

Touching her sword, Ivy glares at him as she readjusts herself so there's no contact between them. Ash knows that, if he could see the magic, he would see that she's built a wall between their legs to stop herself from touching him. Ash smiles to himself, giddy that she doesn't want another male in contact with her.

"That's the thing with having all the time in the world. There is no rush, so I can sleep whenever I want to. Especially after a taxing training session," she tells Baz as she tosses her braid in annoyance over her shoulder and onto her back.

Baz shrugs. "Well, training isn't something that females have to do, you know. Fighting is for males."

Ivy ignores the remark, the silence hanging in the air.

"So, I heard you talking to Jenny earlier," Baz informs her.

"Why are you listening in on my private conversations?" Ivy asks with suspicion.

Baz laughs. "I am Pale, too, you know. If someone doesn't want to be heard, then they bar themselves into a soundproof room."

"Common courtesy says that if a person is not speaking to you, then you should not be intent on listening," Ivy says, sounding like her mother.

Ash ducks a little further into the shadows. *Well, that tells you exactly what she would think of you watching her, idiot.*

"You must have been an adorable child."

"I wouldn't know."

"There must be a picture somewhere of what you looked like. Or better yet, what your mom looks like." Ivy eyes him warily and looks down at her soft-soled boot. Playing with the lace as she says, "My mother died when I was born, and my parents didn't believe in pictures."

"But everyone wants to know about their birth mother," Baz persists.

Interested in how she will react, Ash moves a little closer despite risking that she might catch him watching.

As she lifts her face to Baz's, Ivy's expression goes from suspicion to cold royal in a second.

Ash's heart skips a beat. *She is her mother's daughter.*

"I am not interested in finding out any more information on my heritage." She holds her right arm into view, pulling the sleeve up a little bit. "My mark is all I need to know about."

Baz's eyebrows lift. "There isn't a single thing that you want to know? I can help you find information if there is."

"Nope." Not moving an inch closer to Baz, Ivy quietly leans back to look at the stars. "I'm good."

Baz's expression turns sincere as he looks at Ivy. Ash begins to feel annoyed. *She is not yours. Back off.*

"Were your foster parents nice?"

Keeping her eyes on the sky above her, she pulls a sword from her back and says, "Not that it's any of your business, but yes."

Ash watches as the space between them grows. His ego bounces inside his head at the realization.

"What were their names, if you don't mind me asking," Baz says hesitantly.

Ivy shrugs. "I do mind." She misses the look of contempt that Baz quickly hides with a look of irritation.

"Why are you so secretive?"

Ivy's eyes snap to him and flash to red for a half second. "Why are you so inquisitive?"

"I want to get to know you better. You were fine talking to Jenny. Why won't you let me get to know you too?"

Ivy looks exasperated. "You do know me. In fact, you know more about me than almost everyone here."

"I want to get to know you more!"

Looking at her boot again, Ivy shrugs. "I can't give you more information."

"Why?"

"Because I don't have it to give."

Baz considers leaving but seems to decide against it. "Will you go on a date with me?"

Eyes wide, Ivy says, "I don't think about you in that way."

"In what way?"

Ivy's eyes look to the sky as she attempts to hold her temper. Ash doesn't know what Ivy is thinking. "I don't see you as more than a friend. I have told you this."

"Why not?" His look of hurt makes Ash want to gag. *Take a hint, dude!* After a few centuries of having to turn women down, Ash feels bad that Ivy has to do it not once but twice now to the same guy. "You are beautiful," Baz tells her, "and I'm not bad looking either!"

Ash shakes his head. *Like that is the only reason for two people to be together.*

"Looks have nothing to do with it. If that were the case, I would have married the last boyfriend I had." *What boyfriend?*

"Yes, they do!"

Ivy jumps off the hammock, causing it to thrash Baz off the back of it when it flips. "I am not doing this again."

"Why won't you just let me take you to dinner?" he whines as he brushes dead leaves off his shirt.

Ivy laughs and throws up her hands in aggravation as she spins to face him. "Because, for one, I can't leave the compound grounds and, for two, even if I did want to, I don't have anything more than friendship to offer you!"

Baz puts his hands on his hips as if a mother lecturing her child. "You can learn to love me back."

"Who is talking about love? I can't love anybody! And nobody can love me unless they know everything about me, and no one ever will!"

You are my lifemate, and I will show you love. Ash thinks as he shakes his head at the thought nagging him since they went swimming. He doesn't want to admit the council's accuracy either, no matter his feelings, especially when the council planned the marriage so long ago.

Baz's wail snaps Ash into the present.

"I love you, Ivy. I've been trying to tell you that!"

Ivy barks a laugh that stands Ash's hair in end. "You know nothing about me."

"I know everything I need to in order to love you properly."

Ash can feel the growl starting to build in his throat and covers his mouth to choke it back. *You have not claimed her yet as your wife or your lifemate,* he tells himself.

Ivy lifts like a royal condescending to a subject, and Ash grows quickly uncomfortable. The look of stubbornness on her face in full view makes him wish that he could kiss the look off her face. Half of the coven watches. Seeing them and not wanting to seem unfair, yet far from giving in, she asks, "What is my favorite color?

Black, thinks Ash.

"Pink," says Baz.

Ivy shakes her head no, quiet and waiting for the next guess.

"All women like pink," Baz proclaims.

Ash secretly laughs. *Tool!*

"Not all, because I don't."

"Ivy, you must at least like pink."

"No, Baz. I don't. I like black and green."

Baz edges towards Ivy as he realizes that most of the coven is there. "You are so odd . . . ."

Closing his eyes, he leans in for a kiss.

"Get away from me," Ivy whispers as she backs away from him again.

Ash's gag reflex acts up again when Baz pouts, "We are good together, so no." He goes in closer again to kiss her, and as Ash prepares to step off the roof, almost giving away his sentinel position, she reacts.

"Funny," Ivy says. Her eyes flash red, and Baz searches for an escape.

That's odd. Ash thinks, as he adjust himself in response to her eyes. *Why would that make him back off if he wants her? All I can imagine is her teeth in my carotid.* The thought makes him pulse in pain.

Baz turns to leave but spins right back around to face Ivy, "I'm serious. We would be amazing together, and I am sick that you can't see that."

"Sick in the head is more like it. You need to get over your fascination with me, because it won't ever happen."

Baz kicks a rock and mutters, "Cold-hearted—"

"Bitch!" She finishes. "Yeah, I suspected as much."

Baz looks at her like a puppy dog begging, "Why are you like this?"

Ivy shrugs, jumps up to her balcony, and slams the door so no one can follow her.

Ash can't help but wonder how in the hell a male of the Pale Race can't take a hint. There aren't many females out there, no, but there are enough that if one says no, another very well might say yes.

Ash debates whether to ask her for a one-on-one sparring session but thinks better of it. The last thing he wants is for her to pummel him for things that another male has said to her.

Sitting in the hammock, Ash stares up at Ivy's window. He can't get her out of his mind no matter what he does. He has tried everything from exercise to napping with no results.

Cason approaches.

"I shouldn't be saying this. I said I would keep the information to myself," Cason whispers almost inaudibly.

Ash perks up, taken from his train of thought. "Is this about practice?"

"In a way, but not quite."

Confused, Ash asks, "Well how did she do at practice?"

"She reached for the sword seventeen times. She has agreed that she needs to train without swords for the time being."

"But are there any weaknesses other than discussed, Cason?"

"No. The only thing that happens when she reaches for her swords is a split second of panic that creates a window of opportunity for the adversary."

Ash finds himself upset by the information. "What would make her panic?"

Cason shrugs. "Past trauma, maybe. But that's not what I want to talk to you about, no matter how important."

"Go on."

Cason shuffles his feet.

"Spit it out, man."

Cason takes a dramatic breath. "She asked where you were tonight."

"Okay—"

"She is interested in you but doesn't feel that she is worthy of it. She said she knows that you will protect her but backpedaled and said she can protect herself. Then when we were quiet, she told us not to say anything because she shouldn't be thinking like that."

Cason looks around to check for listeners.

Ash knows she has low self-esteem but never suspected its intensity. "Is there anything else?"

"She has no want for royal titles and feels that she will never find someone who can relate to her." Cason hastily looks around, then continues, "I never said anything about any of this. Nod if you can accept that I will deny it if asked."

Ash nods, smiling. "You are afraid of her."

"No. I am torn between my brotherhood to you and my duty to protect the hybrid. In the brief time I have known her, she has grown on me."

Ash nods. "Thank you for the information. I am grateful."

"If you are in love with her, and I hope that you are, she will be happy. I want her to have that. No one should know the life of loneliness that I have watched you suffer for centuries."

With that, Cason walks away, keeping to the shadows. The act makes Ash chuckle and return to gazing up at Ivy's window.

Ash will no longer let orders sway him from what he wants. *Stubbornness be damned. I will show that girl how worthy she is of love.*

Lying in her favorite place, he contemplates all the ways he can make her believe that duty isn't the reason he wants her to marry him.

Unexpected Solutions

Checkmate

There must be a way that I can get out of this, Ivy thinks furiously. *I do not lose! I never lose. I refuse to lose.* She sees without a doubt as she evaluates every piece that she has, in fact, lost her first game of chess in a decade.

"Checkmate"

Ivy looks up in shock. "How did you do that?" she asks in fascination. She has never seen someone play so haphazardly and still manage to beat her. She looks back at the chessboard, "Shit!"

Ash laughs, the four-inch spikes on his head defying gravity as he covers his mouth.

Ivy crosses her arms in front of her and glares at him. "What do you find so humorous?"

"You definitely don't lose very well!" Ash says, smiling still.

Ivy shrugs and looks away. "No one has beaten me at chess since I was ten."

"Except me!"

Ivy looks out the window in annoyance as she mocks him.

"You are funny when you lose," he says sarcastically.

"Right. Because you would never stomp a foot when I beat you." She eyes him seriously as her eyebrow lifts.

Ash scoffs back at her. "Absolutely not! My loud pants would ruin the effect."

Ivy laughs so hard she snorts, picturing the idea. "We will rematch to challenge that."

"Know that you will lose again." The crooked grin on his face instigates an emotional roller coaster as she watches him. Even so, Ivy won't let him think that he has the upper hand. "Ego much?"

"Hey!" he cries, smiling. "My ego is just fine!"

Yes, it is! she thinks as she pictures what he looked like naked the other night. Her face burns red, and her body responds even as she tries to stifle the thought.

Ivy smiles as she gets an idea for retaliation, "I bet I can frazzle your ego in less than ten seconds," she tells him.

"How much?" he asks as he considers the challenge.

Ivy shrugs. "How about a share-size bag of candy-covered chocolate?" she offers, eyeing the unopened bag of treats next to Ash.

"Really?" he asks as he cocks a perfect eyebrow at her.

Ivy smiles, knowing that she is no good at hiding her scheme. "Yipp."

Ash leans towards her as he assumes his general face and says, with no emotion at all, "Go for it."

Ivy jumps on him in a blur and rubs her hand through his hair in a noogie, then hops back off and sizes up his expression. Ash eyes her with an annoyed look that screams frazzled, and she giggles, holding out her hand.

Ash reaches over to the bag of candy and hands it to her without blinking. Ivy flutters her eyelashes as she smiles and snags the bag from his hand. Then she smells his arousal like a slap to her senses. *He is turned on!* She feels her eyes flash red and blushes so deeply that she knows she couldn't possibly hide her flush.

She tosses the bag onto the table and says sheepishly, "Guess we have to share."

If Ivy couldn't smell the heat coming off him in waves, she would never have known that it was there. Ash hides everything he thinks with a perfect mask even as she looks towards the bathroom. *I need an ice shower and quick. How is he hiding it so well?*

Ash's phone starts ringing in his pocket. He reaches in and pulls it out, annoyed as he sees the name of the caller.

"Who's Lola?" Ivy asks as she sees the name sprawled across the screen.

Ash turns red as he shoves the phone back into his pocket. "A female my mother set me up with. She is a crazy creature. Like worse than Nova."

Ivy smiles with a thought. "Want me to take care of it?"

"What are you going to do that I haven't already tried?" He sits forward with a questioning expression.

"If she's as crazy as you say, she will call back. Let me answer. The more pissed off she gets, the longer it will take for her to call you again. And if she does, you can bring it to my room, and I will piss her off again until she gets the picture."

Ivy shrugs, smiling. "Or you can keep telling her it's not happening, and she can keep calling you."

Ash digs the ringing phone from his pocket as it starts again and hands it to Ivy. "It's not like you could make it worse than it already is."

She pushes the answer spot on the phone and makes her voice as sultry as possible. "Mm, hello?" She watches Ash gulp and feels a butterfly in her stomach as she looks into his eyes, then takes a deep breath and feigns the enthusiasm she has witnessed from rivals in the past.

The shocked gasp of the woman named Lola on the other line makes Ivy smile. "Is Ash there?" Lola asks.

"Yes, but he's busy," Ivy giggles. "Stop that, baby!" she says not exactly to Lola and clears her throat. "He's really not in the—position—to talk right now."

Ivy looks Ash directly in the eye and smiles with Lola evidently speechless. Ivy feels her eyes flash to red as she smells Ash's arousal become stronger at her innuendo.

"Is there anything I can do for you?" Ivy asks into the phone. "I can give him your name when he is—finished." Ivy winks at Ash and stifles a giggle as he shifts again. *You should get him hot enough that he will kiss you!* she thinks.

"My name is Lola. His girlfriend. And I am going to kick your tramp ass."

Ivy smiles brightly at Lola's threat.

Ivy hitches her breath a few times as she remembers all the fornication she's heard from the neighbors in Lesai. Then she sighs delightedly.

"Mmmmm yes. I think getting hurt sounds good right about now." Ivy ruffles a pillow over the phone to make it sound as if she dropped the phone.

Oh, Ash . . . ," Ivy whispers with a feigned gasp.

"Asshole!" shouts Lola as she hangs up.

Reaching over to the bag of candy, Ivy opens it and pops a few tiny morsels into her mouth, then places the bag on the table.

"How long have you been playing chess?" Ivy asks to change the subject as she sucks the coating off the candy in her mouth.

"Hang on. I need to use the restroom," Ash announces as he stands up, his back ramrod straight, and heads in the direction of the bathroom.

Ivy giggles as she asks, "Uncomfortable?"

Ash shakes his head. "Not at all." Ash remains in the bathroom for a full ten minutes, then returns to sit at the chess board again.

Ivy's eyes flash red as she meets his eye, and the air leaves the room as she smells what had happened in her bathroom. *Did he really just take care of business in my bathroom?* Ivy can't help the urge to lift her nose into the air as the erotic scent of him surrounds her.

Ash has total control as he sits across from her and picks up the bag of candy. "Let's say that I learned how to play when the queen was still the ferz," He says, as he arranges the pieces back to starting positions.

Distracted from her thoughts, Ivy scrunches up her face and cocks her head. "What's a ferz?"

Laughing, Ash answers, "The king's counselor."

"Ahh. So when the chess queen was thought to be worth something, they changed the name," she says disdainfully.

Ash straightens up a little bit. "Actually, it was a romantic idea. The queen had little power at all. It was the weakest piece."

"Oh, Elemental Mother!" Ivy whispers in exasperation. "What is it with the patriarchal bullshit that every race has?" she asks herself more than she asks Ash, but recognizing his silence, she says, "Don't tell me you're one of them."

She sits further back in the armchair and stares at the ceiling.

Ash laughs a little. "If you knew even a few of the women I have met in my life, you would understand that there is a reason for it."

She looks at him, but he avoids eye contact.

"So, all females need to be protected because some of them are idiots?" Ivy scoffs.

Ash shakes his head. "I didn't say that."

"But that's what you meant, isn't it?" she asks, trying to get him to admit it. "Women are the weaker sex."

"Nope." he says as he finishes setting up the board and sits back to look her in the eyes. "What I meant is that the women I have met don't give anyone a reason to believe they can do for themselves."

Ivy ponders and looks away. The intensity of his gaze seems to say something she doesn't want to think about. She isn't in the loop of some unspoken conversation of his. "How many women have you met exactly?" she asks.

Ash gapes. "What do you mean by that?"

"I mean, how many women have you met who are unable to help themselves in any way, shape, or form?" Ivy persists. "How about your mother, maybe sisters if you have any? By your words, you are condemning them as well. After all, the women you have met don't give you a reason, right?"

Ash looks shocked. "My mother and three sisters, raised by my mother, are different entirely," he says, gritting his teeth.

Ivy looks away. "I figured as much."

"You have never met my family, so how would you know?" Ash demands. She can see that he is fuming.

"That's the point, Ash. I don't know them and would never judge them based on their gender. You don't know every woman of the Pale Race, so making assumptions on the entire population of females is bullshit. So say, for instance, the only male I have ever met is Baz . . ." Ash reacts, and she continues. ". . . For instance . . . he is the only male I have ever met of the Pale Race. Me being a female who can kick his ass would determine that all the males are equally weak, correct?"

Ash stares at her in stunned silence.

Ivy continues, and knowing that he hears her, she speaks as calmly as her nerves permit. "I have known many women in Lesai who, like Pale Race females, make a problem for self-sufficient women." She sighs. "Hell, if I had stayed in Lesai, not that it was even a possibility for me, obviously, I would have been married to a man of prominence six months after I came to maturity. Here, I have to become pregnant with two babies by the time I am fifty, or I will have a baby by force. The only thing I will get to choose is if I want magical or natural conception!"

Ivy looks up as she hears a growl. She cocks an eyebrow and laughs. "What's wrong with you?"

"Nothing," he says too quickly for her to believe him.

Looking away as she pulls her feet nearer her in the chair, she says, "Like I said at the waterfall, you have a choice. But please know this before you make your decision. I can take care of myself, and I always will. It's who I am. I won't need coddling and entertainment, because I have learned over the years to rely only on myself."

"I am well aware that I have a choice," Ash says quietly.

Ivy gulps, staring at a boot lace as she messes with it. "I know that I can never expect to be happy in life. I made the decision when my dad told me about the match not to allow myself to hope." She takes a deep breath, steeling herself, having never before said what she would say next.

"Hope creates disappointment," she asserts. "I would much rather be fighting and enjoying the things in life that make me happy than worry about the prospect of love. I will do what I must should you decide to marry me as the Pale Council wishes."

In the silence after her solemn words, Ivy stands up, brushes the wrinkles out of her clothes. and heads to her bedroom. Shutting the door softly, she leaves Ash in the living room of her suite to think.

As the first hiccups of sorrow start, she hits the play button on the beautiful violin music she received from Ash. She weeps into a pillow and knows that the well of sadness penetrating to the bone will never be gone. Her stifled sobs awaken her heart to a different type of pain she never before allowed herself to consider.

After having sworn off the idea of hope for her whole life, she realizes that her feelings are exactly that—hopes and dreams crushed before she even knew they were there.

Balancing Act

Training Room

Ash broke inside when Ivy told him she will do what he wants even if she will never be happy. *The girl doesn't even allow herself to have hope for a future because she believes she's unnatural.* Unnerving protection for her bursts from him as he remembers her unwavering defense of women. *Life and the world have treated her so poorly that it's no wonder she feels as she does,* he thinks. The realization of her pain hits him like a lightning strike as he recognizes from her demeanor how, with years of training, she held her temper about patriarchy by carefully hiding her resentment.

He feels like a kicked puppy as he thinks about her bringing up his mother and sisters, every one of them completely capable of fending off anyone who wishes her ill will. In fact, without more than a sharp tongue, the beautiful hybrid put him in his place and made him realize he's a sexist.

It royally pisses him off that if she had remained in Lesai, she would have been married off before even experiencing anyone who cares for her. But nothing compares to another male touching her soft skin to breed her, should they not marry. As he'd sat there watching her refusing to meet his eyes and hugging her long unblemished legs, he felt insanely compelled to touch her. Melancholy echoes in his mind and causes everything in him to reach for her. Considering the moment, he refuses to let her believe herself worthless even as he attempts to figure out his own feelings.

Having never hoped for love himself, he understands how she feels even though she told him she would never need him to care for her. Ever. *I can't allow her to think she isn't worth love.* His heart bleeds as it refuses to listen to his mind. *Be careful. She is the only woman capable of breaking you.*

Not knowing how to ask the important question. he paces around the roof. He has to show not only Ivy her worth but also show the world.

Whether his mind has caught up or not, he freaks out at the knowledge that she is his fated mate. The prospect that the Pale Council could predict the happiness of two people born more than three hundred years apart seems ridiculous to him. Then again, rendering the point moot, his mother and father are almost five hundred years apart,. His mother had also waited for his father to be born because—just as the council had forced Ash to wait—they had also forced his mother to.

She sealed his fate when she stood up, poised and elegant from years of royal training in decorum. Without a backwards glance or a tear falling, she had walked straight into the bedroom and soundlessly shut the door. The Lindsey Sterling compact disc he'd bought her had begun to play as he heard the unmistakable hiccup of a woman in pain. That she would try to hide sadness from him wreaked havoc on all the assumptions he had ever made over the years.

Steeling himself for the phone call he was about to make, he hits the redial button and holds his breath. The phone went to what would be a voicemail if it were set up, and he sighs. *She must be busy.*

Flashing back to the Lola phone call and as heat surges to his face, Ash waits a few minutes. He remembers her face burning bright as she smelled what he had taken care of in her bathroom. Her eyes had flashed red with lust when he emerged, and he again burns for her. It was unavoidable after hearing her fake an orgasm right in front of him, her eyes closing to roll up in imitation of bliss that had sealed his fate.

God, I need her in my life. I need to show her that there is more to life than duty.

Unable to put the call off until later, he refreshes his resolve. Taking a deep breath, he makes his first step to get through to Ivy and make her feel the love he wants to give her. Council be damned, he's going to fulfill his fate even after more than three hundred years of fighting it. He slams his thumb back onto the redial image as, determined, he holds his phone to his ear.

"Hello?" he hears, smiling at the confusion he detects in her voice. His untraceable number can make for a lot of fun conversations when someone does not expect a phone call.

"Um, hi. Queen Diannicalyn," Ash says, smiling as he tries to throw her off.

Confusion, Calyn asks, "How did you get this number?"

"Are you alone?" he inquires in the creepiest voice he can muster.

He can hear her heart picking up pace. "Yes."

"Good. How are you doing, Spitfire?" he says with a grin.

"Asher!" she retorts as she at once recognizes the nickname. "How have you been?"

He can't help but smiling as he tells her, "Well, I am general of the Protectors now!"

"You are very good at chess, so that isn't a surprise to me," Calyn replies.

Quiet for a moment, Ash then says, "There is something I need to ask you."

"Go ahead."

Ash clears his throat and Calyn's heart picks up a beat. "I have met Ivy. She is definitely as proficient in fighting as you are . . ."

Calyn contemplates.

"I would like your permission to ask your daughter's hand in marriage."

Silence on the other end of the line vexes him. "Calyn?"

"I'm here," she replies, and Ash can hear her grin.

Ash laughs. "Are you trying to put me through hoops?"

Calyn coughs to cover up her laughter. "Do you think that she will say yes?"

Not knowing the answer, Asher blows out a breath. "I know that she will say yes out of duty because she doesn't believe that she is worthy. This is a problem. I don't want her to feel that there is nothing between us."

"There is more?" Calyn asks, breathless.

He almost fumbles his response but blurts, "I have felt the pull of a lifemate more times than I can count."

"Are you sure? Because that can be a finicky thing. Some swear they feel it and never get a mark and others get a mark and have never felt a thing, Ash."

"I am positive. Every time our bodies touch, even without expecting it, the jolt happens. I swear, the other night swimming, it was more like a bolt of lightning. Hard core." He enjoys something like the drama he imagines a woman feels during a good gossip session. "And what the hell is up with the territorial stuff? It's weird as hell!"

Calyn thinks for a moment, then asks, "Do you think you can get her to understand that duty is not the reason you are proposing?"

Ash wonders if it's possible for him to get Ivy to accept his truth, and replies, "I don't know. She is so damn stubborn! It's not the normal stubborn of a kid not eating their peas, either. It's the stubborn on the inside that she hides extremely well."

Calyn bursts out laughing, and Ash feels like an ass as he starts chuckling, too. "Do you know how helpless you sound, Ash?" she asks between laughs.

"You have no idea what I am going through right now," Ash says, desperate to get her to understand his predicament.

"Yeah, right! How do you think I have felt for the past two decades? Ever since she began talking, it was nothing but fighting and stubborn arguments about what she was willing to endure as a royal. You have no idea how many people our girl has bitten!"

Ash pictures a little Ivy running around stabbing people with wooden swords with a grin, the thought turning to pain at the thought of her biting him. Changing the subject, he says. "Well, if you are so experienced in all things Ivy, you should clue me in."

"I don't know!" Calyn says with perfected sarcasm. "Hearing how much you are squirming kind of makes a mother proud!"

"Spitfire! You're mean!" Ash complains melodramatically as he shakes off the feeling of her teasing.

"Let's try to figure out a way to get her to understand the actual situation, shall we?" Calyn retorts.

Ash smiles hopefully.

The Terrors will love this!

Ash stands in the middle of the revamped room as his men gather together to see it. He holds the note Ivy left on his door the day before. In sprawling calligraphy, it invites him to meet her in the dining room.

He watches as Soren, Baz, and Jynx pile slowly into the room and look around with wide eyes.

He smiles in satisfaction when he realizes that Ivy has created a sparring room that weirdly enough also includes different acrobatic equipment to work with as well.

A few balance beams placed throughout the room create obstacles. Rock-climbing holds in various places along the walls go toward the soaring ceilings. The floor and lower walls sport giant ergonomic mats with speakers mounted around the entire room.

He sees Jynx's face as she gawks around. Finding a mace, she begins spinning it as if testing it out. Her Russian accent would have betrayed her obvious love for the dramatic, yet she'd mastered English centuries before.

Ash knows that he has work to do, and nothing will stop him from making Ivy feel her worth. Ash wants to punch someone in the face at the thought of a forced conception for Ivy. Even without physical contact, he wants to hurt anyone who thinks of procreating with his lifemate. Even if there were males who would be okay with procreating with a hybrid who can kill them, Ash will never be able to live with himself if he lets her go.

He can only imagine the loneliness she has felt throughout her life. She has always known her differences from others around her and never knew why she is different. Without her ever telling him, he can see it manifested in the room he's standing in. He decides that she has used fighting to block out any sorrow in her life as she has focused all her energy, even while starving, on the future.

Completely out of his element, Baz stands in the corner. Always having been more of a squire than anything, Baz does not have the need for violence in his blood. Soren has always appreciated Baz's mind as he knew how to speak and act in situations where Soren would lose his shit.

Ash nevertheless worries about any male's motives, warrior or not.

Wearing a long-sleeved shirt and pair of tight leggings, Ivy strolls into the room. Ash observes that Baz has no interest, as he's scrolling his phone.

Baz's evident indifference piques Ash's interest. *Why is he like a puppy if he isn't interested in her?* Ash wonders. An unrelenting gut feeling pulls at him as he watches Baz closer. Baz begins typing without even looking up. *He's probably texting another chick,* Ash thinks with annoyance.

Ash holds firm in his belief that Ivy should be with someone who loves her, no matter what other motives they may share. *That's me!* he realizes, startling himself with his own thoughts.

Ash feels a territorial pull as he thinks about Baz's interest, even though Baz at the moment seems indifferent, and Ash freaks out some more.

Ivy grins ear to ear as she absorbs compliments. The tight outfit, meanwhile, does nothing to alleviate the tension Ash has dealt with for weeks.

"Anyone want to break her in?" Ivy asks wiggling her eyebrows holding two staffs. Ash recognizes the design of them but can't place the source.

Soren steps towards Ivy without a second thought, and she smiles. Tossing him one of the staffs, she giggles like a little girl.

Ash smiles to himself as Jynx attempts to sneak up behind Ivy with the mace, baring her fangs in a way that would make most Protectors cower. Ivy senses the movement and smiles as she squares them both up. "Your funeral!"

I need to teach her a better catch phrase! He thinks as he watches them spar. He happily stands on the sidelines as his girl jumps onto a balance beam. Ivy runs as the other two try with a staff or mace to knock her off the slim piece of wood. She taunts them as she moves, inviting more fury in their effort to take her out.

Ash opens his phone and opens the wireless network feature. He figures she installed speakers for a reason in the room. Sure enough, he finds the label sparring room among locations for available devices. As he turns the volume all the way down, he considers the best music to throw her off balance. He decides that some I Prevail will make for good sensory training.

He watches Ivy cartwheel off the end of the beam then jump to catch hand grips on the wall. With one hand, she fends off Soren's attacks, and with the other, she feels for the next handhold.

She's cheating again, thinks Ash. *No one can balance on just feet at that angle, Pale Race, ancient or otherwise, unless using elemental magic to combat gravity.*

Ash giggles, feeling like a child as he presses play on his phone. He turns the sound up a notch, and she immediately looks panicked. Losing her focus, Ivy slams into the mats covering the walls as the elemental magic flees from her consciousness.

Standing up and shaking her head, she waits for her attackers to come at her again. Ash turns the music up to two bars.

Ivy looks directly at him and smiles. Her inner warrior makes her push herself, intent on getting past her weaknesses and not failing.

Ash knows she isn't simply working on sparring without her swords but also getting herself used to loud noises. Her resilience fills him up with pride. It swells in his chest as he watches her make progress in the match. She jumps up to reach a set of uneven bars he hadn't realized were there. Observing that they'd be useless unless training for a confrontation in an alleyway, he knows they're good for strength training.

All this stuff must be what she's trained with in Lesai, he realizes. *Jeez!*

She spins herself over the bar and begins walking it like a tight rope.

Ash turns the music up to three. Her eyes go wide, and she wavers slightly. After a moment of swaying, she loses her balance and falls. Ash runs under where she falls and catches her, glad he was fast enough. She would have landed on her face otherwise.

Aware of the jolt they share, Ash sets her down. *This woman will be mine.*

Ash looks around himself and sees Baz still texting. He hadn't even noticed that Ivy almost broke her face. The fact makes Ash happy because Ivy sees it too, but it also pisses him off because those who care should be vigilant, not to mention that the goal for anyone who knows about her is protection.

"You good?" Ash asks Ivy after he shuts the music off.

Ivy nods, putting her fingers on her temples. "Yeah, that noise is horrible!" she complains. "I've been using rain sounds when I am training to stop the sensitivity, and it works just fine."

"Baby steps only go so far," Ash smiles.

Soren looks at her. "You have been working on the noise issue?"

Ivy nods again. "Yes, but the killer migraines I get suck."

Ash looks at Ivy sympathetically as he admires the staff in Soren's hand. "This is awesome, by the way. Where did you buy this?"

Ivy laughs. "It was a gift."

"It's a damn good gift," Ash says. "So why a sparring room?"

Ivy looks around her smiling. "Because fighting is who I am, and I don't want to see nature's gifts go to waste. All the furniture went to human . . ." she looks to her father for help.

". . . charities," Soren finishes for her.

"Yeah, those."

Ash bursts with something he can't quite figure out. Ivy cares about people other than herself, whether Pale Race, ancient, or not. Ash admires Ivy's reluctance to sit in the limelight long as she walks out of the room with a smile on her flushed face. She evidently doesn't recognize her attributes, only her downfalls, he concludes.

I feed you!

Easy Cheese

She drinks deep, loving the feel of warm blood entering her stomach and branching out as it travels through her arteries to be absorbed by her body. She stops as she feels Nova's blood get sweeter than she likes.

She pulls away and looks up at the ceiling in ecstasy as the pure divine power of blood invigorates her body. Nova's vein makes her soar with more energy than any bottled blood ever could. The nutrients are fresher in that manner of feeding.

Before she can control her actions, she glances over at Ash, and sees the hungry look in his face. The hunger isn't for the blood she's drinking, though. She smells his arousal and licks her lips. The arousal is for her, and the painful pulsation running through her body tells her exactly what has happened since she first laid eyes on Ash.

Her body screams for divine release as she straddles her meal. She fights the urge to touch herself as blood surges to her abdomen.

Ash stalks toward her and crouches to her level as her eyes widen in surprise. He inhales her scent and takes possession of her mouth in the most feral of ways. He nips her tongue, causing her body to pulse more rapidly. She feels his fingers right where she needs them, and she climaxes within moments as he stares into her eyes. She wants so much more.

Ivy awakes to absolute euphoria in her loins from her intoxicating dream followed by a panic attack. The combination nearly puts her in her grave. *What the hell was that?*

She gets out of bed as fast as she can and jumps into an ice-water shower to cool herself down.

243

Ivy looks down at the book she is scrubbing and peripherally watches Ash. He is reading on the first floor of the library while she works on the second floor. The book in his hand must intrigue him, because every once in a while, he smiles or frowns at something he reads. Her eyes find his every move even as she does everything in her power not to stare at him.

She smells the crackers after he opens them, and her stomach starts to rumble with hunger. Perking up, she peeks over the edge of the banister. He squeezes a tube with a nozzle and yellow stuff comes out onto the cracker. Cocking her head, she sniffs the air, and her body follows the scent. Without volition, she walks down the stairs and sits on the couch beside him.

With a crooked grin, he asks, "Can I help you?"

"What is that?" She motions to the tube on the table.

He laughs. "Cheese."

"In that?" She scrunches her nose in horror.

He nods. "The humans invented the tube so it won't go bad as quickly."

"Hmm." Ivy salivates as the smell lingers.

"Would you like to try some?" He reaches for a cracker and the cheese, handing them to her. Ivy tips the tube over, and nothing happens. She shakes it, but still nothing.

Ash laughs and takes the can and cracker from her. "You put pressure on the tip, and it comes out."

He holds his hand out for her to open her mouth, and she does, tasting the cracker on her tongue and then playfully nipping his finger. She falls back dramatically into the pillows of the couch. "Oh, my Elemental Mother!" she purrs. "That's delicious!"

Then she smells his arousal and comes up short. "Why are you staring?"

Ash smiles, "You are totally adorable."

"Feed me more?" Ivy pleads.

Ash shakes his head. "No. You know how to do it now. Good practice for you getting your own."

She pops her lower lip out in imitation of the children in Lesai.

Ash gives in, puts more cheese on a cracker, and feeds it to her. "God, you are incredible," Ash says with a sigh, then looks away quickly. His ears turn bright pink, and Ivy realizes that he's said something he hadn't intended to.

Ivy smiles slyly. "Thank you."

"Anytime."

Ivy grabs the crackers from the table and makes another for herself with cheese. "Where can I get more of these?"

Laughing, Ash opens his mouth for the one she's made. Ivy pouts but feeds it to him. Between chews, he speaks with his mouth full of cracker, "I'll have some sent up to your room."

"Thank you!" Ivy replies with her mouth stuffed full.

"What are you doing up there?"

Ivy shrugs. "Cleaning the books."

He glances up to the area she was standing and back at her with interest. "Is there a reason behind that, or do you enjoy cleaning?"

"Books are a blessing," She smiles to herself. "They shouldn't go to waste or be forgotten." Ash looks at her quizzically. "Trees feel pain, too."

He looks stunned, "Really?"

Ivy rolls her eyes. "Are they alive?"

"Well, yes."

"Just because you can't hear the sorrow of the earth doesn't mean it isn't there." She pauses, assessing whether she should explain.

Thinking that he might understand, she continues. "Do you remember the day you saw my oak tree?"

He nods. "That day was the most painful time I have ever meditated. You see—" she checks to make sure there isn't anyone around and lowers her voice "—the Ancients are made of magic, too. We draw from the Elemental magic, filtering it as we meditate. The magic that we absorb in Lesai is cultivated and pure magic. The magic in the outside world is horrific in comparison. It took five solid meditations for me to get to a point where I can draw without the pain and release without the feeling of defeat. That day when I meditated, I learned that certain parts of the earth are worse off than others."

Ash considers, then asks, "So you were crying because it was painful?"

Ivy nods. "When I was a child, there was a handpicked sect of Ancients whose sole purpose was to pull the hurt from the earth and filter it. But from what I have been able to see and feel, that sect of Ancients is either long gone or not doing their job. No one has cleansed the area around Duneskil aside from me in hundreds of years."

He looks down, brooding, then meets her eyes, "You can feel that?"

Ivy nods, tears welling in her eyes as she realizes he isn't judging her for what she's told him. Refusing to look like one of the sappy, pouty women she has observed on TV as well as in Lesai, she changes the subject.

"What are you reading?" she asks.

"An epic," Ash replies, jumping slightly as if startled.

"Ooh! What about?"

He turns a little red but smiles all the same, "Fate. They are fated to marry for the good of the race. They fight it tooth and nail inside as well as out until they realize they've fallen in love. They marry, then discover that they are actually lifemates."

"I've read about the term lifemates!" Ivy exclaims. "What makes it so special? For the life of me, I can't get more than just the phrase from any of the books I've read." *Maybe he can tell me some more about it.*

Ash's eyes send sparks at her as his blush deepens and she smells his arousal. "I don't feel comfortable having a birds-and-bees talk right now."

He shifts in his seat, cluing Ivy in on just how much the question affected him.

"Oh, sorry." Her face scalds red as she looks at her feet.

"There is no need to be sorry. It's one of those things that you don't really talk about with just anyone."

Ivy nods. Standing up, she grabs two more crackers without cheese before heading back up to the second floor. She can feel Ash's eyes on her back as she goes. She wonders if there could ever be anything between them. The question hangs in the air as she continuously debates whether to marry the man she is supposed to or, better yet, whether he will decide he wants to marry her.

She hears Baz on the first floor calling, "Have you seen Ivy?"

Ash takes a breath as if to answer, and quickly she hollers, "Up here."

"I really don't understand why you waste your time," Baz grumbles to her as he heads up the stairs.

Ivy laughs sarcastically, annoyed with his consistent complaints about her choices. "What is time when you have forever?" Ivy sighs as he shrugs. "You didn't get it the first time, so I don't think you will right now, either."

"What is that supposed to mean?" His chest puffs up a little bit. Ivy wants to pop a hole in his alter ego but really doesn't want the drama. Instead, she huffs, "Only that repeating myself is futile."

"And that is—?" His clueless expression confirms for Ivy just how unintelligent the male is.

"Pointless," she says with a sigh, thinking, *Just as it is futile for me to even converse with you.*

He shrugs, brushing off the diss that went over his head. "I was thinking of going out tonight to see a movie. Will you be my date?"

Hell no! She sees Ash look up at Baz furiously and smiles a little bit as she debates whether to say yes to get a response out of him, but she knows better. "We have been through this already, and I have training."

"How about tomorrow night?"

Ivy eyes him with suspicion. "You just asked about tonight.

Looking at his feet, he shifts. "I want to take you on a date. I don't care when it is."

"I train every night, Baz. It's my job to make sure that I am ready to go with the Terrors when the time comes," she explains. She can see Ash relax a little.

Baz scoffs, "You aren't even getting paid. You can take a night off."

"I've never been paid," Ivy shrugs. "Protecting people for money is selfish and rude."

Baz looks like he has seen a ghost. "Seriously?" His cockiness reminds Ivy of a Pale Race version of Finn. "I can take care of you." She laughs as she sees Ash, pissed, put his book down. *Hmm!* "That's not necessary, Baz."

"But I want to," he pouts.

Ivy looks at him as if he has two heads and says, "I don't want you to."

Baz shifts his weight again. Ivy watches him closely as his anger contorts his features. "Why, Ivy? What is so wrong with needing help?"

"Nothing. But I don't want your help."

"Why are you so difficult?" Baz groans as he takes a step towards her.

Ivy laughs, her annoyance clear in her features. The royal "I don't want you to know what I am thinking" flies out the window as she becomes furious. "That I am self-sufficient, automatically means I am being difficult?" Ivy asks angrily as she shakes her head and returns to cleaning books.

"No. But no matter what I do, you refuse to give me the time of day!" Baz yells almost in her face.

Her eyes flash to red as Ivy unleashes. "Because I'm not interested in more than friends, you ass!" She throws the towel down and lifts herself to her full height.

"Why are you such a bitch about it?" Baz booms and cowers as he tries to hold his ground.

Ivy hears a growl from downstairs, and she grins for a moment as she debates whether to allow Ash to make a move. She decides against it, and not wanting more drama, shakes her head at Ash who sits on the edge of the couch, menace in his glare, the look of doom on his face, aimed directly at Baz. Ivy can almost hear Ash begging her to let him take Baz out.

Ivy snaps her eyes back to Baz. "I have no obligation to you," she reminds him. "You are under me in station." She knows she has pulled the royalty card, but she doesn't care. Enough is enough.

"I *feed* you!" he yells.

Aggravated, Ivy laughs. "You keep saying that, but actually, I am perfectly capable of feeding myself. I don't need a lap dog constantly bringing me the newspaper in exchange for a treat—the treat being me!"

Baz throws his hands in the air. "Fine!"

"Glad we understand each other now!" she yells down the stairs at his back.

Looking like a kicked dog, he turns back as he realizes his job. "Do you want me to bring you someone?"

"Actually, no. I release you from that duty, Baz. I just ate."

Ivy winks at Ash from the banister. Baz turns bright red with rage as, fuming, he stomps out of the library.

Ivy sits down on the floor. "Elemental Mother, that jerk will force me to bite him one of these nights!"

Ivy hears a growl and looks through the bars of the banister to see Ash, also pissed, stalking out of the room. He has squared his shoulders so tensely she can see the ripples through his shirt. *If only I could see those muscles in the sunlight.* She shocks herself and smooshes the thought down: *Shut up, Ivy.*

The books call her, so she gets back to her mission.

Only halfway there.

Don't do it!

K.O.

Ash tries to get the upper hand with Ivy, but her regimen of practice in martial techniques places him on the defense more often than not. He pushes forward for a few blows only for her to push him right back as she uses her other senses to gain ground. Her footwork and balance, better than anyone else's he has ever met, messes with him as he spars. When he considers her soft-soled boots, he wonders if her shoe choice gives her the advantage.

When lightning strikes nearby, she falters. The bolt hits a tree so close that she covers her ears and squeezes her eyes shut during his strike. Ash panics as his assault sends her sailing over a hedge. He immediately throws his practice sword to the ground and jumps over the hedge to check on her. "Ivy!"

Worry streaking through his body, he scoops her up and shakes her a little.

Her eyes open slowly. "What happened?"

"Lightning," he says with a half smile. "You okay?"

Ivy nods, her lids low.

He feels a tingling everywhere he touches her, and he knows by her face that she feels it, too. She stares at her own hand as she lifts it to his face, cups his jaw, and sends the jittering shock of the life-mate jolt down his throat. Every fiber of his being tells him to kiss her, her face within inches of his own. *Don't let her go*, he thinks, his arms tightening.

But against everything, he sets her back down, nevertheless thinking, *You will be mine.*

"Good," he says. "I've got some stuff I need to take care of."

He makes sure she's steady before walking back into the compound. He refuses to see the hurt he knows she wears on her features. Storming out of the library the previous night was bad form, but to consider biting Baz—even if it was because she was mad—made him lose all sense of reality.

"Ash?"

He turns to her and hides his reaction from their touch the best he can. "Why is it," she asks, "when we touch, I feel like lightning is about to strike?"

Ash feels the air leave his lungs. He calmly draws in a deep breath to speak. "You should look it up. I have somewhere I need to be."

Calyn, you had better be right about this! he thinks, pissed and in serious need of a cold shower before he leaves for the bank. Even if Calyn had been right about the food, it didn't stop him from wondering if her plan will work.

ᐁᐁ ᐁᐁ ᐁᐁ

He'd called his dad when he heard Ivy talking to Baz last night. It had never occurred to him that no one was paying her for her service as one of the Terrors even if employment justifies her training with them. Only a select few have permission to know her hybrid status. He also talked with Soren, who also hadn't realized Ivy didn't receive pay, so the two of them got paperwork together to get her human documents. Ash just needed to get to the bank and open her a checking account in order to make her pay from the previous month and a half retroactive from his personal account. As of the previous week, the council's payroll listed her officially as a Protector. She would have her own money going forward.

Ash's hackles rise as he looks out the window and sees Ivy talking to one of the males who lives in the compound. "She is mine," Ash growls as Ivy giggles about something the male says to her as she glances up at the window, smiling. Loud enough for him to hear, she asks, "Want to come up to my room and play chess, Robert?"

Robert gives her an enthusiastic nod, and Ivy blushes. Ash can feel blood drain from his body as raw frustration balls his hands into fists. He forces himself away from the window to sit next to the adjoining door and wait to hear her enter her suite.

The chess pieces shuffle around as Robert and Ivy set the chess board up for a game. *You are torturing yourself,* Ash thinks. *Get out of here, you idiot, or you are going to kill her meal.* Ash shakes his head to get rid of his brain's prattle and listens intently.

"Have you ever played before, Robert?"

"A few times with my grandmother, ages ago."

"Oh." The defeated sound of her voice upsets Ash a little. *I'm going to have to rematch her soon so she stops asking other dudes to play with her.*

The male's voice becomes hopeful as he says, "You could always teach me to play. Or better yet, I could teach you to play some games."

More shuffling and then Ivy's shocked gasp. "Robert! I am not interested in that! I asked you to play chess!"

"I thought you wanted something that I'm a little better at playing."

About to rip the door open, Ash's hand hovers over the knob as the tenor of Robert's voice grates into him. Fumes spew from Ash's ears as he tries to rein in his temper. *She is not yours yet. You have absolutely no claim on her. Get a grip!*

He pulls his hand back from the door and pulls back to punch the door frame when he hears, "You will fill this bottle with your blood, then drink this blood bag, remembering nothing of our time together other than losing a game of chess to Ivy."

The monotone "I will remember nothing" echoes back as Ash hears the hiss of the male biting himself and blood leaking steadily into the bottle. When it stops, the hiss of reopening the wound occurs repeatedly followed by the blood bag opening. The obvious slurp of the attached intravenous port sends his mind back to thoughts of Ivy drinking from himself and not a bottle.

The blood bag drops onto the floor. and the hallway door to her room opens and then shuts.

"This shit blows," he hears Ivy huff from the other side of the door as he imagines her picking the blood bag up from the floor. "I'm sticking to chicks from now on. At least they don't try to kiss me every time. Ew! Like I would really want to kiss him!"

Ash smiles. He wants to punch Robert in the face, but it makes him happy that she makes the decision to only feed from females on her own. His stomach turns at the idea that she will have another male's blood in her veins when he drinks from her. *She will be filled with only my blood, and I will be filled with hers. She is mine.*

"Stupid Ash and his refusal to acknowledge anything," she rants in the other room. "What is he getting at? Watches me and seems like he wants to kiss me one minute and then walks away like a hurt puppy, Elemental Mother! What did I do to deserve this?"

Ash listens closer, but the tub filling with water drowns out most sound. Wishing that he could be in that tub with her as she washes her body, he listens to her for the rest of the night. The thoughts that plague him are worse than any he has ever felt, and the pull of becoming one with her makes his blood burn.

She makes little sounds, and the quick movement of water turns his mind to the idea of her taking care of her own needs. Ash uses the images it projects to take care of himself even if what he hears is not what it seems to be.

🌱 🌱 🌱

The next evening, Ash hears the door slam to Ivy's bedroom. Not in the mood for anything after the night he's been having, he checks on the other part of his career.

The Terrors have been on recon missions for the past few nights, and from the compound, he can't do anything to help. He has orders to protect the hybrid before anything else. That means that his men get to go out into the night to fulfill all orders from the council. Unfortunately, the intel they've come up with isn't exactly matching up, and his orders demand that he stay. *Hopefully it will sort itself out.*

Ash opens his suite door to see Soren shaking his head, absolutely pissed. Ash looks at him like, "What the hell, man?" but takes a step back when the seriousness of Soren's anger shows. The glare coming from the man causes even Ash to wonder what the hell happened. The last time he had seen Soren that angry was almost a century ago.

"Is Ivy okay?" Ash asks.

Soren nods, but his face becomes even redder as he looks around at the heads poking out into the hallway.

Baz comes running down the hall in a panic, worry on his face. "What's happening?" he asks huffing and puffing.

What is he? A smoker? Jeez! Ash thinks sarcastically as he waits for Soren to answer. He glances at Baz and wonders why the male looks overly innocent. *Wait a minute.—*

"Who gave her the blood on her nightstand?" Soren demands. "Who gave her that damn blood?" he yells. He won't accept the silence as they try to figure out what's wrong.

Baz looks between the two of them as if they're idiots. "I did. I noticed that she was out before dawn, so I gave her some of my blood." still catching his breath, he has his fists on his hips in an attitude of "Why the hell is this a terrible thing?" Ash glances down the hall where a bunch of vampires look at each other in concern.

"Watch your mouth, Baz," Ash growls.

Soren glares at Baz. "I explicitly told you which blood to give her." The commander in him shows through to a degree Ash hasn't seen in years as he attempts to keep the situation away from other ears. *What the fuck is wrong with this dude?*

"Ivy told you the other night she doesn't want you feeding her anymore!" Ash yells at Baz. "She is perfectly capable of finding her own chess mates and her own blood bags."

"What's the difference? I figured that she would need something, and everyone else was asleep," Baz says shrugging. "It's not like I gave her pig's blood, man."

Ash silently freaks out. *She did not choose to have another male's blood in her veins.* Still growling, he exchanges glances with Soren, who's also growling. Ash gestures towards Baz. "Dude, Soren, this kid is fucking stupid."

To Baz he says, "How do you not realize what a direct order is? Do you have a brain, or are the cigarettes you must be smoking messing with the chemistry up there?"

Without hesitation, Baz tries to punch Ash in the face. Ash blocks his fist with one hand and smiles. "That is your one and only free shot, kid. Next time, you will live to regret it. When a royal gives you a direct order, you heed it well."

"Fuck off, you megalomaniac piece of shit. At least I feed her."

Ash simmers. "Anyone who feeds a female of the Pale Race their blood without her okaying the offer is a piece of shit, Dude. You fucked up. Don't treat me like shit because you're a goddamned idiot!" *I will feed her, asshole. But she will drink from my vein, not a cup!*

"You couldn't tell her how you feel even if it killed you, Ash. What makes you think that a female like her would want anything to do with a pussy?"

Ash snaps, punches Baz in the face, and floors him as he bares his teeth to Baz's throat. "The pussy is you, lowlife. Ivy is a royal, and you will treat her with the respect her title earns her. The fact that she is friends with the likes of you is testament to how amazing she is, not how worthy you are."

"Coward. Why don't you kill me? I know she would never give you the time of day," Baz spits back.

Ash laughs. "You know nothing about her. This is how I know you aren't worthy. She would kill you without a second thought if she felt you were worth the headache."

Soren puts a hand up, stopping the pissing match.

"Get up, now," Soren tells Baz. Ash lets him up only because Soren's commandership supersedes his own while they are on Duneskil's grounds. *Otherwise, the little shit would be in the ground rotting.*

"So why did she react that way?" Soren asks with obvious confusion lacing his tone.

"What way?" Ash and Baz say in unison, each glaring at the other.

"She reacts in a way that made me get the hell out of there! I wasn't supposed to witness that. I'm her father!"

Looks of realization cross the two faces. Ash's rage explodes as Baz's satisfaction puffs up his ego.

"I am going to kill you," Ash says to Baz with malice, getting into his face. Fearful, Baz backs up a step. *You aren't worthy of her!*

Soren interrupts again. "I am going to kill both of you if you don't shut the hell up!"

Ash accepts that Soren can think straight in the moment, so he backs off. Ivy would slap him if she heard the territorial thoughts running through his mind.

Soren runs his hand through his hair and says, "Shit! I can't go in there." He looks between the two of them and says, "Ash, I need you to go let her know what happened."

Ash shakes his head quickly. "You can't let me in that room."

"Why the hell not?" Soren asks Ash.

Ash looks at Baz and back to Soren. "I don't trust myself to be around her if she is as you say. There is too much of a pull."

Soren's eyes round out like quarters as astonishment sets in. "Are you sure?"

Ash nods.

Baz looks between Ash and Soren and asks, "What pull?"

Neither of the men acknowledge the question. Instead, Soren says to Baz, "Okay then. With that news, Baz, your dumb ass did this, and you can deal with it."

Pissed off, Soren nevertheless accepts Ash's admission. A look of understanding passes between Ash and Soren, and Baz sputters.

You just told your best friend that you feel the pull of a lifemate from his daughter while she is getting off on another man's blood. You are truly an idiot.

"If you are such a man, you should do it, Ash," Baz smirks. "Go tell her that she has felt bliss from the blood of an unworthy."

Ash grins as Soren punches Baz in the face. "You have disrespected my family for the last time. If you live past today and I find out you have forced yourself on my daughter again, you are out of this coven."

Covering his bloody nose, Baz glares at Soren.

"Am I understood?" Soren demands.

Baz nods, though daggers remain in his eyes.

"Good. Go fix this shit. Now!"

Baz straightens his back and forces himself to go to the door. Ash forces his back to the wall as Baz opens it. The scent of her orgasm sets him on fire, and immediately he goes rock solid. *I'm going to fuck that little shit up!* he swears, and he imagines how beautiful she must look as he hears her soft breaths as she sleeps.

Soren closes the door quickly.

"Damn it!" Ash slams his hand into the door frame.

Soren tries to say something to calm him down, but it's lost in the torment Ash faces within. He disappears back into his room, where he paces and worries about what it means.

Am I wrong? Is she really Baz's lifemate? Or does all Pale Race blood do that for her? What will that mean for her true lifemate? Will she ever have one? The questions keep pace with his steps and don't stop until he hears muffled voices in her suite. He puts his ear to the adjoining wall and listens.

Ash hears Ivy ask what happened. The conversation stays too quiet to hear until she begins screaming at Baz. Eventually he hears Ivy leave her room and slam her door.

Ash smiles a little at her temper giving himself a reprise of all the times her eyes have flashed red at him. He thanks the heavens that she wasn't okay that Baz tricked her to drink his blood.

He hears her go directly into her father's office with Baz right on her tail.

Ash leaves his room and waits in the hall for them until their footfalls come back up the stairs. He knows he must look like a kicked puppy, but refusing to miss a single detail of what's going on, he waits.

As Ivy rounds the corner, her tension radiates off her stiff muscles. Ash feels the rage wafting off her in waves as he avoids taking a step towards her. *That's it, baby. Kill him!* Ash chants to himself, the thoughts of giving her space completely forgotten. She meets Ash's eyes and looks to the floor quickly, seemingly embarrassed as she approaches the door to her room.

Ignoring Ash who is looming only a few feet away, Baz comes up behind her and touches her shoulder. She whips around. "What do you have to say that you haven't already?"

"Why won't you talk about this?" he asks sadly.

Ivy scoffs. "Because you fed me your blood behind my back. In every single book I have read about Pale Race customs, all of them say that no one can feed another their own blood without mutual consent. It is beyond wrong on all levels."

"You should be happy that I fed you!" he argues, one fist on his right hip and his left out to the side in exasperation.

"Are you kidding me?" Ivy demands as she backs him into the wall, her eyes flaring brilliantly.

"Your father just proved to you that we can be lifemates." he says, his eyes darting around. "Don't you want to know if that's true?" he asks, not looking into her bright red eyes.

"Why the hell would I want to know?" she inquires with menace. "I made myself perfectly clear—three times."

Baz frowns. "I made myself clear. too. I am in love with you, Ivy."

Ivy throws her hands up in the air in defeat. "Don't you get it? I don't care, Baz. You are a friend and that's all. Actually, you just proved to me that you aren't even that. I have read fifteen books on the history of the Pale Race over the last month and a half. Fifteen! Every single one of them that mentions lifemates says that you know it from the moment you meet. Whether you know exactly what the feeling you have is, it's there and it's strong—irresistible and there is nothing you can do to combat the feeling. Both sides feel it. Not just one. So, the answer is, no. I do not feel it."

Good girl. Ash says, beaming on the inside and remembering that she asked why she felt a jolt.

"But you have bliss from my blood!" Baz argues as he expects to render her reasoning null and void.

Ash watches with hope as she takes on the same stance she uses when sparring. "Don't you realize? I am so different that I can have bliss from anyone's blood."

She looks over at Ash. "Ash, will you give me some of your blood? I'm fairly sure that Soren's blood won't work in that manner because he's my father."

Ash sputters. "Um, sure, but I'm not going to right now. His blood is running through your veins."

She narrows her flashing-red eyes at him, and he puts his hands out defensively. "If you would like to drink my blood, Ivy, you will have to let me drink yours, too."

Her blush floors Ash as he becomes hard as a rock. In that moment, he knows she feels the pull of their bond. She glances down at the bulge in his pants, and he hears her heart skip a beat. *Thank God!*

Baz explodes. "You will let him drink your blood before you let me, even though you know that my blood gives you the bliss of a lifemate?"

Not looking away from Ash's eyes, Ivy nods. "The difference between you and Ash is that Ash would never even attempt to feed me his blood without me fully aware." Ivy glances shyly at Ash, who feels his heart soar with the thoughts of their union.

"Suit yourself, you stupid bit—"

Thwack goes Ivy's left foot as she reverse-roundhouse kicks Baz in the jaw. Her eyes disengage from Ash's only just before her foot strikes Baz.

Ash's jaw drops as she blurs with ancient speed. There had been no tell, no showing at all what she was about to do! *God, I want to take her right now!* He can focus on nothing but the white-hot heat that wafts at him as she makes the air move. *She reacts the same way I do,* his thoughts purr.

Without a second glance back at Baz or Ash, Ivy opens her door, walks in, and slams it.

Pondering what exactly she has or hasn't just agreed to do with him, Ash stands in the hallway. *Does she really want to bite me?* he asks himself, feeling bubbly.

Unavoidable, Baz stands right there.

"You really are a piece of shit, Asher," Baz says, spitting in front of Ash.

Ash twists his face in disgust. "Anyone who thinks spitting on a carpet is the macho thing to do doesn't understand social decorum or self-respect," Ash taunts Baz.

Attempting to punch Ash in the jaw, Baz moves too slowly to make impact with Ash.

Why the hell is he so weak? Ash wonders.

"I told you already that you got your one and only free shot," Ash reminds his would-be attacker and pulls back, Baz in his grip. He knocks him out with one punch, dropping Baz down and shaking his head in annoyance.

Ivy peeks her head out of the door quick and smiles. "Thank you, Ash."

He nods, wanting more than anything to pull her to him for a kiss but instead walks back into his room furious, because even if he wants her to test a lifemate bond with him, he has to wait at least thirty hours for Baz's blood to be out of her system.

It isn't just vampire blood in her system now. It's a male's.

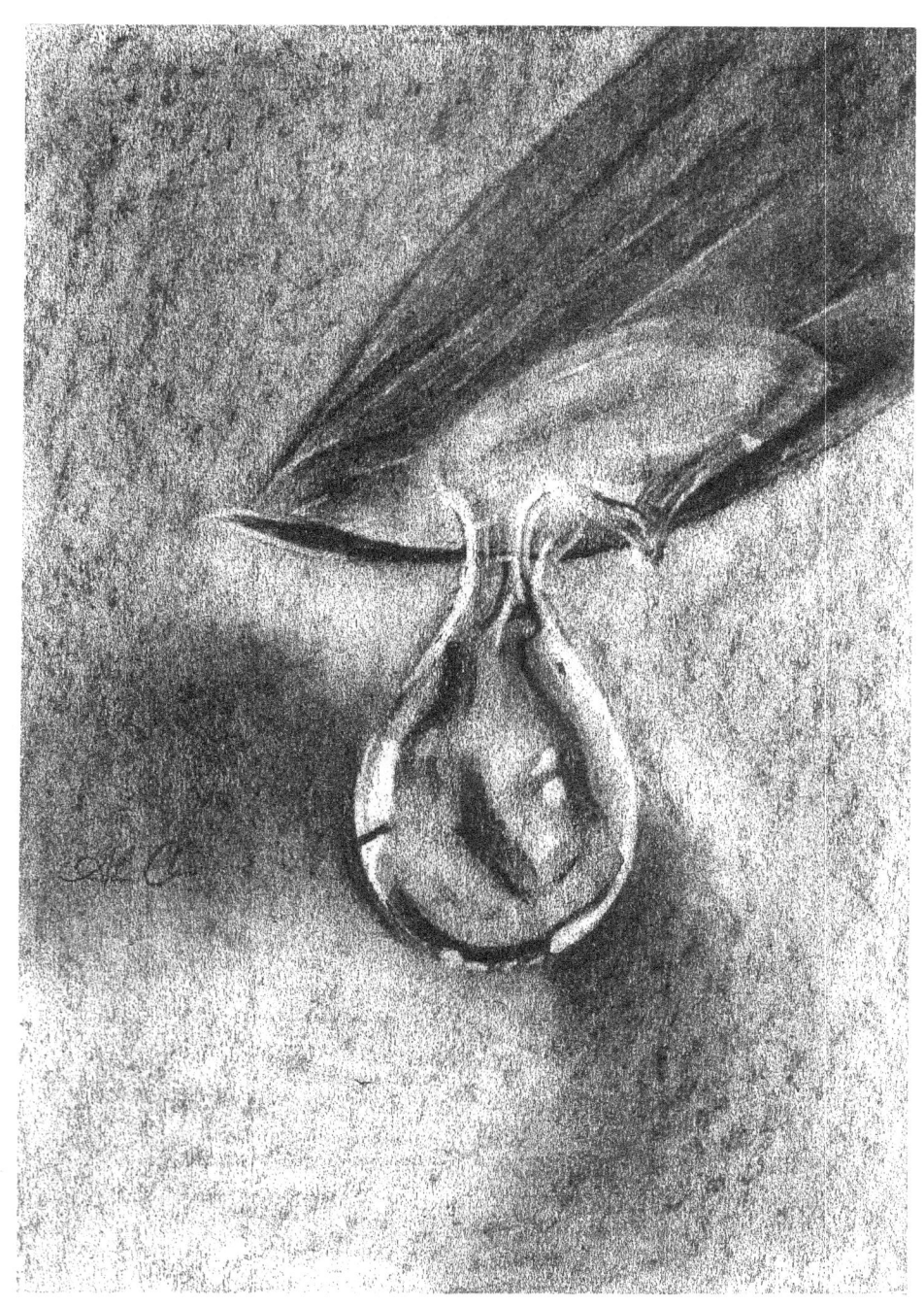

Life Mate

Bloodlust

Ivy grouches to herself in the wake of Baz's deception.

Her father refused to allow her to go shopping due to her inability to apologize to Baz. According to her father, Baz is still his second in command but has made a mistake. Her role as heir means that she must rectify the situation.

Pacing her room, she has had to tell Baz to shove it three times when he shows up with her food. *How dare any man try to force me into anything. That little shit tried to do the same thing that Finn did. Lucky he can't die is what he is.*

Not fully knowing if the whole lifemate thing can be true, Ivy makes the circuit around her room but realizes she would rather be alone for an eternity than with a twit who'd try to control her.

And Ash! He's had her hot and bothered since he arrived but hasn't made a move to ask for more. If anyone is her lifemate, it's him with the way he makes her tingle. He told her to look it up, and she did, but all that came up is something called a lifemate jolt. *I don't even know if he wants to do this whole marriage thing! Why would you consider him a possible lifemate, you idiot!* she yells.

Ivy can handle a marriage of convenience if she knows the other person is a willing participant and on board to make it work. Manipulation, on the other hand, she cannot and will not withstand, and she determines to fight it to the death: preferably Baz's, yet her father told her that she needs to apologize! *This is so screwed up!*

Ivy considers their rain-soaked sparring. Ash, who had gotten the best of her yet again during sparring, came to within inches of Ivy's face.

If tension were a tightrope, it was about to snap. Knowing she shouldn't have wished for him to close the gap but unable to resist the pull, she had touched his face. The tingling as it went down her spine and all the way down her arm reminded her of the feeling she'd had moments before the lightning struck. As Ivy waited eyes closed in anticipation and face red, as she breathed hard from exertion, Ash set her to right and walked away, putting space between them and any fantasies she'd had.

Ivy feels anger well in her. *What in the hell are you expecting? You cannot think about happy endings! There shouldn't be anything that makes you feel like that. Get over your dreaming and get back to the real world. No one can love you. Get over it. You will have children to love you. That's it!*

Ivy pictures little boys and girls stick fighting behind Duneskil. She smiles. Before long in her reverie, Ash's arms wrap around her as, both smiling affectionately, they watch the same sight.

Gah! Knock it the hell off, Ivy!

I am obligated to have children. She remembers her dad's voice as she relives the conversation. Her mother had told her about the fertilization process, but it's not like there were people lining up to teach her anything about it. Finn was the only one who'd ever tried, and she never trusted him enough to allow it.

She punches the door frame in the living room and grits her teeth as she endures the resulting pain.

Asking Ash if she can drink his blood was a ploy to piss off Baz, who happens to be the controller, but yikes, the look of hunger on that man's face was territorial, which made absolutely no sense. *He hasn't even tried to kiss me, damn it!*

She felt something weird when she'd drank the blood the other day. It was unnatural, and in the books, a lifemate doesn't think about other people except their mate in the heat of the moment.

The bliss that gripped her that evening was all Ash as she remembered the tingling of his skin against hers when they were swimming and he'd caught her. She remembered the way he'd watched her when she was on top of Nova . . . all her fantasies of Ash flashed in her head when she drank another man's blood. She hopes something more than the council's determination prevails, but hope is not something she can let back in.

All she can imagine is what he looks like under all those clothes. Coming up with an idea, Ivy decides that she wants to know once and for all if Ash simply wants to do as the Pale Council tells him or if he is actually interested in her. Ash has never tried to kiss her in all the time they have spent together. So much is happening as she considers the calendar where her decision date looms.

Five days. I have only five days to make my decision, and I have no idea what is in his mind.

She keeps hearing Jynx's words. *A kiss can tell a thousand words that a voice cannot.*

Knowing that she must unruffle a few feathers before she can do anything else, Ivy heads to Baz's room and takes a breath. She knocks.

The door opens, and he glares out at her, the giant bruise from the kick and knockout still unhealed and marring his face.

That's weird.

"I am sorry." Ivy says, forcing herself to look at him with remorse even as the scent of decay and mold hits her senses. "I was bitchy. It was a shock. Can we still go to the mall?"

She prayed that he would take the apology and move forward without her having to mesmer anyone.

"Why would I do that? Big man can take you."

The door goes to slam, but Ivy puts her foot in the way.

As Ivy stalks into the room, Baz skitters away from her. Ivy scans the room, her senses reacting as a pungent odor wafts to her.

"You would take me to the mall because I am your better and I asked you to, you asshole," Ivy tells him as she closes the door. "Come to me, Baz." She pushes her thoughts into him and pulls him toward her.

Unable to disobey, Baz floats slowly over to her. His eyes dart around. She waits for his eyes to meet hers again and puts him under a mesmer, saying "You have forgiven me for anything you find offensive. You will take me to the mall with Ash, and I am going to fill my closet. You won't remember me in your room after I leave it."

Ivy steps back and waits for her handiwork to make itself clear.

"You are a bitch, but I forgive you." Baz says with a sideways grin. "Do you think there's a chance that we could be lifemates?"

Ivy shrugs. "Anything's possible, but we may never know if I don't get some clothes to wear." she lies through her teeth. "We leave at two!"

꙳ ꙳ ꙳

Rummaging through her closet, she finds what she's looking for.

Thank you again, Jynx, for your trashy style, she giggles. Glancing at the clock, she knows she has an hour to make her plan work. The little string swimming suit that barely covers anything swings in circles in her hand as she smiles with anticipation.

I am taking that kiss if it's the last thing I do.

She dons the suit, and in the mirror she sees that she's changed since leaving Lesai. She doesn't appear sick or tired. She stands vibrant and full of life.

Wearing what Aster's mother would refer to as floozing clothes, she pulls open her door and walks to the door across the hall where she leans on the casing, She hears him walking from the other side towards the door.

Ash opens the door and gasps. "Jeez, Ivy." He looks down the hallway and drags her into his room as another male comes out of one of the rooms. "Put some clothes on!"

His face is red as he looks away.

Ivy smiles, ignoring the urge to cover her body . "I was thinking of another swim. Want to come?"

"It depends." He says a dark look in his eyes. "Is this to hang out with me or piss off Baz?"

Ivy smiles coyly, watching how it affects him. "There is something hinky with that one. I want to figure out what it is, but I also want to get to know you better. Hang out if you will."

"I'll be right back." Ash says, crossing the room to his stuffed closet. He closes the door most of the way as he changes into his swimming attire. "I thought you wanted to go to the mall tonight."

Ivy grimaces. "I don't even know what the hell a mall is. It was Soren's idea to go to the mall. He says it is a girl's happiness to have all the stores in one place."

She studies him as he emerges from the closet wearing a pair of swim trunks and t-shirt. "It sounds like a waste of time."

Ash grins from ear to ear. "What kind of clothes do you like to wear?"

Ivy shrugs. "Pretty much anything I can fight in."

"So, you want a sporting goods store," he says with a giant grin.

"I guess."

Ivy skirts his room, glancing at pictures of him and his sisters along with family photos. Some of them date back to what looks like the invention of photos.

Ash nods. "After the pool, we will get you some clothes. I must admit, though, I am grateful that you don't need the frilly shit. Shopping for that is hellish."

"I will need a chick's store" she said as her cheeks begin to flush with embarrassment as she recalls the dreams she's been having.

"Done," he says with a smile.

Ivy smiles shyly. "Perfect. Ready?"

"I will be in one second," Ash says, bringing a towel out of his bathroom and handing it to her.

Feeling self-conscious again, Ivy buries it as she puts a hand on her hip and changes her stance. She can smell her own burning heat for him as it wafts but ignores the urge to book it for the door. "You really don't like my bathing suit?"

Ash shrugs, and Ivy smiles to herself as she watches the tips of his ears turn red. "No matter how much I like the look of your body, I would rather it not be on display for the entire coven as we go down to the pool."

Ivy giggles. "Do I sense alpha male there?"

Ash blushes brighter as he holds the towel out again.

She extends her right hand for the towel, and Ash pauses a moment before handing it to her. He sees her entire heritage mark for the first time. "Shit! That must have hurt!"

Ivy shrugs, brushing off the sympathy, but he takes her hand softly and lifts her tingling arm. He searches for the coat of arms as she turns bright red. His eyes travel to the side boob popping out of the bikini, and Ivy looks away, moving her hair to hide her face from him and uncovering her coat of arms.

Ash chuckles, stepping around her. He starts to trace the mark's vines, his touch sending sparks and shivers down her spine.

"Your father can never deny you!" he says, clearing his throat. As he glides his tingling fingers over the mark on its way to her collar bones, he glances down to her cleavage.

Ivy can smell his arousal coming off him in waves, exciting her as she never thought possible. She boils inside and can't take her eyes off his face as his eyes explore her. Then, looking from Ivy's mark up, she follows his fingers moving to her jawline as he brushes her bottom lip with his thumb.

He looks into her eyes, and she stops breathing. Ash leans down and covers her mouth with his in a tender kiss, igniting a fire within her that roars to life. The kiss lasts only moments but feels like forever, then ends on a shaky breath as he withdraws. Ash stills, staring into her eyes as he waits for her to make the next move, his question for her obvious as he waits.

Ivy lifts onto her tippy toes and pulls his head down to her, taking exactly what she wants from him. As if a dam breaks free, the towel goes flying, and all she can feel is hands, lips, and sparks as they explore each other. He lifts her up to straddle him, pushing his need into her with her back flush against the wall. Friction causes her back to arch as every thought recedes to the back of her mind. Every part of her body in contact with his tingles with violent ferocity.

Ivy feels her eyes darkening with need and pulls back in a jerk. She forces him to put her down so she can get away from him. The urge to bite into his neck is so strong that it takes everything in her to hold herself still.

Ivy can't take her eyes off the pulsing artery in his neck as she pants, drawing ragged breaths into her lungs. He approaches, and she feels herself cower away from him. Fear of hurting him consumes her. Her wish for more between them smashes into bits as tears stream down her face.

He tips her head up and meets her eyes still red with the bloodlust as tears fall, preventing her from looking away from him.

"Look at me, Ivy," he demands softly.

She can't speak. Her elongated fangs pulse with pain as she looks back into his eyes.

"You will be okay," he smiles reassuringly to her. "Do you need blood, or can you fight it?"

She hisses as she pants, "Blood. Away . . . from . . . me!"

"I'll be okay. Let's focus on you." Ash grabs his phone out of his swim trunks and opens it. After tapping a couple times, Ivy hears her father answer.

Ash very calmly says into the phone, "Bring the supply you have for her."

A few excruciating moments pass as Ivy stares into Ash's eyes. Her panic increases as her eyes cease to register what is in front of her.

"Blackout," Ivy pants as her eyes roll back.

Old Buildings

Beacham's

"Ivy? Ivy?" he begs as she starts to go limp in his arms, her face falling into a neutral state.

Soren comes rushing into the room and sees his skimpily clad daughter in Ash's lap. Soren has two jugs of blood. He fills a glass with the murky red liquid and dips a finger into it, rubbing it on her lips. Nothing happens. Ash maneuvers to cradle her head as he uses his spare hand to open her mouth.

Soren pours some of it into her mouth, and her eyes snap open, still black and freakier than he has seen before. Her hand takes the glass and drains it while Soren pours another. One after another after another, she keeps drinking. Finally, she stops, her arm going limp with the glass of blood yet miraculously not spilling any. She has emptied two bottles.

She moves a little as she realizes that her senses are beginning to snap back on. Her nose twitches, and she turns her head into Ash's chest, inhaling him so deep that he can feel himself getting turned on yet again. *Her body knows I'm hers, too!* he thinks as his mind turns somersaults.

She slowly opens her eyes and looks around, panic etching her features. "What happened?" She meets Ash's eyes and smiles a little through tired eyes. "You almost got bit, didn't you?"

Soren shakes his head. "What in the hell are you two doing?" he asks. "It took all this blood to get you out of that!"

He waits for an answer, but when he doesn't receive one says, "You two are ridiculous."

He goes to stand, but Ivy puts a hand on his arm. "That is good thinking, Dad."

Ash watches Soren puff up a little as he smiles at his daughter.

"You do know that we need to figure this out, right?" Soren says.

They nod.

"Good. Now both you should get dressed and come down to my office."

"Wait, Soren."

He turns back.

"She just blacked out from starvation after a supposed lifemate gave her his blood. Does that make any sense to you?" Ash asks.

Soren's eyes widen, and he shakes his head as he leaves the room.

Ash and Ivy remain, snuggling and recuperating from the longest ten minutes of their lives.

"I could have killed you," She tells him, tears coming in her eyes.

"You are stronger than you think, Ivy," he says kissing her forehead. "Not to mention—I can't die."

Ivy considers what he said. "No, but if I were to drain you, it would be the same effect." Tears stream down her cheeks.

"I am not worried about me," he tells her sternly as he dries her tears with his thumbs, then lifts her chin to make her look at him.

Ivy nods. "I know." She looks past him. "It's your job to protect me."

Ash growls, shaking her a little bit as he says, "No. My job be damned. I couldn't live with myself if I'd lost you before you know how I feel."

Shocked, Ivy meets his eyes,. "What do you mean?"

"I've been fated to you since I transitioned into my Pale form on my twenty-first birthday, and for the life of me, I am unable to resist the pull I feel towards you." Ash feels the words ripped from his soul.

"You have been so distant. I can smell attraction, but I can't read your mind. It took wearing this skimpy thing that covers nothing to get a single kiss from you!" *That string thing is for me?*

Ash already knows she can smell his arousal from her admission. "You wore that thing for me?"

Ivy nods.

He smiles even more. "If I were to tell you that I really like you and want to know you, what would you say to me? Be honest."

Ivy shrugs. "I still don't believe it, even as it comes from your mouth," she says, touching his bottom lip with her thumb and sighing. "There is no way the council could have predicted this three hundred years before it happens."

"Actually, my mom waited 450 years for my dad," Ash tells her.

Ivy raises a questioning eyebrow.

"They married for duty and discovered when they finally drank from each other that they were lifemates," he says seriously. "The novel I was reading is an epic centering on them."

Ivy's eyes flee from Ash's. "I can never hope for happiness."

Ash pulls Ivy's chin to meet his eyes. "No. You can be certain of it."

"Why?"

"Because," he says, setting Ivy back to sit in front of him. The loss of her touch makes his body ache. "I am making the solid vow of a Protector. Ivy, you will be happy in this life if you choose to marry me. I will always do what I can to show you that you are stunning on the inside as well as the outside. My heart is yours to do with as you please."

Her eyes wide in amazement, Ivy stares at him.

He smiles at her.

"How can you make a vow like that to someone as messed up as I am?" she asks.

"Because you are my lifemate."

Ivy scoffs. "You can't know that for sure."

Ash shrugs. "Not until we try for the marks, no, but I know that both of us get the jolt when we touch."

Ivy nods, admitting that she feels it, too.

"That is how I am certain."

Ivy wonders, "Have you had one before?"

"No." *I told her to look it up!* Ash chuckles as he realizes he must have made a mistake. He should have specified that she should read some romance fiction.

"Then how do you know?" The question is innocent enough, but Ash always finds himself frustrated that she doesn't take his word for anything.

"Cason and everyone else I have asked," he says, looking at the floor.

Adoration written all over her perfect features, Ivy lifts his chin. "You've told people?"

He nods. "Aren't you afraid that they will talk ill of it? You're a royal!"

Ash chuckles. "Why are you concerned about that? You are also a royal and my lifemate whether marked or not.

"But I'm a freak," Ivy says without blinking an eye. "No one can ever accept me if they know everything about me."

Ash looks at her as if she has five heads. "Are you daft, woman?" he asks. "I am telling you that I am in love with you. Like pure, can't keep it in my pants, and head over heels, fall on my face in public kind of love. I dream and think of you every moment and honest—"

Ivy bestows on him a scorching kiss that he never would have suspected part of her repertoire. So much emotion pools out of her in that one kiss that it almost brings him to tears.

When she finally lets go of him, Ash feels a hundred pounds lighter. He pecks her on the forehead. "Good. Now that we have gotten through that, we need to see your dad before he has a shit fit."

Ash watches as Ivy heads towards the door, the sway of her hips mesmerizing him. The door handle turns, and he growls at her. "Where the hell do you think you're going, dressed like that?"

Ivy looks down and sheepishly does the one thing he had expected her to do as soon as he opened the door. Looking uncomfortable, she covers every part of herself that she can. "I forgot."

Ash walks over to her and removes her hands from herself. "You can dress like this . . ." he looks her up and down, ". . . anytime you want when it's just me. I will always appreciate it, so there isn't any reason to hide." Putting her hands above her head with one hand, he leans into her, pushes her gently against the door, and swoops in for a kiss of possession that has him wanting to bring her to his bed. Knowing that they have other places they need to be and satisfied that she has understood his meaning, he releases her trembling body.

"I just want to be the only male to see the skin, here . . ." He traces a line between her breasts, causing her breath to catch in her throat.

" . . . and here . . ." He traces the top edge of the bathing suit bottom, making sure to find the spot where her muscles would spasm under her womb.

Running his hand back up the side of her body, his painful situation begs for attention as her eyes are red with her own arousal. The scent of her wafting at him in hot waves makes him dizzy. "As much as I would really enjoy showing you how much I enjoy looking at you, we would be here until daybreak, and right now, we need to get downstairs," Ash sighs, gazing down into her eyes. She, too, is panting with desire.

"Can I raid your closet?" she asks straight-faced.

Ash laughs at her. "Um—sure."

"Do that again," Ivy begs.

"What?" Ash asks, curious as he idly twirls her long black hair.

Ivy touches his face. Tingles making their way up his arm. "Laugh like you did at the waterfall."

Not knowing how to stop the feeling of his heart about to explode with adoration, he asks. "Can I keep you?" He knows in that moment he will never find a female he wants to hold as much as he loves holding her.

Ivy nods, looking as if she will start crying again.

Ash lifts her closer to his face and kisses her with all the passion he has in him. *Nothing can take you from me,* he swears to himself.

It takes her fifteen minutes to find something she will wear out of the compound. She chooses a pair of seventies pale blue bellbottoms that are much too big and a tank undershirt in black.

"These are pretty feminine," She giggles, examining at her reflection in the mirror. "You really wore these?"

Offended, Ash replies, "Those are pretty comfortable. Because we live so long, though, every ten years, each of the Pale Race has to change up identities to stop the humans from asking questions."

"Does that mean moving, too?"

Ash nods, opening the door to the suite for her to exit. She looks up at his hair.

"How long have you been dressing like a rock star?" she asks, poking a bit of fun at him.

"Actually, my hairdresser is working on the next look as we speak."

Ivy looks up and mouths hairdresser.

He pokes her in the side.

Her erupting giggle makes him smile. "Yes," he says. "I don't trust anyone else with the hair. She would love to help with yours. too!"

Ivy glares at him. "There will be no reason for that. My hair will be this length until I die. If I need to master a few different hairdos, I will do that, but otherwise, it stays this length."

Ash knows better than to persist as he sees a stubborn streak like his own reflecting at him.

Smiling, they get to Soren's office. Before entering, they both put on equally serious looks. The annoyance that Soren had expressed earlier weighs heavily on both of them as they stand in front of his desk waiting for orders.

"Something is wrong. I can feel it," Soren says looking through intel on his desk. "Whatever just happened upstairs needs to be kept quiet for the time being."

Ash switches from one foot to another as he says, "Why in the world would we need to keep what's going on between us a secret?"

"I have no idea now, but call it a hunch. Something has been off since yesterday, and the council is concerned," Soren says scrubbing a hand through his hair. "Actually, I'd like you to go to the mall tonight, Ivy. Take Baz and Ash as planned and make sure that your apology stuck."

Ivy hesitates. "Are they pissed that I'm defective?" Not wanting to see the looks on either of the men's faces, she looks down.

"No, they need you protected. Though I have to say it's probably anyone who messes with you that will need protection," he says with a pointed look at Ash, who blushes. "All the same, I want the two of you to include Baz. Get rid of the hard feelings. We will need him if shit hits the fan."

"I made him forgive me earlier like you asked. He will be down at two," Ivy says with dismay.

Ash looks irritated. "Okay. But if he . . ."

"No," Soren says. "You will deal with him hitting on Ivy as she will. There have been no claims made, proposals given, or marks created."

Ash's teeth grind as he shoves down the urge to fight back. *She's mine!* "Thank you," he reluctantly agrees. "Would you like the Terrors to accompany us?"

Soren shakes his head. "I have other things to occupy their time regarding recon. Will that be an issue?"

"No, sir."

Ash puts a hand on Ivy's shoulder, and she turns to look up at him.

"Oh, and Ivy?" Soren says. "Do not bite anyone. Take the last half gallon with you in a cooler to keep any shit shows at bay, please."

Ivy's face burns bright red as, pissed, she walks out of the office.

Ash feels Ivy's hand, and instead of taking it proudly, squeezes it and lets it go.

She looks up at him questioningly. The fury of having to hide what they have causes her to stomp away like a scolded five-year-old.

I finally got her to agree to be with me, and this is the shit we will have to deal with? Ash thinks.

Baz waits outside Soren's office and Ivy smiles the socially acceptable royal smile, yet her expression changes to one of annoyance as soon as she is past him. She gives Ash a look that makes him fear for the next person to piss her off. He imagines she may go all out crazy on them. "I'm going to grab my swords," she says.

Ivy meets them outside a few minutes later with her swords strapped to her back, and Baz greets her. "Hey, Ivy! Ready for an adventure?"

Ash's expression reveals his displeasure as he approaches his own high-end vehicle. The black, sleek sports car that impresses all the women doesn't even faze his lifemate as she stalks over to the passenger side. Ash doesn't want to think about what will happen if Baz does hit on her. *Will it be her or me to drain his ass?*

"Good morning, Ivy," Ash grins. "Baz," he adds, in an effort to make the encounter a little less awkward. It doesn't help. Ivy is already sitting in the front passenger seat, so Ash has to let Baz climb through the driver's door into the back seat. It's suffocating for the three of them to be in close quarters.

Ash pulls away from the compound. Ivy sits stiffly next to him. He wants to put a hand on her thigh as he drives but can't manage without Baz seeing. *Ugh*

Baz interrupts the awkward silence by asking, "Can I hijack the Bluetooth?"

"I guess so," Ash replies.

Ash observes the look of hate crossing Ivy's features and sees Baz put his hat over his head and covers his face. Ash quickly gives Ivy's hand a squeeze of encouragement. She looks to see if the coast is clear before picking his hand up and kissing the back of it ten times, dragging her fangs across the back of it.

She will get us in trouble! he thinks. *I'm screwed!*

A moment later, Ivy almost faints with the penetrating bass that begins in the car. It forces her to cover her ears and sob. Her ears begin to bleed by the time Ash turns the music down. He growls at the thought that Baz has hurt her on purpose with the loud bass. There is no way that he doesn't know that she has sensitive ears. Especially after her falling in the sparring room.

"Are you okay?" Ash asks Ivy. She slowly uncovers her ears and nods with a slight wince.

"Why'd you shut it off? That was a good song!" Baz groans from the back seat without bothering to lift his hat up.

Ivy grabs Ash's arm as he starts to whip around. He looks her in the eye, furious, and she very softly shakes her head no. "Got any headphones you can use?" Ash growls as he shuts the media player off on the dash.

Baz petulantly stuffs a hand in his pocket, whips out a little pouch, and puts earbuds into his ears. The tiny balls began screeching and thrumming as Baz grumpily lies back down.

"Dick," Ash says under his breath, unable to hold it in.

Ivy sighs. "He didn't realize."

"He was in the sparring room."

Ivy shrugs. "He wasn't paying attention to anything," her eyes wide as she examines the strip malls they pass and people walking around with dogs or kids at their heels.

Ash smiles as she looks around the front of the car to see where they were.

"What?" she asks as she senses him about to say something.

He shrugs. "I don't think I have seen anyone as enamored over a five-minute car ride before."

"Well," she looks into the back seat. "I have only been to Lesai and Duneskil so far, and the first car ride was horrible. Then there was the water . . ." She blushes as her nose flares. She looks at him shyly. "I haven't had much experience."

Is she talking about the outside world or inside a bedroom? Ash wonders. The pain in his groin intensifies as he drives, so he changes the subject.

"I'm telling your dad you think he's a bad driver!" Ash pulls into a parking lot in the center of town.

"I didn't say that!" Ivy responds, slapping him and sending a jolt directly into his heart. Motion in the back seat makes Ivy jump.

Baz smiles at her in a way that says "Scared ya!"

"Ready?" Baz asks. "Wait. Why are we at Beacham's?"

"I thought that Ivy might be as hungry as I am. How about you, Baz?" Ash asks, hopeful that Baz will want to sit in the car.

"I could eat," Baz replies, eyeing the place and glancing around suspiciously.

"Ivy?" Ash asks, not getting his hopes up too much since the place usually pisses women off. Ash hears Ivy's stomach growl at the thought of food and laughs. "I take that as a yes," Ash says.

Ivy nods and looks at the restaurant with an odd expression.

Ash opens the front door of Beacham's for Ivy, letting it close slightly so Baz must pull the handle himself. *I'm not that nice,* he thinks.

He comes up short as Ivy stares around her in amazement. "This place is—old," she says as she approaches the building to touch the wall.

"How old?" Ash asks looking around at the modern feel.

Her hand on the wall, she closes her eyes obviously feeling something he can't figure.

Ivy looks back and meets his eyes, hers lit up as she says, "Ancient."

Ash opens his eyes in astonishment. Everything in the place is round with no ends to pieces of wood. No places where they attach to one another. *Have I been drawn here because it was created by the Ancients?*

He glances back at Ivy, smiling as she touches the table where he always sits. He sees that she has a bottle of ketchup in her hand. She shrugs as she peruses the place. She spots a mop bucket a few tables over and grabs a rag from it, wrings it out, and washes the table and benches.

Her action floors him. Never in his life has he ever seen a woman make such an effort except for family. She obviously cares that something wasn't perfect and didn't just sit down. He can't stop smiling as she explores his favorite place in the Pale world.

"Why this table?" she asks him.

"You picked it."

Ivy's nostrils flare, and he realizes that she chose the table because she knows he often prefers it. *She is tracking my scent. She's mine!*

She sniffs a little more, refusing to sit on the other side of the table. "By the way, whoever that sandalwood belongs to smells mean," she says, wrinkling her nose in distaste.

Is that jealousy I sense? Realizing that she is talking about Lola unnerves him.

The waitress arrives in a flourish, visibly taken aback by the clean table. "Um, thank you," she says sheepishly. Seeing Ivy's heritage mark, she knows that Ivy's royalty.

"It's not a problem. I wanted to sit here, so it was the least I could do."

The young woman looks as if she will faint as she looks first at Ivy, then at Ash unable to decide what's going on. After a couple hundred years into the existence of one of his restaurants, almost every waitress in every city knows Ash.

Ash smiles. "Are you ready to order, Ivy?"

"Yes, but you go first," she says, smiling.

Ash clears his throat. He's not sure what to make of beautiful Ivy sitting next to him. She even makes a female vampire used to the demeaning attitudes of most Pale women feel like royalty. Most of the Pale women he has met make sure that all vampires know their place, yet she is humble. "Um, I would like the porterhouse steak, rare, with mash, broccoli, and a chocolate milkshake."

The waitress nods. She looks at Ivy.

"Oh!" Ivy says, smiling. "I'll have the same. But I would also like some of the French fries I see everyone on the TV eat."

The waitress looks surprised. Ash smiles. Baz also seems surprised.

"I love me a woman with an appetite," laughs Ash. "What are you eating, Baz?"

Frazzled, Baz responds, "I'll do tomato soup and a Caesar salad. Lemon soda to drink."

Ivy mouths "Eeew" to Ash. They share a laugh and joke back and forth while waiting for the food. Ivy's eyes close as she smells the steak cooking. "God, I am in love with that smell," she sighs.

"What smell?" Baz asks, looking around and giving Ash a dirty look. Ash can smell the steak, too, and wonders why Baz can't smell it. *Ivy is probably smelling the blood searing in the pan as well, but Baz should still be able to smell at least the seasonings they add!*

The steaks arrive quickly, since neither one of them really wants them much done. As the servers place the meal in front of her complete with French fries, Ivy digs in. She doesn't wait or keep any pretenses. She eats. If present, her mother would yell at her for lack of manners, but her behavior captivates Ash. Baz instead casts a disgusted glance at her, but Ash is over the moon in complete love over the fact that she is eating.

"You can eat!" Ash says, grinning ear to ear.

Ivy gulps and looks up sheepishly. "You feed me, and I will melt like putty." she says, digging into the French fries.

You should know that, idiot, Ash thinks. *She bit you when you fed her a cracker. It's exactly as Calyn said.* Ash reaches over her and puts some ketchup on her plate. She looks at him questioningly, so he dips a fry in the ketchup and lifts it to his mouth. She watches the French fry as it enters his mouth, and at once he can smell her reaction. She is so turned on that she reaches over to his knee under the table and grips it tightly.

The smell and the touch floor him. *Really? God, I am in trouble with this one.* He glances over to Baz, utterly clueless to what's going on. *How can he not smell it?* Then a thought directed to Baz: *You'd better not smell my mate.*

Baz interrupts with a pouty face, reminding Ash of Lola. "You don't melt for me, and I feed you."

Ivy shrugs. "This is different. There is no food at the compound. I am constantly on the verge of starvation with the nonexistent food there." She pouts back, then dips a fry and closes her eyes as she chews.

Baz is at once uncomfortable again as he tries to keep up with the conversation.

"You should have said something to someone. We could have taken you shopping so you can eat," Ash says with concern.

"I didn't want to be more of a burden than I already am," Ivy says, digging into the mashed potatoes as Ash realizes that she is almost done with her meal.

Ash keeps eating. "Do you want to grab some real food before heading to do the rest of the shopping?" he asks.

"Oh, yeah!" The broad smile and her doe eyes make Ash want to earn the look more often. Meantime, Baz plays on his phone, his plate and bowl of soup barely touched.

What the hell is wrong with this kid?

Eat to Live

Food Police

Ivy's eyes are about to pop out of her head. When Ash had suggested to grab a few things from a food store, she pictured the little shops of Lesai where you can pick up products of latest harvest. The food store is another beast altogether. Bigger than the restaurant, the building seems to go on forever. Her heart starts pounding and she breathes in gasps as she surveys the aisles.

"All this is food?"

Ash chuckles. "For the most part."

Ivy can't fathom being able to pick something to eat when the choices seem endless. Her face blooming red as she realizes she hasn't had enough human food to know what she even likes, she looks pleadlingly at Ash.

"Are you okay?" he asks.

Ivy shakes her head.

"What do you like to eat?" he inquires gently.

Ivy shrugs as she stares at all the humans pushing their way through behind her. "I don't know."

"Want me to grab a few things to see if you want to try them?"

Ivy nods. "Don't even ask if I want to try it." She eyes a bag of chips. "I can't tell by looking at half of this stuff if its edible."

Ash laughs, grabs a shopping cart, and begins pushing it. "Fair enough."

Ivy salivates when she sees something called a cheesecake. Putting it in the cart, she looks up at him sheepishly, "Is it okay if I get fat?"

"No! Women are supposed to be thin and beautiful," Baz says with a sneer.

Ash glares at Baz, then tells Ivy, "Real men don't care about their mate's shell. They care about what's inside them. So yes. Get as fat as you want." He pushes the cart towards Ivy, and whispers, "It makes the babies healthier when you eat."

He looks into her eyes and winks, and she blushes as heat rushes through her.

Ash holds up a can of the cheese she loves, and she nods and holds up two fingers.

"That's horrible for you!" Baz's face scrunches up at the idea.

Ivy eyes Baz, "We are immortal."

Baz looks stunned. "Does that mean you should hate your body by filling it with trash?"

"It tastes good, and if I remember right, you just drank liquid sugar."

Ash smiles at her just to tease Baz as he informs Ivy, "I'll show you what chips and ice cream are, too!"

"Awesome!" Ivy grins with delight, having asked her father for snacks she's seen people eat on TV but hasn't yet experienced.

Baz pushes his eyebrows together and scrutinizes her as he asks, "Why don't you ever take my advice?"

"No reason, really." She reads the label of a drink she's picked up. She lifts it for Ash to see, and he shakes his head. Shrugging, she places the item back on the shelf.

Baz has his hands on his hips and his body language screams. "But you will take his!" he exclaims pointing at Ash in amazement.

Ivy shrugs, "He's old as dirt!" she says, sticking her tongue out at Ash, who pretends to be shocked by the diss. "Plus he feeds me human food, and it's always good. So, shoot me for wanting to taste something other than iron!"

Ash smiles at her innuendo. He pulls things off shelves as he walks. *It's mostly fresh fruit and vegetables in the cart. I'm not that bad!*

"Why are you two so chummy all of a sudden?" Baz asks.

Ivy's eyes get wide as she turns to fake look at another label. "We are friends."

"—ish," Ash adds with a glare at Ivy for not having told Baz they are together.

Ivy widens her eyes as if to say "We were told not to." Ash gets pouty.

Baz's eyes widen in horror. "You two are hooking up!"

"What's 'hooking up'?" Ivy stares clueless between the two of them as Baz and Ash silently face off in the middle of the store.

Ash softly clears his throat and attempts to keep his voice down. "No, Baz. We are not hooking up."

"You two are together. A couple. I am not stupid!" Baz's neck and ears flush a bright shade of red as his arms cross over his chest.

Now look what you did! Ivy chides herself. "I don't know what we are, exactly," she says. "Exploring?" She searches Ash's face for an answer.

Ash growls, "We are fated by the council."

"That doesn't mean you have to marry the jerk!"

Ivy hisses to herself, *Ash is my lifemate! Do not insult him. E*ven though she knows Ash can take care of himself, but she says,. "Knock it off, Baz. You are not an alpha male, so back off. There is no claim on me by anyone, and you had better remember that."

Her voice drops so low that she doubts anyone else could hear it. With humans around, her flashing red eyes pose a problem, though.

Baz looks at her as if she's foolish. "You are my lifemate, Ivy. And you are screwing this asshole!"

Ash growls so aggressively that she puts herself between them. At the same time, Baz approaches her slowly and soundlessly. The life force in him beats wildly as it had earlier that night.

"I am not your lifemate," she tells Baz. "You are destined to someone else. Somewhere else. You think Ash is cool, by the way, and you have no more than friendship for me. You will remember nothing of this conversation, only that I like cheese in a can."

Ivy lets Baz's mind go and goes to the cart. Ash's wide eyes don't blink as he watches Baz for a reaction.

"Was that a good idea?" Ash asks her with evident dismay.

Unable to calm her temper until she feels his hand on her lower back, Ivy shrugs. "It was that or rip his throat out, Pale or not."

Ash smiles at her and bends to kiss her head. She sees him eye Baz for reaction, and without one, he smiles and hugs her tightly against himself.

Contentment flows through Ivy and scares her a little. She nevertheless smiles, closes her eyes, and leans back into Ash, allowing his body to envelop her in a safety like she's never known.

"Where's my mommy?" a little boy asks, interrupting the moment as he tugs on Ivy's sleeve.

Ivy looks around but doesn't see anyone looking for the child. She holds her hand out and guides him to the front of the store. Ash follows with the cart. "Can I get someone in charge?" she asks loudly, attracting the attention of a store clerk.

"I can help you. What is the problem?"

"I can't find my mommy," the little boy says shyly, shrinking into Ivy's side.

The clerk looks around and pages someone. Instantly, a voice echoes on the store speaker. Ivy winces at the volume. "There is a little boy at the front looking for his parent."

Ten seconds later, a woman runs down an aisle towards them shouting, "Stewart!"

"Mommy!" The child runs to his mother, and she holds on to him for dear life.

Uncertainly, she tells Ivy, "Thank you." Looking down at her son, she says, "Don't you ever go running off like that again! You scared me half to death!"

There are tears in the little boy's eyes. "I'm sorry." He looks at Ivy with sorrow as his mother, intent on finishing her shopping, tugs him back down the aisle to her cart.

Ivy startles out of her worry for the boy as Ash wraps his arms back around her. "You will be an amazing mother," he says.

Ivy shrugs, and he squeezes her tighter, resting his chin on her shoulder and breathing in her hair. "Believe it or not, I know you will be."

"There is no way that anyone knows what kind of parent they will be when the time comes."

"Iveliis, you would not have just had a human child walk up to you and grab your hand if he didn't sense that you are mother material."

Ivy strains to turn and look at him, but he doesn't let her. She gives up and huffs, "How long have you known my real name?"

She can feel Ash's body move around her as he shrugs. "Not sure why you don't use it. It's pretty."

Ivy shudders. "Because it is royal, and I am not someone who believes in keeping pretenses constantly. The formality makes me feel like an outsider." For a moment she pauses and smiles. "Plus, there are many types of Ivy, including the poison type."

Ash barks a laugh but stifles it as five humans eye him with concern. His black baggy clothes make them uneasy as he holds her.

"We will have to finish shopping, you know."

"Yes, Ivy. I can hear your stomach growling already, and we just ate."

Ivy smiles. "I might be hungry for something else." She can feel a shiver work through Ash as he pokes her in the back. "Well, that seems to get you slightly hungry, too, I think."

"You have no idea," he growls softly, and she shivers. A pressure builds at her core.

Ash takes a deep breath as he smells her arousal and squeezes her tighter.

"We could always test that theory out," Ivy smiles. "I did almost bite you earlier."

Ash freezes. "You couldn't tempt me in this if I was starving," he tells her.

The cold sound in his voice startles her. She wriggles free and looks into his eyes. "What's the matter? I didn't mean to upset you."

Ash glares at Baz standing at the deli counter ordering more cheese from the sound of it. He looks possessively into her eyes. "When I drink from you, there won't be another male's blood in your veins."

Ivy blushes. "I didn't mean for that to happen." Not wanting to upset Ash any more than she already has with the statement, she looks away.

Ash tilts her head to make eye contact. "What happened this morning is not on you. He forced you to drink his blood."

"But what happened . . . ?"

Ash puts his finger on her lips.

"You are mine." Ash kisses her so deeply that Ivy can feel the store around her start to spin. When he pulls away, she doesn't open her eyes and look at him immediately. "We will wait the thirty hours for his blood to be gone, and I will show you what I mean. Agreed?"

Ivy nods as she continues to spin from the shock wave of heat running through her body.

Ash pulls away a little as he pulls things off the shelf again while holding her against him.

Ivy smiles and thanks Elemental Mother for the support. She knows she will fall on her face if he lets her go. "You are amazing," She tells him.

Ash grins. "The same can be said for you, Ms."

Baz approaches the cart.

Uncertain about how Baz will act, Ivy and Ash shuffle away from each other slightly.

"The least you can do is get some real cheese," he says. He holds up a tub of port wine, and Ivy nods as she smiles at Ash.

"I am totally going to be fat if I don't work out after this feast," she comments. She smells Ash's arousal and realizes the innuendo he's reacting to. "Really?" she asks him by way of noticing his predicament.

He blushes.

"Is that all men think about?" she asks.

He smiles and nods with the shit-eating grin of a little boy who's acted naughty.

Credit

Limits

Ash brings Ivy into a sporting goods store. She looks around, grinning ear to ear like a kid in a candy store.

"They have bows!" she squeals. She jumps up and down, then says seriously, "Dad says I have a limit that I can spend. What is it?" Her doe eyes glitter as she picks up bows and measures their balance. She doesn't consider how a bow would look up against her skin or if one would match an accessory she already owns.

A woman who doesn't care about what she looks like as long as her form is correct brings Ash close to a swoon. He wraps his arms around her shoulders and kisses her neck. He's in his glory for having brought her here. The prospect that just hours earlier she agreed to "see where 'this' goes" does nothing to stop him from displaying the affection he has for her.

"Fill the cart," He tells her. He knows that Soren has given her only a grand to spend. Only. *If she can spend a thousand in one store, then I will gladly pitch in the rest. It's not like I don't have enough after eight centuries of learning what people want. Especially when I have the means to open eight clubs and six restaurants.*

Ivy places a fifteen-hundred-dollar longbow into the cart, and he smiles to himself. *This girl will be the death of me!* She adds arrows, arrowheads, and a quiver.

Never has Ash known a woman to want to work out, yet he can see the wheels turning as she walks down the aisles. Women of the Pale Race aren't about to lose their shape, so they could care less.

Almost pouting but still watching her every move, Baz stands off to the side, Ash shifts a little as he pushes down his alpha male urge to deck him. Baz reacts indifferently to her enthusiasm, and the nagging feeling returns to the pit of his stomach.

Why is he just standing there? He watches her like a hawk, but he doesn't interact with her. There is no way he is interested in her for real, Ash ponders happily but annoyed, as well, because he can't figure out what this kid wants with his female.

Ivy picks two bathing suits, each a thousand times more modest than the one she wore into his room—a one-piece regular suit and one that looks more like something a surfer would wear with shorts and t-shirt attached. The suit zips up the back and he wonders why she would need something like that.

If it's a plan to swim with someone else around, he much prefers her covered, so he doesn't bother to ask. *If I get my way, she will be swimming in a parka.—Unless we are alone,— then—* His mind goes dark with the thoughts of her in the water and his pants become a little too tight.

"What are you thinking?" Ivy eyes Ash with a smile, her nose flaring.

The chatter in the store will hide what they are saying, so he whispers, "About how much I like you covered in public but would love to go swimming alone with you soon."

Ivy turns bright red. "It was dark. It's not like you saw much."

Coming in close behind her, he discreetly puts his hand on her butt. "I saw every bit of you in detail. Back and front."

Her breath catches in her throat as she turns her head to meet his eyes. "I didn't realize that. I thought the water would cover me. Sorry." She tries to distract herself and steps away from him and over to another display.

"You have no reason to be ashamed of your body," he says, watching her closely as she doesn't look at him. He moves closer to her and whispers, "I know you can smell what I am going through right now, so don't be ashamed."

She finally looks up at him. He nods as she leans closer, pushing into him, her eyes widen in shock. He moves a little to let her feel the full manifestation of his reaction.

She giggles. "I guess. Though I do have to say we are being stared at, so back up a bit before I start getting all messed up in my head again."

Ash nods, and she skips away, grabbing this and that, the bill adding up as she smiles.

Heading over to the training gear, Ivy grabs a punching bag, two sets of gloves, hand wraps, four workout bras with bottoms, and a couple of the headbands.

What is she trying to do? Fill the damn sparring room?

Ivy finally makes her way over to regular apparel, and he laughs aloud when she grabs seven pairs of solid black leggings, five black fitted t-shirts, five black fitted long-sleeve shirts, and a ten pack of black socks.

He chuckles as he asks, "Do you not like color?"

"Says the man in all black. Warriors aren't seen."

"But I see you," he smiles at her as she scrunches her face. "All that hair—how do you keep it from snarling?"

"Wouldn't you like to know!" She sticks her tongue out, smiling brightly at him. Then, "Crap. I'll be right back."

She runs into the aisles for something she's forgotten. She comes back with a mounting chin-up bar and all-natural soap, shampoo, and conditioner.

Ash shakes his head. *I am never going to look at a female the same way again.* He picks up the scentless shampoo and conditioner. The soap also has no scent, and he grins as he realizes he will always smell her natural scent.

They stand in line for a few minutes as the cashier rings up the purchases. "Cash or credit, sir?"

Ivy looks questioningly as he says, "Debit." He hands the clerk his card and then makes himself busy putting things back into the cart. "Can I actually have the larger items shipped to this address please?"

In a rush to finish, the cashier nods and hands the card to Ivy. Ash sees Ivy look at the card and watches the wheels turn. Her eyes get wide, and she giggles as she realizes she has let him pay $3,792.82.

He plucks the card out of her hand and puts it in his wallet as his eyes tell her not to say anything.

Baz approaches. "Need me to carry anything, Ivy?"

Ivy hands him the pull-up bar. "Why on earth do you need this?"

Shrugging off the judgment, Ivy says, "Because I like the feeling of a good burn after a long, challenging workout."

Ash feels himself getting aroused by the phrase alone as he imagines her getting a good workout.

She shows no sign that she can smell it, but he knows she does.

"But you are already strong and fast," Baz argues.

Ivy thinks a moment. "I am only as strong and fast as I keep myself. If I get lazy, my senses will be lazy. Humans are known to be able to capture the Pale Race because they go after the women who don't protect themselves. I feel bad for anyone whether vampire, Pale Race, or human who thinks they can take me."

Ash sees a flicker of panic in Baz's expression, and it's gone as quickly as it came. There isn't a reason for it that he can fathom. Ivy intimidates most everyone at times, but it still makes no sense that Baz thinks he loves her when he's afraid of her. *I will figure it out,* he thinks. Not in a mind set to ponder it at the moment, he lets it go.

With the trunk being full of groceries, Ash puts the sporting goods in the back seat. With one stop left, Ash sucks down a blood bag while he drives. He anticipates the pain he will endure in his groin. Ivy sits in the back seat sipping her red drink. Baz stares out the front window, and Ivy reaches her hand to touch Ash's left side. At first startled, he jerks a bit.

"What's got into you?" Baz asks?

"Bit my tongue," Ash replies, smirking as he stares into Ivy's eyes in the rear-view mirror. She honors him with a blush that arouses him more. They aren't at the lingerie store, but he can already picture taking naughty things off her body.

Man, this is bad. How am I supposed to keep Baz from knowing? Oh wait. I have a mesmer for a lifemate. I don't have to keep shit hidden. That thought satisfies Ash in an alpha male kind of way.

They arrive at the store, and Baz says, "I'll keep an eye out here."

"Are you sure?" Ivy asks, trying to make him feel invited as Soren asked her to, but Ash wants to growl at the invite. *Jeez! Cason wasn't kidding about the territorial part. God, if she enters her haze, what in the hell will I act like then?*

Baz nods. "I'm good." He leans against the side of the car, pulls out his phone, and smiles when he reads a text message.

Ash eyes the paint job of his prized vehicle and sighs in resignation. "Okay, man. But it's getting locked." The car beeps once as Baz nods, taking no offense that he won't have access.

Ash and Ivy enter the store and Ivy's wide eyes register fear. "What is this place?"

"It's an underwear store," Ash answers, picking up a pair of underwear comprised of no more than three inches of fabric. He smiles at her and wiggles his eyebrows.

Ivy shakes her head, whispering, "No. This is a sex store." Her face turns bright red. She's mortified.

She looks vulnerable, and he wants to cuddle her.

Ash leans in and whispers, "A sex store in the human world is where you will buy toys to use in the bedroom."

Horrified, she draws away from him quickly.

Her innocence makes him want to take her into one of the changing rooms. "Do you want me to help you find something that actually works the way underwear is supposed to?" he asks, doing his absolute best to hide the acidity of his blood.

Ivy nods slightly and looks down at her feet.

He lifts her chin so that their eyes meet. "You have no reason to be ashamed or feel awkward. You are stunning and, even though this makes you uneasy, it doesn't mean you shouldn't enjoy shopping here. Okay?"

Glancing around the store, Ivy nods slightly.

Ash nods back. He doesn't want her to feel so uncomfortable. He approaches one of the workers, who turns bright red at the sight of him, her lusty response to his appearance comes off her in waves.

He feels Ivy tense at the clerk's reaction, and his ego up, he squeezes Ivy's hand to calm her down. "Can you point me in the direction of actual underwear that she can wear for a workout?"

The clerk stands up straighter. "They all can be," she responds as she attempts to get him to look at her in a new light. She assesses Ivy and finds something like inadequacy, then bats her eyelashes at Ash provocatively.

"That wasn't my question," He says deadpan while doing everything in his power to not allow the clerk's attraction to him piss Ivy off.

"Sure, sir," the clerk replies, cool as a cucumber even as he let her down.

She has them follow her to the back of the store. "This is where we keep underwear for the less adventurous."

The clerk eyes Ivy with a smirk, and Ivy gives it right back. Ivy's grin at the clerk causes the hair on Ash's neck to stand on end.

Holy crap," he decides. *She is just as possessive as I am.* He does a happy dance in his head. Ivy's dead stare and bared teeth encourage the clerk, unable to stand her ground, to scurry away.

Though Ivy's fangs never showed, Ash knows they need to finish their shopping quickly.

Ivy picks her shoulders up a bit and smiles up at him as she hugs him from the front. "She wanted you."

"I know." Ash doesn't make a face.

Ivy tilts her head. "She was pretty."

Ash chuckles. "Not as pretty as you."

Ivy searches for truth in his eyes.

"Did I pass?" Ash asks.

"That depends," Ivy says, her face red.

She lowers her voice and whispers, "Would you like me to be more (she pauses) adventurous?"

Ash clears his throat, clearly uncomfortable as Ivy shrugs away from him. "Go pick out a few pairs you will want to see me in. I'll go look for my boring underwear."

"Are you kidding?" he asks, salivating. He can barely comprehend what she asks him to do as he searches her expression for another test.

Ivy shakes her head. "Nope. Just because I have never experienced this life before doesn't mean I don't want to."

"Where have you been all my life?" he asks adoringly, unable to think straight until she moves away from him.

"I think I should stay by your side, though," he tells her on a quick return.

Ivy shrugs, "As if your tallness can't see my tallness over these racks. Psh!"

Ash glances to where he was heading and realizes that she's right.

"I'll be right over there." He points to racks hung with baby doll lingerie.

She nods, not even looking up. "I will smell you, silly."

Ash feels heat creep into his face, his ears turning bright red at the thought.

When have I ever blushed besides when my mom talks about sex?

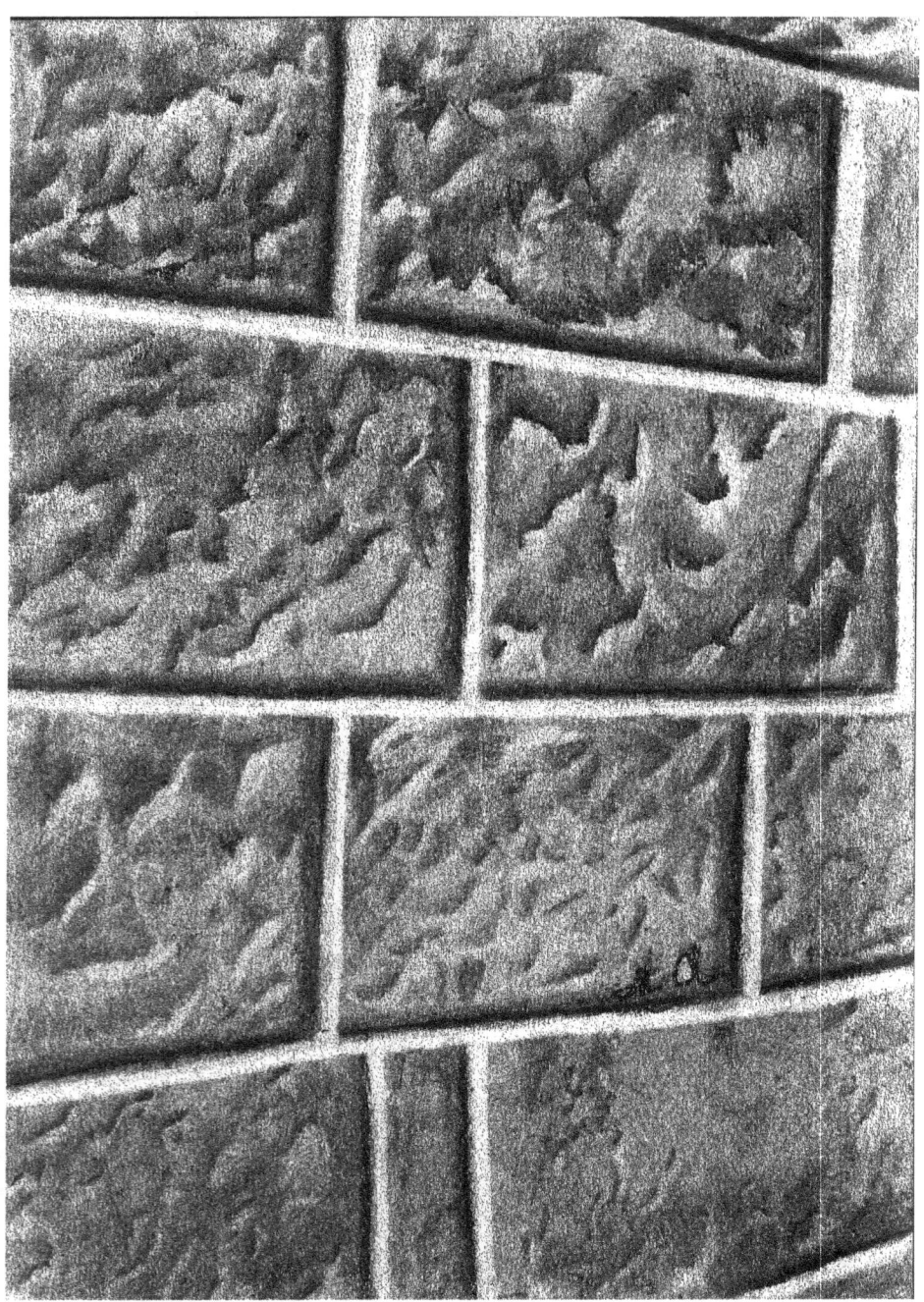

Cat and Canary

Heritage Marks

Ivy knows she won't be able to pick out something as revealing as the bathing suit she wore earlier. She'll chicken out. At least if she makes Ash do it, she'll know he wants to see her in it.

You're walking a line, Ivy, she tells herself. *You're going to hurt him.*

She aims to be fitted so she can pick out a few matching bra and underwear combos. Another clerk brings her into one of the stalls to measure her. In the human world, she wears they call a 34B bra and Size 5 underwear. She sets out on her mission in the back room and finds a few styles that she might like as well as a few she thinks qualify as in the middle of safe and reckless.

She has all the bras and underwear sitting on the counter as she waits for Ash to meet her. He has a few items in his arms and as he approaches, Ivy tries to get a glimpse of them. Ash wags his finger, tsking.

Ivy pouts at him, then asks the salesclerk, "Do you have a bathroom?"

The woman sighs. "No. We share with the rest of the building. If you go out this door, you will see the restroom sign on the far wall. You can't miss it."

"I'll be right back." Ivy says in a hurry.

Ash doesn't look happy about it. "Can you wait a minute? I'll bring you over there."

"It's right there," Ivy says, pointing to the sign out in the hallway.

He relents. "Fine. I'm going to bring this stuff to the car. I'll come back in if you aren't out there in two minutes. I'll walk right into the stall if I have to."

Ivy blushes and eyes the salesclerk gritting her teeth with jealousy.

Ivy nods to Ash and quickly walks into the large hallway between stores. She can feel his eyes on her all the way until she walks up to the door. It takes her a moment to figure out that the triangle with a circle on top is for females. She shakes her head at the sexist bullcrap that all women wear dresses.

She enters the stall and, sighing, relieves herself, sighing. She wipes, flushes, and walks up to the sink to wash her hands. Another woman also washes her hands.

Ivy smiles politely to her in the mirror and finishes drying her hands when she feels piercing pain in her neck. She slaps at it, and a dart falls to the floor with a click. Ivy bends over to pick it up and sees Baz in the stall behind her.

"What the hell is this?" she asks him. She can feel tremors from her fury overtaking her senses.

"I thought you said she was a Pale one," the other woman says to Baz. She looks terrified as she realizes her mistake.

Baz is pissed. "She is! Soren wouldn't lie to me. I'm the second in command." She sees a menacing look in his eyes that she's never seen before.

Virtually clueless to what is going on, Ivy knows one thing. *This asshole tried to dose me.* Pissed, she squares them up. "What was the plan, Baz?" Ivy asks while waiting for another dart to come at her.

Baz ignores her.

"Baz, why the fuck is she still standing?" Panic causes the woman's pulse to race as her eyes start darting around.

"Yeah, Baz. Why the fuck am I still standing? Didn't consider my strength, huh?" Ivy fumes.

Baz gulps as his eyes dart to the door Ivy blocks.

"Oh, poor baby is trapped in the playpen?" Ivy taunts the hyperventilating woman. Ivy imagines the woman must know that she is about to die since her heart beats so fast. It reminds Ivy of a rabbit.

Ivy pounces on her. The woman goes down on her back, and Ivy feels Baz moving silently moving around the restroom, looking for an escape.

Ivy rips the girl's throat out, making as big a mess as she can so the cause of death will be harder to pinpoint. The woman—distinctly human by the taste of her, all iron and water—bleeds out on the floor.

Ivy sees Baz approach her as she blocks the only escape he can take. She feels no air flow into the room even after he's scrambled to find one. She settles herself on her haunches as she waits for him to choose his fate.

"So why did a human want to know why this dart, right here, didn't knock me out?" Ivy asks, twirling the dart in her fingers, her teeth at full length and shining in the fluorescent lights.

Baz doesn't say anything as he fixes Ivy with a death stare. "I'd say I'm sorry, but I'm not. You are a freak of nature," he sneers at her with a newfound backbone. "I should have known that you weren't full Pale Race."

How did I not see this before? she asks herself. *The signs were there, so why didn't I listen to my gut?* The more she thinks about it, the more she realizes spies inhabit the ranks.

"Oh, but I'm much more, you little shit." She smiles at him, and he cringes. "I am your worst nightmare."

She plays idly with the dart, testing the sharpness with her finger. "How did you make my body react to the blood you gave me?"

Baz's eyes widen. "You couldn't know. It's undetectable."

"I suspected. You confirmed it," Ivy says. "So why in the world would you want to trick an unpredictable Pale female into being your lifemate? At any point I figured out your agenda, I would have killed you without a second thought."

"Because I needed you to confide in me," he retorts, bewildered that she doesn't already know that. "Duh."

Ivy smiles as she attempts to put the nightmarish pieces together. There is more to the story but she grasps that she needs to get every answer before killing his sleezy ass.

"So, you're working for the humans who capture and breed our kind for their sick." She grins menacingly, wanting more than anything to rip his throat out, too.

"You know nothing!" Baz screams.

Ash suddenly barges into the bathroom, a feral look on his face. He sees Ivy covered in blood and searches her face for pain.

"It's not mine, Ash," she assures him.

"It never is," he responds with a grin. "But I will always make sure before assuming you're okay."

He glances at Baz, then her, then Baz again.

"You want to tell him or do I have to?" Ivy asks.

Baz shifts his weight from one foot to the other and says nothing.

"He and this blood bag decided to dart me," Ivy tells Ash. "They thought they could take me down like the normal females of the Pale Race."

Ash roars with anger, causing Ivy to squint at the force.

"What?" Ash asks.

"You can't kill him, Ash." Ivy says. "We need to find out what he knows."

Looking for the hole the dart made, Ash moves the hair on her neck. He finds the dart and smells it. "Shit. We need to get him out of here right now. And we especially need to get *you* out of here."

She draws Baz over to her with her eyes. *You will not speak. You will do exactly as told until you are locked in chains.*

Panic in his eyes, Baz feels it. "Hurry up. I have him. Get the car," Ivy directs. Ash hurries out as she tells Baz, "Walk like a good boy." She giggles knowing that she is about to overrun him with her mind.

Ash pulls around to the side door as Ivy escorts Baz. They shove Baz, hatred in his glaring eyes, into the back seat of the car and don't speak until they're moving.

"I have to say," Ash says looking into her eyes as they start driving, "I can really use you in the field."

Ivy laughs. "Duh."

Something dawns on her. "You are aware that since I was five I have been trained for the Scavenger Guild."

Ash nods and looks out the front window.

"I am a fighter," she tells him. "It's in my blood and always will be."

She can't place Ash's odd expression as he says, "You never cease to amaze me."

They drive back to Duneskil as fast as Ash's sport sedan can take them whipping down back roads so fast that Ivy clutches door handle they take corners.

As the two of them jump out of the car, Ash yells, "Soren!"

Soren flies out of the house. "What the hell is happening?"

"Where can we question him discreetly?" Ivy asks, focusing on keeping the mesmer on Baz as they guide him along with them.

Soren comes to attention without bothering to ask further what is going on as he leads the way.

"Follow me." Soren lets Ivy and Ash into his office and shuts the door on any potential onlookers. He pulls a lever when he announces, "This was a speakeasy during the Prohibition."

"Whatever that is," Ivy mumbles, bringing a chuckle from Ash.

"Human history, Ivy," Soren says as he follows a set of stairs from the office down into a dark tunnel. Halfway down, Soren pulls a switch to light the rest of the way, which isn't far. At the bottom of the stairs a large entryway expands out into many rooms. Soren walks to the one furthest from the stairs. At intervals, the walls have chains thick enough to hold even Ivy.

Ivy allows Baz free will once he is mounted to the wall. She is about to fall over from exertion. Ash rushes to her, catches her, and sets her down in one of the dusty old chairs.

"Are you sure that dart didn't mess with you?" Ash asks, concerned.

Ivy shakes her head. "No. But I can say they expected me to go down quickly."

"What are you talking about?" Soren asks bewildered.

Hatred contorts every feature on Baz's face.

"What's wrong with him?" Soren asks.

Ivy recounts the ordeal to Soren, including the fact that she ripped out the human's throat. "We brought him back here so you can figure out what the hell is going on," Ivy says with little energy.

Considering what he's heard, Soren nods. "You say it was a woman he was working with?"

"Yes," Ivy replies.

"And do we know what was in the dart?" Soren asks, impatient.

Ash looks at the ground. "It was pure ancient blood mixed with some other toxin. That is why she wasn't affected like we are. She already has it running through her veins."

"You're an ancient!" Baz gapes from the wall.

Ivy smiles, looking over at him. "Yes, actually. I am."

She watches as the wheels turn in his mind.

"You're the hybrid—like the actual hybrid everyone is freaking out about," Baz says triumphantly.

Ivy smiles as he panics again.

"Wait," says Ash. "Do you think that's why he wanted her to bite him? They wanted to get her venom to test?"

"That would make sense. But why come at her tonight?" Soren asks.

"Because this is the only time she has been off the compound with Baz since she got here," Ash guesses. "He's been begging to take her on a date for weeks."

"Or because Baz, here, realized that spiking his blood so I'd have a reaction wasn't going to work if I'm not interested in him," Ivy pipes in through tired eyes.

"Spiked his blood? How can he do that?" Ash asks her, not understanding.

Ivy thinks back to the history books for a moment so she can put it all together. "Oh, snap!" she says with a look of understanding. "He isn't full Pale Race!"

The two men look at her like she has two heads.

"Females can get pregnant whether the father is of another race, right?" she asks.

They both nod.

"It's rare that any hybrid matures, though." Soren says with reluctance.

"But it can happen. Especially if they are breeding the mother nonstop for the blood." Ivy's blood starts to boil inside of her.

"That's it, isn't it?" Ivy directs herself to the chained-up man on the wall. She goes to him and gets a better look at his heritage mark. Its smaller than the four she has ever seen. She wonders why it's the first time she has thought of looking at it.

Then she looks closer at the coat of arms and sees that it's missing something.

"Ash come over here," Ivy directs.

Ash joins her, and Ivy holds his arm and Baz's closer together to compare them.

"His coat of arms is unfinished," Ivy whispers. She directs herself to Baz again. "Your mother wasn't able to pass her lineage to you completely because your blood wasn't potent enough to take a full change."

Baz swears at her. "Shut up, bitch."

"Do you even drink blood?" Ivy asks him with wide eyes.

"Nope. I never have," he says proudly. "You are all disgusting, by the way. Most of my life has been hell looking after filthy blood suckers who kill people on a whim." He grins at Ivy. "I was so close to getting a new post and a raise. Had I been able to get a royal untainted bloodline into the lab, I'd have been set for life."

Ivy doesn't believe it. "How many times have they forced you to breed with the Pale Race, Baz?"

"None," he says. "I don't need to be forced to help save humanity from illness. It's the least I can do for being given the chance to live."

Beyond her control, Ivy feels a growl starting deep in her chest. "You are scum," she tells Baz.

She sees red and stalks closer to Baz, but Ash and her father pull her back.

"Ivy!" her father commands, distracting her from Baz. "You need to feed."

Feeling guilty that she'd lost control, Ivy nods and looks up at Ash, who says, "You take care of yourself. I will beat the shit out of this asshole for some answers."

Ivy goes to speak but her father pulls her from the dungeon and brings her to her own room. She closes herself in the bathroom at once and takes a shower to rid herself of the bloody mess covering the front of her body. When she reappears, she jumps at the sight of three women and Soren standing in her living room.

The first woman, Jenny, seems the most adventurous of the three. She addresses Ivy. "Soren says you are depressed and can use a few friends and a movie to perk you up." She looks around and then at Soren. "I thought you said she has a TV."

Soren takes the remote from the table between the couches and pushes a button. A flap in the ceiling opens, and a TV floats down into the room. Jenny approaches the entertainment center and starts fiddling with things, to get the movie to play on the giant screen.

"Now that is sweet," says the woman with blond, mid-length, wavy hair as she plops herself down on the couch to settle in. Her popcorn makes a small mess under her as she bounces. "I'm Clara, by the way."

The third woman stands out of the way. She seems not to want to intrude on Ivy "I'm Amanda.".

"Make yourself at home," Ivy tells her, not wanting her to feel unwanted. In so many ways, the woman reminds Ivy of Willow. She looks at Ivy adoringly as she goes to sit on the couch opposite the woman with popcorn.

"What are you doing?" Ivy mouths to Soren.

Knowing that anything he says can be overheard by the other three, he hands Ivy a note that reads: *Have all three of them fill one of the bottles that I left in a bag under your desk. There are also six blood bags to have them drink*

*from. Have them watch the entire movie so it's not as questionable. Drink every-
thing you can and then store the rest in your minifridge that I stuck in your closet.*

Knowing that she is famished after the long mesmer, she smiles and gives her father a kiss on his cheek. "Thank you, Dad."

"You are most welcome."

He turns to go and then stops and looks at her for a moment. "When the movie is over, you should come downstairs to my office."

Ivy nods. "Okay."

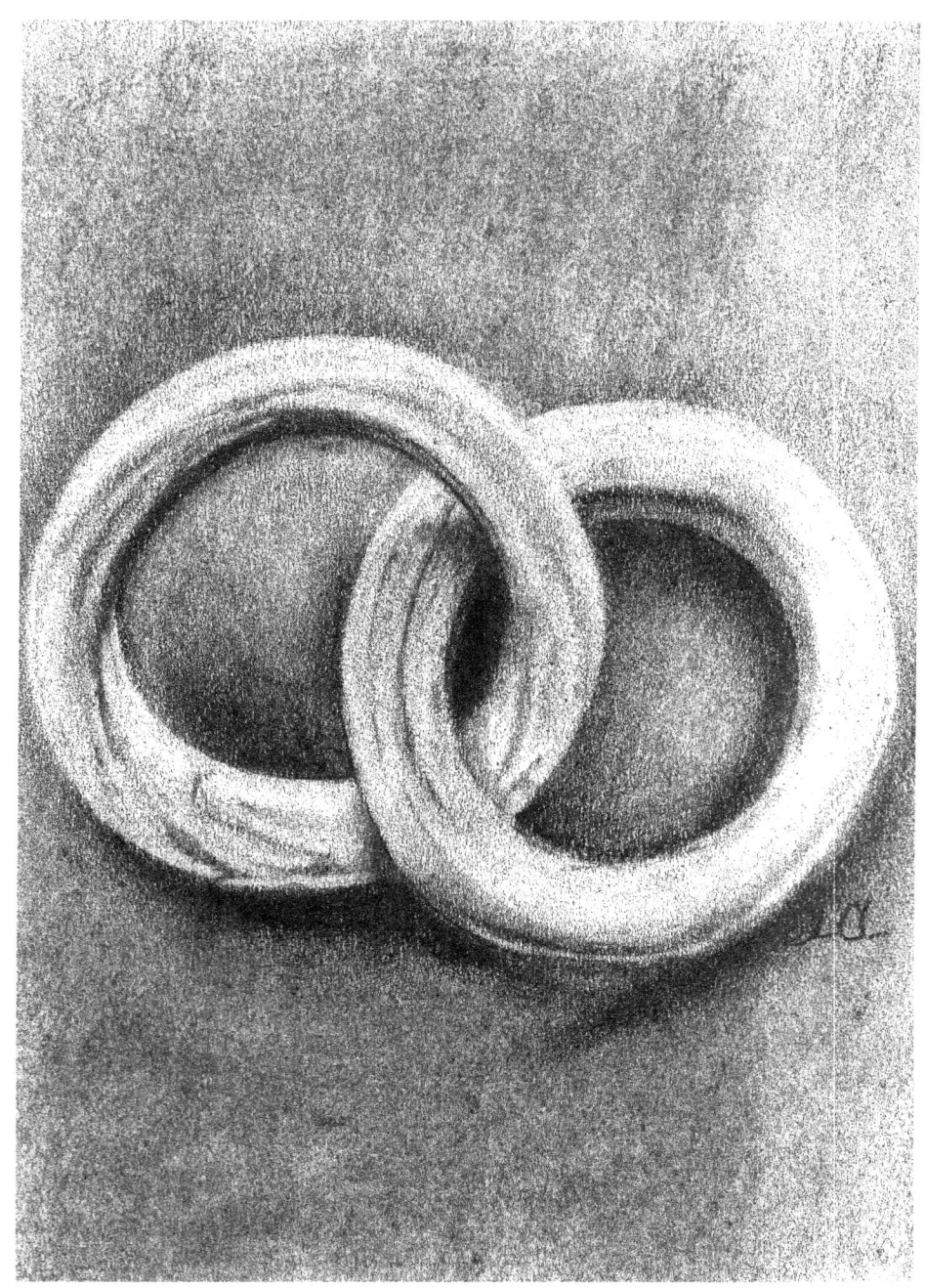

Infinity

Gifts

Ash's hands are bloody from repeatedly battering into Baz's face and body. It isn't as if he can really change a mind that's been made up, but it's making him feel a little better on behalf of the Pale Race. He feels the rage of a male who cannot protect his female and disappointment in himself for letting his duties falter regarding another person's trust.

Soren asked him to stop an hour before, but the urge to keep hitting Baz persists. He feels the overwhelming need to bury the traitor who's betrayed Ivy.

It doesn't matter that she can take care of herself. She shouldn't have to, he screams in his head, pissed at himself as much as he's pissed at Baz. *I should never have let her out of my sight. I knew something was off, but I didn't listen to my gut.*

Baz chuckles to himself with every blow and doesn't feel the pain in his bones the way Ash wants him to.

"You've been at this for hours," Cason says. "We aren't getting anything out of him. Take a break until Ivy gets back."

"Ivy is not doing this!" Ash rages. "It's my job to protect her, and she was almost grabbed by this piece of shit!"

Cason steps back, then musters the strength to come back, "You know what? You are pulling some real alpha male bullshit, and you need to knock it off. That girl can handle herself in a fight, and you know it." He takes a breath. "She is nothing like other females of our race because she was made for only you. Stop treating her like she's going to break!"

Ash glares at Cason, who shrinks into nothing.

"Fine. Be an asshole without a solid plan!"

Cason storms out of the dungeon and leaves the door open.

Ash knows that if they hadn't tried that night, they would have tried another night and succeeded. *Any of those times that Baz tried to get her off the compound for a date could have led to her demise. All because I had my head up my ass about being told who to be with!* The knowledge did nothing to help his mood. If anything, it made him want to hit Baz harder.

They will come after her again. He repeats over and over, *how am I going to protect her? If I can't protect her, I don't deserve her!*

He stops as he smells Ivy approaching. The natural scent of her intoxicates him while causing him to want to hurt Baz even more. *This asshole needs to die!*

"You really don't know how to question someone, do you Ash?" Baz croaks out as he starts to laugh like a lunatic. "What a joke."

"Ash, let me try." Ivy says timidly. He can sense that she doesn't want to upset him but knows she will be the one to get answers. She's the only one who can.

Ash shakes his head no as he throws another punch into Baz's stomach, causing him to cough up blood. As he is about to swing again, Ash feels Ivy's arms wrapping around his torso from behind. The lifemate jolt stops him dead. He feels her shiver as Baz's laughter turns maniacal. His entire body rages even more territorially as he fights to protect his lifemate.

"You need to get out of here," Ash growls at her. He wants nothing getting in the way of what he feels he needs to do. He hears Dayton take her from the room and continues doing what he has always done best.

Ivy's voice gets raw with emotion as she spins back to speak. "Who in the hell asked you to be the savior, Ash? No one. I am the hybrid. If anything, I'm here to save you!" With that, she leaves Ash to his self doubt as she walks away from him.

His heart wants to break. *Why can't I do anything right with this girl? Any other female who has ever wanted me tried to please me where they could, but this one only wants what is best for all concerned. She doesn't give a damn about pretenses and least of all about her own safety.*

After she leaves, Ash all but weeps. He can't stay in the same room with the man who tried to take her from him. Hatred overwhelms his other emotions so much that it takes everything not to kill Baz on the spot—force drain him and leave him to rot for the next thirty years.

Unable to stay still, he goes outside and paces the garden. He lies in the hammock. No matter what he does, however, he can't force the sound of hurt in her voice as she yelled at him from echoing in his mind. The anguish that she'd shown at not being able to help in a way that only she could causes him to curl into the hammock and shed his own tears.

What the hell is wrong with me! Ash thinks, not wanting to admit that something is. I did the one thing that makes her feel like less of a person, the one thing that she can't stand from anyone. *I didn't trust her to protect me when she is supposed to trust me to protect her.* Wiping the tears from his face in irritation, the realization has him landing on her balcony seconds later.

He doesn't do what he knows he must, though, as he peers through the glass doors and sees her intent on writing. Three women sit in the living room watching some movie about a guy with tattoos and a kid, but she isn't paying attention. He peers closer at the paper in front of her and sees that she is writing a list of all the things she will want to know from Baz.

Ash smiles at the thought of her so on task, two empty bottles to the side as she's sipping a third, writing with perfect penmanship. Butterflies run through his stomach and remind him that he will have to make up for it somehow no matter what his male ego demands.

He watches as she finishes her list, the women having left a few minutes before. She doesn't go to the office, though, as he watches her. She heads out to the garden and paces as if to gain the courage she needs to do what she must. She seems to brood as she thinks.

Ash can't take it anymore. He jumps down from the balcony and strides toward her. The feeling of protection washes over him until she is in his arms. "I know I can't blame myself, but it doesn't mean I don't. I am sorry for treating you the way I did."

"Ash. No one could have foreseen this."

He pulls back and, counting on his fingers as he looks her in the eye. "One, he loses his breath upon exertion like a human smoker. Two, he can't smell a steak cooking twenty feet away from him. Three, he can't smell the lovely aroma that comes from you every time I make you blush. Four, he doesn't look at you like I do, and, five, he is afraid of you."

Ash heaves a breath.

"All these things, and he told both Soren and me that he wasn't interested in you for your love. Soren investigated his phone and found love messages to a human girl, so Soren assumed that's why Baz was faking it. He wanted a better title, and the Pale Race doesn't get a better title with a human woman on his arm.

"All the same, we should have been more vigilant and will be from now on."

Ivy chuckles. "You don't realize that this is the kind of thing I am used to, do you?"

Waiting for her to explain and not wanting her to make excuses for him, he would accept her loyalty if she were to explain. Ash looks into her eyes.

She does explain. "When I was in Lesai, I killed the boyfriend I'd had for almost a year. He was only seeking power and was willing to out my mother because he wanted a better position. He knew my mother would never allow it after he beat me during my transition. So instead of letting my mother's guards take care of him, I did the deed myself, draining him and tossing him aside like the dung that he was. Defending myself and protecting my family are what I do."

Ash can't believe what he hears. "You were alone with a male during your transition, and he hurt you?"

"That's what you took from that?" Ivy can't believe it. "This is the past. I am not afraid of anyone."

Ash looks into her eyes. "You will never be alone again if I can help it. There is nothing in the world I want more than to see that asshole rot in the ground, but he is of the Pale Race."

"He is a hybrid human who barely has any magic in his veins," she says seriously. "If there is a way for him to die, believe me, I will find it tonight. But right now, I need to meditate. I need to draw as much energy as I can before I mesmer the information we want out of him."

Ash nods and makes a promise to himself as he tells her, "The Terrors will be within earshot of you at all times from now on. I'm sorry for not hearing you out earlier."

"Just realize that next time I will make you stop beating him so there is enough left for me to mesmer."

Ash smiles, glad that she understands he wasn't in his right mind when she approached him.

"And the Terrors are welcome to hear all our mushy conversations that they want." Ivy says with amusement.

Having prepared for an argument, he smiles at her invitation to terrorize the Terrors. "Now show me how to meditate with you so I can help the Elemental Mother help you."

Ivy looks up at him with wide eyes.

"Seriously?"

Ash nods, unwilling to allow anything to happen to her ever again, whether that means meditating with her or standing in the room with her while she pees.

Ivy brings Ash to a grove of trees, and she sits. She has him sit, legs crossed, opposite her. He has to adjust his pants to allow his legs to bend the way they need to. Ivy laughs.

Once in place, she starts explaining in monotone, sounding eerily like Calyn. "Take deep cleansing breaths. In . . . Out . . . In . . . Out . . . Believe that for every breath you take, you are cleansing the air with your lungs and breathing out food for the trees and plants around you. As you keep breathing, feel the root of the tree that is you burrowing deep into the ground, so deep that it is close to burrowing into the life veins of the earth.

"Those life veins that are filled with molten lava heating the ground beneath us. As our roots grow deeper, our sapling emerges, branching out into the open space above us and growing leaves to absorb the sun's fuel. As our trees grow and our roots go deeper, the elemental magic that flows everywhere around us begins seeping into our roots and branches.

"The fire of her blood, the water of her womb, the air rustling our leaves, and the earth stabilizes our being. As we breathe . . . in . . . out . . . in . . . out . . . , we breathe in the elemental magic that fuels within us and breathe out the magic that feeds the life around us—the energy pulsing with everything that has been, everything that is and everything that has yet to come.

"We breathe until we can breathe no more, and we absorb until we can absorb no more. As we wait in silence listening to the life that is around us, we gather the fuel we need to work the mission of the Elemental Mother. As we sing, we sing to her and let her smile her gifts of blessings onto us."

Then she sings, the melancholy beauty of her voice in the moment scarring his soul forever. Ash feels a pull to open his eyes and knows that the Elemental Mother is telling him what to do. He sees Ivy, glowing in tree form, right next to him. It's surreal, unbelievable, and beautiful. The Mother pushes him to do something he'd never in a million years think of. He reaches into a tree next to him and feels something there. As he pulls, he sees himself looking at a wooden infinity symbol complete with two intertwined rings. None of the pieces have an end, and it is the most stunning thing he has ever seen in his life.

Then out of nowhere he feels himself begin to sing. Not the high notes that Ivy climbs to as she draws energy from the earth but the deeper notes of a choir tormented with a love he is discovering. The music echoes in his ears as the two of them sing together in the night causing the birds and animals around them to sing as well. When the song ends, she leans into him, and the electrical current running through them back and forth has him not wanting to move.

Feeling the approach of dawn, he goes to touch her shoulder. Before he can, she looks at him. Her eyes glow a golden yellow of the elemental magic she's taken into herself.

"Time to go," she tells him.

He nods and smiles at her.

"I should totally take a picture and show you your eyes," Ash says with a smile.

Ivy looks back at him, and he sees her eyes no longer golden.

"Why?"

Confused, he shrugs. "No reason. I just love looking at you."

Her face contorts as she refuses to believe him.

Stopping her in her tracks and grabbing her around the waist, he spins her to himself. "You, my dear, will come to know your beauty."

"Mhmm." She goes to turn, not believing it.

Ash pulls her back to him and gives her a searing kiss that has him spinning, too. Pulling back, he says, "You are." He smiles as her dizziness threatens to topple her. "Do I need to carry you in?"

"No!" She pecks him on the nose. "I will accept that you think I am. That's all I can do for now."

At least you got her to accept that much!

Dark Temptation

Blood Magic

As Ash and Ivy walk down the stairs, the sun coming up over the horizon, every one of the Terrors emits a gasp. All of them sit around a table in what they call the war room. They're there to guard Baz.

When Ash doesn't react to his warriors' shock, Ivy feels the pull of something she can't put her finger on. Ash smiles wide and lands a kiss right on her lips, owning her soul in a grip that she can't understand as he hugs her tightly.

"Get a room!" Graham gags, an ick factor in his tone.

"Shut up, asshole! You're mad that you aren't getting the attention." Cason laughs and winks at Ivy.

Ivy ignores the banter. A shiver runs down her spine as she looks at Ash, and she hugs him tighter.

"You good?" Ash asks, concerned.

"You're here with me, so yes." Her heart wants to explode with the safety she feels in his arms.

Stone gives a fake grimace. "God, they sound like they're in a lifetime movie."

Ash smacks him in the back of the head.

"Ow!"

Dayton elbows Stone in the rib. "Now you have something to cry about."

"Ass!"

In her little bubble, Ivy smiles, thankful that she has her warriors around her for what's to come.

The meditation she and Ash shared causes her to grow emotional for reasons unknown, but for the life of her, she doesn't understand why.

Standing in the middle of a room full of men who come close to kicking her butt in a fight, she feels herself relaxing slightly.

"Also," she adds, returning her eyes to Ash's, "Baz is weaker than a baby vamp strapped to a wall. I guarantee that him not drinking blood weakens him. Think about it."

She watches as Ash fights everything inside of him that tells him to make her leave. Instead, he hugs her back. "I am not leaving you alone with Baz"

She smiles, feeling like the luckiest woman in the world, while gaining the confidence to hold Baz in mesmer for as long as it takes to get answers. The earlier meditation had filled her more than in months, and she is grateful for all that she has received.

"I'd hope not." She kisses him on the tip of the nose and making him laugh in the process, Ivy gives Ash one last hug before stepping towards Baz, still shackled to the wall.

Graham starts gagging in the background. "You two are disgusting."

Letting her teeth out, Ivy smiles at him. "Thank you."

Ash chuckles at her smiling while Graham, always disgruntled when she does it, shifts in his seat.

"Do you have that gift we got?" Ivy asks.

Ash nods, holding it out to her. She shakes her head and smiles at him. "It was a gift to you. Keep it with you. It'll guide you."

Ash smiles and kisses her again. She blushes as he deepens the kiss.

"My God! You two are ridiculous!" Baz complains from his spot on the wall.

With a no-nonsense air that screams "mess with me. I dare you," Soren enters. Ivy, heads over to him with the list of questions she had produced while the women watched the movie.

"I made this up to keep me on track. I don't know how long I can hold the mesmer." She hands the list over to Soren and he reads it.

"You know, for someone who is new to this world, you know so much more than I'd have thought," her father says with pride. "I do have to add more, though." He jots a few more questions and hands the notes back to her.

Ivy looks over the revisions and hands the paper to Ash. He reads it over and nods approval.

Ivy shifts a little, drawing their attention as she again eyes Baz. "There is only one thing. If you have any more questions to follow up with, I need you to write them down. Interrupting my concentration could cause more issues, and I'm not sure how long I can hold the mesmer."

Soren rips the paper, taking the bottom third and a pen to a spot near where Baz is chained up. In the corner, Jynx waits patiently with a laptop. Soren insists on a written record as well as an audio recording of the questioning for the Pale Council.

Ivy sits in a chair in front of Baz, Ivy zeroes her focus to him.

"I'm not telling you anything, bitch."

"Now, now, Baz. You will tell me everything I want to know. How did you get here all chained up?

"I came here because I will do anything you say." He maintains his smug look until he realizes what he's said.

Ivy smiles and looks at Ash.

Uneasy as she looks back into his puffy eyes, Baz peers at her. "This should only take about five minutes," she tells him.

Baz has a renewed sense of fear.

She puts herself inside his brain, and he screams, trying to fight her off, but she only grips harder. He stops screaming and stares at her with a fog over his eyes, as the mesmer sticks. Ivy tests it out to make sure the supplement he took isn't blocking her.

"Baz, break your finger." She watches as he snaps his pinky, roaring as the pain hits his features.

She nods. "You have no pain during the questioning." Baz's features become perfectly controlled, so she continues.

"Baz, what is your full name?"

"Sebastian Blackwell," he says with a faraway look in his eyes.

"Age and birth date?" she asks.

"Thirty-five years old. February 19, 1981."

"Who is your mother?"

"Kamila Knight."

Ivy looks over at Soren, who furiously begins writing.

"Who is your father?"

"Samuel Blackwell."

Completely dismissing what she'd asked him to do, Soren interrupts her and shows her the paper he's written on.

"When was your mother captured?" she asks.

"August of 1891." Ivy watches her father's features as he racks his brain for the right question.

"Why do the humans want me specifically?"

"You are the first female heir to the Knight name. Two names began the Pale Race." *What the hell does that mean?* she wonders, forgetting that she is still in Baz's head. "There were two in the beginning. There will be two at the end. They want to control the end of the races."

"What do the humans know about Duneskil?" she asks

"Everything I do and more," he replies.

Ivy begins to feel scared.

"Who here is also a plant?"

"I don't know."

"How long have you been undercover?"

"Twenty-six years, three months, and eight days." The monotonous sound of his voice is freaking Ivy out.

"Where is your mother being held?"

"I don't know."

"How do you survive without blood?"

"Special vitamins."

Where do you hide your food? she thinks to ask without speaking, then realizes that Soren and Ash also need to hear the questions.

"Pantry hidden in my closet."

"How many other covens are under surveillance?" she asks as she returns to speaking aloud.

"All of them." She feels Ash move from behind her and grabs his hand without looking. She doesn't want him to be any further away.

"Why did you want me to bite you so much?"

"The blood you drank didn't transfer the tracking substance the way it does other substances."

Soren brings her a new set of questions and takes the paper she's finished. "Is Knox alive?"

"I don't know that name."

"How many children have you sired?"

"Sixteen."

Ivy feels like vomiting as she sways, beginning to feel the drain of the mesmer and not wanting to think of all the children born into captivity.

"Is there another of you planted in Duneskil?"

"Yes."

"Who?"

"I don't know."

Soren hands her back the first paper. "How many of your children have lived past fledgling?"

"Five."

"How many have their heritage mark?"

"None."

"If you don't know who the plant is at Duneskil, how do you know there is one?"

"They knew Ivy was coming." Ivy's eyes get wide as she tries to think of anyone at Duneskil who might have known she was coming.

"Is there a plant in Lesai?"

"Several."

Ash whispers into her ear, and she asks a final question. "How much of the blood at Duneskil is tainted?"

"All of it."

Ivy looks wide-eyed at Ash and her father. Panic takes her body as she feels the sickness coming. It hits her like a ton of bricks, and as she tries to back herself away from Baz, she sees that he is coming to. Worried, Ash studies her, but she can't speak to ease his mind. Her whole body is a coiled snake ready to bite.

She feels a type of hunger she hasn't felt before. Roars of pain begin again as Baz snaps out of the mesmer. She can't understand what she is doing as she moves instinctively towards him and raises her hands towards his head.

Aching for the kill, her teeth protrude from her gums. Her heart pounds in a way she has never before endured.

She moves closer to Baz, and he cowers away in fear. "You know everything now. Let me go," he says as if it's that easy. "What's wrong with your eyes?" Then he shrieks, his questions no longer forming words as Ivy's mind flits from blood lust to a new searing need for magic.

She recognizes the pull. She can feel the essence of blood coursing through his veins, and the sensation floors her.

There is no turning back even as she feels both of her Protectors trying to pull her away from Baz. She pulls herself free, relishing in pure power that makes her who she is. Her sight changes colors to a magnetic blue, allowing her to see tendrils of wiggly magic floating through him. As she tries to touch them, they flee, making her grab for them with her mind to hold them hostage before she can feel them.

Ivy feels the pull of the magic within Baz as she tilts her head to look at him She can feel the drum of blood in his veins, magic in and of itself. Like elements, magic can be absorbed.

The magic of Baz is different, though—sinister and potent, not the effervescent beauty that creates the forests and seas of the earth. The magic of Baz feels more intense, and it draws her in with a ferocity she can't control. She can't make herself run as her head tells her to, and the men pulling on her have no effect on her body.

The pull of the magic is too strong as she stares through the lens of his skin and into his blood. She places her hands on his head and forces his attention back to her eyes. He growls fiercely as she mentally erases the memory of her and everything he has ever known. He will never be able to even think again of anything about the place.

There will be nothing but a shell, she thinks as he screams so profusely that by the end there is no breath left, just a limp body and eyes wide in fear. Pulling the little tendrils of magic through his body to her hands one at a time, she smiles as she finds she has to chase each one before it will give in to her. Her body roars to life as she absorbs Baz's blood magic into herself.

Her hands shake with newfound energy that makes her skin crawl while refueling every cell in her body. Her head falls backwards as she feels each strand of magic soiled with the taint of hate. She can feel her body cleansing the magic before allowing it into her bloodstream. As the last tendril emerges from his body, she watches his eyes roll back into his head, defeated.

Who to trust?

Patience

Ash and Soren can both feel the air get thick and humid as Ivy drains the male of his life force. Baz goes from a twenty-one-year-old with the slow heartbeat of the Pale Race to a thirty-five-year-old with the quick pace of a human in seconds. Ivy holds his head in her hands, her eyes glowing blue with the magic that she draws into herself.

As Ivy's skin color returns to its normal alabaster instead of the grey of just moments earlier, she begins to fall sideways. Ash scoops her into his arms before she hits the ground and shakes her to make sure that she's okay.

Her eyes open slowly, and she smiles all that she can with the exhaustion that overtakes her. "He can be killed now," she announces, drifting off to sleep in Ash's arms.

Ash and Soren look at each other with mutual confusion at what she's done. *No one can find out.* Ash holds her tighter. It's bad enough that he will have to explain it to his father, the head of the Pale Council.

"You will have to protect her from herself as well as from enemies," Soren says with a grimace. "There is no feasible way she won't be hunted down if anyone finds out that she got these secrets from Baz."

Removing the hair from her face, Ash looks down into Ivy's face as she softly snores.

"You will need to call Calyn soon."

Ash meets his eye and smiles. "I asked a couple days ago."

Soren takes on a questioning look, and Ash laughs. "I needed a plan that would work. Your daughter is the most stubborn person I have ever met. I wasn't about to tell her that I feel for her. She would never believe me. She needs to feel it, too."

Quiet prevails as Soren takes it in. Then he nods. "I guess you're right. Who better to help you get past the stubborn than the one who passed it to her?"

Soren is quiet. "It took me three years to convince Calyn that she was the person I wanted to spend my life with," he says, shaking his head with a smile. "And to this night, she is still the love of my life, and I will protect her in any way I can."

Ash thinks about it quietly for a moment. Clearing his throat, he says, "I have a confession to make." He looks at Soren with remorse and then back down at Ivy.

"The council told me when I received my mark that my match will be the first female knight with a heritage mark," Ash says. He doesn't want to look up at Soren for fear of the man's potential anger.

"You have known for more than three hundred years that you will marry my daughter?" Soren asks, his eyebrows raised.

Ash sighs. "I was going to tell them to eat it, honestly." He pauses a moment. "I was told at once that, as the prince of the Pale Race, I will have to be matched with the blood of a princess who is my equal. Which really makes no sense when all is said and done.

"You could have told me, you know." Soren says, a look of irritation on his face.

"If I hadn't been sworn to secrecy, I would have told you, but you know how the council is. How my father is."

Soren considers for a moment. "Yeah, he's known about Ivy since she was eight."

Ash looks at Soren surprised. "I figured that out after coming here. My father told me that he'd kept it secret because he didn't think she would get her mark. The hybrid was supposed to be a male."

Thinking, Soren scrubs his hand through his hair.

Annoyed, Ash says, "I found out shortly after I met you that Knight and Vale were the first two surnames of the Pale Race to be born. They were born on the same night and time on opposite sides of the world."

Soren curses under his breath. "You have read the prophecy."

Ash nods. He knows more than Soren does about it, but again sworn to secrecy, he has to keep it locked in the vault.

"But what does it mean?" Soren asks. "I get why the Ancients would be against their magic taken from the earth, but why would the Pale Race want this prophecy to come forward?"

Ash shrugs, trying to keep the chills at bay that always come when he thinks about the prophecy. "I have always thought that the hybrid would be a male, too, but when I put it in Ivy terms, the words patriarchal bullshit come to mind that strength has to come from men."

They chuckle, both looking down at Ivy as she snores softly.

"Is it weird that I know I'll get my lifemate mark if your daughter and I become one?" *Did I really just ask that?*

Expecting to be smacked in the back of the head, Ash glances at Soren. Not wanting to see what will happen to Ash, those at the table of warriors all make hasty retreats.

"No," Soren says with a lilt to his voice that tells Ash everything he needs to know. Soren had met his own lifemate at some point in his long life. He looks down at his daughter in Ash's arms, "She is already in love with you," he says knowingly.

Ash shakes his head, afraid to believe that it could be true. "I'm not so sure about that."

"I am," Soren says with a nod. "Call it a father's instinct, but even if I haven't watched her grow, I see the same look that Calyn has for me."

Ash smiles a little at the reminder of Calyn. "Can we have a lifemate without getting a mark?"

"I believe I have one," Soren says with a smile. "I am not able to love anyone other than Calyn. Believe that I have tried several times to fall in love with someone else. Especially when I thought Calyn was dead."

He looks away, then meets Ash's eyes. "Never take advantage of the time you have. Love can be fleeting or last an eternity. Whichever it is, you will never know."

"Will you idiots shut up? Where am I? And who in the hell are you, anyways?" Baz asks from three feet away, his eyes rolling in his head a little. They look up at Baz, who instantly projectile vomits all over Ash and Ivy. The putrid scent causes Ash to begin dry heaving.

Soren covers his face with his shirt. "You take care of her. I'm going to take care of this bumbling idiot."

"No fair!" Ash says, wanting to be the one who takes his head off.

"Dude, you are turning green, and if I remember right," Soren lectures, "you got to beat him to a pulp earlier. It's not my fault that I waited for my daughter to suck the magic out of him."

Ash laughs. "Fine! I'll take the princess to the tower to pamper her."

"Dumb ass!" Soren mumbles under his breath.

Gagging, Ash carries Ivy upstairs. He pauses as he approaches her bedroom door. He looks down at her sleeping face and opens his door instead. She smells of vomit and decay as much as he does, so he does what he hopes is the right thing. He brings her into his bathroom and strips her down to her underwear, making sure that the vomit doesn't transfer over to those garments. Then he undresses.

Not knowing if it's even possible for her to wake up so soon after the ordeal she went through, Ash steps into the tub he asked Jynx to fill earlier with her. He smiles as she sighs into his arms, though she's evidently not looking close to waking.

As he watches her sleep, he imagines what it will be like to hold her every night before they sleep. The thought creates a swirling vortex of what can be their future if he can convince her to hope. He reaches over to the sponge with one hand while propping up her head with the other as he makes sure that her head doesn't fall beneath the surface of the water.

Ash uses his free hand to wash all the vomit off. He isn't sure how long he sat in the tub with her, but he wakes up with a start when he feels her shivering from the icy water. *Shit! I give her a bath only to give her hypothermia. Yeah, really smart!*

He stands and grabs a couple towels without bothering to dry off until he gets her over to the bed.

Laying her down, he dries her as much as possible. He runs to his closet to get a t-shirt to put on her. When he debates bringing her back to her room, he falls short of the gentlemanly thing to do, tucking her into his bed instead. He goes around, picking up the random things he has lying around the suite before he puts his own pajamas on, that is, a pair of boxers and a black undershirt.

The smell of her is heaven as he crawls into the king-sized bed next to her and pulls her over to him, burying his face in her hair as he falls asleep.

Waking up in the middle of the day has become a habit since he met Ivy. Never has he wanted to be awake in the past so late when he is weakest, but when she is around, it's usually entertaining. The way she works on her sparring or lies in the sun reading a book intoxicates his dreams.

When he wakes up to find that she is still sleeping in the crook of his arm, snuggled up to his chest, his body comes to attention. Her hair tangles around his body and cheek and smooshes against his arm, arousing him despite his best efforts to resist.

He does the only thing that he can think of to stay in control of himself. He gets out of bed. His heart and body on the same page for the first time in his life, but he decides they will argue with his head about it, too. He goes out into the living room and turns the TV on a random channel for background noise as he rummages his pantry for something to eat.

Finding nothing, he sneaks out and gently closes his bedroom door to head to Baz's room, figuring that he doesn't have time to get rid of the pantry that he'd admitted is in his closet. When he enters Baz's quarters, he smells horrid decay. With due diligence, he moves to investigate.

The bathroom is disgusting in a way that even rats don't tolerate. The scum on the sinks and toilet make him gag yet again. Making a mental note to have someone come in and get the room taken care of, he closes the door. He wanders to the bureau and begins pulling drawers, but finds nothing as if Baz weren't even living in the room. It's not until he opens the closet door that he figures out where the smell comes from.

It is covered in rats where Baz's food sits. The nests create a stench like ammonia that makes his senses go haywire and his stomach lurch into his throat. The cot and pillow in there with the food and rats are dingy and gross. Any food Baz had can't even come close to being salvaged.

Rubbing his nose, Ash leaves the bedroom. His eyes water as he wonders how in the hell anyone can live like that.

Sure, there are messy and clean people, but what goes on in that room outstrips anything he's seen since the plague.

Hellbent on finding something to eat, he heads down to the kitchen and finds something new. The kitchen sparkles with cleanliness, and the cupboards contain some food.

When did this happen? Oh! Duh. We got all of this yesterday!

He grabs a couple blueberry muffins and heads back up to the room. He smiles at the thought that he can tempt her awake with something he knows she will be thankful for.

He goes back into his room and smiles when he hears her sigh in her sleep. The sound sends butterflies to the pit of his stomach. Sitting on the couch, he blindly watches TV and considers the possibility of getting her to say yes to becoming his wife.

The thought of what their kids will look like eventually creeps in, and he can't help but laugh when his mind tells him that he can't wonder about that without pain. The truth is that they can both have hope and find happiness in each other. A month ago, both would have laughed in anyone's face if they had suggested such possibilities that now seem endless.

Ash pulls his phone from the table in front of him. It dawns on him that it's been a week since he's last spoken to his boss, his father, about the situation.

Pushing the call button, he listens to the ringing, figuring that he will wake his father up but instead hearing a chipper "Hello" as his dad answers.

"Calling to update." He speaks in his generals' tone to try and keep the call formal. At high noon, there isn't anyone else awake to overhear the conversation.

There is a laugh. "So, I see. But know that during this call, I also expect you to speak to your father."

Ash relaxes a little bit, hearing his father's evident good mood. "There was an incident last night."

"Continue."

"Sebastian Blackwell has been working with vamp-op. They tried to abduct Ivy last night. They did not get the upper hand because they didn't have the knowledge." Still pissed about the entire ordeal, he tries to hide his anger.

His father comes to attention as Ash hears a muffled sound, likely of his father sitting up. "Short and sweet, what happened and the outcome?"

Ash steels himself and takes a breath. "Sebastian and another woman at the strip mall in town attempted to dart Ivy with a serum that was supposed to knock her out. It didn't. Ivy ripped the girl's throat out, and we left her in the bathroom. Ivy was able to mesmer Baz home. Once here, we brought him to the speakeasy, and I beat the ever-living crap out of him. Ivy and Soren produced a list of questions and got the information they were looking for. Ivy then sucked the magic out of Baz, making him killable, and then she fell asleep."

"Why was he working with the humans?" *Why aren't you concerned that she can kill the Pale Race?*

Ash sighs, wishing he hadn't missed the signs. "He is a hybrid human who survived transition. He doesn't drink blood and despises the Pale Race."

"And the answers to the questions?" Xavier is quick to ask.

"With Soren. As he spoke, Jynx also transcribed all the answers on the computer so there would be a written record for you."

"Good. Now you need to give me your answer."

Even though he doesn't want to admit his decision, he does. "I have bought a ring. I intend to ask her soon."

Astonishment comes from the other end of the phone. "Really?"

"Yes."

"But you have been so against it." He argues.

Ash takes a deep breath, as he gazes into the other room where Ivy sleeps peacefully. "It seems that fate has a way of knowing what it is we need even before we do."

"Thank God!"

Laughing, Ash shakes his head. "You have to keep this between us, though. I can't risk it getting back to her. I have a plan."

"You've got it." His father hesitates, then says, "I am proud of the man you are, Ash."

"Thanks, Dad. Shit! There is something else."

His dad waits quietly. "We need an entire shipment of blood sent to us posthaste. You may want to send a few humans. All the blood is tainted by the vamp-ops to track our movement."

"*WHAT!*"

Ash hesitates. "That might have been my first order of business, but I have been charged with protecting Ivy first and foremost."

Apparently his dad thinks for a few moments, then says, "No. You are right. Keep Ivy close and make sure that she is protected. Only leave the room if you must. There is too much at stake. Have Stone and Dayton meet the crew at your place. We have a backup of potentials who wish to earn their place. They are loyal. I will have them there by the end of the week. Until then, everyone will have to nomad quietly."

"Thank you."

"Ash?"

"Yeah, Dad?"

"Be careful. No one can be trusted. Lesai has been abandoned, but you need to keep the information to yourself. We can't have Ivy running off to save her mother and end up killed."

"Copy that."

Pondering the thoughts that have plagued him for his entire life, Ash sits in his living room and waits for his lifemate to wake up.

Small Wins

Sunlight

Ivy awakes to a room she doesn't quite recognize. The features are the same but in mirror image to her own room. She can hear a TV in the next room talking of happenings in Massachusetts and how there has been a murder in a local mall.

That's me! Ivy knows.

She breathes in the all-male scent that is Ash. It lingers in the pillow she lies on. She snuggles further into it, thinking she might go back to sleep so she can stay a little longer. *You have it bad,* she tells herself as she covers her head with the blanket to block out the light.

Ash strides into the room, and she peeks her face out from under the covers. She doesn't know if he realizes she's awake. She ogles his muscles as he struts around looking for something. He wears only a pair of jeans. Her heart begins to race, and she feels the effects like a lioness in heat.

He disappears behind her, and she sulks at the loss of the view of such a perfect piece of art.

She jumps and shrieks as she feels the full weight of him cover her as he snuggles up into her. "You know I can hear your heartbeat, right?" she hears him purr as he cuddles his face into her shoulder. "The moment you woke up, I knew."

"Cheater," she muffles under the blankets. "Now let me up so I can look at you some more."

Ash chuckles. "So that's what's getting you all worked up!"

Ivy wiggles around to face him. "Yes. It's not like there's anything not to like."

Ash looks into her eyes and bends closer to kiss her. Ivy covers her mouth with her hand. "I have morning breath!" Ash goes to kiss her again when she moves her hand, and she turns her face so he can't smell it.

"I don't care if you have morning breath. Kiss me, woman!"

She shakes her head and tries to escape.

"I am going to get my kiss, willing or not!" he says with a challenge as he pins her hands above her head with one hand and holds her chin gently with the other. Ever so gently, he brushes his lips against hers and then kisses her forehead. She feels her eyes flash red with lust, and he chuckles at her. "See? That wasn't so bad, was it?"

"No," she says as she does a little wiggle and manages to flip him over onto his back in one swift motion, pinning him down as he had pinned her down. "It wasn't," She says with a grin.

His eyes grow wide with shock and heat. Then he relaxes a little, and she lets his hands loose.

"I need to brush my teeth," she says with a determined look. "I feel like I slept the night away!"

"You did. No worries. It's noon. You slept a full twenty-seven hours. I brought you a muffin!"

Ivy's expression is deadpan. "I thought the Pale Race sleeps during the day as much as the vampires."

Ash shrugs. "Most do, but I've had my hands full trying to get to know this day walker I met. She likes to go outside where I can't protect her during the day. It drives me so nuts, I can't sleep."

Ivy smiles a brilliant smile. "You told me that I have to meditate at dawn every day!"

Ash looks up at the ceiling with his green eyes. "Only because we don't need the coven to see that giant oak tree that always pops up when you're out there. You really have no idea how odd that looks!"

"I never thought about it much." Ivy smiles pondering. "Though it is a live oak that I imagine."

"I have a picture. Want to see it?"

Ivy nods.

Ivy sees the mist in the form of a giant oak tree and sighs, "You definitely have a thing for this day walker!"

She giggles, covering what she considers her bad breath.

"I think that much is obvious," he says, a dark look in his eyes. "There is an extra toothbrush in the bathroom."

"Perfect! I feel like I'm growing moss!"

She jumps up and stands on the bed to look down at Ash, who enjoys the view. "What are you looking at?" she asks.

Ash grins ear to ear. "The most beautiful girl in the world."

Ivy shakes her head in disbelief.

"Go brush your moss," he tells her.

Ivy goes into the bathroom that also smells like Ash and opens the cabinet over the sink. As if bought for her, a toothbrush in its package sits in its own cup in the cabinet. Mouthwash and floss repose between the two cups. Making sure to retract her fangs and brush those as well, she goes through her routine of dental hygiene, then smiles into the mirror.

She flosses and uses mouthwash, though she hates the extreme taste. *What is a bloodsucker if you don't have fangs to bite someone!* she thinks, imagining a toothless vampire slapping its gums as she giggles.

Ash laughs. "So true."

Ivy stops in her tracks, spits the mouthwash out into the sink, and exits the bathroom to approach him.

"What?" She asks.

"You just joked about a bloodsucker without fangs," he says chuckling.

I did in my head while my mouth was filled with mouthwash! she says to herself so she can rule out being crazy.

"What the hell?" Ash says, his eyes wide. "Do that again."

Do what again?

"That!" Ash says with astonishment.

Well, she thinks. *There is another thing to add to Ivy's freak train. Her thoughts are not private.*

She walks back into the bathroom and puts her head in her hands as she wonders what will happen next. When she finally appears from the bathroom and walks to the bed where Ash still rests, she can see the wheels turning in his head. Keeping herself from wondering if he thinks she is as much of a freak as anyone else would, she asks. "So why in the world am I in your bedroom sleeping, mister?"

"Because I wanted to make sure you were fine after you sucked the magic out of what's-his-face, and your dad asked me to keep an eye on you. You sleeping for so long had me a little worried, though." Ash says it all matter-of-factly. "Plus, I really like you in my bed. You make it smell good."

Ivy blushes. "That's what woke me up. The smell of you."

"Get over here," He tells her, grabbing at her arm to pull her back into the bed with him.

She skirts his grasp a couple times, causing him to groan defeated. "I have something I'd like to talk to you about," he says.

Ivy tries to figure out what he wants to talk about and he finally gets a hold of her arm and pulls her over to him. She snuggles back into the blankets, her nose flaring again at the smell of his bed. She cradles her head on his arm, causing their faces to be about a foot apart.

He looks into her eyes for a few moments. "I have a proposal," he says with a neutral expression.

Ivy stays quiet. She wants to hear more before she explodes.

"I'd like to find out if we are lifemates," He says.

Ivy goes to speak, but he puts one finger gently on her lips to keep her quiet a moment longer. "The only way I will agree to find out, though, is if you agree to marry me when the mark appears."

Ivy thinks a moment. "And if the mark doesn't appear?"

"On the off chance that it doesn't, then I still want to marry you, but you don't have to if you don't want to," he says, a certain hesitation clear in his voice.

Ivy remains quiet for a few minutes as she wonders what she wants to happen. She knows she is in love with Ash, whether he is supposed to be her lifemate or not. There is no taking that away from her.

"How do we find out?" she asks. "I haven't done any of this before." She hides her blush in the blanket. "None of the history books made much sense about the way it happens. Like, is it sex or is it blood or both?"

Ivy feels extreme heat. She feels Ash move his arm to lift her face out of the blankets. "Sex is not necessary for a lifemate mark to appear," he says with a serious face. "It appears when the blood of a match becomes one. It's a sign that the magic in our blood will have the best viability of you carrying our children as well as a sign that means our blood is enough to sustain each other."

"So, I won't have to feed on vampires in order to survive?" Ivy asks hopefully, even though she figures she shouldn't be hopeful.

Ash looks away and then back at her. "There isn't another like you to compare with, but that's the way it's supposed to work. You may have to drink another's blood, but from what I saw earlier, you may not need to drink vampire blood at all, only syphon a little magic at a time without anyone knowing. Until now, that was the only way we thought you could get the magic."

Ivy stares at a strand of Ash's hair she twirls between her fingers as she asks, "So how does our blood become one? "She feels Ash's body get tense as the air sucks out of the room.

Ash clears his throat and says, "First I need you to promise that you will marry me when our marks appear."

"Are they going to hurt as bad as they did on my birthday?" she asks, wincing as she remembered the burn.

"Yes," Ash replies, his voice husky with emotion.

Ivy forces herself to look away from his hair she's managed to stand straight up and into Ash's verdant eyes. "What will my last name be?"

Ash rolls onto her and starts to kiss her. She pushes him up enough to say, "Really. What is my name going to be? Because whether a mark appears or not, I want to marry you, Asher."

"What changed?" he asks her.

She looks away and then meets his gaze. "I was resigned to my fate when my dad told me, but no matter what I felt towards you, I didn't want you to marry me out of duty."

He beams down at her with a look of possession that knocks the breath out of her. "Your name will be Iveliis Vale. You can rest assured, I'm too stubborn to marry someone I don't love."

Ivy squirms. "Asher Vale, husband to Ivy Vale." She tries it out on her tongue before he settles his weight onto her for a kiss, thus opening a dam within her. Untamed heat pours into every fiber of her being, making her hungry for him in ways she has never known existed.

Ivy feels herself grinding into him without understanding why as he growls into her mouth, "That's not fair." Her hips move without prompting, and he adjusts himself, causing her to feel the pure masculinity that she invokes. Ivy's mouth pops open in shock as a blunt object stabs her in the leg. "Sorry." *I can't help it.*

"You have to try," he says gasping for breath, answering her thought. "Instead of kissing me, you should bite me so we can figure this out. I won't be able to hold back much longer."

Ivy kisses him one more time for good measure her own gasping breath lingering against his mouth, her eyes starting to roll back in her head. "What is wrong with me?" she asks.

"Absolutely nothing, beautiful. Now, bite me."

Ivy feels like she will explode. She nuzzles his neck and kisses and licks the pulse in his wrist until finally she can't resist the pull of his clavicle any longer. Her fangs at full length, she bites in slowly, drawing out the moment longer than necessary. As she bottoms out and pulls back to begin sucking blood from the wound, she feels him buck on top of her.

A moment later, she feels the fast pierce of his fangs as he begins feeding. He starts pulling her blood into his body, and the two of them fall together off the edge of the cliff, their arousal and climax all they can smell as they bite each other repeatedly to keep drinking. Their bodies writhe together as they feel their way to another climax that has both crying out as they float blissfully back down to earth.

As Ivy pulls her mouth off Ash's neck, she sees that his wound has begun healing itself closed. She closes her eyes in satisfaction. The afterglow of full stomachs hangs heavily in the air around them.

They both catch their breath as completely clothed, they lay intertwined, hands lacing together. Ash lifts his head to look at her as he rolls off her body. He doesn't say anything as he looks into her heavy-lidded eyes.

Ivy senses it before it hits. "Shit. Shit. Shit."

"What's wrong? Ahh . . . ," Ash hisses as pain sears through their clasped fingers. Ivy holds her breath, as she knows full well that her pain will last much longer than his.

Ivy grimaces through pain.

"Jeez, why is it going so high?" he hisses. "How are you so damned calm?"

He chances a look at her and laughs. "You, cheater!" he exclaims.

Ivy hands a sword to him.

"I can't use . . ."

He clutches the sword as he expects it to zap him.

"What the hell?" Ash exclaims.

Ivy grins. "Ancient blood can wield elemental magic. Focus on the magic and pull," she instructs.

Both grip a sword as the searing pain becomes bearable. Ivy laughs aloud forcefully as Ash sulks.

"What is so funny?" he asks.

"That you will have one giant ass mark all because your lifemate is a freak," Ivy smirks.

"My freak," Ash says, holding their hands up in front of them as vines sear up their arms. "What the hell are our kids going to have for marks?" His eyes grow wide with concern.

"Beautiful ones," Ivy remarks with a smile. "But they will never have to go through it alone.

Ash chuckles and pulls her closer as he hisses from a new round of pain at his throat. "How did you get your swords without leaving my bed?" he asks suddenly.

Ivy smiles.

"I don't need swords to do magic, Sweety," she says slyly as she no longer feels pain. She sits up on the bed in order to see what the last fifteen minutes of hot lava created. She goes to stand, but Ash pulls her back down.

"Not so fast," he says with a grin.

"But I want to . . ." She gestures to her mark and eyeballs as she turns to look back into his eyes. Sitting at the edge of the bed, she notices a little box he holds out to her. She looks at the tiny box, takes it, and spins it?

"What is it?" she asks.

Looking nervous, Ash sits up. He takes Ivy's hand and asks, "Will you be mine for the rest of our long-ass lives?"

Ivy begins to weep. The box pops open to reveal a beautiful black ring, the band thick enough that it won't dig into her finger in a fight. The deep red garnet nestled in it sparkles as the sun shines through the window.

Ivy looks into his eyes and nods vigorously.

Ash laughs. "You have to say it!"

"I want to spend our long-ass lives together, and when we decide we have had enough, lie beside you until the Elemental Mother decides it's time for us to live again," Ivy tells him shyly as she appreciates the stone she knows he picked especially to complement their lives—garnet, the commitment stone, symbol of perseverance and strength.

Ash smiles as he slides the ring into place where her lifemate mark begins. He looks into her eyes and kisses the ring. "Now let's go see what we look like, my love," he says.

He all but drags her to the bathroom mirror, and she sees vines climbing up Ash's arm and around his neck, the prominent Knight coat of arms on his right bicep, and the name Iveliis scrawled under his right collar bone. Ivy licks her name and wipes away the smear of blood she's left from feeding from him.

Still tracing his vines, Ash tugs her hand. "Look!"

Pulling her shirt off and grabbing a towel to cover herself, Ivy turns to face the mirror. Ash pulls it from her hands and sets it back down on the rack. "I've seen you in less," Ash says with a smile, gazing at their matching marks in the mirror.

Asher's name scrawls under her left collarbone and his coat of arms sits at the same height when they stand, so it's near her shoulder.

"I knew that little shit wasn't your lifemate," Ash says to her as he squeezes her to him.

Ivy looks up at Ash and sighs. "Yes. I knew too."

"How?"

"Because when I drank his blood, it wasn't him I was envisioning." She feels herself grow warm as she blushes and pauses. Then, "I guess that means I am getting married soon, huh?" she asks as she looks down at her ring, then up at him with a smile.

"Shit," Ash says aloud.

Ivy looks at him in the mirror with concern. "What's the matter?"

"My mother will kill me," he says, his voice full of remorse.

Ivy looks bewildered.

"Hang on," he says. Ash pulls his cell phone out of his pocket and dials a number. "Hey, Mom. I have some news."

Aurora laughs at the end of the line. "Soren already called me. He knew you would forget."

"Do I have your blessing to marry a woman you haven't met yet?" he asks, looking down at his feet. Ivy lifts his chin so he has to look at her. When he does, she kisses him on the nose. He smiles.

Aurora is quiet for a moment. "Send me a picture of your mark, and I will let you know."

Ash looks bewildered. "How do you know?"

"I have had six phone calls in the last hour about it. Apparently, everyone in the house heard the fiasco." Aurora giggles. "Send me the picture, son."

Ash burns bright red. Ivy finds it absolutely adorable.

Ash shows Ivy how to take pictures with his phone, and after checking that they show all the details, he sends the images to his mother. He knows the exact moment she receives them because she gasps. "Asher Vale, you had better marry that woman. That is the strongest lifemate mark I have ever seen, and you know I have been around for several lifetimes."

"Thanks, Mom," Ash replies with relief.

"Now let me speak to my future daughter-in-law."

Ash seems a bit worried.

"I won't scare her away," she says. "That's not possible. Pass her the phone."

Ash gives Ivy the phone.

"My son has never been in love before, and it's obvious that he loves you dearly," Aurora tells her.

"I understand, Ms. Vale." Ivy says primly. She wants his mother to recognize that she is every bit royal enough for Ash.

After a moment of silence, Aurora asks Ivy, "Do you love him?"

Ivy looks directly into Ash's eyes and with no hesitation says, "Yes." Her cheeks flush red and her heartbeat picks up when she speaks the words, and Ash grins from ear to ear.

The rest of the conversation concerns where she grew up and the life she had before arriving at the compound. Ash finds himself enamored with much of what they speak about yet somehow finds himself drifting into the recesses of his mind. He wraps his arms around Ivy's waist as he half listens to the conversation. After a good hour, Ivy senses panic gripping Ash.

Ash grabs the phone from Ivy and makes a hasty goodbye to his mother, who laughs when she thinks that he only wants to get her back into his bed. Ivy giggles with Aurora about watching him blush, which causes the color to spread even up to his ears. He shoves the phone into his pocket and looks right into Ivy's eyes. "I have been standing in the sun for over an hour."

"I am aware," Ivy says to him looking up through her lashes. "You have been shading me from the sun this whole time." She pauses for a moment, then says, "I like it when you hold me."

Ash sputters, "How is this happening? I was born with the ability to be awake during the day, and I only need to avoid direct sunlight. It isn't even giving me a migraine!"

"I am half ancient, Ash. When we share blood, we share *all blood*," she says. "So, me doing magic probably means that you can too, even a little. The best part is we can both feed from vampires if that's what we need to do to survive, whether that's drawing it into us or biting someone." *We are one,* she thinks. *You only have to be taught.*

Ash doesn't reply.

"You aren't changing your mind, are you?" Ivy asks as sadness gnaws at her.

"Never," Ash reassures her, kissing the top of her head. "I'm just thinking."

Ivy walks into Ash's bedroom and heads to the hallway door. "I need to go shower. I'll be back in a few minutes."

Ash blocks the door in a blink. "You can use the adjoining door if you want. I really don't want to take my eyes off you," he says protectively.

"You know I can take you, right?"

It startles him out of his panic, and he laughs. "Yes."

"Good. As long as you know." Ivy says with a grin. "Now what is an adjoining door?"

Ash walks to the adjoining door off the living room and opens it from his side. She sees another door. "You will have to show me how you do that lock trick sometime," he tells her.

Ivy nods. "That one's easy. You will figure it out pretty quick."

She lifts herself up on her tippy toes and slowly kisses him, though trying not to evoke too much heat, responds intensely as he gently braces her up against the door jamb.

Her mind clouds over as she responds, unable to do anything but love the man who has stolen her heart. The kiss lasts longer than her brain can track, but her body knows that she craves satisfaction. She looks into his eyes and at his crooked grin.

"I can get used to that look," he says.

"What?" she asks absently.

Ash chuckles, sending needles into the pit of her stomach. "I will wait here for you, vixen."

Ivy shakes her head to clear any cobwebs. She can't remember why she's standing there. .

"Um, do you want me to leave the door open?" she asks Ash. He hands Ivy her swords, and she unlocks the door.

"Yes, please," Ash replies, adding "If you are okay with it."

Ivy nods. She doesn't look towards the man who literally makes her forget her name. "I am," she says.

Getaway

Fate Always Wins

Ash smiles from the passenger seat and grips the door, afraid she may total his car. Knowing the chances of her getting into an accident are slim to none doesn't ease his anxiety.

"If I had known you were going to be such a wuss, I would have insisted we take the Rubicon again!" Ivy says, giggling from the driver's seat.

"I'm fine. You will take your next left."

Ivy nods smiling, though she doesn't know where they are going.

The surprise came to him in a dream, another change since getting their marks. Time away from the compound for a little while: necessary. Even considering the stakes and that they are supposed to stay in the room, they've put the entire coven through the hell of their non-stop happiness all weekend. Soren even threatened to send them to the shack for a week if they didn't ease up.

Ivy takes the left, and her nose flares. "What is that smell?" she says in awe as she sniffs a few more times. "I can't put my finger on it, but it's a cross between decay and life."

Ash chuckles to himself. "So, is it good or bad?" he asks seriously as he tries to assess whether she'll like it.

"It's wonderful," she declares, closing her eyes as she sticks her head out the window.

"Ivy!" He grabs the wheel from her, panic gripping him. "I think it's time to let me drive."

Without hesitation, she pulls over to the curb. Ash jumps out of the car, and she slides over to the passenger seat without a second thought. Trying to figure out where the smell comes from, she looks around.

He knows they are only two blocks from the boardwalk, so he takes his time, moving slowly between houses to keep anticipation alive. He reaches into his pocket and feels the gift from the Elemental Mother waiting, and he smiles. He knows that the goddess must have given him the idea.

Ivy's breath hitches in her throat as she leans forward as they approach the beach. The horizon behind them will lose the sun in about an hour, and the sky displays magnificent colors.

"This is the ocean!" she exclaims with the amazement of a child and stares with eyes as big as coins.

Ash pulls up to a parking spot, most empty since humans usually don't swim in the evening. "I thought you might like this. I also wanted to ask you if you would be willing to teach me to speak to you, too."

Ivy smiles. "You've already done it, sweety."

"I mean the way you do it for me."

Ivy gives him an all-knowing look. "The night you taught me to mesmer, you did it, too."

Ash remembers hearing her thoughts that night and blushes. "That's the night I found out you were interested in me." He realizes that isn't what she means. "What did I say?"

Ivy smiles like a little kid with a secret. "Nothing much." The gleam in her eyes causes him to grab her and pull her to his lap.

"Fine." She relents, snuggling into his chest. "I saw an image of me sleeping in the hammock with a book."

Ash blushes again as he remembers the first time he saw her. "Why didn't you tell me, Vixen?" He asks her with a tickle, making her squirm and the car horn beep.

"Stop!" she squeals. "Because I never thought it was more than a fascination with a freak!"

Mortified that she could think like that about herself, Ash stops tickling her.

She opens her eyes to sees hurt on his face. "It's not like I could have known or would have believed you," she tells him. "My entire life has been a game of dominos. Once some of the pieces stand, they get knocked down before I can be happy with the outcome."

She looks toward the ocean and, with a melancholy in her voice reminding him of when she sings for the Elemental Mother, she says, "I'm still waiting for them to fall."

Not knowing how he will save her from the doubt she has been plagued with her entire life, Ash hugs her. "Let's go splash in the water," he says. "Then you can try to teach me your way of mesmering."

"What?" she asks as she shakes her head to rid herself of sadness.

Ivy smiles mischievously. "If you can make that connection again while we hold hands, we can build it to get stronger."

"Really?" He asks, excited at the opportunity to get her back at her own game. Her tendency to push her thoughts over to him in her moments of lust torture him. Once as he sparred with the men, she was in his bed smelling his sheets and pushing the image of him on top of her searing into his mind. After getting knocked on his ass by one of his sparring partners, he locked himself in his bathroom for a half hour with music blaring to hold himself at bay.

Her mischievous grin tells him that she will scorch him at mesmering that night, but he figures it's worth it. "Once you get better at pushing images over to me, we will work up to words," she tells him.

She looks out at the impending sunset. "But first, let's explore." She pulls her boots off and jumps out of the car.

Booking it down to the water, she looks back at him and laughs as he pulls off his shoes and locks the car. "Come on, slowpoke!"

Ash strolls and revels in the sight of Ivy as the breeze whips her hair around. She closes her eyes with her arms outstretched. The image sears into his brain as vividly as his image of her in the hammock. Her marks show in full view as the ring he bought her glitters in fading sunlight.

She splashes into the water, and Ash grimaces as he contemplates getting sand out of his car the next day. *She will be the death of me.*

Ivy holds her hands out to Ash and beckons him towards her already in the water to her knees. "Now I know why you are wearing shorts," she tells him.

He enters the water to goosebumps and numbing feet from the cold. She holds his hands in hers and looks up into his eyes. "You are amazing in all the ways I could ever have dreamed, Asher Vale."

They watch in happy silence, arm in arm as the sun sinks below the horizon. Not until the stars and moon begin to light the night sky does she pull him to a spot in the sand not yet touched by the coming tide. She sits him down with his legs outstretched, straddles him, and smiles.

In all things carnal, this could totally be fun! she decides.

"You will kill me," Ash tells her with desire as he feels himself come to life.

Ivy giggles. "Okay. Now. Start the way you started the first time. Try to mesmer me, love."

Without speaking words, he does exactly what he did that night as he opens himself to her. Before he knows it, he is looking at himself through her eyes.

Shaking his head, freaked out, he hears Ivy say, "Is that really how you see me?"

Ash stares into her eyes. "Wait, that's how you see me?"

Ivy nods, and he does it again, wanting to experience it without the panic.

Immediately, his eyes blur and return to the image of himself staring down into her eyes with a look of adoration he's never known he owns. Her feeling of contentment and safety at being in his arms causes him to pull her in for a hug. He understands that he may be controlling his body, but he knows he is feeling her feelings.

She sighs with relaxation he has never thought possible in her, as her mind whispers, *I love you,* leaving it to echo throughout their heads.

It feels like hours have passed by the time he returns to himself when he hears her stomach growl.

Ivy giggles.

"You are always hungry," he tells her with a laugh.

Ivy grins. "I'm actually not sure what kind of hungry I am, though." She studies his neck. It sends shivers down his spine as he waits for her to ask.

Her eyes flash red, and she looks away embarrassed.

He turns her face to look at him. "What's the matter?"

Ivy shrugs, her eyes getting misty. "I don't want to make you feel like I'm with you only to eat."

"Are you kidding me?"

She shakes her head no and tries to look away again.

"Ivy, soon-to-be Vale, you will bite me and drink when you are hungry, whether we are home in bed, cooking regular food, or in the field.

"But what if I take too much?"

"It's not possible if I'm drinking, too." He pulls his gift out of his pocket and holds it up to her. "We share blood. We are one. Just like this." Ivy nods, but it doesn't appear that she will take a vein.

To convince her of his intention and commitment, he pulls her shirt to the side and, without hesitation, bites into her. Her hiss and lust roar through him, and he loses all sense as he drinks.

Still she hasn't bit him.

He looks up to see that he has misjudged the situation entirely. Her eyes flash red, and the searing heat of her arousal all but knocks him out. Without asking if it's okay, he kisses her everywhere he can land his mouth He tears her shirt off her, and she unbuttons his pants as she shimmies her own down and maneuvers to take a leg out.

He reaches down, rubbing in circles to feed her the way she wants, exploring a little further and finding her hymen.

Ivy hisses in reaction, and he jumps.

"Shit." The innocence he detected the other day didn't mean she's inexperienced. Her hymen has never broken. It's still there.

"What?" she asks, still seeking satisfaction with the friction of his hand but finding it isn't there anymore.

He gapes at her, unable to believe it. "You're a virgin!"

The idea that she has never been touched sends his mind racing through hoops.

Ivy turns bright red as he's stops moving. *What's a virgin?*

"You have never had sex before," he says, as the thought *Mine!* roars through him, gripping his insides in knots as he thinks of every reason he shouldn't.

Ash pulls her face to his and kisses her so deeply he gasps for breath, inhaling the air as she exhales. He can't think of anything but her.

Ash feels her hand unconsciously grip him firmly as she leans forward, her breasts in his face. In a moment of pure ecstasy, he feels himself sheathed in the tight grip of her virgin heat.

He roars, tipping his head back as he instinctively bites into Ivy's shoulder to focus her pain elsewhere. She calls out as her pulsing begins around him. As he feels the climax ebbing, she nuzzles his neck blindly in search of the vein she loves so much.

He guides her head with his hand as he begins pulling her blood into him. She finds her spot and, as she bites into him, his body jerks and begins moving instinctively with hers. His climax happens soon after, bringing her over the cliff right with him. both of them sated and covered in sweat.

Water washes over them in waves., He pulls back as one drenches them. Ivy sputters as the wave forces her to remove her face from his neck.

"It's so cold!" she shrieks.

"That's what you get with the Atlantic!"

Ivy scoffs at him with a laugh.

He hears her stomach growl again. "Really? That wasn't enough food for you?"

Ivy gently taunts him. "Are we close enough to go to Beacham's again?"

"Yes." He smiles. "We are always close enough. Anytime you want to go, I'm game."

Ivy laughs. "What do you, own the place?"

It surprises Ash that she jokes about it as if that is out of the question. He nods.

"Seriously?"

"Yes. There are six of them actually." He waits for a reaction.

"So that's why you don't care about money! You are loaded!"

"Kind of." Ash looks down sheepishly. "Is that okay?"

Ivy nods, "Is that something that makes you feel good?"

He nods.

"Then I'm good."

Ash pulls her in for a devastating kiss, and she pulls back with a serious look.

"Just don't tell me you own any of those sex stores you told me about."

The ick factor sweeps across her face, and Ash giggles like a kid.

"No, But I do own a chain of clubs called Vines," he says with a shrug. *Did fate mess with me that way too?* he wonders, realizing that Ivy is a vine.

Ivy smiles brilliantly. "You did it!" She launches at him and knocks him on his back as a wave comes crashing over them.

They both sputter and shiver, and he asks, "Did what?"

"Fate does have a way of bringing beings together. You were obsessed with me before I even existed!" Her self image soars through the roof, and that is all he can see in her eyes.

Ash smiles. "Let's go get food, Vixen."

"I'm buying!" Ivy smiles brightly. Ever since Ash gave her the debit card and her human documentation, she's been experiencing the I-buy-everything phase.

"Fine by me!" Ash says smiling, knowing that he's been direct depositing every dime back into her account for future use.

They walk hand-in-hand back towards the car, their lifemate marks intertwined by their clasped hands.

Acknowledgments

I would like to acknowledge the following people who supported my writing *Hybrid of the Pale Race* and bringing the novel to publication:

My children for giving me the drive to succeed and prove myself.

Marcia, my publisher, who put up with my active voice and busy introvert antics.

Aunt Noreen, who told me not to stop writing no matter what they say.

Scotty for reading and re-reading my manuscript to his beautiful wife and giving me feedback.

VampireBear, the beautiful young woman who allowed me to borrow her face for the cover photo.

All of my chosen family and friends who accept my oddity without judgment.

And, finally, all those who have given my mind a reason or need to escape reality. I'd have never known I had it in me if I hadn't felt so dejected.

Amelia Adams Clark

About the Author

As a child, Amelia lived down the street from her grandma's farm, Adams Farm and Slaughterhouse in Athol, Massachusetts. Having six siblings, three of whom lived with her, she says she learned to love self-isolating, abhor SpongeBob, and nevertheless dearly love all her siblings.

Though hard on her, Amelia says, her parents out of love taught her self-sufficiency early. Amelia spent her childhood and teen years creating as a form of therapy every moment she got the chance. Through reading and writing to drawing and oil painting, she embraced every emotion she had and transformed it.

Amelia says she sometimes got into trouble while reading a novel while walking on the side of the road, and it's certainly understandable that she has walked into parking meters without realizing it. Always "in the clouds" while remaining steadfast in her determination to succeed, she received the plaque for Most Outstanding Achievements in the Arts from Athol High School in 2006 upon graduation. She did not use the attached scholarship to Massachusetts College of Art, but she continued to create works of visual art and writing.

A mom of two and stepmom of four amazing kids, Amelia says she will continue to show by example what persistence and passion can achieve, even if passion wasn't her main source of income. Having worked in factories, her grandma's slaughterhouse, pizza houses, hotels, and more, she has driven school buses and public transportation vehicles before settling into a role as an autism specialist.

Amelia says that sometimes, for some people, their passions bring more fulfillment when deadlines don't dictate a timetable. That said, she adds, she will continue her heart-happy career and proceed to enjoy her passion projects as ideas come to her.

Colophon

Text and captions for *Hybrid of the Pale Race* are set in Adobe Caslon Pro. William Caslon released his first typefaces in 1722. Caslon's types were based on seventeenth-century Dutch old style designs, then used extensively in England. Because of their remarkable practicality, Caslon's designs met with instant success.

Caslon's types became popular throughout Europe and the American colonies—printer Benjamin Franklin hardly used any other typeface. The first printings of the American Declaration of Independence and the Constitution were set in Caslon.

For her Caslon revival, designer Carol Twombly studied specimen pages printed by William Caslon between 1734 and 1770. The OpenType Pro version merges formerly separate fonts and adds both central European language support and several additional ligatures. Ideally suited for text in sizes ranging from six-point to fourteen-point, Adobe Caslon Pro is often chosen for magazines, journals, book publishing, and corporate communications.

Titles are set in Colonna MT, originally an advertising font developed by Monotype in 1927. The inline roman face has some elegant letterforms.

Ornaments at chapter headings and content changes within chapters are from the Bodoni Ornaments collection created by Sumner Stone. He based the ornaments those found in the *Manuale Tipografico*, compiled in 1788 as an inventory of types by Giambattista Bodoni, an Italian printer. *Manuale Tipografico* includes 291 roman and italic typefaces, along with samples of Russian, Greek, and other types. A second edition of his book was published by his widow in 1818.